In the Lair of the Fox . . .

"I want to tell you Dick Fox," she leaned toward him with an impressive confidence. "I ran off from a peer of the realm tonight, an actual earl, because I didn't choose to give in to what he was askin' me." Why was she bothering to tell him all this?

He worked the empty mug gently from her fingers without replying to her boast, and said, "One good stroke of fortune deserves a second," and motioned her to the straw bed.

She would have questioned him, tested her ground but somehow her mind stopped dead. The bed was more good grace than her world would ever hold on another day. She would not dare to think ab[illegible] tomorrow or Harry Watkins or even wha[illegible] [illegible] [illegible]ox might do to her in her sleep.

She toppled in a hazy [illegible] the long, soft rectang[illegible]

For a moment she [illegible] across her breasts, waiting for [illegible]uch and feel of his approach, watching [illegible]tensely . . .

THE FOX AND HIS VIXEN

The turbulent searing saga of a woman who would die for her man . . . who took him to the depths of hell and the heights of ecstacy to win her place by his side.

THE FOX AND HIS VIXEN

Viveca Ives

BALLANTINE BOOKS • NEW YORK

 Published in the United States by Ballantine Books, a division of Random House, Inc., New York, and simultaneously in Canada by Ballantine Books of Canada, Ltd., Toronto, Canada.

Library of Congress Catalog Card Number: 77-6205

ISBN 0-345-27325-7

Printed in Canada.

First Edition: December 1977

The fox went out on a hunt one night,
He prayed to the moon to give him light,
He had many a mile to go that night
Before he reached the town.

Many a mile to go that night
Before he reached the town.

Folk Song

THE TREATY OF AMIENS brought a peace in 1802 that seemed lasting. Heroes swaggered home with tales of the Nile and cheers for Nelson who saved their channel shores. Mums and sweethearts of the fleet hung on their boys' necks, put away dread, and ran to their kitchens, chuckling over the hearth flames and roasting in their conversations that French frog-eating devil driven off forever behind a wall of British naval might. *Huzza* and *long live the King!* who slept in his God-fearing bed. Clear-eyed merchants of the city glimpsed a rising time and rushed to open their stuffed warehouses for Paris trade while their Lordships of the Realm wakened for play, sensing in themselves a stirring taste for continental frolics.

Chapter One

IT WAS a bitter January night in 1803 that stopped the water in the leaden turncocks and froze the cloaks of men into stiff wings. A wine-colored carriage with a small crest creaked along Thames Street beside the black, swollen river, four gleaming bays struggling behind the muck-ridden wharves, breath crackling in the fog. A commotion had started inside the carriage. Two shadows rose across the drawn-up shades and tumbled about with each other, crossing, countercrossing, mingling, and breaking suddenly apart with a girl's defiant scream and a startled masculine: "Damme bitch!"

Jolted by her own brazen act, the girl fell back immediately and blinked at her companion, who was touching his bitten face. A caged fire struggled inside her and flashed erratically in her straightforward glance and flushed complexion.

"Meanin' no disrespect, y'r Lordship. Ain't goin' to have no more. No more, I says. Keep y'r hands off me now, please m'lord. Keep 'em off . . ."

"Now, missy. Now, Meg. What's this?" He wiped the blood from a tooth mark beside his lip and studied two ruby smears on a white gloved finger. "You're to be a good girl."

"Good girl I ain't," she panted. "Good girl I never can be no more."

"But did you not promise the magistrate?" He sat back and passively watched the blazing, prideful gray eyes of this wild street cat in her just-held-together finery—snatched, no doubt, from a rag fair—squirming before him along the silk-lined carriage walls. "You have stolen an apron and that is a serious charge." He stretched his muscular legs out across the seats and caught her frail waist between his iron calves.

Gasping and swallowing, Meg stared at the white-stocking trap, watching knees bend and herself drawn in closer and closer to his perfumed chest.

"Listen t'me, y'r Lordship. I ain't a *good* girl, if you get the drift. I swear it. You'll not find what you want in me." A bruising, searing desperation compelled her to continue. "No! Let me go, y'r Lordship. I heard what y'likes to do to girls at certain days of the month."

"So much the better that you know." He smiled brightly. "And there's a guinea in it for you. How many pails of porter will that buy? Eh, Meg?" He let go his leghold, pressed a gold coin into her palm, and grabbed her in a bear squeeze with his arms. "And hot eel pies? And winkles?" She felt wet, relentless breath against her ear. "I'll bring you home a bauble from Paris," he whispered urgently. "I'll keep you drunk for a lifetime."

"Never! Never! Nevermore!" she croaked, and wrenching free, jabbed an elbow into his teeth. Her auburn hair fell forward over her terrified face.

He growled with a sudden temper and dug claw-like, jeweled fingers through her woolen shawl. She winced and she glared wildly around the silk prison, searching for escape. A sheen of golden tufted walls . . . one pale violet shade . . .

"Don't fool with me, Meg Watkins," he demanded roughly, the voice deep now and commanding. "I have paid well for you tonight. And if it weren't for my generosity, you would be beating hemp in Bridewell or being whipped as you deserve."

It was true. She knew every inch there was to know about him, yet she could not grit her teeth and yield one more time. It was too much to bear again. The very horses themselves seemed to hear her need. The carriage creaked around Tower Wharf and picked up speed, pitching her across the small distance to the door.

She heard the rip of her bodice just as her icy palm

closed upon the door handle. It happened then that the door swung open with the carriage sway, and out she traveled on a long slide that propelled her into darkness. The earl himself half came out with her, but the gallop never stopped even as he cried up to the driver. The horses, sniffing a smoky, reeking gallows, turned reckless and bolted with slipping hooves onto cobbles sunk in mire. Thus grabbing some support, they flung their great weight forward into an explosive run and clattered out of control.

The earl's hallooing rolled back to her through the slimy air as she tumbled and fell, skidding, fighting for a balance she could not maintain, and finally flopping chest first into the crackling mud. The momentum of her fall spun her over, and bits of gritty things stung her flesh. Yet Meg sensed in this her escape to new freedom. An insane joy sang in her bones, relaxing them so that she bounced like a babe, bruising the skin but hurting nothing down deep where it mattered, in either her vitals or her soul.

She lay where she came to a halt, with her cheek squeezed between two cobbles, eyes shut tight, groaning hot breath against her arm. Shocked from its senses, her body wanted nothing more than to stay where it fell, quiet and inert. She remained still, giving in to it, aware only that nothing mattered . . . and that her life had leaped, somehow, out of the hands of her enemies.

How long she lay she could not tell, but after a while her mind did strange things to her. Her ears picked up the creaking sounds of masts from the forest of ships on the river, and she sniffed the rank stench of ebbing tide. Squeaking, scurrying sounds emerged from bales of food closer by, as though speaking among themselves and ignoring the presence of the intruder who had dropped into their midst.

Her attention began to clarify and soon focused on her body. Tentatively she stretched her legs. Rolling onto her side and resting there, she gazed with interest at low, sagging houses that loomed briefly out of the murk when touched by a faint trickle of moonlight, then were hidden behind swirling, acrid drifts.

Meg, you fool! said an inner voice eventually. *He's going to beat you again when he hears what you did!* The pale, goatish face of her father loomed up, bleating oaths at her and glaring with milky-blue eyes. She pushed it all away and sighed and started gingerly to try to sit up. Inch by inch she did it well, feeling her elbows, her ribs, and discovering that everything worked as before, though she ached fiercely.

Now, finally standing, she tottered a few steps for the sake of movement. Her high crest of definance was gone now and left her only the despair of being utterly alone and far from any welcoming bed.

Behind her a low signal whistled. Then the rapid patter of footfalls gathered. Here and there stared the bleary orange eyes of lit tobacco. One . . . two before her . . . three . . . a fourth on the left. Street sense rushed to her and began to draw her muscles together into a defending wall.

Someone chuckled and coughed hoarsely. "Place me a bet, Jack, that I takes her afore you c'n raise a single finger."

Raucous laughter ringed around her.

Meg hurried onward with her chin down to her bosom, scratching her shoulders to find and bring up the missing shawl.

She felt a sudden yank of her hair behind her. Her chin jerked up and then relaxed. Far away in the distance, the faint glimmer of a street lamp struggled to find her. She kept her gaze on it, telling herself that she must run into that light.

"Moves like a greased kitten, don't she, Rob?"

"Chirps like a sparrow, though. What d'you make on't?"

The voices followed her at an easy trot, letting her run where she pleased. In an icy film of recognition, she realized the dread end of their game. Suddenly it made sense to her not to move at all but to stop dead and let them see that she was bruised and filthy and nothing to want. The veil of hopelessness that gave this advice seemed reasonable and was no stranger, after all.

Meg Watkins, you're a damn fool, said her inner voice again, speaking out as though they were safe in some room and could talk.

Harry Watkins loomed again in her exhausted brain. *Killing's too good for you. Deserting your old dad!*

She was standing still inside a tight ambush. Her head swiveled this way and that, peering at the misty shapes of her oppressors floating through the gloom. They waited as though in a marked circle. A steaming stench of gin mingled with sweat congealed on the frosted air. An icy ripple rolled over her naked shoulders and down her rigid arms. She threw her head back then and laughed with the bold frenzy of an animal that knows its throat will be slit.

"What can you do to me, boys, that ain't been done to me a thousand times already?" Her laughter was the street sense talking. She hardly recognized the pleasure of her supreme separation from fear, for she had leaped out of that pain into another world of numb savagery the match of these men.

"Awwwright," said the man called Rob. "We watched yer tumblin' from the lord's sweet arms. What he give yer there, sweetie? A guinea for yer trouble?"

"Bastards!" she screamed. "Ain't got a bloody farthing in my fist! Here! Here, looksee!" She held out her torn, bereft palms. "He gave me ache and misery and the guinea rolled away into the mud. Run back there if y'want it . . . and leave off chasin' after me!"

She sensed around her a hesitation.

"I'll go, Rob," grunted one.

"Stay here, y'lyin' swindler," growled another. *"I'll* go."

"T'hell y'will."

A tangle of two thick bodies scuffled away into the dark.

"Now, now, now," said Rob to her. "Those loony louts'll chase a copper to hell. That leaves just you and me. And Jack and Bert and Keltie. All poor, wicked cadgers that knows what's what."

They began to gabble among each other, with guarded voices but in a street slang that she could not decipher.

"Here, here," she called into their babble. "What's it worth to have your good times on me? A night's lodgin'? A bit of the bed y'sleep on?"

They stopped short in their mutterings and started to grumble, as though in some way she had offended or disappointed them.

"Y'trotted away from us so fast," called one. "We thought y'was a . . ."

". . . virgin," spat Rob viciously.

"Virgin?" she shrieked, laughing.

Madness that they could think so! But she heard them pacing in restless, growing anger, turning mean. Uneasily she began to eye again the street lamp, some fifty paces off on Catherine Street.

Something told her what to do, a primitive sense of timing in the face of destruction. She broke away abruptly and ran for her life, but running nowhere that could save it.

They reached her easily. "Hey, there! Hey!" At the street lamp they grabbed her and banged her head a few times against the metal pole, mocking her futile hope for safety in light. Rob jabbed out a hairy fist and jerked her chin up, squinting down into her face from two narrow, close-together eyes. The hair on his mottled cheeks grew black as bedbugs and seemed to crawl.

"Look at this 'un, Jack," he breathed, staring at her face in startled admiration.

Jack waddled over quickly, a short stump on thick bow legs. He squinted and whistled over his tongue. "Bet his Lordship did give 'er a guinea right enough!"

Admiration did not prevent the brutal grab of her shoulders that pinned them back, curving and stretching her into a painful arch that lifted her breasts and made of them twin flags of invitation.

She jabbed a knee up, kicked, and spit full in Rob's face, hitting him smack on an eyelid.

"Let go of me," she commanded with all the high, imperious claim she had mustered in the carriage. But now it was a strange, vain insanity. The same insanity that had landed her here would drive her lower into heaven only knew what depths of anguish. The likes of Jack and Rob were no strangers to her experience. Her father used their kind sometimes, too, just as he used her . . . as favors to some generous peer with a taste for unspeakable amusements.

A skinny thing, his greasy gray neckcloth flapping, dove at her from the shadows. His face, pointed as a rat, aimed directly for the side of her throat. She saw him from the edge of her vision but had no time to dodge or fend him off.

His nose butted against her neck; then the rough, scraggled chin scraped down across the softness of her bosom, plunging and chewing at her as she became a succulent, ripe melon discovered in the snow. The insult was more than she could bear tonight. She started to lunge and bite back blindly, but her wrists were quickly jerked and pinned together behind the pole, held there like a trussed-up cow at market.

The rage of frustration burst in screams from her burning mouth, yet threatened no one. They heard her and flicked dark, nervous looks from her to Rob. Rob yanked his felt brim down to his eyebrows and directed scowls at the man who attacked her.

"You don't go ahead of me, Bert." He rushed in and pulled the nibbling animal away, flinging him down to the scummy ground and striding up close to Meg. She caught the jaunty, lusty glare as his eyes devoured her, measuring and anticipating what she had to offer.

"I likes ter be a gentlemun," he rasped close to her face, as though confiding a secret. "I likes to take me portion in me own sweet time . . . and has no use for the leavin's."

"Stinking son of a bitch," she cried just as softly, relishing the words and spitting them at him. "I'd rather frig a dog than you!"

"Oh-ho-ho, ha—ha—haaaah!!"

The laughter knifed back, but it didn't come from Rob. It jabbed at him instead, flung by the others and flying in his face. He heard it, and his body seemed to swell and expand with a surging fury. To Meg the laughter became a most dangerous sound. Rob never once turned back to the others or gave a sign that he cared. He leaned forward and rose to his toes, rocking, teetering at her, looking blackly, teeth clicking together slowly like the sound of a creature poisoned and rallying his remaining strength for the kill.

In that lightning moment she saw that the real menace to herself was more than rape and mere physical brutality. She saw herself face to face with the changing force of a crazed creature who believed she must be destroyed at all costs.

The grip upon her wrists was still total. She tried to wiggle her fingers and felt their numbness, while sounds that she could not understand burbled darkly, far back in the thickness of Rob's throat.

Finally his head and muscles stopped jerking. "She's a wise 'un," he said. "A beauty and a wise 'un. . . . Let go on her, Keltie. Let's see her run!"

She knew then what he wanted, and her chest contracted with tortured anticipation of their crazed game. Slowly she began to rub her wrists, stalling for time, warily glancing from one to the next, panting out her bravado in sharp, wheezing breaths that stuck painfully in her ribs.

"You'll not play ringing the pig with me," she cried defiantly. "I'll see myself in hell first before I run."

A small, gleeful giggle behind her told her she was amusing them. Keltie flapped about her in a smock too large for his arms and thin chest, dancing like a scarecrow and imitating the sound of her voice. The others, too, began to caper, expecting to tease her on by tweaking her breast or jabbing her behind.

All except Rob.

He had fallen silent and stood at a distance, slightly removed, observing her from some private, satanic depth that she could not begin to fathom. She felt no terrors except when she looked at him. Felt no care for her own life until she absorbed his brooding need to avenge himself upon her in some maniacal way that would satisfy the mockery. It was Rob and Rob alone who taught her, in flashes of shivering anguish, the intensity of strength and hope that coiled in her muscles . . . that would flail out even in the face of death for the sake of some dimly perceived honor that had existed mute and unrevealed during the full seventeen years of her life.

"Run," Rob said. "You will run."

"Looks like she ain't able to budge a single toe there, Rob."

Rob took one small step away from her, readying and aiming his body, like a rifle, with her own.

"Run."

Behind him the two scufflers were still tumbling in the dark. One of them called in a muffled, distracted voice, "Where the hell are you, Ed? Ed?"

"Run."

Jack sidled up to her. "If I wuz you, sweetheart . . . I'd run, sure."

She ignored the advice and stood her ground. There was no chance for her in running and none in standing still. No chance for her, no matter what she did. In that pale, raging face she recognized the threats and their fulfillment. In those compact lumps of muscle was packed all the wretched superiority to her female weakness. She drew a breath and spat out: "If anyone's t'run, mister, then it's you." And she spat with all her strength again, as far as the arching spittle would reach. A glob of saliva fell short and landed at Rob's feet.

From the darkness behind them came a loud, amused laugh from the scufflers, deep and rolling.

"She likes t'spit a lot."

"Shut up," Rob called uneasily.

He seemed no longer able to speak but scratched his head and the back of his neck once or twice, shifting the bulk of his shoulders inside his shirt.

Then, with a decisive jerk of his stomach, he started barreling toward her till his chest and loins were touching hers. His arms hooked around her waist and locked there. The solid, viselike grip of forearms jerked her to him hard, where she felt the rigid, curving line of his body.

Breath squeezed out of her. The others, afraid to join in, waited where they stood. But soon Rob grunted something and laughed as though relieved of the affront to his pride and called, "Come along, boys. Come closer and take a piece for yersel's."

Meg's ears were ringing as he spoke. Her body braced itself like a band of steel, ready neither to feel nor touch nor respond but simply to exist . . . to *endure*. Around her they swarmed, touching, pressing, feeling, all of them squeezing in upon her, smothering her with the breathy stench of gin and sour, pickled belches. They trampled her with their hands and nuzzling mouths. Rob held her fast all the while and stared down with a wide, steel-faced grin, feeding upon her as she panted, her heart thundering achingly like a trapped bird or rabbit in the field with the suffering she could not hide from his eyes.

That was the worst of it, his watching her.

"A full-breasted beauty," sniggered one.

"And soft in the arse," squawked another.

She stared back at Rob as stiffly as she could, swaying or wincing only when the prying fingers hurt too much or found a secret, private place that startled her into recoil.

"One day," she called to him steadily in a hoarse whisper, "one day, you can depend upon it, I'll have a curved knife in my hand and I'll spread your legs apart and cut—"

He flung her hard to the ground and flopped down upon her. The breath whacked out of her chest, and she disappeared beneath the smothering heat of his vicious, driving attack. The agony searing through her sweating flesh was like nothing she had ever felt before.

The others, taking their cue, dropped upon Rob

and pummeled him aside, kicking and squealing, hen-like, in their mounting lust.

Meg closed her eyes and screamed inside herself: *I'll live through all of this and more! Yes, I will!*

Chapter Two

"SSSSSSTTTTTTTTTTTTTTTTTTTT!!!!!!!!!!"

The soft promise of a saber blade cut through the air and leaped from the shadows. With it sailed the huge, lean body of a man, arcing catlike, arms and legs extended to hurtle himself upon the mob. Dressed in something darker than the fog, he was a giant shadow of energy, and from his waist flew out the trailing fringes of a scarlet sash.

Meg, blocked by the faces and bodies upon her, saw nothing of him, but she heard the steady warning note with its terrifying intent, and before the pile of men could sense what happened, the attacker landed.

"Oow . . . oooo. Uhh . . wazzzziz . . . ouhhh." Gobs of air flew about, and instantly a melee of arms and legs tangled as cries filled the shrouded night.

The stranger, pummeling into the mass and plucking bodies from the heap, went about his work with a single-minded will. Having the advantage of surprise, he rapidly peeled his way down to the victim pinned in the sodden earth.

"Eh, what's here?" he said, crouching and peering into Meg's splattered and astounded face.

Meg wasn't quite sure at first what she saw. Her blurred vision could make out only one more masculine form, a larger tormentor, among the many.

While he studied the coughing, mud-mottled features, he grabbed her behind the shoulders and lifted her slightly to get a better look in the flickering street lamp. Before he could fix her in a satisfying position for his curiosity, Rob, recovered from the attack, sprang with a vengeance and dropped like a bat upon the neck of the stranger. The unknown intruder fell into a curve, bending with a sudden shift of his balance, and tumbled easily forward so that Rob was propelled ahead and landed several feet away.

"Stand aside, you sluggish bastard," called the stranger with an odd nonchalance.

The others now began shooting at him like cannonballs from all directions, their hard, resentful bodies pounding him with broadsides that landed solidly enough but with small effect.

Meg, watching in confusion, rallied her addled brains just enough to begin to move her body. She rose to her knees and began a gradual crawl away from the exploding fracas, hoping to disappear before anyone noticed. Glancing back warily as she went, she worked herself far enough into the darkness to be able to stand up and run.

Just as she had reached around to the far side of the lamppost, an icy fist caught her by the ankle and yanked it sharply, dragging her back, scraping her stomach on stones buried in the mud.

"Y'don't run out on Rob Raffy."

A row of snaggle-edged teeth bit into her ear.

She screamed and clawed out at the brutish face, finding in herself the strength to kick and scratch, drawing upon the reserves of a second and third wind each time she thought she was going to faint.

Three men were standing and tottering, uneasily looking about them with dazed, bobbing heads, then listed toward Rob.

"You bastards will never have enough!" cried the stranger, sailing into them as they stood in a huddle.

They fell backward into the street lamp. Seconds later came the tinkle of shattered glass. Slivers of the protective dome showered upon them, and with a hissing noise the dim flicker was extinguished.

"Blimey . . ."

"Can't see the friggin' sucker . . ."

Thwack . . . thwack. Striking fists resounded in Meg's ears. She held her arms around herself to fend off any blows that might land in her direction.

They were no match for the stranger, of that much she was sure in the rising tide of her cold terror. He had about him the unerring ease, nerve, and calculation of a soldier accustomed to battle; a terrible will to conquer. He was just home from the war and still had the war's blood-lust boiling in his veins, she suspected, admiring him yet fearing him even more than the pack. At the same time she focused hard on the shadows and managed to follow the snaking flash and sweep of the red waistband as he whirled, leaped, straddled, and pounded the gang into a breathless hash. Meg swallowed and pulled herself tightly together, cursing first the brutes and then this hugest brute, not knowing what outcome to pray for. In whose hands would she be worse off?

Then she heard a terrible rapping noise of heads being knocked together, and a double crying out.

"Blasted cokernuts! Help me!" screeched Rob in a terrified howl. "Kill 'im, boys. Peel the skin from 'is bones."

Even as he screamed, the futile frenzy of his fear seemed to infect his mates and stir them to desert him in his need.

Someone bawled, "Dammit, Rob. This ain't no match for the likes of me."

An echo of agreement came from another and another, accompanied by the patter of feet stumbling and slipping away into the dark.

"Eh, boys? Ehhh? Come back!" rang Rob's voice dismally. "Come back, I say. We'll lick the bloody baaaastaaaarrddd!!!" He threatened thus as his own legs began to move, and he, too, started to back off while keeping a careful watch on his attacker.

The unknown source of destruction began to laugh sourly. He loomed close to Rob and could easily have reached out and lifted him by the neck to swing him up to the heavens.

"Go on, Rob," urged the chuckling but gloomy voice. "Run after your mates. Get 'em. Get 'em. Ha. Ha. Ha. Where are they off to, eh? The river boats? Hurry. You'll catch 'em if you've a mind for it. Go on. There's a copper yet to be won tonight."

The encouragement sounded strangely genuine, even though exhibited with the free spirit of nonchalance.

Meg listened and bit down on her lower lip. Her skin began to crawl with apprehension. Any moment this monster would turn his attention to her. Should she again try to run? Might she succeed this time?

Even if she didn't, wouldn't it be worth it to try? And to keep fighting?

She turned at the same time as she decided, trailing away into the murky stew of swirling grime that rose from the docks. The air was like a rough blanket; it covered her and would hide her if she could get enough of a head start.

Her sandals sank into the freezing slime as she stumbled away from the banks into the first alley that appeared, running like a river rat down its hole. On either side tumbledown houses, reeking of dank sewage, closed protectively in upon her. The passage snaked off into crooked streets, making byways complex enough to hide anything that sought refuge in their mazes. This was not the first time that Meg had run from a tormentor, run with the sharp mind of a hunted creature intent upon winning its own life despite the hopelessness of the contest. She no longer thought of her chances but continued numbly, her feet miraculously finding their way from sinking mire onto the more secure footing of cobbles, while the breath stuck in her ribs and she ignored the pain.

She dared not spend the strength to listen, to hear if he followed her.

And then abruptly, as she swung around a corner, there were his footsteps chasing after her.

"Wait now, wait!" he called. "Wait."

The closer his voice the faster she went, impelled

by the strength of an awe she had never in all her life known. *I must lose him. I must . . . I must.*

"Don't run from me, girl . . . come back."

His puzzled voice resounded from the walls, bounding off the old bricks and wood of the houses. She felt sure that she had lost him in the dizzy twist of streets, but she refused to stop and hide in a doorway for fear that he might accidentally tumble in upon her.

"Where are you?"

Her breath came up in harsh wheezes. She tried to stifle the sound and felt her heart pumping harder. All was madness around her, and she the maddest of the lot. *He'll not find me, he'll not . . .*

"Ah! So there you are, little vixen."

She blinked up at the broad expanse of ruffled shirt front blocking her passage. The blood pounded in her ears. Where had he come from? How had he found her so soon?

But it made no difference. She put both fists up and held them in front of her chest, preparing herself to do battle to the death.

Grinding her teeth in readiness, she considered where to attack first. The mute blur of her desperation impelled her into the hard belly ridges, while she drove her knee up along the inside of his thigh.

"Och! Oh! Ow! Devil!"

She felt herself being lifted from the ground in the swooping grasp of mighty arms. His ability to lift her with such ease was a fierce insult, and she kicked out widely, hoping to get him in the gut.

"Put me down. Down!"

"Yes. I'll put you down if you can behave yourself."

She couldn't figure out the musical quality in the voice or how to respond to it. Gathering all her self-control, she made her body quite limp, as though obeying his order. That was the way to do, with men. That was the secret she had learned early in the game of pleasing men against her will. Obedience won the day most quickly. And what she wanted now was her freedom.

As soon as she quieted, he lowered her back to earth. Mute she stood, until she felt his fingers gradually releasing their grip on her elbows.

"Now, there," he said softly, cautiously.

Slowly she rubbed where the pressure marks of his fingers had brought up red bruises. Slowly, slowly, she continued to stroke herself, as though cowed by him, while biding time till she could catch her breath. She dared not look up into his face . . . and it was so far above her. The great tower of his body loomed like a church spire, but she thought of no churches with him. Her mind veered instantly to the tales she had heard of men raping women in the countries they captured. She would not be *his* prize of war.

Her breath returned with agonizing reluctance, and was followed by her first ounce of strength, and she darted around him into a twisting black lane.

"Damn," he called after her. "Is this what you do when I trust you?"

She was swift, but his long strides covered three to her one.

"Listen . . . listen to me."

She could not outdistance him a second time, and darted into a doorway, starting up a flight of creaking steps that swayed as she bounded them two at a time.

"What are you up to in there? Come down. I won't hurt you. I swear it."

The more he promised, the less she believed. He was too intent. Stubbornly, she would not even answer him for fear of giving away what little advantage she held in the shadow where she huddled. She shut her eyes tight and waited. If luck were with her once in her life, he would tire of the sport and go off, seeking some other, easier pleasure than what was to be found with her body.

"Are you coming down to me?"

She pressed her palm to her mouth to stifle any giveaway sound of anxious breathing.

Then came the slide of his boot on the stair, reluctant, casual, sure of its mission and of the reward. He coughed once. It was surprisingly close. A pulse throbbed at the back of her eyeballs. She tilted her head and glimpsed where the staircase ended at the blind of a doorway boarded and shut off. There was no other room to run to, no way to the roof. If she could just find the roof she would jump off. But no. In her blind rage to save herself, she had trapped herself instead. She was caught and held fast by the curve of three walls around her. A seep of water trickled through cracks overhead. As she pressed her back to the wood behind her, the cold mildew stench spread through her thin dress. Yet she did not shiver. As her mind fixed on the approaching menace, she felt as though her fate and her being had already united and become one.

He reached the last step, and from the depths of her vital, living soul, Meg knew she must take one last try for herself. With the clamor of an untamed thing, and the courage of a wild animal going to its slaughter, she flung her body at his, hoping to topple him and for them both to tumble down the steps.

She took him by surprise and he slipped, catching at the wall to steady himself, dropping down a few steps, boots clattering along the edges, heels ringing.

With her arms clinging round his neck, she swung her weight and struggled to unbalance him.

"No. No, don't do it!"

But she *would* do it. Break both their necks, if necessary, so long as she also broke his.

She felt their balance going like a pendulum this way and that as she kicked toward the abyss behind him. He cried out and braced his back to the wall, bent his knees, and let one foot slip down a few steps more, straining the thigh muscles to work against her weight and counterbalance the effort of her body. She felt him leaning in the opposite direction to her flinging thrusts. She pulled at his hair in hopelessness and from the depths of that unhappy, suspended state wondered how to murder him. Gradually she could no longer sway him very far, and he was winning out over her, her weight insufficient to do the battle of her will.

Inside his torn shirt ruffles she could feel the rippling tide of his chest counteracting the meager force of her own life. She understood the masculine body well, and this one that she gripped was exceptional in many ways. Now the gasp in her throat held something more than fear, and she released him suddenly, letting herself tumble down the stair bend, rolling over and over, the ample folds of her muslin skirt cushioning the hard edges that struck her flesh and bones as she fell. She was dimly aware of him clattering along beside her, cursing her for being so pigheaded. When she landed at the base of the stairs, he was right there bending over her.

"This comes to an end now," he muttered. "Before you kill us both."

There was a new tone in him, a determination that had reached the limits of patience with her. Hot humiliation spread through her flesh as she realized how he had been toying with her all the while . . . allowing her the reins to see how far she would gallop. And it had come to this . . . to naught for her. She shut her eyes and turned away from him, unable to face his triumphant look as she felt herself being scooped up like so much straw and packed away in the crook of his arm.

"Wherever you live," he said, "is your own business. But you'll not get home tonight in safety, my fine lass, if you try to go alone. And since I have no horse to take you, worse luck, you'll have to tuck away your temper and come with me."

Chapter Three

HOW COULD she let this happen? It was impossible. Carried under an arm like so much baggage to be shipped away. Meg held her stubborn silence, determined not to give him the satisfaction of her defeat. She would close her mind to him, and so prove that though he could murder her in her sleep, she would never cringe or cry out.

The night's skirmish had shaken her wits, yet she determined to keep track of their path in case by some miracle she could make her escape in tomorrow's new light. As though reading her mind and wishing to make it easier for her, he swung her up and over his shoulder but kept a firm grasp of her legs just above the knees. Alertly, she waited to see how much higher his hands would go and meanwhile tried to count the numbers of the street crossings they passed.

On and on he tramped, past Burr Street and Henry and Nightingale Lane, going along the snake of St. Catherine's docks rather than inland. All the while his hands never moved in exploration, except for the once or twice that he patted her behind when she squirmed, as though reassuring her.

"There's a good girl," he said soothingly. "Hang quiet-like, and we'll be there shortly. Three minutes up the road and it's home. D'you have a name, m'girl?" he asked from time to time.

But she did not once reply, taking a perverse satisfaction in her silence, for he could not force her to talk. When she would not answer, he simply grunted and continued on the march.

Bouncing on his broad shoulder, Meg lay very close

to his head. While she pretended to ignore him, her sharp senses took in the thick quality of his matted, curly hair, pasty with sweat from the fighting, with raven-black glints.

A faint scent of hay rose from his neck. Her palm brushed along the shirt back from time to time, and she felt where it was ripped in places and crusty with blood. But despite the wounds, he walked with a springy, vital force, the relentless, all-powerful tide of an ocean captured in a mere human frame. Exhausted, she could imagine herself drowning in him and did not resist the picture, as though something of fate were in the notion. His endless strength was like a great wave that had crested and rolled in, rushing over her, dragging her with the tide of his will out into deep and dangerous places. The fear of being bedded by this brute turned to something else that she could not name. Her skin prickled with the anticipation of how she would fight him off when he forced her to her back. She became aware again of a shifting, silvery delirium . . . of being obsessed with the need never to give in . . . never!

"Here we are now, sweetheart . . . a king's palace. Good enough for old George and Charlotte, I warrant, but not for the likes of you."

He had stopped at a low lodging house, one in a row of several of the meanest sort, but did not set her down on her feet. She realized he sensed instinctively that she would bolt from him if given the breath of a chance. With a natural ease her captor gently kicked open a door that wobbled on a single hinge and tramped inside.

A pale yellow gloom, the color of weak tea, hung over the splintered remains of banisters torn off for firewood. Meg heard heavy snores through thin walls that followed them up to the first landing. Could it be that this man did not live alone but shared his bedroom with others? If so, would that be a saving grace? Or another dreadful lark?

A second door opened to his foot in the same way,

nd she saw immediately that they would be alone ogether.

Releasing her with one hand, he slapped the door closed behind him.

"I'll stand you on your feet now, but don't do anything foolish."

He slipped her gently from him and she tested her shaky legs, not quite sure of her balance or of the peace that surrounded them as the room flared into view, welling up in the flickering uncertainty of a single tallow candle that he lifted from the floor. The taper itself stood upright, stuck into the head of a cabbage, its leaves held together by layers of drippings. He touched this light to a second and stood them both in their vegetable bases, smoking upward on either end of a long mantel which was quite chipped and split and seemed to sag beneath the weight of a single mug. There was enough light to see by with ease, which struck up Meg's first glimmer of cheer. To see something clearly—not in hazy shadow—was to rob it of its worst terrors. Immediately Meg flung her attention upon the swarthy river pirate to face what she inevitably must.

"Well, then?" he said to her, meeting her eye directly.

For some minutes they stood stock-still, staring and studying each other and saying nothing, except for a grunt of appreciation that escaped his lips without his knowledge.

Meg, for her part, found more than what she had expected. He was younger than he looked, worn tough by war. Blade-steel eyes, very level and open-lidded, seemed to flow like glinting liquid from the depths of a tan, darkly mysterious in winter, with the narrow white slice of a scar tracing across through the left eyebrow. A bony, straight nose with curved nostrils held the arrogance of a prince, an arrogance that carried down to the full, sensuous bow-curve of the lips and into the broad, blunt, forward-thrusting chin that bristled slightly with a shadowed growth. She was startled to find him so handsome, and straightening her caked skirts with rebellious defiance, she sent a cheeky, intense challenge that told him his amusement, his careless ways, and his manners held no charms for her. But then the sash attracted curiosity. She could not understand where it came from or what it meant. Her gaze kept sneaking back to the long strip of scarlet satin swaying round his narrow black breeches, as though she were facing some wild Egyptian-desert devil who had leaped out at her from a fanciful dream. The sash was embroidered with intricate gold leaves that twinkled as he turned on his heel and took down the cracked mug from above the sputtering hearth flames. He noticed the meager fire and poked it with a crooked tong. Fumes of burned wood became heavy, but not smoky on the air. Meg inhaled a sweet fragrance which was nothing like flowers, certainly, but with a bloom . . . a bloom of warmth. It was the warmth that she crept toward, that thawed her brains and enabled her to quickly scan the room and take in cluttered piles of paper on a table and in corners on the floor.

"There you have it," he said. "A nice, hot dish of tea for your troubles."

She looked down into the dark, invigorating brew that he extended toward her with a steady hand. Where was the second cup for him? But not to ask questions. She felt an urge to snap the brim to her cracked lips and swallow the steaming heat down in two washes. But she had promised herself not to let him see her needs. No. Not a single one. Not even her exhaustion. And so she paused and hesitated, as though considering whether it was poisoned, then finally giving him the benefit of the doubt that it was not, gulped the scalding liquid and felt the release of heat through her grateful insides.

"Why, thank you, Mr. Fox," he said for her mockingly. "How nice for a spot of tea on so bleak a night."

She lowered her lashes and peered at him through the thick curve of their forest, sipping at the tea with her frozen palms around the hot mug, her body relaxing, her feelings confused. Should she venture a word to him? What would it be?

In two strides he was at the far side of the hearth, observing her with a devilish glint of interest kindled in those amazingly changeable eyes. The cruelty was gone from them, and so was the determination. Meg recognized something else much more familiar that impelled her not to say a word in his favor. She turned her gaze to the flames while she stood there under his investigation, feeling his thoughts like hands upon her body. Only a matter of time before he would do what she expected . . . and she had already felt the largeness of his loins pressed against her in the scuffle.

"That hair of yours is an odd tint of red, you know," he mused with interest. "Not quite red . . . more titian. The color of elm leaves in autumn. A bit of Venetian, too, reflected by the fire." He strode around the room, staring at her from different angles. "And what are we to say about those cheekbones? And the way you toss your head like a court lady? Intriguing. A mass of contradictions." He waved an arm as he spoke and seemed to grow more fiery, more within himself.

Meg did not understand the language and lifted her chin with a haughty thrust to show him that she was not made uncomfortable and did not fear what he had to say about her looks. She remained silent in the strong light of his inspection, which had passed far beyond the surprise of his first findings. His scrutiny hung upon her like star beams. She would be looking for trouble to face up to it brazenly. No good could come to her thereby, she sensed with thrilling premonition.

"Listen to me," he said softly. "Move over into the light, a little this way." He motioned her leftward, where the shadows were somewhat softer.

Uneasily she did as he asked but shifted her appraising, questioning glance to a row of battered books on the floor along one wall. Near them stood a tall, square easel firmly planted on a stocky base, the only solid object in the room, it seemed, and beside it, a flat table with a bucket holding brushes in a smelly brew.

What was this place? What was he doing? Meg saw a meager patch of rye straw on the far side of the hearth. A bed of sorts. The usual kind of bed that poor men slept on. Yet she sensed it was his alone . . . and she had never, never slept on a whole bed for herself an entire night. What would it be, she wondered with agonized yearning, to fall down upon that soft bit of thatch covered with its scraps of cloth and simply sleep, altogether undisturbed, until light came through the window?

Her gaze traveled with her thoughts and found the single small window with its broken panes. One was stuffed full with smeary colored rags. Another had a squarish bit of paper stuck fast in it. At first she assumed it was a tear of newspaper. But then she noticed a drawing scribbled across it, in broad, humorous lines, of a boar's face, strengthened around the snout and eyes in such a way as to resemble Napoleon! Her eyebrows drew together and a great guffaw sounded from her lips.

"Ah. She speaks."

Instantly Meg clamped her mouth shut and rolled her gaze ceilingward with perfect, innocent indifference.

"Oh, do favor us with another word, my sweetheart."

She brought the mug back to her lips, determined to look neither at him nor at the pictures but directly into the dregs of tea. Yet it was much too hard on tired eyes to do that for very long. Soon she was peeping up again at the curious, interesting pull of the walls around her, covered from top to bottom with drawings and more drawings. Some had been done with black burned sticks, others with red chalks. Profiles of faces she recognized. The prince with his high waves of brushed and brilliantined hair. A full front view of the square, sullen, slow-eyed king. Chubby-cheeked Queen Charlotte. Each face reflected a convincing, inner spirit so that the eyes seemed to gleam and follow her. Even though they had all been sketched over the words on white newsprint paper, she fancied she could make out the complexions, the very quality of the skin that went with each personality. Still, there was more and more of interest: a horse rearing in battle, mounted riders with sabers clashing over a hill of corpses. The wall of sketches became a wall of life: country pastures; rivers; gorges and castles in the distance behind billowy trees; waterfalls with their steeply dropping spill had a flow to them. Meg fancied she could almost hear the gurgle and roar. Some scenes were quite large and were accomplished with simple strokes. What is this all about? she wondered with awe.

"I see you enjoy my art work," he laughed. "Those you are looking at right now are watercolors, I suppose you can tell as much. I did them on a walking tour through Scotland near the River Dee. If you look closely, you can find a young man fishing from the riverbank, and his rod is bending because he has just hooked a salmon."

She peered in closer, and true enough, there he was, seriously gripping the rod with strong concentration, a large fish well hooked, she could tell, by the angle of his body and the way the rod curved over. A rush of the water swirled over some rocks and a wicker fish basket lay open in the high grasses.

"Those are quick sketches," he explained, "but have some faint interest of their own for me."

"Salmon," she breathed, hardly realizing that she spoke, and wondering how salmon tasted. She had often seen men eating it with a dab of green dressing. The last time she had tasted fish was in the downstairs kitchen of a baronet who was amused to indulge her fancy for it. How she had promised to do anything for some dainty fishes on toast, and how he had known it! One tiny whitebait had arrived, teasing and tempting her floating tongue. She remembered the sensation of his lips nibbling on her neck as she tried to stuff her mouth with the succulent morsel.

"Yes. Salmon. I've a taste for it, too, in the right season, of course," he added, easily reading her fascination. "Now look over here. At these more complicated paintings. They are in oils. Do you know what oil paintings are?"

She nodded vehemently, never having seen one quite this close. "Of course I know oil pictures. They are . . . them."

"Yes." He smiled at her with a gentle amusement that took in the full length of her compact but voluptuous body with its back arched very straight and her dirty fingers gesturing with unself-conscious grace. He drew in a long, yearning breath, then sent his gaze swiftly back to the subject. "Oils are the enduring backbone of painting," he continued with relish, rubbing his hands together in the warm radiations of the meager flame.

"Backbone, eh? There's bones in paintings, I suppose." She was laughing at her joke and at him in turn, gathering her courage, now that the ice was broken, to speak up.

"I could mean bones as you and I have bones." He left the painting now and was upon her with a full survey, talking in a brisk and earnest style that she half suspected and listened to with reservations. "By the bones of a painting I mean its enduring qualities. When Sir Joshua Reynolds did a portrait of a great lady, for example, he would fix her image in oils. Her proud and appreciative husband would then mount the picture upon some properly lighted wall in one of his country houses . . . and there begins immortality. She will become a mother and a grandmother. Her youthful beauty will fade. But generations thereafter will stand and admire her upon the wall, in the brushwork and genius of Sir Joshua. Just as someday," his voice fell to a husky growl, "they will admire mine."

Her glance flicked over to the blazing, hawklike intensity of his sunburned face. Sometimes as he talked he would prance about, as though the world living inside him might burst through the mortal bonds. At other times he stood solemnly, his broad fingers clasped behind his back, head tilted so that a lock of hair fell forward from the widow's peak over the high, furrowed brow. The room was always too small for him, and when he paced, soft leather boots creaking, their heels clicking on the wide floorboards, he seemed ready to fly at any moment to the source of some cherished, calling voice.

"You did all these pictures, then?"

"Every one."

"Mm."

"And what do you mean, *mm?*"

"Is that what I said? *Mm?*"

"Mm."

They smiled at each other. The smiles grew into grins.

"It's all very interesting," she said.

Her voice trembled with exhaustion, but she fought not to give in. What if she stopped talking? What if they stopped talking about painting? She understood too well what else was occupying his thoughts behind their conversation. She must do everything to keep things back there behind their curtains, till daybreak.

"I've had all this marvelous tea," she said. "And you've none."

"Well, though." He brushed it aside impatiently. "What do you think of the paintings? Are they no more to you than *interesting?*"

What did he want her to say? She was suddenly not quite sure of *everything* in his turbulent mind.

"Sit down," he ordered brusquely, pushing a stool at her as though suddenly seeing clear through to the tired marrow of her bones.

It was the single chair in the room, a rude construction of thick legs and flat seat, very squat, with some of the cross slats missing. Everything that she noticed was an only item. He had no brothers, no sisters, no family living here with him. No wife. No sweetheart. She could tell these things. He was a loner of the world, one of the bad debts that her father never tried to collect from.

"Yes, I'll sit down," she said, and dragged the chair a bit closer to the fire's glow.

As the weight came off her legs and she relaxed, she nearly fell asleep exactly as she sat, the little shadows of the blue-tipped flames sliding and winking, while the wood chips and bits of coal snapped away into ash. All her strength now went into the business of keeping her eyelids unstuck as wave after wave of sleepiness passed over her, which she fought against with the same might and will she had used earlier against this man. "Fox," she said, trying it.

"Dick Fox." He smiled with an exaggerated bow. "At your service." He poured more tea from the pot into her dish.

"Meg Watkins," she offered softly, glancing up from her mud-caked slippers to his face, which held more interest for her just then than the paintings.

"Meg Watkins deserves better than to be roaming among ruffians."

"Not roaming at all, but parting from the presence of a gentleman," she said, blushing, then changed the subject. "Tell me about *that* picture, for instance. The one in the corner, high near the ceiling, with the angels and the harps."

"That's an early one," he replied easily, happily distracted. "As a very young man, I learned to work by making copies from the Italian masters."

"Well, it looks familiar to me, you see," she replied seriously, wagging a finger at him. "I saw its mate someplace. Now just let me think."

"Its mate, eh? There is no mate. Maybe you saw the original." He watched her with a kind of long-held wonder. "Where might you have been, Meg, to have seen it?"

She laughed aloud and grinned at him with gleeful, childlike triumph. "You think I never seen pictures before yours here? To the contrary, I seen many of them hanging near the gloomy green curtains . . . in shadows in the great houses. I been to great houses in my time, not like most." She pressed one fist strongly to a thigh, her legs wide-spread beneath their skirts, the mug resting on the other thigh. "I've been in the company of your Graces and such, who has these pictures by the score hanging there, one above the other, like I said."

His lips grew suddenly grim before the brunt of her cheer. "Did you work in those houses, Meg? What sort of work did you do?"

"You don't want to ask me that," she replied with low and flippant ease.

"No, I don't," he said kindly.

He turned slightly from her and she saw the curve of his back suddenly bowing a bit, slumped like a man who had lost a great gamble. Somehow that didn't sit well with her. "Now cheer up, Fox," she said merrily. "I have a proper trade, as you might say, working with me dad. Yes, me old dad. You wouldn't want to know the likes of Harry Watkins too close, but not the world's worst work most of the time." Her voice rang valiantly. "I'll tell you right out what I do, Fox, and set your mind at rest. I help the old devil collect debts. What rich men lose to each other at cards or at the horses is fair shocking." As she spoke, as she tilted her mind around to recall the adventures of her life in the light of this room, why, it didn't seem quite so rotten as she had believed! Not a bit. "Listen to me," she said, smiling, her eyes glazed over with sleep. "I could talk to you all week about the oil paintings I've seen in my time and never have to stop. I seen French paintings and Italian paintings and Greek paintings. Yes, Greek, how about that, enough to make your eyes pop. Why, the sailors bring 'em home every day of the month to their mums, but not anywhere near as good as the ones already here in this room."

He turned back to her slowly with a warming twinkle. "I can see it, Meg. You're an educated and sensitive woman in your own style. One to be listened to with care and appreciated."

She hung suspended at his words, waiting to see if he would burst out laughing, but nothing of the sort happened. "Well, it is true I saw all those pictures, though to tell you exactly the idea, I wasn't paying much attention to 'em at the time. There was other things on a girl's mind, to be sure."

"To be sure, Meg."

"But I don't mind telling you, Dick Fox"—the words

grew rapid and warm on her tongue—"that I can see you have a real fire for this line of work. Art, isn't it? And I would have the right to tell you, seeing as how I've seen so many pictures, that you could stand up in their company and compare."

She felt herself rattling on and on, enjoying the attention of his steely eyes leveled straight at her, watching her as though there were something of interest to be found in her dirty, stiff skin, her mud-thick, wretched hair that she kept shrugging away from her cheeks. The mugs of hot tea were just the topping to her spirit, she realized. And she was sitting down, safe enough from Harry Watkins, at least for the time being.

"I want to tell you, Dick Fox." She leaned toward him with an impressive confidence. "I ran off from a peer of the realm tonight, an actual earl, because I didn't choose to give in to what he was askin' of me." Why was she bothering to tell him all this? Would it stop him? Delay him? Affect him at all?

He worked the empty mug gently from her fingers without replying to her boast, said, "One good stroke of fortune deserves a second," and motioned her to the straw bed.

She would have questioned him, tested her ground, but somehow her mind stopped dead, a horse shot in bright sunlight and fallen to its knees upon the highway. The bed was more good grace than her world would ever hold on another day. She would not dare to think about tomorrow or Harry Watkins or even what Dick Fox might do to her in her sleep.

She tottered in a hazy slow motion and fell upon the long, soft rectangle of crackling straw. For a moment she lay on her side, hands across her breasts, waiting for the inevitable touch and feel of his approach, watching for him tensely with final, feeble efforts at wakefulness.

The last thing she remembered was a snuffling, snoring sound coming from her own mouth, and an answering snuffling snore drifting to her from behind the chair at the far side of the settling hearth.

Chapter Four

HAUNTED FRAGMENTS of memory snatched her from sleep in the cold, dead-still darkness of dawn. Meg lay trembling inside the pent-up fury of her life, sniffing the dead ash, laughing and crying inside with a vague hysterical sense that she had left her father's house forever. She was never one to pause very long over sour milk or to try to save it. There was no one at home she would miss. With her mother dead and her brothers in the navy, only Harry Watkins and she were left. And now she had run away, so it was only she herself. She hugged her shoulders together for a bit of sustaining warmth. Harry must get his pig's fry dinner for himself, without her. And she would damn well do the same without him. Gingerly she stretched out one leg and then the other, the bruised, aching muscles crying for mercy in the dream of his beating her. Then, recalling last night's actual struggles, she chose to dwell only on the interesting parts . . . the curious kindness that had come her way in the disguise of a swarthy-faced artist.

Her ears picked up the easy sound of his breathing, rather too light and shallow for sleep. As she lay with her back to him, a certain gentle quality stirred and she knew, without having to look, that he was watching her from across the floor. Her skin began to tingle with mixed anticipations. She waited, wondering how long it would take before he came and dropped upon her like a dog in rut. But that old defensive stance ended quickly as she realized he must have been watching for quite some time but had not come to disturb her. In the early break of light upon the room, her heart felt lighter, too; her lips, stroked by fingers of calm, parted slightly in a smile. She didn't want to move but rather to lie here for hours, with things remaining exactly as they were between her and Dick Fox, each one very conscious of the other yet not doing anything at all, and certainly not being brutal.

Her knowledge of men was only of that: brutality. She had heard tales of affection between people, but never in her life had there been such a luxury. For her, love was earning a living. They were one and the same, and she had been lucky that men found her desirable or Harry would have kicked her out soon enough. She believed, therefore, that spreading her legs was where everything began and also ended. She didn't think twice of herself or her own pleasures, and so, at this delicate moment, she had no idea what to feel or expect, for she held no experience of anything like it. A somewhat feathery and illusive turmoil began to tremble inside her. She lay half on the verge of sleep and half waking, unsure of which as she drifted and softly sighed from time to time, content in the knowledge that she had ceased to think or plan any more escapes. She lifted one hand and stroked the hair that lay about her face in tangles, unaware of the modesty in the gesture or of the deep, hungry desire for the fulfillment of unspoken, unexpected beauty that dwelled within.

A board creaked where she knew he lay. She held her breath. Heard him moving across the floor. Now he crouched behind her, stretched out beside her. She felt the outlines of the hard, full length of his body touching her own, lightly brushing against her, utterly aware of her dreamy, drifting state and not wishing to disturb it. The smile that had lain on her lips slipped with a warm glow down her throat and into her breasts in a bath of languid ecstasy that he was being *careful* with her. Cor blimey! Was it true? Yes! Yes! Still, her brain fought against believing and accepting this strange, disquieting reality; he was just a man after all. Yet she reached behind her and felt about to find his hand and stroke the long fingers, touching on the tops of each of the distinctive shape of knuckles, the soft tufts of hair, the rounded nails. It was delicious to see him through her sense of touch.

He edged in closer. She smelled the gin and the sweat and the mud on him, and it was the same as her very own flesh. He rested his mouth gently on the curve of her jaw just beneath the ear lobe, and his beard prickled from the pressure of the weight of his head.

"I've been up for hours," she sighed, needing, perversely, to tease him a bit.

"No, you haven't, wench." He laughed gently on her cheek.

"Been watching me?"

"Most of the night."

But she had heard him snore, too. They were both liars.

"Don't you ever sleep?"

"When I'm in jail."

His lips were exploring now, moving along the sides of her mouth, nibbling lightly, tasting. She sensed with amazement that he reined himself. She had never known a man could. Or would, if he could.

"Dick Fox," she whispered.

"What is it, sweetheart?"

"You're a curious thing."

"You hardly know the half," he chuckled.

I may yet know the whole, she thought, deciding it was wiser, however, not to let him hear her mind.

He took his time with her and rolled her into his arms, not turning her around yet but remaining behind, their bodies forming into mutually molded lines. The room was an ice island, and there was nothing left to put upon the fire. The heat from his huge body radiated an intense warmth, an animal energy that she leaned into, deriving strength from it as though he were the source of life—the sun—and she a seed absorbing and readying herself to open. Yes, it was all very curious how she sensed that she existed . . . that Dick Fox and Meg Watkins were together without either being master or slave. She had performed unspeakable acts with men or for them, but somehow she had always protected herself from the brunt of the experience, distracting her mind by thinking of other things when she could, or by fuddling her wits with gin. This was so different. She responded to every breath, every stroke, concentrated in an unusual way —as though for the first time in her life her eyes were clear and she could see. She reached up and pressed her hand over his fingers as they spread across her shoulder. She brought those fingers in front of her face, examining what an artist's hand looked like close up.

"The hand of a prince of pleasures," he laughed. As she joined him in the chuckle, he slipped his other arm beneath her and turned her toward him.

In a moment the languishing sun was blotted out by the heaving, possessing thrust of loins against her stomach.

She laughed raucously with a triumph of familiarity and lapsed into her old guardedness.

"I wondered if you was a man," she cackled, grinning, willing to show him what she could do to please.

He had no time for talk. She wondered if he had even heard her as his mouth plunged greedily and sucked her tongue out to answer the restive searching of his own. But he did not hurt her. Completely, tenderly, he captured her in his arms. She drew breath and gave way, vanquished, freed at last from the tormenting bonds that had always held her passionate nature caged. Her mouth responded to him as her body rose in a flourish of gorgeous, throbbing desire. Desire that boggled her. She could not think what to make of it. For all the bodies she had known, this, her own, was a stranger. Friend now! Herself her own friend! The fleshy globes that men had chewed and mauled sprang into new worlds of thrilling sensation. The hands she had fondled reached beneath the scraps of her dress and lifted out her breasts, covering them quickly with his palms and then his fingers and finally his mouth. She felt herself shiver wherever he touched her, shuddering now in deep, devastating contractions. *For all you've been used, you were never a woman,* she thought with her eyes closed. Her girl's features twisted into the bittersweet anguish of desire, escaping into joyful glories of expression.

He hunched over her, rocking hard, a stallion stretched out and galloping free. She reached out and caught hold of the risen masculinity, thick and long and bull-like, tilting at her, exuding a sweet perfume all its own and sticky to her touch. Beneath it the hairy sacs swayed, wrinkle-skinned and hot, possessed of the nuggets of life, driven to release inside her. His eyes turned to flame and watched insatiably her every movement while those fingers that she loved reached down to fondle her at the cave of her thighs.

And here came something else new and fresh: they did not tear her tender flesh, did not drive deeply in, but played at the edges with a tantalizing, teasing exploration. Leaping thrills suffused the area, and her body gave off a liquid film that spread over the inside lips of her entrance.

"You're ready," he whispered reassuringly.

He knew more of her body than she herself, and with a sudden trust she gave over into his care her passion, soul, and survival. She caught hold of his fleshy, nubbed stick and slid her hips forward. The touch of the helmet-tipped head nuzzled its way inside, working with slow, advancing circles. Gradually deeper it sank. Her hips soon responded with a special will, lifting and shifting to catch the full drive of him. His hands slipped beneath her and held her steadily in place.

"You're very, very tight," he said, surprised and pleased.

"Yes," she chuckled. "Even while I laid with the whole world, there was something special I was keeping back for you, Dick Fox."

"Does it hurt?"

"Nothing hurts me."

"Of course not. Does it hurt?"

"A bit."

"I'll be easy."

"You can do what suits you."

He hung there cradled by the insides of her thighs while she tightened her knees around his narrow waist. If he didn't move, everything would be just fine, but it could never work that way.

"You're not going to tell me you are a virgin, Meg?"

"Lud, no!"

He grunted something skeptical.

She grabbed hold of his hand and pressed a few fingers to the opening between her other cheeks. "Most men I been with like it better in here."

"I see. . . . And you yourself?"

She didn't want to tell him that she never liked anything till right now. Before she could think of something to say that wouldn't pop his eyes out, he lifted her to him, taking long, driving motions into her that stretched her and sent himself up to the hilt.

"Eeeeoooh."

"It's the only way to do it, luv. Quick and clean."

"It's fine. I don't mind," she panted, clinging to him, feeling the sweat begin to sprout down her back.

And it was so. The pain was a mere flash that shot from head to toes and out and away forever. She blinked and realized that he had driven himself all the way home. She could tweak her inside muscles and feel the full length of him hovering there in the wet cave of her being. She liked that idea. She began to swivel her hips in short, experimental strokes, seeing what it actually felt like, doing it for fun now.

"What a curious feel," she said aloud.

"Is it good?"

"Dunno yet. Wait a minute. Oh. My. Ohmy." She shivered and clawed him. The ability to form words slipped away. Something soft and gasping cried out from her as he continued to move. She held on and kept herself swinging in the concentrated action that he controlled at a steady pace. He wasn't running away with her but maintaining a rhythm that she could manage and follow easily.

"This is good," she grunted, wanting him to hear it. "Stay so."

"As long as you wish."

Yet for all his obedience and concern for her wants, she knew for certain that there was another side to making love with passionate, careless, greedy prizes and that Dick Fox would show it to her one day.

Bits of thoughts came and went while she continued to ride beneath him. Old pictures. Boys poking her as she lay asleep. Old men pushing her head down on limp gizzards. She embraced Dick, galloping along the underbelly of her mighty steed. Her stallion knew where they were going . . . was taking her away to a better place . . . where they could live and be free. Free!

They had, together, in silent harmonious assent, increased the speed of their movements. Her thighs trembled from the tension of gripping his hips. They were all wet and greasy from last night's mud melting in the heat of their love. The dirt that was her own smeared and mingled with his, but their mouths were clean and their kisses like crystal, washed by the fresh, flowing waters of their passion.

Then certain quirking, jerking movements began to occur harshly, demandingly, without warning.

"You're ready now," he rasped at her. "Do it! Do it now!"

Her body heard him with total willingness, and the magic in his commanding voice swept her away. A large convulsion drowned her in its hot, curving wash. Round and round she swirled, tumbling over herself inside, stretching, contracting, spilling sweet treacle.

As the roaring tide began, it dragged him along, and she glimpsed in a split second of revelation her own being, *her own power over him.*

Mind-shattering to watch the little nicks of scars across his face and chest, pale beneath the nut-brown tan, as he was drawn, compelled, controlled by her body to respond with huge shuddering contractions of his own. The animal grunts rising from the very roots of his soul told her how good she was for him.

Unbearably, deliciously, the sensation lingered, growing more intense and possessive. It twined them together in vines of invisible bondage, stronger, more enduring even, than the mingling of their mere limbs.

But soon, too soon, she sensed the delicate crest begin to weaken and slip, subsiding lower and gradually flowing out into a vast sea of calm. She would have called it back again if she could. To let go of him seemed a terrible admission of defeat and loss. She wanted him always and forever as they were, with neither past nor future times to interfere. *Fox . . . Fox . . . Fox. . . .*

He lay on his back between her and the ash, poking it occasionally in hopes of uncovering some lost spark. Only gray wisps tumbled over and rose in clouds. On the mantel lay a film of frost.

"There'll be icicles dripping down from it in an hour," Dick muttered, and began to wrap her up in what was left of her clothes. On the far side of the cracked wall echoed a din of hammering.

"Ah. The old hen is at work," he said with increasing cheer. "We'll have some heat in a minute." With the side of his fist he rapped on the wall, calling, "For God's sake, Mrs. Bannish, let it be!"

"Is that the likes o' you, Dick Fox, home at last?"

"Home it is I am," he called, imitating her Irish accent. "And freezing to death with my woman."

"Lord be praised, I have your meaning, Fox! I've half an armful here beside the good boards and y'r welcome to take what you please." Then came a hesitating cough. ". . . *if* you done the job for me!" Her voice was lower, intimate, as though there were no wall between them.

"And so I have," he replied. "Or would I be callin' to you in vain."

With that he gave the wall a final slap, and hitching on his breeches, snatched one of the drawings from the pile scattered on the floor beneath the window.

"I'll be back in a flash, my love," he said with a conspiratorial wink.

Meg had no idea what Mrs. Bannish intended to do with the picture, and hoped she could hear more of his conversation when he arrived next door. He slammed out of the room, and she heard the fall of his heavy-booted stride pass through the other door.

"So there y'are at last, you old rogue," called Dick's voice.

There came a silence then, as though the two friends were hugging or kissing each other. Meg sighed in frustration, wanting to be part of it. She crept closer to the wall and touched her cheek against it, pressing her ear mightily and closing her eyes.

"Now let's see what you've done for me."

"There it is," said Fox. "Good for a sporting print and fifteen guineas. Will Feargus pay me half? You'll make your fortune on my genius before too long . . . and who will know it, Maundy? Who will know?"

There was chagrin and anger in his voice, a tone Meg had not heard before.

"There, there, Fox. It will all come right one day, and the world will know you for the man you are."

"I say it," Fox continued, calmer.

"You think you ought to say it, that's the fact. Ought to say it more than mean it in your heart. Fox. What you want, and *all* you want, is to do the drawing. You've such a blinding passion for the work, for the work itself, that you never could tend to the business of it. Which is how come such as I can earn a few coppers from your flesh and blood."

"Flesh and blood it is, Maundy. And I don't begrudge you."

"I know that, boy. Now listen and look here. . . ."

There came a sound of heavy parchment or canvas crinkling, of something large and cumbersome being unfurled.

"What think ye of this?"

"Why, that's a copy of a Correggio."

"Sure and it is, Fox. A beauty, aye? Old Feargus snuck into the Duke of Glewster place in Piccadilly. Yes. All the way out to there he crept. And here is what he finds hanging in his home. This very forged scene itself."

"Come, Mrs. Bannish. I don't believe your tricks.

That wise old sack of gold wouldn't have a phony on his walls. And stop blinking at me!"

"Bend an ear close to me, Fox, and listen. Feargus seen it with his very eyes. No, not this copy, I imagine. But one very like. Old moneybags *has* been duped, I tell ye. They got to him, too, at last, and sold him what he said he wanted to have. Hee, hee. You understand me, Fox? Glewster couldn't bear to believe it. None of 'em does. That all their money and their influence with this throne and that doesn't buy the best there is in all the world. If Napoleon could snatch out the finest pictures from underneath the noses of kings, says Glewster, what is stopping he? Heh. Heh. Heh. I heard wind of it only a month and a fortnight gone. And then comes old Feargus with his paint and his brushes and his two failing eyes—and wuff! wuff! wuff! barks out a fine Italian picture that we sells to old Glewster with the color still wet upon the canvas. And he doesn't blink a flicker."

"Poor dumb horse."

"That may be, boy. That may be so. And old Feargus thinks it's time for you to climb down from *your* high horse and do some more work for us of that soft sort, too."

"Anyone can do the Italians," said Fox with disdain.

"You're the only one I know of doesn't care a snap to earn a living. But how about this one?"

There came the crinkling sound of more unfurlings and a quiet, self-satisfied chuckle from Mrs. Bannish as Fox said, "Well, now, that's a little different," sounding openly enthusiastic. "I don't mind selling the lords of our land some paintings done by their own French cousins. And besides, it's time for me to work in a lighter-toned palette."

"You'll do this Frenchie, then? That's a fine boy. Now take your wood. Take all you wants of it. There's more where it come from."

Meg leaned her back to the wall and folded her arms over her naked breasts, engrossed in the meaning of what she had overheard. She cared less that Fox should find her where she stood eavesdropping than that he explain the business he was engaged in with Mrs. Maundy Bannish, obviously a shrewd old hag.

He came swinging in with the rolled-up picture under one arm and some hefty slats and banister poles in the other.

"Well, Meg," he said, catching her preoccupied expression. "I'll introduce you to the witch herself one day, if you like. And we all three can be friends."

She flung him a dubious glance. "Is this how painters earn their bread?"

He dropped the fags into the fireplace and bent to set them alight, not deigning to answer her. She realized immediately that she had ruffled him. Had touched a tender nerve end of pride. For all his flamboyance and nonchalance, his painting was not something she could make light of.

"What I do for bread and what I do for myself are far and away worlds apart," he replied. "And so it may always be, for all the Lord knows. Still, I have myself a fine time . . . and a warm time," he added, grinning, dragging her close to the rising, spluttering flame. "Now toast yourself well," he said. "What a rosy, clear skin you have. How these shoulders glow in the light."

She fell into a throbbing silence as he traced a finger over her skin. Eagerly she would make love to him again, for it had happened too quickly and had been too wonderful to understand all at once. She wanted to be in his arms, to kiss and be kissed—everywhere—to relive the freshly discovered gift of giving and taking pleasure.

And so she stood too close to the fire, feeling it grow and burn upward while she swayed idly. But he moved suddenly away, and her thoughts traveled and flitted after him as he rummaged among the contents of a large, shallow wooden box on the floor beneath the window. He crouched over it, tossing out bits of rags and bread and slivers of burned sticks and an oval palette. He laid out flat pans of color with much more care, separating the blues from the yellows and the reds. She enjoyed watching him putter among his beloved things while she absorbed the heat and was finally warm enough to sidle up to him.

She slipped her arms around his waist and whispered, "Sweet one, kiss me."

He swung around and kissed her abruptly, absently. The lack of attention startled her. She began to question him, then shook her head, opening her mouth but remaining speechless as she remembered his words to Mrs. Bannish: *my woman.*

"You *are* beautiful," he breathed. "Truly. Now stand over there. You see where that streak of light is? Yes, along the window but to the left a pace. That's just right. Stay still. Stand. Can you find a more comfortable position?" He laughed. "But you're exhausted, and I'm forcing you to pose standing up. Now, that will never do. How's the chair? Put your dress on it. Drape your stockings over the back. Yes, carelessly. I want you to be entirely natural about everything, that's the secret. Nature. Draw from nature. Paint from nature. Learn from nature in every respect."

She heard him rambling and realized gradually, with an impudent satisfaction, why he had bothered to have her warm herself. Why he had troubled to go next door in the first place and handle the shrew with the babbling mouth.

"You don't mind posing for me, do you, my sweetheart?" he asked, not really listening for an answer as he set out his painting things on the deal table beside the easel.

"It's better than going back to Dad," she replied with a saucy glint, and thought: *If only I can please him!*

"I said sit."

His voice was a bark, but she knew it wasn't meant for her directly. She had ceased to exist as a lover to him and had been transformed, miraculously, into a kind of art thing. An *objet d'art* was the French expression she had learned from a sailor one night in a tavern, who laughingly told her that brothel whores in Paris called themselves *objets d'art.*

"The shadows aren't falling well across your bosom. Swing around."

Where had the love gone? There was so much concentration, so much busyness. And there was no talking to him as those penetrating eyes began to go through her, picking out the framework of her skeleton, as he explained it, and the lights and the shadows—and the way the muscles hung on her legs! Muscles hanging on her legs? There came upon her a peculiar but thrilling feel of transformation. One moment she was a breathing, living person. The next, she was the object of his intense search and study. She fancied her likeness appearing like magic. A picture on a canvas, just like the French portrait of "La Duchesse," which she remembered seeing in the hallway of some earl's mansion. Wouldn't that be a lark? Copies out straightaway. In pretty colors that showed her auburn hair and the white teeth she was proud of, with only one missing, and that one so far back it could not be seen. What if a picture painted by Dick Fox could become famous, and it was a picture of Meg Watkins? Then the two of them, she and Fox, would be forever linked together in tales and history.

She sensed his high, brooding energy flowing out from behind the easel, feeling her all over with his eyes. For hours he was silent, flinging back his hair, occasionally scowling, mumbling to himself, but in other respects quite unaware of his surroundings. She felt that he had created a tunnel between them, through which a portion of him traveled, scooped up a portion of herself, and returned with it for placement on the canvas. As the idea of her was caught and fixed, he began to talk in short sentences that soon grew more complete.

"Posing is a tiresome business," he said. "Tell me about yourself and the time will go faster."

"There's nothing much to say," she replied, honestly at a loss, her attention settled completely upon this man with such intense, compelling urges. Before it was the love. Now it was the drawing. She had no idea which was more important to him.

There came a short knock upon the door. Before Dick answered, it burst open with the explosive presence of a great-sized, billowy-chested woman in dark skirts and a smeared white smock, salt-and-pepper hair piled in a topknot, red face pudgy as a carved potato, clear black eyes gleaming shrewdly.

"So this is the reason for the wood pile," she said with a knowing glint, not at all concerned that she had interrupted.

Fox pointed his brush at her like a rifle and was at her side in one swift stride. "Maundy Bannish. Out. Out. You know my rules!"

Meg watched him spin her around and march her from the room with a no-nonsense strength that could turn back the tides to France. The door shut with a bang before Mrs. Bannish could open her mouth to protest.

"Never mind it," he said casually, resuming his position at the portrait. "She knows by now never to interrupt me in my work. But she had an idea that I was on to something with you, and she wanted to see it for herself."

"Me?" Meg said, burning with flattered curiosity.

But he was lost again in some rapid brush strokes that ended the conversation.

By midafternoon she was fainting with hunger while Dick was still going at it with a will.

"Take heart . . . take heart," he called to her at intervals. "This is it . . . this is it, exactly."

It was hard, at first, to conceive that her body with its dirty, unwashed streaks could be so interesting to a man for so long. Yet when she began to squirm, he plied her with spice buns, ale, new bread, and old cheese. Her starved belly gave way to a certain lightheadedness. She sat back in her chair and let her mind roam.

"Did a fine painter like Sir Joshua"—she remembered the name from the night before—"ever care to paint his wife?"

"Of course," snapped Dick, in the center of his whirlwind. "Any subject that fascinates is fair game."

"Was this Sir Joshua really very good? He couldn't be better than you, I warrant."

"If he was, then it's not by far," laughed Dick with a flippant deviltry. He put down the brush and inspected her from head to toe, comparing what he saw with what he had painted. "One small difference has to do with the Royal Academy," he muttered, winding down from the picture he had evidently concluded for the day. "I'll tell you of the Royal Academy if you want to hear it."

"Don't I know it myself?" she boasted happily. "That's the place of fame and reputation."

"A collection of meager idiots, for the most part, banded together with their stolen supplies and hiding out at old Somerset House on the Strand. What niggling and bickering and petty disputes! Reynolds despised Gainsborough and Gainsborough despised Reynolds. Wilson was all animosity toward them, and Barry would have nothing to do with anyone less of a painter than himself. Yet how does it all add up in the end? One day while Sir Joshua was painting the portrait of the Marchioness of Hertford, he felt the sight beginning to disappear from his left eye. He set down his pencil, sat for a while in mute thought, and never lifted that pencil again. Within two weeks after that attack, he was totally blind."

"Tush. That would never happen in your case, Dick Fox."

"And if it did, if I did lose my sight, I'd continue to paint ne'ertheless . . . and would be the first great, blind painter in history."

Meg sat quietly, pondering the meaning of Dick's passion, watching him as he contentedly cleaned his tools and set the drawing of her beside the window to dry. But then she could not resist going to it, her nakedness forgotten, and looking down upon the likeness of her flesh, gleaming and wet and smelling with the pungent, nostril-itching scent of turpentine. The day's waning light fell poorly on it, and she reached to bring a candle in more closely.

"No, no," he warned, snatching away the flame. "You'll set us ablaze with that mixture."

He tilted the portrait for her to see it as best she could, and the likeness made her flush with its voluptuous discoveries.

"But I am not that pretty!"

"You are even more so."

Now satisfied with the day's work, he swept her into his arms and carried her off to their love bed of straw.

He was an animal with ever-changing hungers, in ardent exploration of desires. Meg, enfolded and burning with the glory of new lust, yielded deliriously to this strange creature with whom she was beginning to feel an alliance.

Yet, lying on her back, stroking his head resting between her breasts, she dared to think of the day when Dick became a recognized painter. To her mind it seemed utterly natural that he should already be one.

"If I understand you rightly," she mused, twisting the curls at his neck and sending her fingers downward to knead the tension from his shoulders, "you are bitter against the Royal Academy. What has it to do with your career?"

"Bitter? Perhaps. Angry, more likely."

"But why? Do you need them?"

"Who does *not* need them . . . in the social manner? Every painter or sculptor or engraver who wishes to make his mark *needs* the R.A. letters after his name. It is the insignia, the stamp of approval. What patrons who have the money to spend would go elsewhere than to an R.A. for portraits of his family or his horses or his great house?" His lips slid upward along the side of her jaw. "Any bungling fool can bulge his pockets with guineas once he is elected to the Royal Academy."

"You do not wish it, then, for yourself?"

"What are you saying, Meg? You don't know anything about it? Such innocence you pretend! You have the face of a child but the mind of ten such devils as Mrs. Bannish next door." He laughed calmly. "You understand me perfectly. You have already concluded that I am determined to manage. And so it shall be, I tell you, without the tyranny of patronage."

"I do not see how else you are to go about it," she persisted, in the same determined tone that had first disconcerted him.

"Go about it? No, I cannot do bear dancing in a funny suit at Royal Academy dinners. Of course I would *go about it,* as you say, if I could bring myself to that distasteful task. But it is not my nature."

"It requires very little of you, I should think?"

"It requires a whole new spinal column for kowtowing and . . . phew! just to talk about it makes the blood pound."

"I see."

And she did see. This creature in her arms would rather thieve and swindle and God knew what else, than struggle for the compromising trappings of fame. To paint was all he really needed, as Mrs. Bannish said. To gain a reputation was quite an unimportant matter. Her mind began to kindle as she considered this aspect of his career. She was willing to wager that his social circle had never carried very far up the ladder, and this was the hopeless barrier to his advancement. But she, on the other hand, could easily tick off the names of seven peers of the realm she had lain with in the course of seven successive nights. Had she ever, in her wildest notions, dreamed that she could put to use the brutes she had known so intimately?

"I can tell your mind is very busy, little vixen. Don't you take on any ideas for me or my art. They won't work. Personally, you may handle me as you wish. But . . . but . . . BUT . . . I am not to be harangued or—"

She put her mouth over his to cover the temper beginning to rise and which she felt instinctively could be dangerous to the growth of their fine understanding.

"I don't wish to do anything," she replied sincerely, "that will displease you."

He bit gently into the cushion of her palm until she let go of his mouth. Then he lowered his face to hers and she felt the insistent, urging pressure of his stiffening maleness spring into steady, pulsing life. Their conversation, which had nothing to do with love, had inflamed them both. The mere act of talking, of being together, of physically touching, was what mattered. She had no interest, really, in the business affairs of artists. Nor did she care whether or not Dick Fox became rich and wealthy . . . so long as whatever he did pleased him, and somehow included her.

Yet her mind could not turn away from the challenge suddenly placed upon it to rally all her resources for the advancement of her man. A parade of earls and dukes and baronets presented themselves for consideration even while Dick lay behind her, approaching between her wet thighs from the back, and she arched herself to wiggle upon him, until the ardent drive of her craving consumed her busy occupation with strategies.

Next door the commotion had started up again, a scuffling, banging, and rattling, a ripping of wood and sometimes a hurl of fond curses that Meg could not clearly make out.

She arched beneath Dick's rib cage and released the full throes of her lust, aware that she had tumbled into a very odd world, indeed, by finding him. A world that she had never dreamed of or imagined could exist, yet flourished here in the very sewer of London. What did she know about him? Where had he come from? Why was this talented, driven creature caught in such miserable circumstances of poverty? A pile of guineas lay heaped in a golden sheen, tossed carelessly beside his breeches and shirt on the floor, enough to keep an ordinary man in food and lodgings for half the year. Yet obviously Dick had need of even more than this merely to maintain himself at this wretched level.

On and on turned her mind, serving up pictures and speculations dredged from the darkest corners, but she could piece together nothing of any great significance. What she knew positively was her own joy and fulfillment. She had found her man. And she must contrive to keep him.

Yet keeping him was not enough. How does one keep a dark soul like Dick Fox happy? That was the problem. She must see to it he had a good time with her. That he got what he wanted. Then, with the smallest effort, grand and amazing vistas passed across her mind's eye. She saw great houses filled with his brilliant portraits. Herself in silk gowns, entertaining titled guests. A world filled with kindness and beauty became suddenly possible, the result of having been transformed in one night from a beast of burden into a full human being. The sense of her flowering self sustained and animated her. Those vague but irresistibly rebellious urges that she had suffered through the years, ever since the arrival of her maturity, were now turned and harnessed in a good direction . . . the proper direction for her. She felt the stir of an eagerness something like ambition; a great and noble calling, not for herself alone, but for this man trembling and contracting in her arms. This rock-hard, sensitive creature taking his pleasure upon her flesh, who was like no other . . . this mystery, this challenge . . . this *lover!*

I will see to it, she vowed, *that Dick Fox gets his chance. I will see to it that some wealthy patron views his painting. And then, one day, he will sell his portraits. Not fake paintings but his own true work of which he is proud and to which he signs his name. Yes. He will sell his pictures and take home with him a great reputation. He shall be knighted by the king.* She then imagined Dick kneeling before the stolid, serious-faced royal German. *Sir Richard Fox. And I will be there. I will be the cause. I will be the start and the cause of this man's rise to fame. When he goes up in the world, as he surely must, and I am the cause, why, then . . . so shall I rise in the very same light.*

The satisfaction that came upon her with these thoughts brought with it an exhilaration that warmed the cold floorboards onto which they had rolled in their love.

"You are very restless," Dick observed languidly. "What bug bites you now?"

Meg laughed, aware that she must not confide her

plans. She knew him but one night and already understood the changeable nature of his temperament.

"Will I be put out on the streets if I tell you?" she asked, flirting.

"You shall be put out on the streets if you don't." He pointed with exaggerated warning to the windows rattling from the hard gusts outside.

An unexpected, delicious shiver passed through her, for Dick was telling her in his own style that she was welcome to stay with him, at least for a while.

How much time do I have? she mused. *How much time to start him on his way before he tires of me? But he shall never tire! I will see to it that he . . .* and her mind danced off in the dazzling glitter of all the chances London spread out before them.

"I will tell you my secret." She smiled, confidently tracing his lips with a forefinger. "I am starving to a skeleton this day."

In her own way, this had been so. Starving to death for something. Now it was filled. Her love for this man would fulfill her. And her devotion to him would fill the world.

Chapter Five

FOR FIVE DAYS they trotted after each other, voracious and inseparable. Meg, spinning in a world of adoration, bathed obediently in a tin tub borrowed from next door, posed for him with tireless vitality, then flung herself upon him for her payment. She watched him closely, trailing after the smallest turns of his brush strokes, needing to discover every nook and cranny of his mind, his likes and dislikes, his needs, his aspirations. They went out only for cans of porter or a mutton chop or to a color man when the cadmium yellow ran unexpectedly dry. Dick required nothing from the world, it seemed, except to be left in peace to work.

On the sixth morning Meg wakened and stretched with a well-rested yawn, hailing out a chirrup of good-mornings to the echoes in an empty room.

She looked around at his paint things with an instant, alert reaction of nerves. He's gone for some oat cakes, she told herself, and did not want to wake me. But there was no comfort in lying. She rose at the same instant and dressed in the pale blue chemise, a stylish and expensive affair that Dick had procured from Mrs. Bannish, along with sandals, comforts to protect them from the slush, and a Spanish cloak the exact color of his beloved sash. She reached the door and stood there in consternation.

"All dressed up and nowhere to go," came the sympathetic voice of Mrs. Bannish from her own doorway.

There was kindness and understanding in her tone, which slowed Meg down a little. The wild pictures of Dick deserting her became preposterous. She smiled crookedly with embarrassment and slid the cloak from her shoulders.

"Come inside, child. You'll not find him on the docks this day." Mrs. Bannish beckoned good-naturedly with a motion of her bulbous chin. "Come. You must be starvin' to death the way he never thinks of food. You'll have a fried herring with me and we'll chatter a bit."

The offer was reassuring and irresistible to Meg's lonely confusion. "You know where he is, then?"

"I do."

Relieved, Meg followed the woman into her room, intending to draw out every thread of information she could from Mrs. Bannish, who evidently knew many things of value about Dick Fox.

Meg had been curious about the noises that came from this side of the wall at odd hours of the day and night. She looked about her with unabashed interest and saw a room the same small, square dimension as

Dick's, filled with the evidence of a fierce occupation also related to art. Piles of wooden frames lay pulled apart. There were stacks of matting boards and scraps of oil paintings torn or cut from their original scenes, boxes of nails, blunt-headed hammers, scrapers, priers—everything needed for the quick dismantling or reconstruction of a picture. Mrs. Bannish, ignoring the fascinations of her factory, stepped among things with alacrity, her thick shoes moving as nimbly as her fingers that became busy with cook pots over the lively hearth.

"A herring fried in oatmeal, a dish of strong tea . . . never mind what they says about coffee. Tea's the thing." She waggled a salt herring in the air, shook some vinegar from its glossy tail fin, dipped it deep into a wheaten-colored gruel, then flopped it into a fry pan that was soon sizzling over points and peaks of the fire. This was her center of personal comfort, decked with two green velvet rockers that stood back from a carved fruitwood table scrubbed clean. Against one wall stood open cupboards of herbs and simples, goose eggs in a crock, tins of rusks and toasts, and a dish of dried white daisies.

"You've known Dick a while?" Meg said immediately, perceiving—expecting, really—that Mrs. Bannish could easily read her mind and discontent.

"Oh, yes. My dearie me, yes. Sit down, child. Over there in the rocker. He'll not run away from you. Sit down." She was smiling with a show of blunt yellow teeth and the sympathy of her own memories of a long-ago love. The tea had already brewed, and she gave Meg a steaming black dishful, patting her on the shoulder and saying, "Here. Let's take that beautiful cloak and hang it up away from all the mess. My, what a pretty face. Deserves a poke bonnet for a frame. Did he not think of getting ye a bonnet, my dear?"

Meg shook her head, unable to speak about such trivial matters while her mind and heart twittered away.

"No, of course not," Mrs. Bannish replied to her

own question. "He's waiting for just the right one to catch his eye. Well, then. Here's our tea and there's the rocker and the herring will be done in a turn. I've known your Master Fox since he was no higher than this." She slapped her behind with vigor and the skirt folds whispered over their petticoats. "He was never no different. Touched by some strange elf in his mother's womb, is what I make of it. Father worked a healthy barber's business up in Chelmsford and the boy grew in the fields. Never was finer people to work for. I was the housemaid then. You'd think the sweet air and his good home would keep the brains clear, but never did. Oh my, no. Was scribblin' little faces of piggies or the old horse at the cab rank when it was rainin' and he couldn't go out. That's right. He could see the rank from his parlor window. And one afternoon, I remember, there he sat, with his legs curled under, working away fierce as you please, when along come the cabbie and throws a blanket over Noggins. Well. Up goes a roar from young Master Fox fit to lift the roof." She tossed the herrings over with the three tines of a huge fork. "The picture was spoiled forever." She laughed good-naturedly. "And he wouldn't talk to none of us till supper next day."

Meg tried to concentrate on the tender details and felt herself privileged to hear them, but the passion of her immediate distraction was too overwhelming for her to stay quietly polite and listen. "Yes, but where is he this morning, Mrs. Bannish?"

"You'll never find him. And you'll not disturb him. So don't ask me to tell ye that." She spoke with a firmness that was almost severe.

"Has it to do with his painting?"

"Yes, of course. It's givin' away no secrets to tell you how he goes out every day at first light, weather permittin', to sketch in the fields or to work from one model or another. There's precious little light in these rooms."

"Model?" Meg flushed uneasily at the thought of competition. Her hand sprang to her bosom as though to pluck the bullet lodged there.

"Oh, I know he's been workin' with *you*. But *you* are neither beginnin' nor end to his interests." Her tone was sly, challenging, yet direct in its realistic observation.

"I was worth a week to him."

"Yes. A whole week, and that's more than most, I can tell you. For him it's the worth of a whole year." The herrings dangled now from the fork, all brown and crusty and fragrant. She set one each upon a plate, good china plates with leafy borders in gold and green, then carried them to the small round table and added pieces of ornate silver, an unexpected service that seemed to have left its brothers and sisters at home in a duke's country seat. Extending her widened nostrils above it all, Mrs. Bannish sniffed the aroma and nodded with approval. She dragged the table forward slightly so that Meg could reach it from where she sat.

Meg stared at the beautiful food without appetite. Her mouth felt dry as old cotton. The fear she had tried not to deal with must now be faced.

"If I'm no use to him as a model," she confided matter-of-factly, "I must find another way. Do you know what it is, Mrs. Bannish? I'm no *ornament*. I've always worked for my keep. I want Dick Fox to need me, somehow. I don't care how." She leaned forward heatedly. "But I must be worth something to him. And he must know it. Value it. There must be something I can do. He's not climbed yet to the top of the tree. He must need help or some service in his art that I can offer." Her voice was a plea as she studied the woman's attentive expression. "You know him so well. If you have any idea . . ."

"To try to help that boy is madness," Mrs. Bannish offered with blunt affection for the subject. "Who hasn't tried to help? But he takes nothing from no one. And what he does take, he finally throws away. Here's another notion for you, however," she said, putting a fork into Meg's fingers. "You can work for me."

The silver paused in midair. Meg's head straightened slightly with a first taste of self-respect. "Can I do something to earn my keep, Mrs. Bannish . . . and still remain here with Dick?"

"Exactly what I had in mind."

The air around them became close with hope as the two conspirators huddled to explore Meg's prospects and capabilities. She would do anything, make herself capable of anything that could in some way advance Dick in his career. It would not matter at first if her influence was not direct. She had much to learn about the art world in its trade and commerce. A very different and calculating world, far removed from the personal, passionate involvement of the artist himself.

"I know the very thing," said Mrs. Bannish with a snap of her rough fingers. "But first I must explain to you what our business is about." She looked around her meaningfully. "This is a flourishing livelihood, make no mistake. These humble surroundings are a protection for us. You're a smart girl, and there's a sort of polish to you that tells me you've been around with your eyes open. Sure, we make fakes here. And who would think to look for us on the docks? Who would *find* us, eh? Now. The thing I have in mind for you, to begin with, is the deliveries. Come. I have a bundle for Feargus. And it's time I was goin'. You'll meet the very man who makes connections between our painters and the High 'n Mighties. You'll see how art marries with money. And *that'll* teach you your ways and means of staying near Master Fox. Might even improve him a little," she snapped with a good-natured jibe. "And he wants a deal of improving."

The plates were soon scraped and hidden beneath a loose floor plank, and Mrs. Bannish tucked herself into her fringed shawls and bonnet before Meg could think about what she was attempting. She felt certain that Dick would always be connected with this woman in some way, which in itself urged her to stay close by.

She had not been outdoors for a week. The windy, gritty air slapped up her vitality as she hurried beside the large woman, who sailed through the crowds of tradesmen and hawkers like a ship of the line. The tides of commerce parted around them. Mrs. Bannish wove among the bundles and crates being hauled up into gaping hulls of tall schooners. She elbowed aside duffers waddling to and fro and frowning beneath their flat hats. Flunkies of the captains scurried with their ledgers clutched to their coat buttons. Whistles and calls and shouted directions rang up to an incomprehensible din that frightened even the larger rats back into their holes. The sharp scent of coffee beans gave a silky, flavorsome aspect to the bedlam, which carried past Salt Peter Bank and White Yard along the crooked byways and people-packed alleyways where children and older prostitutes hung over their sills, hawking a different, more delicate kind of ware. There had been, this year, a great increase in reports of stolen children. Meg, who knew the ways of that life too well, suddenly felt the secure grip that, for the first time, she held on her womanhood. She sucked in her breath and plunged on through the melee til they reached White Chapel Road, a more civil sort of street, where Mrs. Bannish hailed a coachee, huddled high on his box like a great stuffed hen inside his layer of five capes.

They bundled up into the coach and Mrs. Bannish gave a North London address near Queen Anne Street "Yes, that's where old Feargus lives," replied Mrs Bannish to Meg's questioning surprise. "In the very heart of respectable soo-ciety." She hauled up a small reticule at the end of a long string ribbon dangling somewhere inside her clothes and plucked out a glass vial. "Now, child. Dab on a bit o' this in case there's a gentleman present."

A firm scent of rose water fluffed at Meg's nostrils but she dutifully did as requested, certain she would stop at nothing now to make a success of her intentions. Second only to Dick Fox, in her estimation, was Mrs. Bannish, for whom she would smell like Versailles —she had heard what Versailles smelled like—rather than disappoint.

When next she glanced out the window, they were driving past wide, straight-row brick houses, constructed by order of the prince. With peace, the façade of London had begun to change. Money loosed from the Exchequer was blossoming into these red brick experiments, pristine and symmetrical, of obvious fine taste. A sign of good spirits and hope for the future reflected her own hope. Yes, why not? Meg thought. Why not live here one day? With some servants and a fine studio for Dick to work in.

Old Feargus, whom she had expected to find hoveled in some stew behind the Haymarket, actually lived in one of these fine buildings?

"Yes, this is the place," Mrs. Bannish assured her, paying the fare and pushing Meg before her toward the scrubbed stone stoop and the black door with its bright brass knocker. Overhead, a filigree rail at the second story formed a crescent-shaped balcony where two children stood at a long window and gazed out upon their fine, organized street.

The knocker, dropped from Mrs. Bannish's thumb, resounded inside with a will. Almost instantly, a slender young woman in a bright green bombazine dress opened the door with a modest squeak of delight.

"Grandpapa is upstairs waiting for you," she said, with dimpling, flowing smiles that also welcomed the new caller as she took their wraps.

Meg, in her eagerness to be friendly, could not manage very much in return. She allowed her hands to be squeezed, exchanged names, and glimpsed the brushed brown hair and brown eyes, all the while very much aloof from social ease. She had business before her and Dick on her mind, and old Feargus to learn about. This other girl had comforts and pleasures and a quiet life. With an eerily vivid realization, Meg knew that her life with Dick would never rest in such a sensible, middling state. This girl, Hetty, had certain fortunes on her side. But Meg did not envy her position. In fact, she could feel sorry for every other woman for not having what she alone must possess—and never mind the cost of possessing it.

Hetty lifted her skirts to her ankles and showed them up a winding, carpeted staircase with beautiful mahogany banisters that reflected in their gloss the French cut chandeliers overhead. The modest reserve of the exterior of the house became modestly berserk indoors, responding to the latest fashion in decor. Meg glimpsed Egyptian heads carved into the feet of tables, gold-painted seraphs twining as chair back supports. A wafting aroma of baked white bread warmed the atmosphere and softened the glamorous effect of lights refracted from huge wall mirrors in many shaded hues of the rainbow. Parquet and marquetry woods glowed with a deep, rich polish, catching what was left of the dazzle and taming it.

"He's in the workshop," Hetty explained, charging past the second story toward the attic.

Mrs. Bannish arrived slightly breathless, and Meg no less breathless behind her, touching her hair and smoothing her dress in preparation for she knew not what.

"Come ye in!" boomed squeakingly to the callers. Hetty, at the sound, retired down the stairs while Mrs. Bannish proceeded forward with the greatest enthusiasm.

Meg had expected nothing like this room, nor like the little man pacing about it, two curly gray bagwigs in his left hand and a chestnut-brown frizz wig over the knuckles of his right hand. He stood halfway between Meg's height and Mrs. Bannish's, straight and ancient as an oak. The pink, bright, smooth skin of a toddler gleamed wherever skin could be seen, and mostly on the perfectly domed head above a bright black fringe that grew, like the texture of crow's feathers, in a curve from ear to ear.

"A fine marnin' for all good things, eh, Maundy?" He spoke with a fresh, tinkling sound to Mrs. Bannish while blinking an elfin smile over tiny round spectacles framed in gold, taking Meg in at a glance to the very depths of her secrets, eyes the size of filbert nuts sparkling at her.

Meg, who didn't want to stare, found herself staring at everything, the dozens of coats and britches hanging from hooks around the walls, plain brown businesslike wools, others with flowered paste buttons in a young buck's high style, satins of pale tea-rose pink, short ugly spencers, country squire boots, and city men's beavers. It struck her that this was no wardrobe but a collection of costumes. They were all obviously the same size, made to fit Feargus appropriately for any appearance he might wish to effect.

"But why do we stand here in this closet?" said Feargus, pointing his nose with its bright red beacon of a pimple out of the alcove and into a larger aspect of the room.

The widened area, built toward the rear, took light from an overhead domed glass, which today was in a filthy grayish condition tempered by a niggle of sickly sun. The smell of printer's ink rose from rough muslin rags, and acrid smells came from bottles of yellowing liquids that stood on shelves carefully placed out of reach. The room was a display of glinting copper plates, pointed needle tools, pans of inks, and blotted picture proofs drying on soft, damp paper. Meg studied the hatching and crosshatching strokes done in smaller and smaller dimensions to imitate the lights and darks of a Venus and Psyche attended by cupids, another of Oliver Cromwell dissolving the Long Parliament, and various invitation cards for a regatta ball at Ranalegh, showing old Father Neptune on the Thames.

"Here, study this one and see what you make of it," urged Feargus, removing a spirit lamp from a chair and holding it over a print stippled in red, titled "The First Lesson in Love."

If Meg knew little about painting, she knew less about the engraver's trade. Yet something in the two etched faces caught her. A pair of very young girls stood beside a wall covered with vine leaves, their faces uplifted to watch two doves sitting close to each other in obvious affection. Beyond the wall, watching the girls but unobserved, poised a youth, half hidden by the abundant shady foliage of a tree that partly concealed a cottage in the background.

"Read what is printed, Miss Watkins."

Meg nodded. " 'Coelia, behold yon pretty doves, How sweet they bill and coo. Were I and Lubin wedded loves, Would we not do so, too?' "

Meg purpled in confusion but held her tongue while banter rained around her head concerning the monetary value that prints gave to paintings.

"The money's in the trade of it," said Feargus. "And where the money is, there's the happiness."

"Dick doesn't feel that way," she murmured in a soft but spontaneous outburst, aware that Feargus knew all.

Feargus's sharp ears caught her up. "Dick is plain daft," he replied with decision. "And there's an end to it. If the man had sense, he'd let his paintings go for engravings. See these? And these? And these?" He snatched up prints and flung them down again. "From famous pictures, all. And hanging on thousands of walls of our countrymen. Why, half a dozen such as these, and he could retire to his castle."

"If it is as you say, then he must have good reason not to do it," she replied firmly but in a lowered voice, glancing at Mrs. Bannish.

"Aye, there's love," sighed the woman. "But come. Tell the girl the truth. A hundred copies of something makes each worth less than if but a single copy existed, and so we cannot expect high emoluments from printing. On the other side, if we thought to make a large profit by selling thousands of copies at a very low price each, as publishers may sell a book, we cannot do that, either, for it doesn't go. Which catches us right in the middle—neither unique nor commonplace. And there it is. A living to be got in a middling way."

" 'Tis better to be a painter," said Meg decidedly.

"If one is fortunate to have large-handed patrons," said Feargus. "But better still, as Dick will tell you, is to be out from under that yoke. To have paintings and prints *both* can well free a man from material cares."

"And there is a way to it," rallied Mrs. Bannish, who put herself to the task of pouring tea from an octagonal silver pot into some cups from a sideboard. The confusion of elegance and workingmen's tools had set them all at ease with each other. No pretense could live long in this climate. "But we've not come here to talk of Fox. I've brought you Meg Watkins because she is pretty, as you can see, and trustworthy and easy to be trained." Mrs. Bannish gazed at her in a motherly, prideful way and at the same time confidently assessing. "We need a woman to work with you in the shop, Feargus; you've said it yourself."

"Trustworthy, you say?" Feargus cleared his throat with the tea, then went off to a large decanter of port. "How much can you drink, girl?" he asked easily, pouring a tall bumper glass full and handing it to her.

"I can drink or leave it be," said Meg, staring at him steadily and ignoring the garnet-colored sparkles that tilted at her but in no way enticed. Yet she knew he could tell that she had been gin-soaked in her time and wracked by the blue ruin.

"A rare one," Feargus concluded after some moments of eyeing her steadily. "I'll trust you, girl," he snipped. "And you'll live to lord it over Master Fox."

"But will I be useful to him?" she pressed with growing expectation.

"Oh my, yes," laughed Feargus, polishing off the port himself with relish. "If gold in the waistcoat pocket can be useful to a man."

The urge to explain her real ambition struggled in Meg's breast, but she kept silent for fear of somehow tainting Dick Fox in their estimation. Whatever she did on his behalf, she must do quietly. For it was not her own reputation that mattered, but his.

"Walk her this afternoon upon the Strand, Feargus, and introduce her to *Mr. Widley,*" said Mrs. Bannish with a meaningful nod. "This is what you will do, my girl," she continued, facing Meg and touching her on the back with intimate attention. "Follow Feargus closely and watch how he squeezes information, in his seemingly mindless way, from the gossip you will hear around you. There is a wild thirst for Italian, French, and Flemish masters, and soon you will learn to pull from conversations who it is that wants which pictures. But you can't learn it all in a day, of course, and meanwhile, Feargus will give you other valuable work to do." She patted Meg's cheek. "I can leave you in his care with an easy mind."

Meg had not expected matters to take so many complex turnings so quickly, and she felt a pang of regret at Mrs. Bannish's departure. Yet she understood that Feargus was a real power in some underhanded way, and he was about to offer her interesting chances concerning Dick. Most importantly, he moved among the people who bought and sold paintings.

Left alone with Feargus, she allowed him to fight off her reserve, and she fell upon a pair of mutton chops that Hetty brought up for them before they were to venture out into the penetrating damp.

"The numbers that die from influenza because they're ill-fed," he sermonized, sliding his fork beneath the peas. "You'll not be one of them."

She stuffed herself happily and after a while, when he seemed to have filled himself halfway, said, "I suppose you know Dick Fox since he was this high?" She patted her hip.

As she had expected, Feargus smiled, recognizing the gesture as one of Mrs. Bannish's, and admitted that he knew the boy even longer.

"We're a family in some ways, y'see." He poured more wine and turned the glass round and round, enjoying the play of light on crystal. "Now, Dick lives in the lodging house because he cannot keep his mind upon business." He wiped his spectacles and dabbed at his red, tired eyelids. "He wants a patron and kicks 'em all in the arse when they tells him the kinds of pictures to paint. *That's* why he gambles at the rat catching and whores and pockets money from the filthy beggars at the bear baiting and lives from day to day. Oh, he likes the adventure of it all well enough. After Egypt, I suppose London is pretty mild. But in the end"—he shook his head, stroking his skull gently, lovingly—"it all comes to naught for 'im. And he's back in his hovel when he could be *here* in such a place as this, working in comfort."

But not in fame, she thought. "We are going out to the Strand today, Feargus. Is not the Royal Academy close by?"

"Aha." He sat back with a laugh, enjoying her. "So you wish to climb that mountain, do you?"

He was chiding her, but she would not be baited. Calmly she poured herself a fingerful of port and slapped it down her throat. "I see no wrong in it."

"If it is social traveling you enjoy, I would like to introduce you to some gentlemen," he said tentatively, leaning back in his chair and talking as though in random exploration. "Important gentlemen. Gentlemen who go to Epsom side by side with the prince. Gentlemen who lend him money . . . and who have an eye for lovely girls."

So there it was.

A faint disappointment washed through her but was quickly replaced by resolve. "No. No more," she replied with a small, steadfast smile. "And I am sure to know those gentlemen already."

"Do you? I should have guessed it from the different accents in your speech. Ah, then, good. We shall proceed to the Strand and so on as Mrs. Bannish wishes. It happens that this afternoon we have an interesting engagement. And if you can participate in the encounter with all your wits, might, and main, you will gain much to your advantage."

"Yes. I shall." She felt the blood pulsing up in her as he rose from the table and motioned with a gnarled little finger for her to follow him.

"The mingling of commerce with art lately breeds a fast-scurrying mouse, you see, but one that is willful and stupid and will bite at any cheese."

While he talked he sauntered back and forth from the closet alcove, appearing now in a conservative, powdered bagwig, then in dark blue breeches over a ruffled shirt, and finally in a bright green swallow-tailed coat with gold buttons flashing and a round gold watch upon a fob, the domestic grandpapa and wily dealer in art transformed into a prosperous, conservative tradesman.

"You see before you, my dear, Mr. Jonathan Widley, Esq., of J. S. Widley's Continental Trading Company, furnishers of books, catalogs, prints, currants, and figs to the public. No, don't be shocked, my girl. Mrs. Bannish says I am to trust you." Even the gait had changed, as Feargus, evidently relishing his role, charged about in a solid, substantially wide, rolling stride to gather three panel-sized paintings and fix them into a protective portfolio case.

Meg, realizing that these were not costumes of a fancier but *disguises* that Feargus affected, settled down to study the shifting winds of artistic fortunes. She was more at home, to be sure, in an atmosphere where wits won the day.

"See these beautiful sepia tones? These burnt umbers and Venetian reds and scarlets? See how they glow? It's in the mystery of their glazed grounds. Top o' the line, my dear. Fakes to be proud of and sold with the head held high." He drew his brows together and waggled a finger at her nose. "And hold yer head high, y'must. Or the dupes will *feel* themselves being duped, yes they will. And won't take to it very kindly. It's one thing to be fooled, but quite another to have one's nose rubbed in the droppings. Greed never likes to look itself in the face." As he talked, he warmed to the subject and grew youthful, feeding on the flesh of those who would feed on the likes of himself, the painter, the engraver he had been, once upon a time, long ago. "Now we put on our coats and bundle up warm and go to the marketplace with our wares." He pulled out the fob and studied the watch that swung against his palm. "It will be four o'clock exactly when I arrive at the shop. And you must come by exactly five minutes after. No more, no less." He looked at her face and smiled approvingly. "I see you have a heart for this work. So much the easier. Now we ride along in my carriage and I will explain your part in the job at hand."

Meg held her silence going down the staircase. Her

heart pounded with expectation to meet all the challenges rising so quickly. Was this life? Was this art? Was this love? Tonight, when she saw Dick Fox again, there would be stories to tell. He would find her amusing and worth staying home to talk to. But more importantly, she hugged to her heart the throbbing secret of her ambition for him, which she must not reveal until the day she would bring it to pass.

On the broad Strand, the very fashionable center of London, strolled the young bucks to their clubs. They eased along in their yellow gloves and their greatcoats, poking away with their canes a dastardly wind that curled back upon itself and lost heart at the feet of such admirable high style. It was four o'clock exactly, and the prince would never show his face in public daylight before four. Thoughts of courtesans abandoned behind the gauzy curtains of warm beds . . . of Cyprians, kissed and promised and lied to . . . faded in the twilight expectation of deep gaming at Boodles.

Meg came down the steep carriage steps and saw these men as she had never seen them before, not as her tormentors but as her prey.

She turned away from the weather and sauntered close to the bow-window shops, going at a regular pace, neither hurrying nor dawdling, and paying no attention to the appraising eyes of younger and older gentlemen who turned to follow the pretty face as it sailed past them. The wind paid a compliment to her hair, tossing up the deep, fire-colored curls and playing with them back and forth across her shoulders. The mutton chops in her belly were an unexpected comfort. They lay solid and stabilizing. *This is what it is,* she realized, *to feel like a spoiled kitten.* She fancied that if she glanced over the rooftops she would find Kensington Palace and the Palace of St. James waiting with front portals open for her. The smoky shrouds spilling over the crowded London season could not dispel from the air a chilling sense of her great age of enlightenment.

At exactly five minutes past four, she reached J. S. Widley's, a pair of twin shop windows containing prints, books tooled in leather rococo bindings, and china figurines of doves and fawns, all arranged in a genteel symmetry to cater to a leisurely taste. She paused and casually looked in at a room of cream and robin's-egg blue, long and narrow with bookshelves to the moldings. She strolled inside with hardly a pause, keeping a hold on the most casually elegant face she could imagine, the same one she had practiced outside: a faint, not-too-interested seriousness, tempered by the will to conclude some prearranged obligation. As she stepped almost halfway down the center aisle, a youthful clerk appeared among the browsing patrons. When he reached Meg he held up two scrubbed and earnest fingers in an urgent yet hesitating eagerness to attract her attention.

From the corner of her eye she saw him and pretended not to, lifting a book here, a porcelain there, thanking the shade of her mother for teaching her to read, and praying with an iron determination that all would come to pass as prearranged.

"Missss . . . Missssss Benningott."

Meg raised her head slowly and gazed about in her own good time, finally settling a cool query upon the clerk's voice.

"Miss Benningott?"

"I am she." This sentence, which she had repeated over and over in the carriage, sounded full and musical to her ears, much more so in this larger space where it could echo.

"Miss Benningott, will you do me the honor to come with me? Mr. Widley is expecting you in his office."

She nodded in unsurprised recognition of the request and found, as she took tiny steps forward, that some of the browsers backed away to let her pass, exactly as Feargus had predicted. At the farthest end of the room, beneath the staircase to the balcony, a polished door was already opening for her welcome, and she breezed in on the fragile but steady breath of her own well-being.

"Miss Benningott? I am *sew* happy to meet you at last."

"Ah, Mr. Widley, I assume? How do you do." She smiled at Feargus, amazed to see that, in the space of the five minutes since their separation, he had managed to grow a rounded paunch almost as full as the Duke of Norfolk's, beneath which a child might stand and not be seen by the possessor's face above it.

The door closed and they were alone, with small glasses of the finest pale claret and a view of some valiant little shrubs beyond the window.

Feargus winked at her as he proceeded to open the portfolio case on top of an ornate desk carved all over with grapes and cherubs in the Italian fashion. "Here it is," he said. "This is the Van Dyke that your father and I have discussed so often. I tell you it is a miracle that the painting has come upon the market. An auspicious and lyrical time for us, this peace. Let us pray that Bonaparte will continue to enjoy it as well."

"I so very well agree," replied Meg, glancing from the sluggard, ticking clock on the mantel to Feargus, who, in his turn, glanced at the clock and continued the patter, shrugging at her to take heart and be patient.

They managed to chatter thus with the burden of the talk mostly shouldered by Feargus, who seemed tireless as a carriage wheel, able to roll on and on into the distance.

Just as Meg had given up all hope and was glancing about her for a place to flop and rest her feet, a faint-hearted knuckle rapped, then once again hesitantly.

"Yes, Charles?"

The clerk poked the side of his ear in and announced, "The Earl of Haversham's son, sir. Lord Albert Hallwhite."

"Yes, yes, yes," boomed Mr. Widley with an extreme blow of enthusiasm. "Do show him in to us."

Lord Albert, who had come strolling along meanwhile, insensitive to any possibility of rebuff, was instantly inside the room, his cane caught in the bend of his elbow and smiling systematically around at no one in particular. Swollen eyelids fluttered fatigued lashes over bleary eyes. His hefty winter wrappings seemed to float in space over gleaming boots.

Meg glanced at Feargus, who continued unremittingly to regard Albert with the utmost of solicitation and respect, bowing about him and introducing Miss Benningott, "from the Irish line of Benningotts. Perhaps your father may know them?"

"I daresay he must if they are anybody," drawled Albert, his breath rising with difficulty beneath heavy coat lapels. "But do show me the picture, sir, and have done with this," he pleaded, standing bundled in a long, woolly mantle but trembling with occasional fits of alcoholic stress that shook the hat brim pulled low on his forehead.

"And here it is, m'lord. But a glass of port for your health?" inquired Mr. Widley.

"Mm, yee-es."

When he had poured one and then another, Mr. Widley again set the case upon his desk and opened it with loving, caressing gestures that removed the glossy treasure.

"My father says it is one of the finest Van Dykes to be painted," fired Miss Benningott directly at Lord Albert, but with a retiring little simper, well-bred and utterly unassuming.

"*My* father agrees," replied Albert, slightly disconcerted by the intrusion. "Shall we settle, then, for the five hundred guineas?" he said, hardly glancing at the prize.

"But *my* father has settled for eight."

"What? What?" His eyes opened painfully as he forced them to look upon the swarming annoyance. "This picture is promised by my father to the Comtesse de Fassier, who is desperately exiled and is now living with us."

"Eight hundred guineas," Meg repeated.

"No, not a bit of it. *We* have settled for five, and there's an end."

"I fear I have the advantage of you, m'lord. *We* have settled, and *there's* an end."

Lord Albert could brave it no further. "Mr. Widley, what say you to this? Have we an agreement or have we not? Am I to trust your integrity, your word as a gentleman? Or do I report to my father this shattering disappointment?"

"And shall I?" echoed Miss Benningott.

Both young people looked for justice to Mr. Widley, who came around from behind his desk with an extremely slow and thoughtful waddle, ducklike and somber and weighted down by the woesome dilemma. His bushy eyebrows jumped about as though on the hot rim of volcanic considerations. A deep crease wrinkled his nose, into which the bridge of his glasses sank and seemed to disappear, making each eyepiece appear separate and standing by itself, stiff and unyielding beneath the weight of the problem. He was all fairness, intensity, regret.

Miss Benningott opened her mouth once or twice, as though to say something of additional evidence, but then the mouth closed again, shutting sweetly yet with total, sincere dependence upon the outcome. She looked from the claret glass, delicately held between thumb and forefinger, to the picture, sighed at it, and sighed again.

Albert spun away from them both and faced the set-to with his very broad back, which revealed mother-of-pearl buttons at the waistband. The shoulders and collar trembled once so violently that they threatened to come away unstitched from the lapels. One polished boot heel tapped the marquetry floor with a solid and insolent click. Then the cane tapped the floor beside the heel.

"This is a terrible, terrible impasse we have reached," moaned Mr. Widley. "My friends, I am horribly embarrassed."

"Nine hundred guineas," said Albert.

"Oh, nine hundred guineas?" gasped Miss Benningott. "What shall I do?"

"A bit more claret?" Mr. Widley came with the

decanter, bending over her with one hand suspended at her cheek. " 'Twill certainly give comfort to the blood."

"I doubt it ever so much, Mr. Widley, but let me try." She tasted the claret with eyes rolling to the downy-skinned cherubs floating in sky-blue ovals on the ceiling. "What ever, ever shall I do?"

"I suggest," said Albert in a very bored voice barely exhumed, and with his back still to her, "that you retire from the field."

She made a small squeak that fluttered on the verge of tears.

"Will never do," said Albert to the fire. "I suggest that the subject is closed."

Mr. Widley graciously produced and fluttered a handkerchief that Miss Benningott snatched in her free hand and applied with pressure to her quivering lower lips. "*He* will never forgive me," she mumbled into the handkerchief folds.

"Yes, yes, he will," soothed Mr. Widley with a gallant assurance of chivalrous generosity in the male species. "Shall I call you a cab, my dear?"

"Perhaps I should . . ."

Albert swung around at once. "I shall write you a draft for nine hundred guineas if you will give me your pen."

In response to a pulled bell cord, the clerk entered as gently and as silently as a butterfly.

"My carriage for Miss Benningott."

"Perhaps I should . . ."

The pen scratched busily, scattering ink in high, imperious splatters.

At the final sprinkling of sand upon the signature, Miss Benningott, miserably defeated, rushed from the room, directly down the center of J. S. Widley's Continental Shoppe and out into the waiting black carriage that immediately took off at a canter for the respectable house on the street next to Queen Anne.

She sat beside the window quite demurely until the horse had galloped out of sight of the shop. Then, with bursting giggles, she flung herself about, swaying and rollicking and slapping the walls, lifting up her skirts and kicking the stocking tassels, which action only made her giggle the harder.

"Whatever shall I *dew?"* she shrieked, laughing. "Whatever shall I *dew?"*

Soon the laughter abated and she lay burned out upon the jogging seat, dreaming of the gold coins soon to be her share for the afternoon's transactions, and confident that with some little study she could be a duchess or a grand czarina of Russia should Feargus need one. It was but another instant's thought before she sat bolt upright and knocked upon the driver's box, calling, "You must take me home by way of the Royal Academy. Call it out to me as we pass."

When the driver said, "Somerset House beside us," she leaned her face into the window and studied the old, rusticating red stones facing the Strand on one side and the Thames on the other, devouring with greedy, fascinated eyes the ornate façades and stately columns and pilasters, thinking: But *here* is where I shall come. Yes. One day I shall walk inside *this* place, this place . . . and be known by my very own name.

Chapter Six

IN TRIUMPH she dashed up the lodging-house steps, shaking the guineas in her purse so they would jingle and Dick would hear them and wonder. He must be home now, she knew he must, for he did not draw after dark, and daylight had long since faded. "Dick—Dick—Dick," she called as she ran. Heads popped out of doorways, echoing "Dick—Dick—Dick" after her, annoyed by such signs of happiness in their midst. She heard no one, saw nothing, complete in the glowing circle of her expectations.

She flung the door wide and "Here I am!" burst from her with a grin as she saw him bending over some length of panel board, scrubbing chalk marks from it with a bit of bread.

"Yes, there you are," he replied with preoccupied pleasure, not looking up from his work.

She stopped, and with all the self-possession she could muster, shut the door quietly behind her. It took a world of strength not to fling herself onto his neck, but she knew better than to interfere when he was concentrating. Slyly she reached for her little bag and shook it once, twice. Paused and shook it again, allowing the unmistakable clink to speak for her in its own powerful but unobtrusive style.

"What's going on, eh?" he said, smiling, still at the board.

She saw that he recognized she was up to something and took a tiny step closer, creeping up at him like fog on silent feet.

"Where've you been?"

"Oh. Out of doors."

He blew chalk dust from his fingers and gazed across at her from beneath locks of hair that had fallen over his brow. When he studied her this way, with half a smile hovering like sun just come up at the horizon, she shivered and had to struggle to maintain her wits. He flooded over her and through her merely by looking at her, and she didn't want it revealed. Again she ventured forward another tiny step, shaking the purse behind her back and watching him expectantly.

"What have you got there?"

He recognized the game, and was playing it back to her, willing to frisk for a moment, but for how long she could not tell.

"Nothing."

"Nothing, is it?"

"Mm."

"I've been home for an hour and you've been gone half the day."

"How do you know that?"

"The same way I know you have nothing behind your back."

"But nothing's there!" she insisted, and shook the bag more strenuously.

"Oh, ho."

He lunged for her, tackled her around the waist, and brought her down, cushioned, on top of his body. Over and over they rolled, he roaring laughter, she protesting a tickled innocence. They halted finally in the same position they had first fallen into, she prone upon him, panting, her weight supported by the hard, ridged contour of his chest and stomach and thighs. Hands pressed to his shoulders, she arched back and stared roundly down into the magnetizing eyes. His fine, aquiline nostrils flared slightly, taking in breath. Her hair fell forward and curtained them while she rapidly kissed the separated lips, pressing them back slightly with the urgent vitality of her being. As she kissed him, she realized her relief. How frightened she had been that he would be gone. Far back in her mind, she had really imagined that he had left her, and the loneliness had been too much to face. Now her joy was a fountain. Love bubbled up in vast wave after wave. She had all she could do to control it and remember her more practical intention. The coins jingling in her struggle served to remind her. She hauled up the bag and laid it lightly on the ruffle of his shirt front.

He lifted his head and peered at the silk pouch, his arms still holding her tightly, pressing her to him so that her breasts began to firm at their points.

" 'Tis remarkably like the one Mrs. Bannish carries," he observed with a mocking study.

"Does it, now? Well, it is hers."

"Stealing?" he grunted in a disapproving rumble.

"Who could steal from the likes of her? Not I, surely."

"Sweet generosity, then?"

"Not that, either." She was still giggling between times, loving that he frolicked with her and about matters that to others could seem so ponderously grave.

He darted his head up and pecked a kiss from her mouth. "A mystery of noble proportions."

"Will you guess?"

Something flashed too quickly, like a blade across his eyes, and was gone. "Need I guess? And why guess?"

She began to see how he misunderstood.

"I've *not* been out there turnin' over for the buggerin' bastards, if that's what you think!"

He watched her, suspended between disbelief and the convincing force of her passion.

"All right, you haven't."

"Don't you want to hear?"

"If you care to tell."

In consternation, she lowered her head and bit his upper lip. "You make me so furious! I won't tell you at all. Not until you ask me in a sweet, generous way."

"All right, my darling, in my sweetest, most generous way . . . what are you doing with Mrs. Bannish's purse?"

"I got it, actually, for old Feargus."

The name worked like something magical upon him, she saw, as all his playfulness turned to steady, directed attention.

"How do you come to Feargus?"

She felt the breath stirring a trifle faster in his belly, as though he were waiting, almost with apprehension, for what she would reveal. She sensed Dick's suspicion of what Feargus might have done with her and then recalled the original offer of gentlemen friends.

"Never fear," she said placatingly. "I set Feargus right, straightaway. And no man laid a finger on me, I promise you."

She then recounted the day's events and triumphs, repeating every detail as Dick asked for it, leaving out no speck of the profitable story, from her lessons of deportment in the carriage to receiving her agreed-upon and fair share later, at his home. "There is something about Feargus one must respect," she said. "He has a knowledge of human nature to make a person gawk. He explained to me, before we started, how Lord Albert would not think about the fakery of the picture if there was someone interested in bidding up the value. It is a question, as Feargus explained it, of where one directs a man to concentrate his attentions. A sleight-of-hand trick, but in a mental way."

As she talked on, she found herself surrounded by the warmth of a new admiration coming from Dick. The sparkle that she loved rested full upon her, steady as a summer sun.

"What a quick-witted wench you are," he breathed finally, after he had asked and she had answered a number of questions. How much money she had actually brought home did not seem to interest him as he focused upon her spirit and capacity to bring off the affair.

"Well, I'm a good actress. My mother had a touch of it, too," she said, unable to resist a moment of boasting. "And can talk like the best of 'em when I set my mind to't. I've surely been amongst 'em often enough, the bloody beasts. But see! Here!" She lifted the purse and shook it again. "Don't you want to count what I've brought us home?"

"But it's yours."

"Mine?" She stared at him, flabbergasted. "It's for both." She quickly yanked wide the strings and sifted out five gold coins upon his chest. "Why, an under-housemaid can't earn this in half a year of service. And I can stay with Feargus, and work with him . . . and we can move out of this—place. We'll take a nice, clean lodging up near Portman Square, and a studio where there's light in the daytime so you can work without killing your eyes."

Her words broke as he grabbed her in a harsh embrace, interrupting her thoughts and filling her with the heat of his being. They rolled over slowly until she was beneath him, until she lay smothered happily, contentedly, by his broadness . . . and the coins slid from him unnoticed and rolled away.

"I have found myself a *woman,*" he rasped heatedly against her mouth.

She could not reply. Her heart pounded in her throat. But he knew! He knew! She would walk the plank for him into the jaws of sea beasts. Wild, spinning ideas of what she would do for his happiness conjured up pictures of the utmost fancy. But as he kissed her repeatedly, they subsided into a continuous throbbing of contentment with him. Whatever he wanted . . . so long as she could be there and share it.

"Listen to me, dearest," he said as they lay locked and entwined. "You must save it for yourself. Every ha'-penny bit."

"You make me angry, Dick."

"No, I am serious. What you do with Feargus is your own affair. You'll not learn to depend on *him* and count on *him* because of me."

"I don't understand you," she protested. "Why must you make this difficult?"

He cradled her head in his huge palms and lovingly stroked her hair, watching the hearth light fall upon it and following the shifting shadows with his fingertip. "I am far from settled, as you know," he told her soothingly. "And cannot be counted upon—who can judge how long? Meg, you mustn't look to me to take care of you or to be steady."

"I understand. But what has that got to do with Feargus and all this money?"

"Nothing, I suppose. Except I know that Feargus is himself a bitter man and so not to be trusted."

"Because of the Royal Academy?"

"He told you, then."

"No. But I sense these things in all of you artists. He talks always of commerce and art. Art and commerce. How trade's the thing."

"Feargus was an engraver of the highest sort. Yet the Royal Academy would not elect him a member. The rule there is based on the notion that no engraver can do original work and so deserves only to be allowed the rank of *associate*. Feargus fought it for a while, insisting that engravers deserve full and equal rights. He went about on Sunday mornings, tea-drinking with the members. He poured his heart out to Farraday and Opie and Benjamin West, all outstanding, influential men. But to no avail. Finally discouraged, he let the matter drop and turned altogether from the Academy. His pride would not allow him to accept an inferior position. Soon he began to work more for the caprices and demands of the market than as a purveyor of his own best, artistic interests. Now, instead of crusading against the inferior level of art to which our country has fallen, he takes advantage of the greed. Feeds upon it himself, and feeds mighty well, as you saw when you were at his home."

Meg thought about this for a while, staring into the fire and recalling the pretty, twinkling grandchildren. Hetty, unscathed by struggles in the world, no doubt posing in her flower garden in the summer, with her stringed bonnet, her spaniel and boxes of pure French sweets. "I dare say there is something to be said for comforts," Meg sighed. "And I do not see what you can have against them. What glory is there in scratching and scraping when a man can take his ease? I saw *his* copy of Bell's *Anatomy,* and it's all of a piece. *He* can read the letters and pore over fresh, clean plates. Why shouldn't you? I think I shall go out and buy you a brand-new copy myself."

"Would it were as simple as that," Dick said thoughtfully.

I will make it so, Meg thought, holding his head between her hands and kissing his eyelids. *The whole plan of my life is your career. You have given me direction.*

"Do you yourself not trust Feargus? And Mrs. Bannish? Who have known you since you were this high?" She slapped her behind in the familiar gesture.

"So they have been talking of me, have they?" He smiled. "Mrs. Bannish has her own ambitions and knows how to take care of herself, that's true. But we are at swords' points forever. She would domesticate me if she could. Keep me like ducks in a puddle."

His voice was easy, for he had no fear of being roped in. "Do you want to know a secret, Meg? My heart is really with her in the matter. If I could be cool-headed like my father was and a happy family man, I'd be a fool to turn it away. But I am not made so. Whatever it is that drives me does so with a will. I am not a responsible man. Cannot take care of money . . . nor be trusted by any woman."

She heard the warning in his voice, trembling there sincerely. *He loves me! He does! He would do for me if he could, or why would he talk like this? He would make me a queen!* She grew higher and higher on the scorching sensation of their intimacy. The mutual bond that united them, invisible though it was, needed no commitment of marriage, home, or children.

"I want only you," she said softly. "However you are. I want only to see you content."

"I do love you, Meg," he whispered. "If that can please you at all, know it. I love you for your honesty and your courage. I love you because you are beautiful and the beauty shows on your face. Do you know about that? I have painted many women, hags with perfect features but half dead. Meg, you have heart! And that is the rare thing. I will always treasure holding you in my arms. Touching you."

Her flesh began to thrill. Cold prickles of delicious joy came to life wherever he touched her and sprang through her limbs. Her heart leaped like a deer, limber and racing up mountainsides in the full glory of its nature. With Dick's hands upon her and his mouth upon her, she was transformed. Her strength was his . . . her blood of life his . . . her courage his. All the long-stifled need for living and loving *he* had set free. Did he not know how thankful she was for his nature? And that she would have him no other way?

She gripped him then to tell him how she wanted all . . . all. His maleness responded instantly, and she heaved a great sigh of pleasure into his mouth while her fingers fondled the endeared object as it grew firmer and stiffened into readiness. He had taught her body to know its own cravings and to glory in the expression of love. Her hunger, during the past week with him, had grown apace. Whenever she thought of him she could desire him. And when she touched him she became a lioness of need. Her hands, free to roam as they pleased upon his flesh, had learned to have eyes in the tips of their fingers. She had learned that, too, from him. To know through touching. To see and hear through touching. And to taste through touching. Yet she wanted to taste with her mouth. She wanted it all . . . with her tongue and lips. She began to graze the edges of her teeth along his chin and then moved her mouth lower, feeling the soft curling hairs of his body as she slipped along. He was all dark, warm masses. His flesh that contained the mysterious fire was hard, yet yielding. Poised above him, she craved to do what others had whipped her into doing. Was it the same act? How could it be so different? Her taste buds came alive as her tongue molded to its object. She was strong and eager and sure. The scent of him was musky and enticing, while the taste of him was slickly smooth along these special curves and pulsing ridges. She drew in a sharp take of air and shivered from the hot, personal taste of him. She was swallowing his very being, alive.

He could not resist her. She felt it in the grip of his hands upon her breasts. Those firm, exploring fingers told her she was made of some precious immortal stuff, a liquid, human gold that he could form, like a sculptor, into the shape that he most desired, that pleased him beyond his wildest, most imaginative dream. His voice crooned at her from time to time, imbuing her with the confidence of his pleasure. And she rejoiced in that pleasure, for his delights were her army against the world, protecting her. She had no past now. All the hurts were gone. And the present moment of embraces enthralled her with a poignancy that permitted no thinking into the future. Flesh was all. Flesh was everything. Flesh held nobility and hope even beyond the unknown limits of love's amazing ecstasy. They clung to each other, somehow naked, somehow perfect.

They had learned to please each other in agile, unself-conscious ways. They lay together on one side . . . and then she sat crouched upon him, riding the steed as far as it would travel.

She was not surprised, however, to waken and find him gone. It was morning, probably, and she had overslept. She rolled and stretched and yawned, studying the grime on the windows for some sign of light. And yawned again. And did not know what to make of it. On the far side of the wall was silence. No hammering racket from Mrs. Bannish. Only the welled, throaty cry of a cat somewhere outside, calling for a mate.

Well. Wherever he was, he could not be with another woman. Not so soon. She smiled complacently.

The cries of hawkers in the streets grew and mingled. She began to dress, pulling on her best white stockings and the slippers that she carefully kept clean. Next door the knocking started, but soon it stopped and Mrs. Bannish came in to her, absentmindedly holding half a frame in one hand and a small white corset with stays in the other, as though she had stopped in the midst of a thought to come and share it with Meg.

"I wanted to tell you, child, what a good—but here, see for yourself." She thrust the undergarment at her.

Meg stared at the wired shape hesitantly. She had never worn such a thing in her life.

"Take it, take it," urged Mrs. Bannish, pressing it into Meg's hand. "Only the finest ladies wear them. When I was drivin' home yesterday, thinkin' of you paradin' the Strand, I decided you was a girl that deserved the best."

"Thank you," Meg replied uncertainly, hearing an undercurrent in the other's voice, a prelude to some further explanation. "I did do a good job, didn't I?"

Mrs. Bannish beamed. "Feargus had only compliments, and he's a hard man to please when it comes to business. A stickler for perfection."

"Like Dick in his way."

"Och. Not like Dick at all!"

"Mrs. Bannish, I want you to understand something." Meg stood flicking the corset about in the air, swinging it as if it were an angry cat's tail. "I'll hear nothing but good about Dick Fox, from you or anyone."

"Why, now. There's a fine girl's loyalty. But of course I meant nothin' evil, how could I? The boy's like me very own son. But could I help overhearin' the ruckus between you last night? And money rollin' all over the floor?"

Meg shook her head to stop the misdirected chatter.

"Mind me, Meg. Blind as you are with love this very minute, he, too, is blind, but with other things."

"Oh, I know about his work and I'm prepared. No jealous heart lies here," she said dramatically, punching her chest. "I like him to paint. It's good. He feels the better for it, and so do I."

Mrs. Bannish exhaled a long sigh. "That's not what I mean at all. And would I be speakin' to you if it began and ended with the paint brush in his hand? No. It's his wary approach to Feargus that's my concern. Influencin' you against earnin' your fair bread and butter."

"He does no such thing, and I'll do what I like in any case," Meg snapped, but her voice trailed away in confusion. She wished Mrs. Bannish would not interfere. She could guess what was coming and did not want to be caught between this marvelous old woman and her lover. The choice, of course, would be clear. But she would regret having to make it.

"Meg, I've not come in to pull yer ear to pieces. Only to warn you. Now there's a sixpence on it, your Master Fox won't be home tonight. Nor the next night after."

"And why should he not come home to me?" Meg flung out with a defiant bravado she did not much feel. Mrs. Bannish had the edge on her. She knew Dick's secrets and perhaps some that Meg herself would never uncover.

"You'll see." She smoothed up her topknot, and the plump features seemed to fix themselves in a sad, superior look of satisfaction.

Was there punishment in the words? Was there teasing? Did she merely want respect?

"Even if he does stay out a while," Meg struggled valiantly, "I shall wait for him till he returns. There is plenty for me to do. Look at this room! Look at those books thrown around. And those chalk-stained shirts. And things to buy!" She chuckled, expanding with recollection of her new financial power. "And should I not learn to make frames, Mrs. Bannish, so I can help *you?* And won't Feargus be wanting me again?" Every word came out like gunshot. But the powder did not explode. Her truth felt wretchedly thin and seen through.

"Very well, m'girl." There were no further words Mrs. Bannish would waste upon the matter. "Now try on that corset and let's see how y'look in't."

With an empty heart, Meg obediently climbed into the unyielding item that lifted her breasts from underneath and thrust them straight ahead of her. They seemed to grow six times their natural size as all the flesh with its rosy points sailed directly on, twin warships out to do the battle of the sexes.

There was a small artist's mirror upon the mantel that Mrs. Bannish took down and held while Meg twisted and turned sideways to squeeze the sight of herself into it. The admiration was predictably flat, however, both from herself and from Mrs. Bannish, since neither of them could stop their thinking upon other, more preoccupying matters.

"I will leave you to walk around in it and make yourself at ease."

Meg exhaled a strangled gasp. "I could never get used to these sticks! And what do I need them for?"

"We'll see. We'll see," said Mrs. Bannish, her ruddy forehead still wrinkling from other dissatisfactions.

Left alone in the aftermath of her first disagreement with her friend and benefactress, Meg pulled herself out of the garment, then sat for long minutes in a depressed silence. She could not understand what had really caused the rift between them. Why must she take sides? Not wishing to give in to the down-sinking sensation, she jumped up and dressed and set about the domestic arrangements she wanted to complete before Dick next arrived home.

The money still lay scattered around the floor, though Mrs. Bannish had deigned to ignore its presence, glinting there in mute evidence of Meg's very first experience with Dick's indifference. Of course it made no matter. If she felt content to take care of all purchases herself without Dick's cooperation, it was no concern of Mrs. Bannish's.

She quickly bent to pick up the coins, yet with something less than the energy that had fired her bringing them home to proudly show him. She found the little purse tucked carelessly into the straw and sifted the gold pieces back into their safe place while she thought about all the new anatomy books and paint colors they would buy. For *those* he would be grateful! Dear, selfish beast. He would gobble down everything she bought him for his art.

Rapidly she finished straightening up, brushing crumbs from the pewter dishes into the fire, then went outdoors into a dense drive of February's fine, powdery snow. At a nimble run she picked her way around muffled footsteps of horses pulling dray carts, their wheels grinding black the slush kicked up by old lady bunters gathering dog dung for sale to the tan yards at the edge of the city. She hurried round the bone grubbers, rag gatherers, and hawkers of pickled whelks, the bargemen and coal heavers, the blind, Scottish crossing sweeper to whom she gave a farthing, and the two-penny post boy, all eking their bread, as she was, from Mother London. The city somehow fed its own and she mingled, passing through the lanes and into a cab, directing the driver to a shop near the Strand vending artist's colors.

She had come too early. There wasn't an artist in the place, but the room was inviting, a frenzied organization of papers stacked in pigeon niches and display trays of every earth brown, yellow, red, blue. She recognized some of the names and began to put together cobalt with its own quality of blue and vermilion with its very special red. She roamed about studying boxes of lead pencils, wooden stands, small plaster casts of limbs, being careful not to touch things with the side of her new muff, till an ancient gentleman approached her, saying, "These are not for yourself, Madame," with the utmost discretion. Wrinkles of experience well taken made delicate webs through the broad face beneath its short, ocher-colored wig.

"No, certainly. For my husband," she replied with an open smile that invited him to talk.

"Just so. What errand has he sent you on, or do you care to look around a bit?"

"But I am so distracted," she said with a flutter, "that I fear I shall need your advice. We are expecting to exhibit at the Royal Academy."

"Ah, yes, in the spring."

"I suppose you go every year?"

"When I can get away, of course."

"And have you seen the Academicians?"

"Not many are a social lot when it comes to mixing with the public. A thousand visitors can come on a day, and that makes a crowded company."

"Indeed. But you must have met one or two of the famous painters. I couldn't believe otherwise for a man of your standing."

"Well, come to think of it, Mr. Fuseli does drop by now and again to have me make him some pig-bristle brushes."

"Fuseli?"

"Henri Fuseli. The Swiss bear, they call him. Not many likes his work. They say it scares them, all those flaming dragons and women in the claws of eagles. But it gives me something to think upon. And tickles my youngest boy, who has a natural love for devil paintings."

"Fuseli must be a fine, fine painter," she said, telling him with a sparkle that she respected his opinion and would be glad to listen further.

"Getting on, of course, as I am."

"And sends an assistant now, I suppose, to buy for im?"

"Not while he still can walk. Quite a peculiar, enrgetic sprout. And particular. Always feeling the paers and testing the brush-hair tips. And comes here ecause here is the finest."

"On special days?"

"That's hard to say. You know he's soon to be Keeper at the Royal Academy, if rumor means news. And has his hands full trouncing the students. A owdy lot."

"Perhaps one day I will see him here," Meg replied nthusiastically, with a flush.

"You will. You will if you keeps at it. But I can give ou no warning when to come, I'm sorry."

"Well, thank you very much. I'll take the Indian ed, it looks a beautiful thing."

" 'Twill go well with your hair, Madame, when your usband paints your portrait. Good day to you."

A thrilling sense of the inevitable vibrated around er as she left the store, for Meg realized that she had topped floundering and had found the beginnings of plan. She must contrive a way to meet this Henri 'useli. The name rang through her all afternoon while she went about town, purchasing brushes for crubbing, papers of tea, plum buns, and thick pease oup in case Dick should arrive home late and be hunry.

The snow froze into a pelting sleet, then dissolved o rain, which had altogether passed by the time she eturned to their room. Walking the city alone had iven her a strange turn, raking up old, unwanted recllections in contrast with her present life. She could carcely believe that she lived here, unmolested. Was a dream? Was it borrowed time? One day, would e not walk smack into Harry Watkins and have o face her punishment for desertion? He knew these ack yards and courts like his hand. His cronies and is gambling habits were right here in this very eighborhood, too. He must be looking out for her to recapture the cut-off source of his income. But sh must not think of that! She brushed her cloak an wondered how Dick would take to a scrubbed-dow floor and hot food waiting for him, and the book c Reynolds' *Principles* and a new *Anatomy of Dissec tion,* with its drawings of unborn infants in the womb that she had accidentally come upon and bought i happy expectation of his surprise.

Her courage failed her, though, when she thougl of all the changes she had already made about th place. What if he liked things exactly as they wer grime and all? What if she disturbed him and be came, thereby, an intruder? She dropped her good in tentions, not willing to risk it any further, and fell t reading Reynolds' *Discourses,* intent on discoveri what it was that drove painters so.

Absorbed, she did not watch the hours. A no came round to her from Feargus, marked "Wedne day." Had a day and night gone by?

My new dear friend,

I will see you again, if you like, tomorrow at half after one.

Yr. Obdt. Svt.,
F.

Wednesday?

She thought about the content of the note and tl day of the week with mingling concern and curiosit Dick had not come home last night. She stirred tl soup in its pot over the hearth and prayed it would n get black before he was home to try it.

He would not like for her to see Feargus tomorro of that she was sure. If he came home, *when* he can home, she would tell him that she intended to se Feargus, anyway.

Thursday morning.

She had slept fitfully, and the straw stuck lil thorns in her flesh. She plucked bits of it from h hair. The god-awful hammering next door wou never stop. She wondered that Mrs. Bannish didr own half the crown jewels from the result of all her industry.

At half after one, she was back to reading Reynolds, her career with Feargus at a decidedly low ebb. How easy it was to admit her cowardice at certain times. She could face the monsters of Loch Ness sooner than miss being here when Dick finally arrived. His absence lay in a siege upon her heart. And now she must swallow her pride and go next door to Mrs. Bannish for some wood.

"The things that one does for love," said Mrs. Bannish kindly, "have excuses in that quarter they can find nowhere else. Of course you wait for him. But starve t'death or freeze t'death while y'r doin' it? No need of that. Have a bit of rabbit with me and a drop of this hot elder wine. We've not much in our poor way, but we do."

Meg sat down in the old, comforting rocker, accustomed now to the protestations of poverty that were part of Mrs. Bannish's life. The woman had already told her the truth: that she lived here to keep the wrong eyes off her business. Since the day with J. S. Widley, Meg was beginning to piece together how the partnership worked.

"Yes, the pictures are fakes, but my frames are real enough," beamed Mrs. Bannish. "And that's a tellin' point. Now you must take this one here to him very soon. It's light and easy to manage and worth more than its weight in gold for hoaxability."

"No, I couldn't go to Feargus." Meg closed her eyes stubbornly. "I know it's a mistake, but I couldn't. Not now."

"So Dick has worked his poison upon ye after all," she clucked without surprise.

"How long do you suppose he'll be gone?" Meg asked with the open admission of her restlessness.

Mrs. Bannish sipped her wine, tasting it with relish, swirling it behind her lips, rolling it over her tongue and finally swallowing with a throaty appreciation for a calming, nourishing drink. "Don't ask me that, I couldn't say."

The abrupt truth sounded crueler than was meant. Meg, flustered, resorted to the drink in her own glass for consolation and something to do. "I could go look for him, but that is hopeless. I could stay here for days, if he has forgotten me. Perhaps weeks. Am I abandoned so soon?"

"He'll be back."

"I won't sleep alone another night."

"You ought to be grateful for a place."

"Hah. I could tie in with Feargus and buy myself better than this," she retorted with empty but resounding pride.

Mrs. Bannish nodded vehemently in agreement and smoothed some of the scrape marks on her fingers. "Which is what I recommend, exactly."

"But I won't," Meg concluded, engrossed in her own thoughts and hardly hearing the other's. "If you will but give a hint of where he is," she pleaded, "I will never say it came from you."

"He'll know in any case, for who else d'you talk to?" she laughed.

"I can't stay here another night. I'll die of the palsy if I stay."

"Well, well . . . all of that. When I was your age I loved a dairy farmer who used to leave me by myself for the cows. When it came calfin' time I was a grass widow year after year. These days, city men leave their women for the gambling halls or the rat-catching barns! There's one close by behind where the cat's meat man stands with his skewers." She jerked a thumb to the west wall. "If there's a moon tonight you'll find it easy."

Chapter Seven

MEG POISED in the doorway, clutching her pelisse collar close and observing that, just as she hoped, there was a full round moon riding high behind thin, scudding clouds. Shadows of houses were strangely clear as she sped along the street with her shoulders hunched. The snow and rain had washed away some of the grit, and now the down-sliding shapes of things were polished by silver. She ran, less in fear from the streets than with misgivings. Having no idea how Dick would greet her, she again worried that he would consider her arrival as *interfering*. She hated the idea of being a burden to him, or of *not* being one but his thinking so. Still, she must straighten out what they were to do, how they would live. In any case, she simply must see him and reassure herself that he was close by.

The night crawlers of the neighborhood had by now learned that she belonged with Dick. There came an occasional call to her from a drunken strong-man or a crippled beggar, which she answered by name if she knew it.

She had not far to go, and before her breath wore out, she reached a street where some dark, dock-tailed bloods pranced in restive restraint before a large, sway-backed barn of a building with an uncertain pitched roof. Random boards popped loose from their pegs and curled back in a warp, outlined by some passing rays of the moon. She arrived at the entrance and heard voices inside yelping and attacking each other with accusations about cheating.

A bulky man guarded the door, and she called up to him, "I'm going inside to Dick Fox," certain that he would be known here.

"Well, 'ee's inside, all right," replied the gruff voice. "Three shillings a seat."

She paid and pushed past him into an acrid area stuffed with a mixed bag of humanity crowded around a rectangular floor space and hoarsely trading bets. Ragged, disabled soldiers in caps askew rattled on as equals with gentlemen in needlecrafted coats. They, in their turn, happily shoved and elbowed boxers with bluff whiskers and faces like street dogs. Everywhere cans of porter were handed around in a foaming slosh. She squinted through the thick hordes, determined to find Dick. Exhilaration whipped her blood as she pushed her way to make room, carving a place for herself at the edge of the first row of benches that climbed in a rickety frame toward the back of the barn. Candles flickered and bent dangerously along the walls. Patches of moonlight poured through the holes in the roof, and the smoke lifted out as through a flue, the only salvation for this oblivious pack that kept it from suffocating in its own steamy breath. A miasma from unwashed bodies saturated her new clothing. Her dress would never be the same. Scanning around for Dick, she saw a sprinkling of women crushed among the men and drinking with them as cronies, grabbing up cans of porter from their fists and slurping long drafts that left a foam bubbling upon the lip. Some were flashily dressed in layers of red flounces, overrouged, with their breasts puffed high—like the sight she herself would make had she worn Mrs. Bannish's corset, an attractive, wenchy type, the kind she most often noticed clustered in the Haymarket with their pimps, looking to go off with some gent behind the crumbling colonnade. The crowd was a show of its own, like the horses at Vauxhall Gardens or Ranalegh, and she despaired of finding Dick right off.

"Ladeez—and genelmun!" Into the arena lumbered a man with a sturdy gray terrier trotting behind him, bristling from nose to tail and glancing nervously about as though searching for something. *"Ladeez*—and genelmun!" He held up two stocky arms to the crowd. "Here come Terrible Billy . . . who warrants and

swears 'ee will put away—before your own very eyes—one hundred enormous and fearful fightin' rats within the space o' ten minutes . . . not a second more."

Into the hoots and shouts of the milling audience stalked a man from a side room, holding fast to a large sack flung over his shoulder that at first seemed bulky with potatoes. The lumps began to move, however, in a turmoil inside the rough, torn cloth. Then a shrill mewling and squealing intermingled with preliminary growls from Billy. The hushed audience *aahed* with pleasure.

Billy, alone for some moments in the arena, glanced about him. Spying the man with the sack, he recognized his presence and tensed, ears alert and eyes, shining and beady, fastened upon the sack.

With a quick motion the man flung the sack forward, untied the cord around the mouth, and emptied its contents to the arena floor. A pile of rats fell tumbling over each other, sliding out onto the boards. Some of them, stunned, stood quite still, whiskers quivering. Others instantly bolted to the walls.

Exactly as the first one moved, Billy tore into them with a ferocious, businesslike dispatch. Shiny red bubbles flew about in a spray. Rats, flung to right and left, piled up in silent pyramids of dull fur.

"Thirty pounds says 'ee does it."

"Forty says no!"

A blistering argument started, with money rattling and crinkling in the air as hands waved wildly. Through the pungent smoke Meg glimpsed the flick and swirl of a red sash, then Dick, pushing back the curled brim of the beaver hat she had bought him and running down the rickety staircase to a man in a flowered jacket. They poured money back and forth into each other's palms with a white-eyed urgency of passion.

"Dick!" An impulse to run to him was quickly squelched by a cold wash of good sense. *Let him alone just now*. But she could go slowly, perhaps reach him when the betting and slaughter were done. Pots of beer spilled around her as she made her way toward him.

Once the betting was over, Dick, aloof to the calls, hauled out a pad from inside his jacket, and holding it firmly, began sketching rapidly, searching among the animals for the poise of haunches and tails, the sway and curve of spinal bones. She understood it. Knew that he was seeking the perfect single gesture for design of light and shade to create the essence of battle.

"Four meeeen-utes. Four minutes and a haaafff!"

Blind to the caterwauling, to the squalling bloodlust around him, Dick sketched on with intensifying concentration.

"Nine mee-e-e-e-nutes and forty-five . . . TEN! . . . And Billy's done 'em all in, ladeez and genelmun!"

To the general yelling and thumping of floorboards, the man came out from the corner and began tossing the dead rats back into the sack from which they had come, moving with an easy sweep of his long arms as Billy leaped about him, blood glistening on the tips of his ruff, evidently hungry for the second act to come.

Meg reached Dick in time to hear the man beside him say, "Well, sir. You've bet against your luck tonight and lost it all."

But Dick did not seem to hear him, either. The pencil still rushed about on its page, his eyes narrowed, cutting a glittering swathe through smoke and passion to discover and dig out exactly the effect of nature that caught him.

She came to stand between the gentleman and Dick, waiting quietly till he should finish and notice her.

He put down the pad and saw her at the same instant, for her body was in line with the final movement of the pencil.

"Meg! Is this what you think to do with your hard-earned guineas?" He stared at her, half laughing in puzzled interest.

She remained silent, not daring to say that she had come here to follow him. "But I'm a gambler of sorts, too, you see. Never knew that about me, did you? It's time you found it out."

"Is that so?" One dark eyebrow rose suspiciously. "Then why would I be here?"

Dick shrugged and slipped the pencil away. "I haven't the foggiest notion," he replied in utter, continuing bafflement.

She enjoyed the idea of his perplexity and saw how it gave her a handle to the situation. Dick, who knew nothing of her habits and tastes, could well believe that she was a gambler, if she said so. And could she not become one, if that would keep her by his side? As they left the barn she searched for some common meeting ground, not wishing to reveal herself a rank beginner.

"Harry Watkins always dragged me to the bear baiting when he came into money from a big debt collection. We used to live high and low. High and low is how it went. But times are always good for bad debts, aren't they? If one can figure out how to collect them, it's an easy life."

They had knocked back some gin and were huddling in the glow of a street fire that a peddler had built near a crossing. Only six blocks from home, but no point in trying to drag Dick away to a warm bed. He was drunk now and cheerful and didn't feel the cold. There was no money in his pockets, but she still had four guineas.

"Filthy torture, bears. Ought to be a law against cruelty to animals, and will be one day. But if you want to go to 'em, you're on." He waved an arm and swung it round her neck, dragging her face in close and kissing her with a surprisingly happy gentleness. He was a strange sort of drunk. Vulgar but not brutal like the rest, nor clumsy when it came to touching her. She was afraid that he could see right through to her thoughts even with those bleary eyes, still secretly sharp. She could almost believe that he wasn't drunk but pretending.

"Y'know, at the bears, men are really daft to win." He played with his sash, fingers fumbling through the fringe. "I could make back a hundred pounds just by starting with this."

"Your sash?"

"My good-luck belt. Always with me. Always comes

back to me, since the day I took it from the dead Frenchman. 'Twas with the Twenty-third Light Dragoons in Egypt. Ask me one day and I'll tell you about it. My good-luck belt. Most swindlers, when they've bet their best pants away, use their neck cloths for a last try at the game. When there's nothing left for me, I always have this sash. It comes back. Always." He hiccuped mildly. "My very, very, very good luck." He kissed her full on the mouth. "I'm glad you reminded me, sweetheart. . . . To the bears we go."

He sounded so happy. Meg felt her stomach drop with sick dread, but she dared say nothing to interfere with Dick's hope to regain his losses. She could not back out now. And she knew where the place was as well as she knew the map of her own face. Surely Harry Watkins would be there, too. He never missed a match.

They seemed like the same coarse mob who thronged to the rat catching; but there were more of them and packed more tightly together, if that were possible, beneath a dangerously wobbling slat roof.

Dick pushed sideways before her toward a stand of slab benches. Meg followed, at first inside the protection of his arm crooked around her neck while they shuffled slowly through the dense swirls of cigar smoke. Nervously she glanced over the crowd, searching the restless and edgy faces, hoping to find her father first and thereby avoid him, somehow. Beside her, Dick was growing tense and eager, taking on an irritable, driving urge to bet and reverse his losses.

"Make room for a lady," he said, forcing space into a crowded bench where there was none.

"Lie-dy, is it?"

Meg faced the froglike stare crawling down her body. "Bet your animal, sir. Three guineas."

Dick leaned across her shoulder. "Hear the lady, don't you? Bet your animal, she says. Three guineas to receive five if the bear ain't finished with six minutes to go the hour."

"Took."

Attention was suddenly diverted from the crowd as it exploded in a great roar, answering the sound of another roar—from the bear the crowd had come to see.

Meg turned and watched a giant, brown shaggy Russian bear. It was much larger than any of its kind she could imagine. It walked hesitatingly on hind legs but sometimes fell down onto all fours as it was led into the rectangle. Then the bear would rear up again at the goading of its master and menacingly draw its lips back to bare large, yellow fangs. The bear did its best to appear vicious and threaten the hooting crowd. Led and tugged by a rope attached to a heavy neck collar, the animal swayed within its limitations but seemed to know how far the lead could go. The small eyes grew lusterless while it roared more loudly, ears flattening, snout grizzled with saliva, as though it understood the torture in store.

Meg shrugged uneasily, taking no pleasure in watching its great display. Queasily, she kept looking around through the crowd, searching for the milky-white goat face she despised, taking its pleasure in the cruel entertainment.

The master of ceremonies drew a deep breath into his chest, waved a hairy, shirt-sleeved arm, and bellowed: "Genelmun . . . genelmun . . . y'r attenshun . . . You see a'fore y'r eyes the giant lately come to us from Petersburg . . . Brutus the Czar . . . who will attempt to fend off our famous Leo, Master of Hounds, and his brethren. Leo . . . Leo promises to bring down this great and fearsome brute before the first stroke of midnight or . . . be dead hisself in the effort."

The crowd clapped and stamped. It dawned on Meg that she was trapped here through the bloody contest. She had never intended this—never intended more than to impress Dick with her bravado. Yet here she sat, in the very pit of folly and revulsion. She peered at Dick and found his profile craning alertly in every direction, drinking in the shapes and passions of the crowd. He leaned over to the man who had taken her bet, whipped off his sash, and called, "Add this to the pile, sir. One more guinea against the lot."

A pack of short, brawny dogs bounded into the arena and immediately set to in a cluster, growling at the feet of the bear, who gave a startled grunt and backed away a few inches.

"Show 'im the teeth, Brutus. The teeth!"

"C'mon, Leo! Nip 'im. Nip 'im in the arse!"

Shrieks and commands thrown heatedly at the animals drowned Dick's voice. He pressed his leg protectively against the side of her thigh as the thick-muscled dogs began darting at the legs of their victim, tails whipping with brisk joy in the sport. One of the pack, a spotted creature with a low-slung, rolling belly, nosed closer than the rest. He sprang in a sudden leap upward, irritably testing his prey and at the same time nipping into the thick fur at the chest. The mob let go a shrill croaking.

"Ecod, there's a pair of jaws for 'ee! Ecod, like t'match 'un against Pretty Blazer!"

"C'mon, Leo," a voice in the mob howled. "Show 'im y'r gob!"

As though catching his name, Leo perked up in every hair. He whirled left and began to trot, circling around the bear who, coming down on all fours, swatted out at the tormentor. Black, curved claws hooked across the dog's rump, but Leo wiggled away from the blow as it landed and merely glanced him.

Meg tried not to watch the proceedings too closely, but the horrible fascination kept her from missing a single motion.

Behind them a man poked Dick's shoulder. "Five pun' . . . six . . . seven. A guinea goes a long way, sir. A guinea on the battle."

Dick, who had bet away his last possession, nodded.

" 'Tis a queer set-out," cackled a woman's voice. "Rammin' their heads against his belly like billy goats."

The baying dogs began to make shorter, bolder rushes. One dashed sideways, caught at a swiping arm, and held fast to it above the elbow. The weight of the heavy belly and swaying haunches pulled the growling bear down in helpless ferocity onto all fours.

once more. Instantly, attackers were upon his head, snapping and tearing flesh from the vulnerable snout. Red fountains spouted over the dirty gray fur of the dogs. The blood-lust of the throng exploded in shouts and hooting and thumping of feet. Gentlemen's sticks pounded upon the creaking floorboards.

The bear staggered back. The dogs, sensing their advantage, snapped at him again and again, blunt, tenacious jaws clamping deeper into the fur and hanging on longer. The brown hairs became soggy with dark, oozing color matted down. The substance smeared itself freely across the muzzles of the smaller animals. They shot their tongues out to lick themselves clean. The taste seemed to make them more vigorous, hungrier for the finish. They leaped at him directly now, like balls shot from a gun, at eyes and ears, with no care for their own protection.

The bear's beady stare focused on an assailant. Jaws lunged and snapped shut. Yellow fangs disappeared, crunching along the spine of a dog. It yelped with surprise and outrage, hind legs trembling in a paralytic way as it was lifted and tossed high into the air, then plummeted with a squeal and one heavy, finalized thud, to lie motionless where it fell. The audience squalled and whistled shrilly. Others of the pack ignored its fate or were enraged further. They dashed at the bear from every angle and gradually backed him, trapped, into a corner. Meg could not tell now which animal was the leader. The collective onslaught was too relentless. Kept down for longer periods of time, dangerously down on all fours, the rough bear's head with its death-dealing fangs was lowered into a weaker position. The tiny eyes became glazed. The ranging head swung in a last fury. Sensing the kill, the dogs lunged again and again, sinking into an ear, an eye, a cheek, wherever their frenzied brains propelled them.

Meg could not see which animal in the tangled heap gouged the final blow to the throat; she faded back onto the bench, breathless and perspired.

The fight, bet upon to last for some hours, proved

to be hardly a contest. Voices from the side of the arena bawled, "Unfair! 'Twere unfair!"

A crooked black cane swung high and poked through the swarm. A forehead followed, deathly pale above a bloated face, eyes and red lids swollen with gin, lips twisting in fury, every feature shaking within a frizz of cream-colored curls rusted at their tips. The bull shoulders, glittering in a frieze jacket, pushed arrogantly through and gained access to the front line of spectators.

"Murder! Murder!" choked the voice, gravelly and besotted. "This beast has been bled and poisoned beforehand." He poked the carcass with his stick.

Meg felt her heart swell into her throat. She clutched Dick's sleeve and froze, mute, as there in his usual place stood the creature hated and feared for so long, having his pleasure, bawling, howling, waving his cane, totally unaware of being watched by her.

"What is it, Meg? Tell me."

She could hardly swallow and pulled at Dick to take her away. But he would not budge.

"What is it?" he demanded again. "You must tell me."

"There. Across the way," she gasped finally. "That's Harry Watkins."

"Is it?" He peered narrowly for long, thoughtful moments. Then, grabbing Meg's wrist and springing from the bench, he thrust forward, the great size of him head and shoulders above the others. Like an ax cutting a trail, he pressed people aside, fairly hacking out of the way those who ignored his onslaught. Meg, at first unwilling, tried to pull back. But then, protected in his wake, she stumbled along just ahead of the crowds closing in behind her. She caught her breath with amazement and security in his strength. A thrill of pride in him overcame her as she saw how it was possible to drown in a sea of humanity that became, in multitudes, strangely liquid.

Their distance to Watkins was hardly three horse lengths. Yet the effort spent to reach him consumed time that saw him growing more fiercely pugnacious.

Ie reached for the master of ceremonies and swung im around by the collar, rapping him sharply on one houlder with his stick. "Murder, I say."

The man was not to be intimidated by hiccuping ies from one rakehell bailiff posing in starcher and lowered paste buttons. He wrenched the stick rudely rom Watkins's fist and grunted, "Be off with ye, y'r Highness."

Watkins's eyes bulged with fury at the insolence. He ould not take the hint but, seeming to realize that is own legs wobbled, grabbed the arm of a tall, attered wretch on his other side and bawled, "D'you ee that miserable, cheating face behind me? Smack im roundly and teach him a lesson!"

The tattered one obviously mistook Watkins's in-ention. His sunken cheeks twisted in a grimace and he long, mottled nose curved down, pecking like an nraged parrot toward Watkins's eye.

Dick, striding, leaping, twisting through, still would ot reach Watkins in time before the blows would tart. Meg's skin prickled with quaking anguish of what was to come that could not be avoided.

No sooner had she thought it than the first violence rupted as Watkins jabbed his fist into the belly of one nd his knuckles into the jaw of another. They were oth stunned but reacted instantly, springing back with ellish curses, then falling simultaneously like an ava-anche over Watkins, burying him from Meg's sight.

Her stomach rose with revulsion and she clutched at er throat. Thank heaven the gang on either side of he scuffling three was more intent upon the dead bear han on the safety of humans. She saw them being lrawn only gradually into the fray as Dick swept the orce of his own tide closer and closer while she clung leterminedly to her place behind his heels.

A volcano of human eruption spewed tangles of rms and legs. With one warning yell Dick plunged n and began pulling them apart, as though tearing mall trees out by the roots in his search down to the owels of the earth for Watkins.

Tears of fury stung and blurred Meg's view. Convulsed torment overwhelmed her as composure began to shred. The hunched body of Dick digging down relentlessly was all she could see that made sense to her. Yet she felt strangely settled, in one breath aghast at his animal energy, in the next, crazily exultant. What an odd beast she watched before her, with that broad neck straining its tendons and that tousled head gleaming. Those rippling bands of arms. How delicately they could hold her around the waist. She shivered at the unexpected memory of their lovemaking. Heard herself groan for mercy in bed, to deaf ears. And not mean it. And be taken. And taken again.

He roared, "Watkins!" and the exhausted crew around him moved aside, not wishing further battle with the maniacal earnestness so dreadfully intent upon its announced purpose. They fell away like snapped bracken and Dick lifted a moaning Watkins into the air.

He was altogether limp, head swaying back, mouth open and gasping. Meg could not tell if this were mere drunkenness or dangerous bruising. The flattened curls drooped against Dick's chest. The knees gave way and would not stand, so that Dick had to hoist him up like a sack and lay him over his shoulder. Then, reaching back, he clutched Meg by the elbow. His hand slid over the length of her forearm. Hot, iron fingers closed round her palm. Wildly, she felt possessed in every part by the mere touch of her hand to his. Burning droplets sprang out along her spine. She gasped for lack of air.

Thus the three of them moved away and through the door.

Outside, Watkins began to get his bearings, and Dick stood and held him till his eyes rolled and focused. Then Dick grabbed him by both ears.

"Harry Watkins." He shook him. "Watkins!"

"Whaa."

Gradually, Watkins came around and gazed blearily at his daughter. "Meg . . . You . . . *You* . . ." he spluttered. "You . . ."

"Don't say a word to her, Watkins," Dick rasped.

"I saved you inside to tell you this. If you ever see her again and try to touch her, if you ever threaten or frighten her . . . by the Lord that made us all, I'll snip your balls off with my knife . . . as I learned how to do in Egypt."

Then, setting the man down on the curb, he grabbed Meg's hand and pulled her off beside him through the dark.

"No, no, we forgot something," Meg cried, yanking her hand free and running back.

With all the zest of a new fire kindled inside her, Meg advanced upon Watkins fearlessly, conscious now of a thrilling strength that would enable her to face anything.

"Y'old bloater," she mumbled, diving down on him and rifling through his pockets. "Where's a crown left on you?" She almost despaired of finding so much as a ha'penny but came, finally, upon a fistful of coins that in his drunkenness he had forgotten to bet.

Without stopping to count them, she dashed off back inside the barn. Her eyes burned from the wall of smoke that had collected during the contest. Laboring through the crowds, she squinted into corners and huddles, determined not to leave the place until her mission was accomplished. Where had they been sitting? Third row. The man could not have moved far away since.

Agonizing moments sped by till she saw it, and a hungry smile of satisfaction came to her mouth. Pushing her way through, bull-like and sure of herself, she waved the money at him, all the while keeping her eyes fastened upon the end of the red sash dangling from the gambler's pocket.

"Sir! Sir!" she bellowed, yanking the precious sash into her own possessive grip. "This will make up the difference. It's more than a fair price for a bit of silk cloth. And come next Thursday, I'll give you another chance if you think you're cheated."

The man laughed at her and let her go. "Take it, dearie. For a kiss."

She raised up onto her toes and planted a full, beautiful smacker upon him with iron-hard joy.

"Wish I had a second sash to match the first," he called after her as she fled back to find Dick.

Waving the red garment, she flung herself into his arms with it, and winding it carefully around his throat, murmured, "*Now* we can go home."

When, safe in their room at last, he had fallen into an endless drunken sleep, she pressed a guinea into hiding in the straw, thus always to have a ransom for his good luck. And snuggling close to his stretched-out body, she whispered, "Always come back to me. Always come back."

Chapter Eight

SHE HAD EARNED the right to be with him and was his comrade at last. Comrade and lover, a powerful spirit between them that, she felt, could beat down the world.

"Am I going with you tonight?" she asked gently, not to insist.

"You'll never stay home again!" he roared, jingling the roll of crowns and half crowns in his palm and pressing half of the coins into hers. "Take these for yourself, my sweetheart. You bring me luck."

She went out proudly beside him, running three steps to his single long rapid stride. He took her to the barges along the river where thieves crouched in a circle, tossing and calling through the night, eyes burning with the lust to win. On miserable, windy March days of rain, they gathered indoors in taverns spreading cloths upon the tables to play in hidden silence, voices rasping, "Tails! . . . Heads! . . . Tails!", eyes bobbing magnetized, hour upon hour as the game went on. Sundays there was a special gambling near swampy grounds filled with rubbish where the Life Guards went occasionally to exercise. Men and boys gathered with their wages, losing in an hour what they had gained in a week and impatient to return the next Sunday. Quarrelsome they were among themselves, but cooperative, one always standing the lookout for interference from strangers. She joined Dick, groveling on the green with him behind the Chelsea bun house and learning a curious quickness of hand, flipping the sixpence from her thumbnail in such a way that the toss would come up as she called it. They scraped together silver and gold, by the handful sometimes, and others staggered home drunk with nothing to their names except bellies full of gin. They lay drunk together for days, singing "God Save Our Noble King," and took no notice of the world, sleeping and making love and slopping down the soup that Mrs. Bannish brought them, a mix of barley meal, Indian corn, and four red herrings pounded in a mortar. She fed it to them with many a cluck for their ill-fated ways. Yet, through the murk of booze Dick would always stagger up at first light and crawl to his chalks and papers.

" 'Tis a miracle his hand is so steady," offered Mrs. Bannish, eyeing some sketches of hunting dogs in a field.

"No miracle," replied Meg. "That's Dick."

"So it is. Can be drunk from Michaelmas to Lady Day and wake up to paint at dawn."

They staggered through weeks of wicked, yellow miasma that rolled in with the tar-footed geese and turkeys herded up from Norfolk for London dinners, a fog that brought on the spleen to make people hurl themselves from bridges.

"You must learn that money is round," warned Mrs. Bannish, sniffing a nasty mess of rice, milk, butter, and spices that Meg was hoarding in a pot. "One day it rolls to you. The next to me. Keep your eye on it, girl, if you're smart."

Through the curtain of her daze and her joy at being with her beloved, Meg nevertheless heard Mrs. Bannish clearly, though she didn't heed the advice. In her nightly dreams she waited to hear from Henri Fuseli regarding Dick's pictures. And she imagined Dick vividly, accepting fame and fortune among the Royal Academicians. She dreamed the same dreams while awake, though kept them secret.

The sun shone for brief spells as April began, enough to dry and warm the sprouting green fields. Her Spanish cloak was ruined. Dick bought her a new shawl and a flaring straw poke bonnet and a fichu with lace handiwork to wear with her new dress. They went off to Hampstead Heath in the daytime, where she ran with the chickens and children upon the common while Dick sat beneath an oak and drew her at play. Breathless after a day's sport, she fell down beside him in the shade, gasping with her eyes closed, "This must never end!"

Springtime, and London was a circus. They pushed and pulled each other everywhere, past draped gambling halls and the stringy-haired dandies trotting in or out, some with their forgotten coats still worn inside out for luck at the tables, yet whitely starched and ruffled, following the new fashion for cleanliness.

One morning, crushed in among two thousand others outside Somerset House, Dick lifted her upon his shoulders for a glimpse of their Majesties with two of the princesses and attendants arriving in three coaches to view the Royal Academy exhibition before the rooms would be open to the public. She studied the dark clothes of the king and the paired, cream-colored horses, her ears ringing with the roar around her of "Huzza! Happiness to your Majesty." The king's square face appeared pleased with the enthusiasm of his people as he bowed several times. The crowd's joy was due to the sight of the king's going unaccompanied by guards, but Meg thought that distant man looked more like a portly father, confident and pleased in the midst of his loved ones, giving and receiving protection and happiness. She could envision his studying

Dick's paintings quite solemnly and commanding him kindly to do a portrait of the royal family at Windsor.

"One day we will meet them, you'll see," she said to Dick, sliding down his body and squeezing his arm.

Dick took up his scrapbook, and they tramped off to sketch the redcoats conducting carriages across Blackfriars' Bridge on the first leg of travel to the continent.

"Dick? What is it?" she said, watching him as he gazed intently at the departing caravans.

"There go some men I used to know," he mumbled. "We sketched together in a drawing class from the life."

"What of it?"

"Nothing."

"But tell me."

"Can't you see?" he burst out, chagrin darkening in his narrowed eyes. "They are off to visit the anatomical studies being conducted, as we all have heard, with great enthusiasm in Paris."

"We have our own anatomical studies here," she countered, hoping to lift his spirits. "Have we not heard praise to the skies for the antique marbles Lord Elgin has brought us home from Greece?"

"If we ever get to view them."

"Yes, we shall. We shall do everything. Wait and see!"

She pulled him off to draw other things. They haunted Pidcock's Wild Beast Show at Exeter 'Change, an old wooden house in the Strand, where lions and tigers confined in upstairs cages paced before walls painted as tropical scenery and gave out roars that frightened the horses in the street below. At Dick's arrival erupted a hearty " 'ere 'ee cums, our jolly painter fellow!" Dick climbed with the menagerie men to a special vantage place above the crowds where he worked, drawing the beasts with fascinated, high seriousness and engulfed by the eerie, implacable loneliness of jungle sounds in London.

"Yes, Feargus, I have been careless of our friendship, and perhaps I have even abused your kindness toward me." Meg spoke with the proper degree of penitence to attract him while placing his neglected letter to her upon the table. "But you may count upon it, I am in want of money and have learned my lesson well as to where it will dependably come from."

Feargus tilted his head to scrutinize her over the glasses that slipped down his nose. "Yes, my girl," he said, patting her ear affectionately. "To watch the charm of your display this instant, I am certainly convinced that you have learned well your lessons in deception." He nodded with pleasure and poured some strange-smelling amber decoction into a pair of tumblers. "Here, you may want to taste this Tokay. I will give you an idea of how the privileged live, which should calm you."

She had become accustomed to the acid aromas o his workroom and sat comfortably in the wide chai that looked toward Queen Anne Street East, where pale, snowy fog drifted down upon the slow-movin horse traffic. "Will you forgive me?" she said simply with a round, vulnerable look.

"Forgive? I never blamed." He drank off the win and cleared his throat. "I merely thought you ha more stuff in you and I admired it. You carried off ou first encounter so well that I foresaw a future loomin brightly."

"And is my future turned all topsy-turvy in so shor a time?" She laughed coquettishly, mustering all th elegant turns and phrases they had practiced together "Surely there is another Lord Albert on the horizon."

"Lord Alberts there are aplenty these days." H passed his hand over his forehead. "But sad to say we do not have paintings enough to go around."

"Is that really so?" she protested softly, at a loss "And yet I hear Mrs. Bannish knocking them up da and night."

"The days are numbered, nevertheless. My eye are not what they were for making pictures, and wh else is there to do the copies? Engraving is just bread-and-butter sideline, as you know. And even tha takes the sight of a younger man." He loosened th cravat and massaged his throat, appearing suddenly weak and pathetic. "Surely there are dozens of hack painters daubing away all over London, but not good men, you understand me. It is one matter to blotch a picture for some splay-footed farmer in the shires, and quite another to deal with our well-bred peers who early go out and learn the world."

"Then you need a man like Dick," she said quietly, hoping to set Feargus up for the bargain.

"I don't know, any more, about Dick," replied Feargus, casually sharp. "He refuses me too often and I grow tired."

She sipped her Tokay and watched Feargus without protesting, feeling the shift and flow balancing the argument between them. He wanted something and, at the same time, knew that so did she.

"I do not think I can convince Dick to do anything that goes against the grain," she mused. "But he has some fine Italian masters already copied."

"Yes. Early works and quite beautiful, Mrs. Bannish tells me."

"You have never seen them yourself? They would enthrall you." She spoke with a lusty grin, suddenly realizing that she had hit upon the very thing that Feargus wanted. "I could convince Dick to turn them over. They serve no use in his life now, from what I can see. And he is piling the place with new pictures every day . . . that is what breaks my heart. Everything is half finished, then tossed aside and never missed. All for want of eyes to look upon them. Oh, if only I could get some good advice about his work. If only I could have a man like Henri Fuseli give me an opinion of how to proceed." She extended her glass boldly now for more Tokay.

"Fuseli, is it?" Feargus brightened in a wide winning smirk and swung round to the bottle with a waking energy that lifted his blue coattails. "Why did you not say so earlier? Do you not know where you are, girl? Why, this is the parish of St. Marylebone, the very center of London's artworld. Would I live anywhere else? And Henri Fuseli is just a few doors from us. I see him often. And Mr. Turner is within a short hop, too. Why, you can meet Shee and Stothard and Opie and all forty of the Royal Academicians, if you wish, for we have all worked together collecting the charity fund dispensations for widows of impoverished artists. I am your key to the world, Meg Watkins. And it would be my pleasure to delight you with introductions."

"You are too kind, Feargus, too kind." Meg tossed her head back, laughing at all the pomp without the position. "And I shall never be the widow of an impoverished artist if you will see to it that the work of Dick Fox reaches Fuseli's eyes."

"You lay too much weight upon artistic merit," Feargus said, suddenly intense. "One must also have the character for such a life. Sir Joshua Reynolds did, and lived as a gentleman in a fine house in Leicester Fields, with an income of close to six thousand a year and a gilded chariot in which his sister drove to take the air. When he died the greatest nobles mourned him. You may say that his honor was due to his genius." Feargus lifted his glass in tribute. "But you must also remember his kindness to everyone, his charm and his fine manners. For Gainsborough, you see, who painted nearly as well, never did nearly as well in society . . . or in his accounts."

"But I must try," Meg replied doggedly. "I must, don't you see?"

"Yes I see." Feargus studied her with a brief alarmed smile. "And so I shall gain you access to Fuseli. Depend upon it. The new works and the old works of Dick Fox shall be sent to him by my hand, personally. And I will include some engravings to make an all-around show."

The letter arrived while Dick was next door, lazily working out a deal with Mrs. Bannish.

Meg knew instantly, by the ornamental script with its fanciful swings and curlicues, that only a man such as Fuseli was described to be could write like this. She gasped and hid the page inside her bosom, to wait for a safe moment when she would read it in privacy. But patience was not one of her stronger virtues when it came to matters concerning Dick. She rubbed the thin material of her dress and felt the paper warming from the heat of her flesh. Before she could think of alternatives, she poked her head in next door and said, "The hawker is calling boiled puddings. Shall I bring some for you, Mrs. Bannish?"

"No, no, girl. Suit yourself."

As Meg predicted, they were both too busy to be bothered, and away she flew down the stairs, racing up the block and into the protected doorway of a ship chandler's shop where she could safely stand and read the letter.

My dear Miss Watkins,

I have the etchings, drawings, and painted scenes in my hand, all of which I agree are to be greatly admired, as you do. The real misfortune to this species of etching, however, is that it is being taught and spoken of as though it were a kind of legerdemain trick, and thereafter, every booby who can hold a pencil and pour gum spirit over a plate of copper congratulates himself on possessing The Secret. In consequence, Europe is deluged with our worthless productions, while the error of those who imagine the attainment of riches to be the proper end of art is leading to the dangerous folly of confounding national wealth with national happiness. Again and again I hear the knowledgeable public lay this fault to want of an ascertained Constitution of National Art at the time of framing the laws of the London Royal Academy, but I take no part in that mainstream and confine myself, in my age, to painting and to teaching the laws of painting to my charges.

I do thank you for interceding on behalf of your friend Mr. Fox and reaffirm that I have the India proof of Bonaparte here in a case at Berner's Street; and if you will come to me on

Wednesday next, at two in the afternoon, I will be happy to discuss with you what you call your dilemma, and at that time I will return the portfolio to you flat and safe.

Yr. Obt. Svt.,
Henri Fuseli

With her temples pounding, Meg walked the streets, stumbling around the charity children being led in a line, and generally blind to everything except what she and Mr. Fuseli would work out on Dick's behalf.

Damn Dick's stubbornness! She knew it was going to be murder all the way. No compliments would change him, but perhaps an offer to show at the exhibition next April might turn his energies to work that yielded a productive reward. She was tired of his pictures being sold for farthings in the dives where they took dinner. And disgusted, too! Not for her sake as much as for Dick's pride. Yet, confound it! His pride was the size of a prince's!

"I'll tell you what I need from you, Mr. Fuseli," she said aloud, practicing. "I need an assurance that members of the committee will vote in favor of the paintings I submit. . . ."

She was still saying that sentence to herself on the following Wednesday as she looked for the golden lion on the right corner house on Berner's Street that Feargus had told her would mark where Fuseli lived. Soon she found herself before the door, and deliberating upon the knocker for a minute or two, at last lifted it with such a determined effort that it stuck in the air. Banging it down with firmness of intent brought a parlormaid instantly, who opened the door to her with a startled face that did not relax until Meg had announced her name.

"Ah yes, miss. He is expectin' you."

Meg followed after her into a gallery room filled with paintings of huge dimension that almost leaped off the wall with chaotic urgency. Malicious witches and galvanized devils brewing incantations, Satan bridging Chaos and springing upward in a pyramid of fire, Lady Macbeth washing blood—every humor, every tremor of pathos, murder, terror, mortification met her glance. She half expected the floor to sway and open beneath her slippers as she imagined Fuseli to be a giant in scaly-green skin.

She heard some footsteps. Small, bony white fingers felt and slid their way around the edge of the door. Then a fragile, white-headed man with a wrinkled lion's face appeared in an old flannel dressing gown tied round the waist with a piece of rope. Upon his head stood a protective cap that looked like the bottom of his wife's work basket.

Is this the very one? thought Meg. *Why, I can deal with him.*

"By Gode, Miss Watkins," he exploded in a strong Swiss accent, shuffling forward in a pair of bedtime slippers. "Your fellow does his painting at least with energy. He studies anatomy and he is right."

"Mr. Fuseli, I am grateful to you with all my heart, but . . . as I told you in the letter . . ." She fumbled with embarrassment, then found her way. "I have a problem with Mr. Fox not easily got around."

"Problem? What problem is there for a man who can draw like an angel? And does he always *paint* his studies? Why did I not hear of him before this?"

"Perhaps that is a good sign," she said ruefully. "Perhaps he will get on to the right foot with you."

"Right foot? Right foot? Of course he is dere already. He draws from nature, and yet one can see in it the GRAND STYLE. *That* is a talent!" He shuffled around the room, glaring up at some of his own productions. "For me it is otherwise. I am the only one who has the right to put six toes on a model and call it Nature . . . or Nature as it *ought* to be. But others. They have no business to make Nature as she never was. And your Mr. Fox has the genius to realize and respect Nature! Well. But I must meet your friend. I can do wonders for his career, Gode bless me. He paints pretty subjects. But I shall give him subjects that astonish! confound! and terrify! for if it do nothing of those, then nothing it *is,* by Gode!"

The harangue stirred an ardor in Meg's blood that flushed up into her cheeks and pounded away. For some moments her vision would dim and then clear again, as though she were sailing in and out of fog. And she was in a fog . . . a conflict of emotions that locked horns in her consciousness with no immediate signs of resolution.

"But why do you look upset? Here. Here. Take this." He handed her a glass of cherry cordial. "Have you dined?"

"Thank you. I am not hungry," she muttered. "My problem is . . . how valuable *you* are."

Fuseli laughed. His small eyes, hidden beneath shaggy tufts of brows, darted from her stricken face to her trembling hands and back again.

"Excuse me for being so vague," she pressed on. "I can hardly find the words. But it is this! There is a place for Dick Fox in the Academy. I know it."

"And I can agree. If he studies. And works well with me, yes."

"But I cannot bring him to come around."

"Not bring him to come around?"

His words went off like gunfire. The dreaded secret knowledge that she was never to tell was now revealed.

"Every lad who can hold a pencil wants to come to His Majesty's Academy. They walk in from miles out of the country. Miles! They come with letters of introduction, begging at my doorstep."

"Yes. Yes, I am sure." The more Fuseli ranted on Dick's behalf, the less hope she felt.

"Well, it is so," he concluded after a while into her silence. "Many *do* despise the ways of Nature. And will have nothing to do with modern art. Let your young man, if he does not wish to study with us, go off to the clear light of Italy. Nature will teach him there, Gode help him."

"And his career?"

"Career! There is no career for a man who cannot commode himself to the classical taste . . . and to his peers and his betters."

She sat exhausted, the untouched glass catching lights from the chandelier that seemed to gutter, then blaze up again. "But there must be a career."

"Then, young woman, you must take heart and apply yourself to a woman's job. You must show Master Fox what you see for yourself!"

"Yes, I must do that," she murmured, and echoed these words while walking down Berner's Street and forgetting to hail herself a carriage. "I must show him what I see for myself."

The pictures sent off to Fuseli with such high expectations she now carried to Feargus in a fit of despair. The trouble lay not in the meeting with Fuseli but in the terrible conclusion that she had realized from that meeting, of Dick's utterly impossible personality. Her head was steaming like a kettle ready to pop the lid. She dared not go home to Dick in this condition for fear of spilling out to him what she had done behind his back.

Feargus, on the other hand, could afford to be circumspect and was, therefore, a safe place to get it all out of her system.

She found him sporting around in his attic, swinging the swallow tails of a fawn-colored dress coat as he tried out a new combination of walk and gesture.

"The point of this," he explained, indicating the silesia cravat, florinelle waistcoat, and contradictory country-style boots, "is to appear as a squire just in from one of the south country shires, with plenty of money to spend, willing and ready to be duped. *You,* Miss Reddingame, will this time be the seller."

"Oh, Feargus, I can't listen to that now!" She dropped the picture case in his hands and pressed her face to his shoulder, releasing a shower of tears that lasted but a moment and was then restrained by an iron backbone of good sense.

"What are these? What are these?" Feargus said, handing her his handkerchief while fussily pretending to examine the pictures. "They are Dick's hand. But nothing *copied.*"

"No, no, they are quite the originals," she sobbed. "And Mr. Fuseli has just seen them and assured me how marvelous they are and what an outstanding chance Dick has to reach the top of the tree . . . and that the Royal Academy awaits him."

"Did he, now?" said Feargus in a soft voice, gazing around at Meg and smiling, his pink face wrinkling like a ripe fruit skin. "And you believed all his tush and tripe, God bless you. Just as you believe that Mr. Fuseli can dub Dick Court Painter to His Majesty in three weeks of powerful work. Well, it's not the case." He harrumphed. "Not the case. I tell you that from my ancient years of experience. Was I not a silver chaser in Maldon when Dick was born?"

"Oh, you don't understand! Why doesn't anyone? I feel like such a fool gabbling and raving and trying to convince all of you, and it's so beyond me. Here. Read this for yourself. He writes *exactly* the way Dick talks. The same morals and ideals. The same high hopes for art. The same mother-hen protectiveness. The same fits of painterly passion. Dick would be right at home! Why doesn't he give himself the chance? Why not? Why not one little *try?* That's all I would ask of him. Meet the man. *Try.*"

"We have all tried a little," Feargus said kindly. "And not won." There was something crisp and definite in his attitude that pulled back from any romanticizing of ambition. Meg recalled that Feargus, too, had taken his share of punishment on behalf of artistic ideals.

"I don't know what I am to do with these pictures," Feargus said. "They are so beautiful. So completely felt. No one will buy them, of course, from an unknown painter. Except for a few shillings."

Meg stared at him, at the fine faker, businessman, and practical conveyor of reason. What was she doing ere? What could she hope to gain here? Or any-vhere?

"Then sell them for a few shillings!" she snapped. At least Dick's name will be signed at the bottom!"

Chapter Nine

HE ARRIVED BACK at the lodging house in a temper hat knew no bounds, for it encompassed and hid a lisillusion that she could not handle. At first, she hought she must kill Dick when she saw him face to ace, but then her mind went blank with the fury.

"Mrs. Bannish, where is he? Why isn't he home?" he called through the wall, even as she stared around he room, eyes burning with held-back tears. Then, vhen no answer was forthcoming, she fell down on the traw and buried her face in it, venting a sorrow that verwhelmed her. She did not know what, exactly, he felt sorry for. First it was Dick, but then, why he? *Ie* was happy enough in the life he had chosen. Dash-ng about at his own convenience, gambling and paint-ng and wenching, probably, when she begged him to et her be for just a few days. Sorry for herself? But vhy that? Had she, too, not chosen her own life? Chosen Dick? Was she not grateful for his love? For he friendship they had combined with the love, that are condition of bliss that came to so few? But the orrow was there. True enough and very blue.

And still the mystery of it remained even as the lespondent pool grew deeper. *But this will not do!* she hought, struggling to pull herself together, slapping epid water over her face and combing her hair with a ne horn brush Dick had bought her as a gift for their nniversary. She smiled at the comb and kissed it impulsively, realizing how, in his own way, Dick was a sentimental lover. To remember themselves monthly. And how she loved to celebrate it! And while she laughed, she was crying again, and amazed at her tears, confused beyond all hope.

"What goes on with you, girl?"

Mrs. Bannish had finally come in, sucking a bit of blood from where she had mauled a forefinger with a nail.

"I'm disgusted, that's all," Meg moaned, not willing to reveal the whole, impossible state of her nerves.

"With what?"

"Life."

"Och. Y'must be hungry. I've a chop on the fire."

"No. I don't want any *fooood,"* she wailed.

"Then a strong whiskey. How about that?"

Meg looked up at her roundly. Mrs. Bannish was not one to encourage drink before midnight. "You're being very kind to me in my temper," she said suspiciously. "That means Dick is gone off someplace, doesn't it? And he's told you not to tell. And to keep me happily amused till he returns. Oh, I know all the tricks! And now I don't give a damn about them, for once. He can go where he chooses, as he likes. He can go to hell, and never confide it in me!"

"There, there, there. Shhhh. What's this?"

Meg stood up, trembling. "Not a decent chair to sit on. Fog stink creeping in through the windows day and night. Tallow dripping over onto my best dresses. And I don't mind a bit of it. Wouldn't mind if there were some good *reason.* But there's none. It's just round and round and round like a game at the fair."

"You have somethin' to tell me," Mrs. Bannish soothed, putting her arm around Meg's shoulder. "Are you to have a child? Is that what's causin' this upset?"

"No! I wish it were so simple. If I were pregnant, I could simply jump in the river and spread my legs till it drowned," she said with a whipping cruelty.

" 'Tis easy to say that now. But you likely wouldn't if it were Dick's child you carried."

Meg hesitated in the face of truth. She had twice

thought herself pregnant, anyway, and it had come to naught. Perhaps she could not even have a baby.

"What has this to do with Dick?" she snapped.

Mrs. Bannish took a cloth and slowly wiped Meg's perspired forehead. "You tell me and then we'll know."

But she wasn't to be outwitted by diplomacy, nor put off the track by kindness. Kindness too often felt good but had no use, and the luxury only made her more impatient, more alert and careful.

"Where is he?" she demanded.

"You've come a long way," Mrs. Bannish said without affectation, "and I can tell you with no fear that you'll run and do yourself harm. He's up to Maldon for a week or two."

"Maldon? Near Chelmsford? His family?" She stared at Mrs. Bannish in amazement. "Dick never cares about his family. Never talks of them." Tells *me* nothing, she thought irritably.

"No, not family. There's another, different sort of one lives there. The man who helped Dick get started in his drawing. A Mr. Dufferin. James Dufferin. A gent of vile renown, I might tell you right away."

"Vile renown?" Meg stared at her with curiosity. "What has Dick to do with vile renown? He, of all people?"

Mrs. Bannish scratched her head and picked up some of the odd stockings and chemises flung in disorder about the room, hanging them back on their pegs. "Dufferin is a grain farmer with a big house in his field . . . where the dissections go on. Yes. Dissections. Cuts up animals. *Carcasses*. He's the one taught Dick early on to draw from the life."

"You mean draw from dead things?"

"That's how it works, they say." She raised both eyebrows and rolled her gaze to the ceiling. "And Dick goes there. Not regular. But every time he feels the need. To sharpen himself up again, he says."

"It has to do with perfection," Meg mused. "When did he leave?"

"Sometime early today."

"And you say he will be gone a week or two?"

"Depends on all manner of things. How well he feels the work is goin'. Sometimes old Dufferin flies into a temper and whales the hide off Dick, yellin at him, is what I mean. Speakin' of perfection, the two are a pair."

"Dick must love it."

"He *adores* it. A babe to mother's milk."

The sorrow returned again and again behind the face of anger. "I'm going to him."

Mrs. Bannish stared at her with a puckered, disgruntled mouth but held silent.

"Don't look at me," Meg yelled. "That's what I said and I mean to go."

"I told you in confidence."

"And in confidence is how I'll get there."

"But why spoil it, child? You've been living, the two of you, like a pair of cooin' lovebirds. Go there, and he'll never face you with the same look again."

"That's fine," she said with spirit. "I may never face *him* with the same looks again. I've got to see him soon and there's an end to this talk!"

Mrs. Bannish seemed to know when she was defeated by blind foolishness. "Well, gettin' to Maldon is no secret. It's only thirty-seven miles off. There's a coach leaves daily at five in the mornin'." She clucked her way out of the room on a trail of misgivings.

Meg waited in the courtyard of the George Inn pacing through the rough gaggle of guards, ostlers stableboys, cooks, porters, and chambermaids scurrying around the red-wheeled coaches arriving and departing in the mist. A number of times she heard the braying of long brass horns and the rumbling thunder of hooves as travelers arrived from distant parts of the country, to creep stiff and bleary-eyed to the cozy coffee room that beckoned them. At last the guard began to toss up mail bags, and the porter threw up parcels, bundles, and luggage into a mountainous pile on top of the Maldon run, and she embarked with four others into the dark interior behind the door with its royal coat of arms.

She wanted nothing and had taken nothing except a small portmanteau lent by Mrs. Bannish with the distinct admonition to bring it home safe and *clean.* Meg had been on the point of refusing it altogether, except that she wanted to carry a fresh shirt for Dick in case he, too, had run out with nothing more than his chalks. And that was likely.

The swaying coach had a soothing rhythm to it. Each passenger sat muffled inside his own thoughts, so that the twelve-hour journey was like one long waking sleep that ended in another cobblestoned yard with sweet country air and public rooms. Meg settled at a large round table away from the fire and attacked a grill of glistening kidneys with buttered biscuits, toasts, and lattice-faced tarts, leaning into the rising aromas as she intended to lean into Dick, with a will. Some inquiries of the keeper brought information that she could reach Mr. Dufferin's farm on a half-mile post, or ride in the cart with his son, if she wanted that comfort. Stares from half a dozen faces followed her every movement when she said, "Lisson Grange," but no one dared to call out what was on half a dozen minds. She realized, then, how far in looks she had come up in the world. Yet, from sordid beginnings she had learned how to fend for herself, and that was needed now.

As she jounced in the dog cart, watching the green slopes and the erratic sheep upon them, it seemed to her that chasing after Dick had become such a natural part of her life that she would miss just this in a less-adventuresome type of man.

The white-washed, balanced gable roofs of Lisson Grange opened onto a field of rich farmland vibrating with the sounds of pigs and sheep and gossiping women washing clothes in huge bellied coppers that glinted in the late afternoon sun.

"Goin' to the *barn,* miss?"

As she nodded, the boy clucked his tongue in malicious expectation. He let her down and waited while the door creaked open to her push.

She smelled something strong before she saw very

much. A dizzying, nauseating stench neither human nor dead but of flesh preserved in a manner that did not quite do the job. A dozen or more men huddled so intently over their sketch papers that none looked about or seemed to hear her entry. Her glance quickly found Dick among them, his dark, concentrated face radiating happiness, the very energy of his life transforming the light that filtered down from open spaces between the high beams. In the center hung the objects of every student's attention. Hoisted upon tackles were dead horses in lifelike, prancing postures, dissected down to various groups of muscles or blue-black veins. Meg's gut came up in a great heave. She stood, shocked, swallowing the retching rise of her dinner.

On the platform, moving among the various anatomized specimens, was a smooth-shaven man who watched her with mild attention from innocent, peaceful eyes. He wore a farm laborer's smock that came down to the knees of his breeches, buttoned along the front and with sleeves to the wrist, every inch of the cloth covered with reddish, brackish smears. He wore a rusty, protective felt hat, the brim turned down, also stained with the same evidence. Meg clamped her teeth together and made her way among the scattered chairs, going deliberately up to the platform. She leaped upon it, mustering all the strength of self-control she possessed not to continue staring in horrified fascination at the corpses.

"Mr. Dufferin?"

"Yes, miss?" he answered sweetly from a soft face with a puffy underjaw, surprisingly gentle-mannered. Intelligent blue eyes were alive with love for his work.

"Mr. Dufferin, I have no doubt but that you are engaged in a right honorable profession." Her voice was breathy, and she seemed to be speaking from a dream in which she had no control of her fate but a terribly clear vision into her future.

"Please state your business, miss," he said, more crisply now.

"Meg!"

Dick's astonished voice sliced through the air, echoed up and down the spattered walls. "Meg!"

She whirled on him. Till this very second she had no decided intention, but had floated free. Now it came through, the mission, the purpose of traveling here.

She dropped the portmanteau and started to rip her clothes down the front, tearing them away from her body quite coldly, without shame. Trembling, her eyes focused on Dick and only Dick as she saw him leap from his seat and dash toward her.

"Here!" she yelled at him. "Here is something to draw that's alive! If you want to dissect, dissect *me*. A human body! Face the facts, Dick, and work from Nature." She stood half revealed, then entirely nude, breasts trembling but proudly held high, their pink points darkened to a deep raspberry, her flesh glowing in the sun. "Nature is the thing, Dick . . . Nature . . . Nature . . ."

He reached her in half a dozen streaking bounds and swept her up in his arms. She felt his cursing, hot breath upon her face, spitting furious, heartfelt oaths at her.

But she wouldn't be held in his arms like a child who could not take care. Squirming and wriggling, she kicked herself free and bit him in the cheek till he was forced to drop her. On her feet, she continued to taunt him. "Dead horses, is it! Dead horses make dead pictures. Draw me!"

The students, recovered from their shock, had jumped up from their seats. Laughing, they cheered her along. "That's the thing, Dick! She has it. Draw from Nature."

Meg felt powerless to stop herself from working to antagonize and upset this foolish man who must throw his life away upon old-fashioned ideals that no one cared for. Half crying, half laughing, she poked her behind at him, then wiggled her breasts.

"Lunatic!" he called. "What are you doing!"

She dashed off, and he chased after her but in a

moment had caught her by the wrists and dragged her, kicking and yelling, from the barn.

She was out in the daylight and naked, stared at by the round, brown eyes of cows who lowed softly as though they alone understood her.

Sobbing now, she flung herself into Dick's arms. But in a second she recovered her spirit and began slapping him.

"Worthless, worthless!" she shrieked. "Why do I love you? Why do I care? Painting bloody messes, you must be mad!"

"You're the one that's mad. Where are your clothes?" He pulled the smock off and wrapped it around her, bundling her tightly to hobble her legs and arms.

"I won't have any more of this," she whimpered, shivering. "I can't stand you and the way you do things."

"Nor I. No more of you!"

He closed the top button of the smock. "Now stay here, if you're not absolutely crazy, and I'll get your things."

She stood staring after him in quavering humiliation, not because she was sane but because there was nowhere else to go. Somehow she had gotten it out of her system. But to what purpose? Watching Dick dash off at a jerking, angry trot, she realized, in a backwash of scorching remorse, how much she had embarrassed him among his colleagues and how she had interrupted the thing he loved most to do. And how she had promised herself not to get in Dick's way. Oh, she never would. Never!

Expecting that she had bolted, Dick returned, breathless and wary, anger mixed with bewilderment in his eyes.

"I'm making you miss your work," she babbled.

He flung the portmanteau at her feet and dropped her ruined dress on top of it. "Have you anything else to wear?"

She shook her head.

He didn't believe her and bent and opened the

ase. Lifting out two of his own shirts, he stared up at her with utter resignation.

"Meg, what are you trying to do?"

"I can't bear it," she wept, turning away from him and pressing her hands to her face. "Can't take it any more."

"What? What in God's hell are you jabbering about?"

"It. It."

"What—is—*IT?"* he cried desperately.

She heard him swinging at the end of his tether. "Oh, go back inside," she moaned. "You're missing all your lessons. All that blood."

"Never mind my lessons."

"Oh, Dick, can't you see?" she wailed dismally. "You don't need to draw cut-up animals. You need to do women in beautiful gowns, and men on their fine thoroughbreds."

He stood at a distance, regarding her for some time in amazed disbelief. "You'll go to the ends of the earth for this, won't you?"

"But you *know* it."

"Never really, Meg," he said, deflated. "Never like this."

What she imagined to be his disappointment ate her alive, burning into her heart with its destroying acid. Regret was no use now. How could she make it up to him? Or explain what she meant without revealing to him her visit with Fuseli? And that betrayal. Yes, betrayal. Everything was tangled in a confusion of ambitious need for Dick and fear for his safety . . . and a wild, consuming pride over him . . . and love . . . and . . . and . . . there were no words to explain to him . . . to somehow have him know.

"Meg," he said, "Meg, I thought you understood that was . . . *me."*

"I thought I did, too. And I *do."*

"Well, then." He sat down upon the grass and crossed his legs under him, waiting for her to explain. A cat ran out from somewhere and nuzzled along his knees, then went to Meg and, sniffing the smock, leaped up at the hem where crusts of blood had congealed.

Horrified, she pulled back from the cat, realizing, as she looked down at herself for the first time, that she was dressed in the signs of death.

"I know what you're going to say," she continued unsteadily, but intent on her purpose now. "I know that you *need* anatomy. But why must it be here? In this isolated village. Where even the innkeepers are hostile and their sons think it all a dirty joke."

"Do I care what anyone else thinks, Meg?"

She shook her head vehemently in rueful acknowledgement that this was the trouble between them. "And I *know* you want to go to Paris. And we haven't seen the Elgin marbles. And the Royal Academy only has casts from the antique."

"You always know so much." He shook his head with weary admiration for her persistence.

"Because I get around," she flaunted with renewed fire. "*I* get around to all the right places. *I* see the right people."

He sighed and the conversation ended abruptly, as though they had fallen into a hole in the ground and were covered by an avalanche of earth. Ashamed, she felt silenced forever, and could do nothing but face the fact that her good intentions had ruined a perfectly fine week for him. Was it possible, she wondered, that those very same intentions could ruin both their lives?

"You're a strangely marvelous little troublemaker," Dick said, his voice flickering with affection, returning to life. "Let's just forget what happened today . . . even if you never understand what I'm trying to do."

Chapter Ten

EVER UNDERSTAND! Hellfire burned a hole in her mper. Dick was the one who never understood! Born pig-headed! She could taste the change in their rtunes if only he would go to see Fuseli. But she ared not mention *that*. Especially not now, after aking such a mess of things, embarrassing him before is friends. She became quietly acquiescent, letting im come and go without question, without tagging long like a donkey tail, sensing the rift between them nd dreading what it might do to their relationship. et sad though she was, contrite she could never be. nd dammit! She had a right to her opinion, her ambiions, too. Living with him had made her conscious of er worth. They were like two halves of an orange, either one complete without the other, and she must old up her part of the combination. If she could only nd a way agreeable to Dick.

"There's no use to it, child," Mrs. Bannish said, ropping silver from her reticule into a tin box that he hid in a hole between the floorboards. "He's been ike he is. And he'll *be* like he is. You'll be a fool to hink you can change it."

"I don't want to change anything," Meg protested, er voice haranguing and irritated. "I just want him o use his opportunities. Is that so wrong? What does e do with his pictures when he's finished them but ile them in corners where the world can't see. Isn't rt a sharing thing? I thought it was."

"Sounds like you're gettin' to be an old shrew in our young years. Sounds like you can't leave your nan the way you find him."

"Well, can you?" Meg's eyes glittered with outrage "Don't you and Feargus always try to make him dc the copies he hates?"

"Me?" jabbed Mrs. Bannish, poking her ampl chest with a thumb. "I'm not bedding the man. I car say what I please. But in the end it's live and let live. You'll find out."

Meg fell silent before the voice of truth. Perhaps that really was the answer. Live and let live. But i was no more in her constitution to flap about unconcerned with her lover's fate than it was in Dick's t idle at the prince's supper parties, hoping for a portrait commission.

Though she kept the peace, her forehead seeme made of glass, and Dick could see exactly what sh was thinking.

"You know, Meg, it's not that you're wrong or tha I wouldn't like to do it, especially to please you. Perhaps one day I will be able to train myself down t some civility."

They were walking home across the Hampstea fields, beneath a rare sky with stars and a slice o moon, and silver chinking in their pockets. She leane against him with her arm around his waist, unabash edly feeling the interlock of their motion, of his lon muscles swaying as he moved, enjoying the leannes and the strength, reveling in their evening's conques that meant he would buy the canvasses he needed fo himself and a new dress for her that she didn't nee at all.

"Oh, Dick, I don't care," she said feelingly. "I jus want us to be happy together and for you to work th way you want and feel satisfied. If we're to be penn toss-ups all our lives, I'll learn somehow to accept it.

"No, you won't," he laughed. "You're a heroi little wench, but not self-sacrificing to that exten And who's to blame you?" He squeezed the side c her breast with his artist's hand, which felt her in way very different from anyone else. She shivere nowing how he *lived* through her flesh, always hun-ry for her, always attentive.

Yet she began to feel edgy and looked up at his ark, silver-washed profile, alert for what was coming ext. The rumble was there in the narrow line of the outh. The storm was soon to follow. "To be with ou is not self-sacrificing," she said simply.

"You know, there are some women who never let eir men go, except if they are off to the wars."

"We're at peace, Dick."

"Yes, so it seems. But only weary men believe it. he papers report every day that Paris is in ferment. egotiations are bound to founder on the problem f Malta, mark my words, and then the gates of Paris ill again be closed to Englishmen."

"Perhaps. And what has politics to do with us?" she sked with apprehension, despairing of what she knew e next would hear.

"I must see what Bonaparte has stolen from all of urope," he said, squeezing her with the ardor of his xpectations. "I must get to the Louvre."

"Must you know everything that every man has ver painted?"

"Yes!" he fired like gunshot.

She held her breath while they walked, sensing in im the stir of his driving devils against which they ere both powerless. "Tell me straight out what you ean," she pressed quietly, unable to stand it any ore.

"I'm going," burst from him. "Somehow I will get ere."

"You have the money now for passage," she said atter-of-factly, aware that she could no more stop is flow than lava from a volcano.

"No. That stays with you. I'll manage otherwise."

"Stays with me?" Her startled voice was harsh. You mean *goes* with me, don't you?"

His silent face became a wall. She felt suddenly ill ith the fatalistic sense of a new direction to their ves.

"There's no way I can take you with me," he said

at last, and she searched for the regret in his voice "It's a rotten, difficult trip at best. And Paris thes days is no place for a woman. Not one that I love.'

He swung around and kissed her, exhaling the ver vapor of his life into her. She grasped the cloth of hi shirt and twisted it in her fingers, thinking that if sh could just hold on hard enough, he would have t take her. Behind them, the sleepy cry of a Charlie i his box called the dreary hour.

"I'm going," she whispered, her mouth presse against the center of his chest, arms tight around hi waist. "And there's an end to it. I won't hear your ex cuses. Don't you know you *need* a woman? You don' do well without one. Why not let it be me?" Her fin gers fumbled with the silken sash. "It'll save you th trouble of having to find a housekeeper on the street And besides, I know your habits. I don't get in you way very much, not lately. All I would do, Dick, i take care of our place and make things more comfort able for you to work in. Nothing will happen to me i Paris, I promise. Duchesses go there every day; we se them ourselves." On and on she rattled, eyes tightl closed against the emptiness, talking uselessly agains the dark tides. Talking to herself.

The conversation was too painful to continue fc very long. But it was not something soon to be for gotten, and it hung in the air around her, a miasm poisoning the pleasure of her days. At night she woul awaken with a start and look around for him, fe beside her for the reassuring touch of his thigh o back. Feverishly, her mind worked upon differer plans and schemes to convince him she would be a asset.

"I tell you what I can do," she said brightly, "I ca be your model in Paris. Pretty girls can get in any where now, I understand, with this new equality. I' make life easier for you. You'll have more time t paint."

"You'll make life easier for me by staying her with Mrs. Bannish where I know you're safe."

He could not be budged and she yielded.

It was only a matter of time.

They hadn't spoken about it for a week, and the idea seemed to have drifted out of Dick's life. She was coming home from an interesting tour de force with Feargus. Miss Benningott had won the day, effecting the sale of a boatload of etchings, aquatints, and lithographs after having charmed the breeches off a middle-aged marquis who was returning to Paris after ten years of exile in London since the Terror. Her cheeks were flushed with the fun of it, her mind bubbling with stories to tell Dick. For she had learned that there was a certain harmlessness behind the greed of the rich, very different from the starving greed of the poor. And wasn't money a thing to be passed around in the world?

"Steak and kidney pie tonight, sweetheart? Or cutlets and curaçao like the prince?" She kicked the door open with her slipper and tossed the poke bonnet ahead of her, swinging her hair like the mane of a sorrel horse. "Dick?" Her gaze took in the empty room. "Dammit, why aren't you home?" She dropped a sackful of gold on the bed for him to fall on when he got back, and started to undo the fastenings of the expensive dress, a gossamer, lilac-colored creation with a high Grecian waistline, all the rage. The side of her vision grazed the mantel and glimpsed the folded, ruby-red heap upon it. Before her mind made sense of it, her breath caught instinctively, knowingly, and stuck in her ribs. The shining day behind her went black. For a long moment she stood with her back to the hearth, not willing to face what she knew, rubbing the cold knuckles of one hand into the sweating palm of the other, waiting for the brunt of the terror to pass. At last she sifted a searing breath through her teeth and turned to the mantel. With trembling hands she took down the sash, letting the folds slide between her fingers. As it unwound she saw the note pinned to its other end: *My dearest love. Keep this safe for me till I return.*

Hot and cold prickles chased across the back of her neck and rippled along her spine. A swaying, fainting sensation curled inside her belly and fluttered upward behind her eyes. She wanted to shriek, but her throat was numb. She grabbed up the mug, the old cracked mug that first had fed her, and flung it with all the willful force she could manage into the hearth, where she heard it shatter in clinking slivers, to disappear in the fire.

"Traitor! Traitor! Traitor!" she screamed in miserable release.

Then she staggered and fell down upon the bed, clutching the sash to her mouth and staining it with furious tears.

"He wants me to stay home and wait, but who does he think he is, telling me what to do? Feargus, do you know any British gentlemen driving to Paris?"

Miss Benningott was seated with Mr. Widley in the office at the rear of his Strand shop, but the determination burning in Meg was that of a one-time street urchin meaning to survive against all odds.

"Shhh. You must keep a tight hold on your reserve," warned Feargus with watchful sympathy. "It's the only thing that will save you. And why don't you stay with me and amass your own pile of gold to welcome him home with when he finally returns? You know he will come in tatters."

She hated the reality of Feargus but could not fight what was so. She knocked back one cherry cordial and then a second, which Feargus handed to her, then poured a third herself.

"You needn't be concerned," she said coldly. "And stop hovering over me. I'm in perfect control." She motioned for him to sit. "There's nothing to talk about except how I am to travel. I know half a dozen earls and baronets from the old days. But if I contact them, they'll have me bouncing in their beds and waste my time. I thought Miss Benningott, the old-maid virgin, might stand a better chance."

"Is Miss Benningott truly above reproach?" asked Feargus with a calculating glint.

Meg fixed upon him a steely look that felt like Dick's. "I will do anything to get to Paris," she replied steadily. "Do you hear me? *Anything.*"

Feargus filled a large tumbler with port and sniffed at it thoughtfully. "In that case, rest assured. The female advantage you have is a large one. Now let me see." He set the glass down, lifted the old bagwig from his neck, and scratched beneath it with slow strokes. "William Bleslake is in Scotland . . . The Duke of Sudbury is marrying his mistress, of all things . . ." His lips tightened before the enormity of the task. "Meg, it will take me time."

"Time is what I do not have," she snapped. "The longer I wait, the further away he gets. And tracking him in Paris will be difficult enough without giving him more time to go . . . who knows where else . . . the Alps, mayhap."

"Yes, I agree with you, and I shall call around. Expect a note from me tomorrow afternoon upon the matter."

Meg left him feeling both disappointed and impatient.

When Mrs. Bannish heard she said, "But what else is there to do? Give the man a day. You can't go back to your father, can you, to look for those very people who abused you? And what makes you think they would take you to Paris even if they were going? A slovenly whore of a girl. That's what you were when you first came to us."

"Yes. The Haymarket," she said, thinking aloud. "That's where they're all bound to drop by after the theater. I'll find a dozen faces that will remember me."

Mrs. Bannish could barely listen to such talk. "But what of your body? What of your pride? What of your good, practical sense? Stay home, Meg, where you are safe and can earn your way so comfortably. I tell you, it is a godsend for a girl of your kind to be off the streets. Go back to it now and you know where it will end. Misery and ruination! What man is worth it? I have been married to three and outlived them all. A woman must keep her independence."

Meg was too distracted to hear reason. "Dick is the only thing that I ever had that was mine, and I shall go after him to the ends of the earth," she said softly, with total conviction. Her mind was already hurled into action as Mrs. Bannish left her to juggle her calamitous plans alone. Possibly she would meet her father near the gin mills hawking another youngster, but he meant no more to her now than a weed.

A knock came through the wall as she was changing into a yellow dress with plum-colored ribbons at the high waist and hardly any bodice to speak of.

"Wear the corset," called Mrs. Bannish. "The corset."

"I'll do better in one naked-looking petticoat." Meg smiled wickedly.

"Don't you go lookin' like every other whore!"

In a second Mrs. Bannish was there again, holding the unyielding item while Meg struggled into it. She gagged as the laces were pulled tightly behind, crisscrossing from the bottom of her wiggling bottom up to the topmost rib, holding her breasts out and adding a *kilo* weight to each.

"Breathe shallow," advised Mrs. Bannish. "And walk slow. You'll survive. There. Turn around. Mm. Shapely. You'll find yourself a lord or two or three, no fear. But what are you puttin' on that sash for? It changes the picture."

"Does it?" Meg said with a ploy of innocence.

And out she went into the night in a swishing cape with piles of white ruffles around her face that somehow opened down at the bosom, revealing the heady fragrance of rose water and a pair of snowy orbs the match of any.

Lud, I don't want to sleep with half the peerage before I find me one that's off to Paris, she mused in the carriage jogging her along to the center of London's night life. *How else am I to do this? Well. Since there's no other way, I must resign myself.*

She would go about it like a business venture,

orderly minded like Mrs. Bannish, and ready like Feargus for the kill. Since they were flocking like flies to the continent, as she knew so well from Dick, it was merely a matter of time and mingling with gentlemen, listening to the gossip and availing herself of the right offer.

At the Haymarket she was a loner, and hoped that this would cause a riot. The crush of high-life swells made a froth of humanity around red-faced madames leading their gaggles of prostitutes from one theater lobby to the next to be stared at in the hissing glare of the gas lamps. They waited about with their hands deep in their raggedy muffs and peered, pig-eyed, at every top hat that slowed near them.

I'll just stroll down the hill, thought Meg, *and see what I can see. It's easy pickin's.*

Before she had reached the Drury Lane, a youngish gentleman was keeping step beside her, whistling softly and tipping his brim, his dress jacket swinging open as he smiled at her over a fancy starcher.

"Dear me, the Earl of Blount."

"No, Madame, the Duke of Ledcastle's second son, Jamison Haunt, at your service."

"Yes, exactly so. 'Tis you and not the other. My dear me, what fog can do to change a face."

"But not yours, my lady. A bite of supper, perhaps?"

"Very pleased, m'lord."

The game would always start like this, with its comical brilliance of gallantry, but there was something new in it for Meg. Thoughts of Dick lay behind every affected simper that carried her full sail into the stranger's embrace.

"Why, you are too pretty to wait upon in an alleyway," he panted urgently. "Come, I have a room in Mosely Street."

"Such a respectable and safe address, m'lord."

"It is my tailor's."

The reply was serious and Meg suppressed a smile. The cut of a coat could make or break a career at fashionable salons.

In the cab riding away from the hubbub, she opened her cloak to his curiosity, not brazenly as a street wench but bravely, with a purpose that seemed to charm Jamison in affecting ways.

"You have a sweet fragrance about you, mmmmm." His appreciation rose muffled from between her breasts.

They fell together in the jouncing carriage and she gave herself up to being tangled and tossed. His hands flew swiftly, sure of what they wanted to explore, and were satisfied. The face dived soon after. He was sober but newly so. She felt the tremors in his weakened flanks and thought she could make him spend right here in the cab before they ever reached a bed.

"Don't touch me." He quivered. "I won't lose it yet. I am an inside man and that is what I want."

"Jamie, I like you. You have a way. Tell me, are you thinking to stay in London?"

"Why, where else should I go?"

"Nowhere . . . nowhere . . . Paris, perhaps?"

"Oh, not I. Not with that gloomy Corsican hanging about and spoiling people's fun."

"Oh, sweet James. I have such a headache. It comes upon me with no warning at all."

"Never mind, my dear. I'll cure you of it at the apartment. I have a way." He laughed with something of a giggle.

"Do be patient, ducks, and take me home, tonight."

"Oh, no, no, no. Not before you taste my remedy."

Meg sighed and wiped her lips with the lace edge of his perfumed handkerchief, deciding it was best to go along rather than to fight her way out. Word traveled fast in small circles, and she could not afford a sour reputation.

Mosely Street had a clean look to its byways, with a flare of light and respectability. The rooms, rather well furnished in the old-fashioned Adam style, seemed ornate and a trifle heavy, but more comfortable than any tailor's digs.

"This must be your sister's," said Meg.

"Oh, not at all. She stays with Mum in Piccadilly."

And he was upon her, tackling her to the goose-down sofa cushions, knocking the breath from her and altogether twisting himself around her hips in the most incredible, lascivious style, with no respect at all for her headache.

"Why are ladies' fashions so ornate?" came with a spit of ribbons and laces from somewhere below her waist. "Brummel counsels men to simplicity. Women should have the same wise advice."

"Oh, yes, yes. Let us talk about fashions. Tell me, I hear he has criticized the Duke of Aberly's coat."

"No. Let us not talk!" A shoe heel toppled his hat from the table and rolled it onto its brim in a slow crescent over the apple-green rug.

"I would so like a cup of tea."

"Don't be a spoilsport!"

"My headache."

"*My* headache, dear!"

"You are not to be resisted." Meg laughed with good nature. Having lost this particular bet, she decided to pay up as quickly as possible. "Now I will show you how to tackle a woman's underclothes so that you don't drown yourself in the laces. . . . Here. Pull away this bow. What would you do if stomachers were still the fashion?"

"Kill myself. Dive from Blackfriars' Bridge."

"Silly thing. Put your hands on my breasts and feel how they move as I undo this. Go ahead."

"You are a wicked madness."

"Kiss me."

"Delightful . . . darling . . . oh . . . oh . . . No! I said don't touch me. Yes. All right." His voice quavered, weakening. "Just enough to make it stand. There you go. Once. Twice. Quite enough. Don't!"

She had him gripped now and was working at it, laughing and making the game irresistible.

"Please. Please. Lie down. Lie back! Quick. Be quick . . . Oooooh."

She watched his eyelids sink closed while the behind muscles inside the rumple of trousers squeezed together so that he seemed to shrivel as he shuddered.

She held him in the crook of one arm, bracing him against her bosom as he shook his head back and forth between her breasts, undecided which nipple to hang on.

She felt the spray of hot slippery juice upon her wrist, and at the same time, he relaxed and cuddled down in a ball at the base of her belly.

She let him rest on his side for a while, waiting to hear if he would snore.

"I told you not to do it that way," he mumbled grumpily.

"Whose fault is it if you can't hold back? But can you tell me you didn't enjoy it? Why, it was sitting right on the prow, ready to cast off."

He blinked at her in sheepish silence and began to straighten his clothes with one hand while swigging port with the other. The moment he let go of her and stood, she wiggled into her chemise, ran to kiss him, and said, "I must go home now. Really I must."

"I'd like to try this again, my dear. But in a better fashion. Tomorrow?"

"Oh, tomorrow." She cast a disappointed glance at the floor and sighed in regret. "Tomorrow I sit with my uncle Magnus. He has gout in both hands, and I have agreed to do his correspondence for him every Tuesday."

"When do you say, then?"

"Jamie." She was intimate now. "Give me your card. You have friends, I suppose, and parties to go to. I am so dejected and need company."

"We are having a cold supper Friday next at nine o'clock," he said with alacrity. "Do you polka?"

"What I don't know, sweets, you will surely teach me."

"Well, then, be a good girl." He kissed her on the cheek and pressed some gold pieces into her palm.

"Oh, no, Jamison, not for *money!*" She pressed the coins back again while he stared at her in astonishment. "Will you call me a cab?"

Riding home and massaging a strained tendon in her right wrist, she thought: *Now am I launched.*

Men streamed through the city from west end to east, and she peered into every face, hunting for a likely traveler to the continent. At the party she met a dozen of Jamison's friends of all ages, every one content to go stalking for deer in Scotland at the end of the London season. Meg sighed, at a loss. Luck, and luck alone, would connect her with her guardian traveling angel.

"I must sift through the quantity, there is no way else," she groaned at Mrs. Bannish.

"Let us keep an eye on the mornin' papers for the schedule of ships to sail the Channel. Perhaps we will see a name in the social columns connectin' with some such journey."

They scoured *Bell's Weekly* and the *Morning Chronicle* each day before she went out. Her circle of friends was rapidly increasing, and from lack of sleep she lost a pound of flesh where she didn't need to lose it.

"I must learn some French phrases."

"You must learn some French fashions. Do you know they wear see-through tunics? Listen to this."

"You are to read me the shipping, Mrs. Bannish. My dress will take care of itself."

"So may you suppose. But competition is fierce in that city. It says people are still flockin' in from everywhere." She rattled the paper warningly. "You'll need all your wits."

"God knows I need them right this minute. Where am I going to find my escort?" She stamped around the room, hands on her slender hips, staring absently at some drawings Dick had left behind. Snatching one up, she said, "Feargus expects me today. I might as well bring him this to do an engraving after. As long as Dick isn't here, he can't even call it stealing, though he never noticed what I took. And that's what bothers me. He has to learn to care what happens afterward."

"Stealin'? Heaven forbid the word," cried Mrs. Bannish, lifting a righteous eyebrow and taking up a dress to hem that had been ripped in one night's fracas.

"Honor among thieves, eh?" Meg laughed calmly. "I think I shall go to Epsom and try the racing circle there. Oh, but it's all the same after all," she sighed with wistful distress.

"Come. Have a slice of barley loaf and cheer up. We'll go on a sunny afternoon together. I'll pack us a picnic lunch." Mrs. Bannish smiled encouragingly. "And if you like, we can take Feargus. The three of us together will surely find a fish."

On either side of the race course flowed a colorful spill of society that gathered around the tumbling jacks and the young acrobats performing for pennies on the grass. Horses with their jockeys aboard pranced about in circles, preening before the fond admiration of their hopeful bettors. One vast apron of din spread before Meg and her two companions. It was a merry-making, companionable crowd that lingered, waiting for the fireshot and perhaps the arrival of the prince, who had a knack for borrowing handfuls of gold at the last instant to bet on the favorite. But how should she spot a proper prospect? Meg wondered, caring nothing for royalty, nothing for horses, nothing for the cheerful, wandering cronies who found each other and split apart and mingled again in noisy camaraderie. Must I sleep with all of England and then for naught?

"Look, there's Lord Albert," muttered Feargus, jabbing Meg. "And with the Comtesse he keeps at his home, do you recall it? There's a good chance for us. I hear his father is giving hospitality to five hundred exiled abbés."

"It is Albert," murmured Meg with a shiver. "Let us go, Mr. Widley, and try our luck."

But Albert, like the others, was reconciled to play host to all his Gallic friends while safe at home in London, and Meg was just as happy to get away from him soon thereafter. She squinted up at the sunlight, frowning and certain that she walked under a cloud of hard times on the matter. Mrs. Bannish, who had a more systematic approach to obstacles in life, left Meg with Feargus dividing a joint of mutton between them while she went forth and rounded up, like a sergeant major, half a dozen prospects who claimed they were onsidering a jaunt to the continent sometime this ear.

"But I want it this week," Meg insisted. "I shall go lone. I certainly can. On my own two legs."

"Madness. Suicide," reported Feargus, dusting some ebble marks from his jacket elbows.

"One last week, I give it. Then I go."

"But try these gentlemen first." Mrs. Bannish ressed a bit of paper upon her. "They all live near ach other in Grosvenor Square. And perhaps you can ianage a few in one night."

Meg flung her a look that told Mrs. Bannish she ad missed her calling, but she folded the paper away arefully, nonetheless.

The running footman caught up with her in Picca-illy Circus, his blue and buff livery as clean as the nest linen, his face only slightly perspired beneath his eavy peruke. "Pardon me, m'lady. Pardon me. I'm ure you know my master, the Marquess of Kell?" He pened the top of his cane and gulped some swallows f its contents. "There he is, if you look. You can see im on his terrace, can't you? He asks would you do im the honor of taking some tea with him today."

"The Marquess of Kell?" At this distance, Meg ould barely make out a face, the body hidden inside annel blankets and protected from the elements by huge striped umbrella. "Why, yes. I am sure I do now him. And I shall come with you directly."

The old man waited for her with a toothless grin alf hidden behind a brown polka-dotted handker-hief that smelled of herbs and simples.

"My dear, my dear," he chirruped. "Do walk in-de. I have been on the lookout for you all day long. Iy nephew has a message for your ears alone. You now who I mean? The youngster who is going to aris?"

"Why, m'lord, Paris?" said Meg, sitting down with n agitated sigh of relief. "You know your wish is iy command. . . ."

The bed of the Marquess of Kell was surrounded

by curtains five inches thick that he said kept out diseases of the lung and any wicked dangers carried by fresh air. He kissed her on the mouth, barely glimpsed her naked beauty before pulling the cover to his chin, and said, "You must turn your head away when you cough."

"But I do not cough, m'lord. And neither do you."

"Because I never breathe when I can help it. Forty-nine years I wasn't married. And when I did it at last, my wife was dead in a twelvemonth. She took us into the country and that's what laid her out. One should stay at home."

He dropped down upon her like a wet sop of milk, his white hair fluttering, his white mouth bubbling with passions he was not sure it healthy to fill.

"No. I never . . ." He mumbled over the words, aware that what he was doing now also brought diseases.

"You take yourself in hand, m'lord? Shall I?"

"Have cousins aplenty for that. You can do something else for me. Have you gargled?"

"Yes. As you directed."

"Then here. Let me see your tongue. Blasted light!" He cursed at the wavering tallow. "Here. Stick it out, girl. Stick it out. Now." He squinted in the gloom and seemed satisfied. "There's nothing green upon it in any event. We can take the chance."

"Shall I go beneath the blankets?"

"That would be excellent. Most excellent. But don't uncover my legs. Fourteen children have died in this family from influenza. All my brother's babes, but one."

"You shan't catch a thing. I promise."

"Be quick about it. I feel a draft."

She foundered down into the darkness and crawled the tunnel between his legs, determined not to suffocate or cough a single time. She kept thinking of the off-hand remark that had fallen from his lips as they sat together on the terrace. A nephew going to Paris. *Which one?* She found him surprisingly upright for his years. Neither faint nor sickly as she had imagined.

In a moment she had him squirming beneath the racticed swirl of her lips, which had performed serv- e upon the best. Now and again he patted the uilting over her head that separated her from his roaning joys, to adjust her speed or position as she orked him onward to his goal. At the final moment, e clapped both hands strongly to her ears and held er head in place, catching her between his night shirt nd the coverlet. She believed her last breath had been ken. But his desire was quickly abated and she umbled out from the cottons and wool in the nick of me.

"Ah, yes." The marquess smiled. "I shall live rough it. I *have* lived through it." The smile became atific. He closed his eyes and hummed the tune of me stately gavotte. "King George's favorite, this bit f Handel," he murmured. "Has played it on the organ r me many a night. Seems to soothe away the mad- ess, it does."

Meg cuddled beside him, careful to turn her back hile they lay together so that as she questioned him e would not feel her breathing and become uneasy.

"You mentioned something earlier about your ephew. Was that in connection with His Majesty, 'lord?"

"Nephew? What nephew?"

"The one you said had a message for me."

"Oh, no. Oh, no." He chuckled with satisfaction at e success of his ruse. "Ralph needs no introduction ladies from his old uncle Jimmy. That was just 'game, girl. Do you forgive it?"

"I find that uncles are better than nephews most ten," she replied with bland good nature. "But for e sake of truth, have you no nephew and is he not ing to Paris?"

"Oh, I do have. And he is."

"In truth?"

"In solemn truth," laughed the marquess. "Why ould I make up a tale?"

"And who is he, then, if you don't mind saying? I ve an errand to Paris that wants a fast messenger.

Something of the deepest importance to me concerning my mother."

His cold hand, which was solemnly rubbing he backside, paused in speculation. "Now don't upse yourself. But Ralph won't do for an errand. Not at al Has enough to remember his own name. A whirligi boy and worse."

"But going to Paris?"

"Doesn't every lunatic with half a crown in hi pocket go?"

"Yes," she answered vehemently.

"And Ralph is one of their number."

"Then he must do, for my purpose."

"You are barking up the wrong tree, I say. But i you can find no better means, I pity you."

She reached round behind her back and squeeze his thin clammy knee. "You are an honest mar m'lord. And I bless you for helping me."

The marquess coughed nervously and went into trembling quake at the sound. But in the face of s ardent a compliment to his being, he rallied. "I wi give you his card and you can send your messag round to his home. It is not far. The second hous on Grosvenor Square. Renning Hall."

As Meg dressed in the eerie glim, the recollection c Renning Hall rose with a ghostly reminder of othe horrible times. It flung her back and seemed to ro her of her adult presence. She felt her throat begin t knot and a perspiration spread between her breasts.

"Do I read this rightly?" she called with stiff harsh ness meant to mask her trepidations. "Ralph Carsti Earl of Eggleston?"

"The very one," said the marquess. "Sounds to m like you know him."

"I do," she replied flatly, and thought: I must g round to him this very evening. If I remember th devil rightly, he will not mind my intrusion.

Chapter Eleven

EG KNEW HIS HOUSE as she knew her father's house . . . a place of childish nightmares. The faces of the wo men seemed forever intertwined, bouncing on oints of hell and calling to her with enticements she ould not resist. They were part of the torture of her outh and had nothing to do with the present, she told erself, fleeing toward the tall brick building with its ghted windows staring from the topmost floor. Fate ad played a cruel trick by bringing Carstip back into er life. But if it were a challenge to test her love for ick, then fate was in for some surprises.

The stabled horses behind the house clattered rest-ssly and griped at each other as though they had been dden and whipped and were complaining now of eir wounds. She could see Ralph's face at the sight f her coming here of her own free will, and she stiff-ned herself for the satisfactions he would indulge ecause she needed him.

The great, gold knocker thundered. Almost in-antly, a frail woman in an old-style mob cap ap-eared, her startled expression indicating recognition.

"Does the earl expect you, m'lady?" The voice was igh-pitched but barely audible.

"Tell the earl—Miss Watkins," she replied with a ip of haughty firmness, of the kind necessary to have nything accomplished in this house.

"Yes, miss. Will you wait in here, miss?"

She knew where to wait, as she had waited trem-ling and defiant so many evenings before, near a ina cabinet of monkeys, mandarins, serpents, shells, nd other odd, undusted things. A strange collection from another time, in keeping with the old-fashioned Chippendale decor, very heavy and depressing to the spirit. Yet in the past she had never noticed that this receiving room was also filled with fine old paintings done in gold and russet tones, portraits of prize-blooded horses and King Charles spaniels, which could have lent a sporting cheer to the room were it not for the earl's dominion. His mood was everywhere, black as chimney smoke corrupting the night. She wondered how a man so young could be so peculiar. Spoiled since infancy. Petted. Catered to. The marquess had given her a glimmering into Ralph Carstip's life. The only child who had survived in a house of fifteen! That must have twisted his mind. Given him the weird belief he held in his godlike powers.

She sniffed something sweet, like lily-cum-valley and turned her head and saw him.

"Why, Meg Watkins. I could hardly believe my good fortune when the girl told me it was you."

He came forward enthusiastically, with both hands extended. The fingers were like branches, knotted and gnarled at the joints where a premature gout from much drinking had swollen them out of shape. She had always considered him tall but realized now that he was only of the middling height when compared with Dick. The silk morning dress he wore at midnight fi loosely, swaying with his light, erratic step. She had evidently caught him in the midst of something, bu she couldn't begin to guess what. The faint revulsion of her memories receded as he approached her. H did not seem quite so powerful as she had recollected

"The odd coincidences of life." Meg smiled. "Onl ten minutes ago I was speaking with the Marquess o Kell about you, and I thought, well, I must come se you immediately."

"Oh, yes! So that's the source. My old, balmy uncle how is he? Still sitting on the terrace watching the pa rade?" He winked with a twinkle that put two and tw together. "We'll have a drink to Uncle Jimmy." H chuckled, twisting the top from a decanter. The stoppe had swollen and stuck fast, so that he lost his patienc with it in a second and pulled it forth with a petulant wrench of surprising strength that snapped the cork. He handed her a glass of visney and bent over, kissing her on the bridge of her nose. "Dear girl," he breathed. "I'm always so glad to see you. I was sad when your father told me you had flown, and I wondered if you would keep contact with me of your own wish. Now here you have!" The pale lashes fluttered with a quickened intensity of eagerness over his milky, burning eyes. "We've had some good times together, you and I. I could never forget them. And see? Neither can you."

Meg, seated in a high-backed chair, felt her spine stiffen against this coming true of all her worst predictions. Inside himself he was rubbing his hands, hoping to get on with it . . . with her. "But I believe our friendship will be interrupted once again. This time by you." She smiled unhappily.

"How do you mean?" he said with quick apprehension, wetting his lips with the liquor and rolling it around on his tongue for a long while before swallowing, sucking out the very last dregs of flavor in a way that seemed to torture his tongue.

"I understand you are going to Paris." She looked into her glass so that he would not see her eyes. She could not risk his discovering her nervousness.

"Paris," he sighed. "Yes, I do have some plans. But never mind that, Meg. We have three days, at least."

Three days! Her heart leaped with joy. "Three days!" she echoed. "Yes, Ralph! We can surely get to know each other again in three days."

"Drink your drink," he said, squeezing her hand. "Shall we have some iced champagne upon it?" He took away her glass and dropped it into the fire, listening for several distracted moments to the small explosions of the flame. "Come, old friend," he whispered. "We'll go upstairs where the servants won't be tempted to listen."

They walked side by side. He lay his arm around her shoulder with the easy, friendly intimacy of a brother for his sister.

"I really can't tell you how delighted I am," he kept repeating.

She could feel her stomach knotting into fists each time he spoke his affection. The soft light from the sconces threw an orange glow over his sand-colored complexion, reflecting there the sprinkle of fine pockmarks in his drawn cheeks and high, curved nostrils. She could think of a dozen reasons for his eagerness, since he had been the first ever to get his hands on her. That was it entirely. She had been so much a child, with breasts hardly pointed. He had thought to pull them into maturity with his insistent mouth and had succeeded in bruising her till she bled. Other memories she pushed aside, finding them a deterrent to the game she must play now and to what she knew she must endure, though for how long it was impossible to predict.

His bedroom windows faced north to the green countryside. A damp scent of earth came in on the night breeze, stirring the drapes and playing provocative fingers upon her flesh. He shut the door and embraced her without a word. She pulled him close with her eyes open. Hat boxes stood in tumbling piles upon the wardrobe; whips and gloves and cravats and bottles of skin lotions and pomatum jars lay scattered about in piles, reflecting the distracted mind that would trust no sullen servant in here. While he held her, she thought of Paris, felt her heart beating like a bird ready to lift away. His cold fingertips traced upward along the bones of her neck to her skull, and she sighed with the pleasure of another's touch remembered.

"Ralph, let's have really fine times together." She spoke huskily, intimately, against the side of his throat. "Let's you and I . . ."

". . . find ourselves in each other." He finished the sentence with a poetical satisfaction.

Meg smiled slyly to herself and continued to kiss him in a long chain of insinuating touches, preferring to work upon him where he was most vulnerable rather than to talk too much. Words were to be avoided wherever possible, for his temper was a flare that could explode at the most harmless expression. He could twist anything into murderous attack, she had learned. And those early bitter lessons with Ralph Carstip were not easily forgotten.

The fingers toying with her were always searching for some exotic response, some novel sensation, while the jaded, young blood lay torpid and dull. Small cooing noises from him told her she had made a chink in his boredom this night. She could hardly believe his oblivion to her disgust. Yet luckily, his imagination worked in her favor. Her chemistry somehow ignited him, and therefore he prized her, would continue to hold her dear as a stronghold against boredom.

"Do you recall that story I told you of the Indian raj and his harem?" He was undoing his banyan and removing it. Beneath, he wore a shirt with long tails that hung to his naked knees.

"Oh, yes, the harem girls and what they did every night to forestall the limpness of his . . ."

A thundering clatter in the yard of coach wheels and yelling drowned her voice. The noise circled below the windows.

"Halloooo, Ralph . . . Ralph . . . Wake up there . . . Ralph, I say . . ." And then, "Come to life, *mon frère* . . ." A jumble of young voices, English and French, continued battering upward in a chorus of hearty anxiousness for Ralph's attention. Whips banged at shutters. Horses whinnied with frenzied vigor.

Meg watched, astonished, as Ralph burst into smiles and strode quickly to the overlooking window. He thrust his head out and called, "Come ahead. Come up, then. What are you waiting for?"

"No. You must come down!" the Englishman demanded.

"It is tonight. We leave tonight," shouted the Frenchman. "In this coach. Put on your hat and hurr-eeeee."

"Tonight?" Ralph echoed blankly, startled.

"We will tell you on the way! But run! Run! It is urgent! And take your visa!"

Paling, then purpling, Ralph would neither deny

nor forestall them. He ducked back into the room, blinking with mute frustration at Meg.

"What is it?" she gasped, hardly daring to hope.

"Paris," Ralph groaned.

"To Paris tonight?"

He nodded with difficulty.

"But you mustn't leave me," she cried, joyously flinging her arms around his neck. "Now that I've found you, I must stay at your side. Why must you go?"

He seemed to sink beneath the warm weight of her breasts pressing against him.

"Oh, my darling, darling," she breathed. "Then take me with you. You will protect me. I'm not afraid."

He stared at her quickly, deeply, his yellow eyes blazing like a cat's in darkness. "Would you come without a passport? Would you trust me with your safekeeping?"

"Of course! Without passport. Without baggage. Without clothing. Just as I am, I would go to Paris with you. Stow away and find life. And love. And strange pleasures never heard of before. Oh, please. *Do* take me. Do!"

It took him a moment to accept that she meant it. Then the soft thin lips twisted with savory expectations. "Yes. We will find a way to hide you aboard." Not bothering, in his self-absorption, to reply to her further, he leaped to his wardrobe and pulled out gray breeches, dressing rapidly and sloppily, without concern. At the bottom of the closet lay bags of silver or gold, the size of large fists. He hefted two and thrust them with his papers into pockets that bulged over fragile hips. With tousled hair and clothes awry, he looked like a robber or a madman on the run but took no notice. He was accustomed to doing as he wished when he wished, protected by his immense wealth and family connections.

He grabbed her elbow and pulled her toward the door as she wrapped the sash securely around her. "Those are my friends downstairs," he said offhandedly.

She did not know what he meant by friends or why he bothered to tell her, but the idea of what they must be like chilled her blood. She stayed close beside him, however, as he took the steps down two at a time, using a back stairwell that circled steeply. They reached the servant's door and were out into the warm, vaporous air.

"Quick-lee," breathed the Frenchman, head bobbing at the carriage window.

He took small notice of Meg, dragging her up and inside by the waist and pulling Ralph after her.

"Eh, *allons,* Ned," he called to the driver. "We go!"

A whip snapped in air. The horses wheeled, backing and twisting onto the road. With a gathering clatter, they lurched ahead and Meg sank back, hardly daring to believe her good fortune. She found herself squeezed in between Ralph on one side and the Frenchman, in a strange tricorne hat, on the other. Two more of Ralph's cronies lounged opposite, one with his arms folded over a heavy redingote made for colder weather, and the other mud-splattered in shirt sleeves and tasseled Hessian boots.

She could make no sense of the motley crew. Nor did it matter.

The Frenchman tilted his narrow head and smiled at her from a fleshless face, very long and bony-nosed, with jaunty, almond-shaped eyes that reminded her of a bird of prey no longer mighty.

"Mademoiselle?" He tipped his hat in an elaborate gesture, but curtailed to the space in the carriage.

Ralph slipped his arm around Meg's waist and squeezed it. "My dear, this is the Comte du Beauharvais."

"Victor to my friends," said the comte. "In these times of change, it is all *egalité,* is it not?"

"Yes, change." Meg nodded, half in delirium, thinking ahead to Dick with every gallop of the hooves. "I am so eager to see the new Paris."

"And I," replied Victor, "am not so sure to say the same." He tipped the hat to his eyebrows and blew up softly at his nostrils. "Ten years I am *émigré* in your fine country. I have run for my life, you see, like so many othairs. And now to return."

"You will be seeing your home."

"Yes, that is true. And what will I find left of it? The lands confiscated by that . . . that opportunist. My vineyards." He lifted his shoulders and held them rigid. "Who knows? And my mother . . . Of course she takes care of things beautifully. She says everyone in Paris is now friends with every othair one. It is all mixed up together, the classes of people. And she says that is good, can you believe her? My father is dead, of course. They found him in Dijon and cut his head off. Why? Because he had no certificate of residence signed by nine witnesses. But really, it was because he was a nobleman of the *ancien régime*—and an enemy of the new. That was six years ago. And still, yes, still, despite everything, I am eager to return." He talked on and on while the carriage jounced them, drumming along as though his sadness had finally burst and the feelings must pour out.

The thick man in the greatcoat opened the button tabs at his neck and said, "Go to sleep, Victor. You have had too much wine," hiccuping and belching, rubbing his palm over the scattered strands of his flat hair. "We raced Mr. Browne to Haversham and stole his coach." He giggled tiredly. "Didn't we, Tom?"

"And now we are chasing down to Dover in a stolen carriage?" Ralph said irritably. "We could have used any one of mine."

"Sit back, that's not why," interjected Tom. He lifted one bandy leg and pulled the knee to his chest, stretching worn and aching muscles.

"Well, then?" snapped Ralph.

All the while he listened to his cronies, Meg felt Ralph fondling her behind her back where no one could see, slipping his fingers lower along the curve of her behind.

"We got the drift o' some stolen goods coming in from Calais, eh, Humbert?" Tom continued nudging the greatcoat, grinning and wetting his lips.

"Wine." Humbert burped from the depths of the

collar. With methodical, slow movements he rubbed one palm heel into his eye. "Casks and casks of vintage wine."

"Due in sometime tonight, before dawn," Tom leered, wiping sweat from his lip with a thick forearm.

"Has Ned been driving very long?" said Ralph, listing slightly against Meg's side.

"He's the freshest of the lot," Tom replied with a grunt.

"That's not saying very much."

"We'll get there. We will." Tom leaned forward and pinched Meg's knee. "Settle down, darling, and rest easy."

She glanced quickly to Ralph to see what this strange man's touching her had ignited. To her amazement, she found that Ralph hardly seemed to notice. She had thought of herself as Ralph's exclusive possession. But was she mistaken? Was she to become communal property? Especially here, in these close quarters, it would be easy for one hand or another to make its way to her for some touch of comfort or titillation.

Victor had toppled to one side, and his cheek pressed against a corner of the wall. Humbert had stopped belching and was snoring in starts that rose or sank according to the pits and ditches of the road. There was nothing much to see outside, except streams of rooftops racing by as they plunged along, six miles an hour, southward toward the Thames and then the Channel.

Tom leaned across, hands on his knees, and looked up into Meg's face. His tiny, bulging eyes flashed once with reflected light from a gas lamp. "Who's the fancy creature, Ralph? Who's the pretty one?"

He squeezed her hand. She saw his wet tongue flick and salacious hunger crinkle in his cheeks. *These brutes are the king's gentlemen,* she thought with no surprise. She wondered if this was the side Dick saw when he railed against the tyranny of patronage. If these were the men to whom he would sell pictures, there was no blaming him for turning away.

Ralph's fingers had now stolen in beneath the

bottom of one thigh and were trying to flip over so that his palm faced up.

"Meg Watkins," said Ralph with a gentle wheeze of excitement. "This is my very own darling Meg. Meg, say hello to my good friend Thomas, Viscount of Rothiegate."

"Meg Watkins, is it? Nice bit o' baggage to the boat." Tom chewed his lip with appreciation. "And drop it at Dover, eh?"

Meg glanced quickly at Ralph, feeling with a shudder the helplessness of her position with no passport, no money, and Ralph's good will alone to depend on.

"She comes with us," said Ralph. "To Paris."

"Paris? We've only booked for four."

"Never mind," Ralph grunted irritably. "Never mind."

The horses reared to one side of a cart rumbling slowly through the darkness. Ned yelled a commanding curse and Tom tumbled to his knees on the carriage floor, his chest snapping forward onto the tops of her thighs. He started to lift himself off and then, thinking better of it, stopped and sniffed longingly into her skirts and let his head rest there. "All the way to Paris," he sighed. "And dump it in the Seine."

Meg held herself rigid, arresting her instinctive urge to knee him in the chin. Tom's nose crept upward, inch by inch, worming along, finding its way in sure but easy stages. She knew how far he would go and where he intended to stop. She wanted to swat him with the side of her fist to his skull. But Ralph, who was also watching Tom's progress, sniggered about it from time to time, and Meg had no idea what Ralph had in mind. The fingers beneath her were finding their own way incessantly.

Humbert snored fully now, in huge broadsides of stinking breath. He thrust his booted legs up onto the seat between Victor and herself. Victor, in his own dreamy world, shifted sideways, squeezing Meg even closer to Ralph. She jumped and her legs parted for a second. That instant gave Ralph the opening he wanted.

"Ahhhhh," he sang out unabashedly with a spreading grin. A trickle of perspiration glistened on the sides of his nostrils and slid down toward his lips. He flicked a tongue at both edges quickly and slumped backward, fingers groping deep and pressing dress material into her.

"Tom," he said. "Tom. What do you like best in the world to do?"

"Devilish question," Tom replied, muffled in her skirts. "Devilish difficult to answer."

"Try," said Ralph. "There are so many equivocal positions we take in life. Try. Don't sit on the fence all day. Try."

Tom's laughter between her thighs came in hot gasps. "I've reached the top of my position and am content to pause a while."

"But would you not like to bare some facts to us about it?" laughed Ralph, watching his friend disappear into a triangular cushion as her skirts were raised.

No answer. A groan of distracted ecstasy.

"I see," Ralph murmured, "that you are concentrated on the core of things."

Meg listened to them and let it all happen. She was nothing but a rag doll played upon by the forces of a fate that was nevertheless taking her where she wanted to go. This was her paid price to her destiny. But she supposed that in a moment or two Ralph would be looking for her to exhibit some signs of passionate response. He expected that all a man had to do was fumble about with a woman and tickle her a few times in particular places and she would quiver, foaming at the mouth, to be poked all the way. His self-absorbed nature had never learned there was life in anyone else. His fingers, trilling over the harpsichord of her bottom, had become increasingly urgent. The idea of bouncing her upon him, of being helped by the carriage sway, added a zest of the unexpected that sharpened his appetite.

"Meg," he said to her, as though asking for a bit of jam, "grasp me."

He was a fine one for prolonging the starters. Meg

knew that she could fondle and stroke him until her arm went numb, and nothing would come of it until he decided it was time.

Tom said, "Jack him off, sweetheart, but don't let him spit in my eye."

The sleeping Humbert seemed to hear this and burst out laughing. But Victor delicately kept his silence.

Meg, still taking her orders from Ralph, kept a wary eye upon all his responses and found him growing more intense. The soft mouth became grim and smaller, carved out of rock rather than fruit. His knees slapped back and forth against her hand, urging it to speed up the process according to some inner need. He reached for her bodice and plunged hot fingers inside. She felt the scrape of nails on her tender skin and she knew he purposely meant to scratch her.

"We should stop at an inn," he cried, "and make the most of this among us all."

"No!"

"We can't miss the wine," rumbled Humbert instantly.

Ralph laughed with sour objection. "We can't miss the wine," he repeated. "What lunacy. Of course we can."

"No, we can't!" The voice came louder, tense, threatened.

Meg shifted slightly and snaked her arms around Ralph's neck. "We'll have all the time and space we need on the boat," she whispered reassuringly.

His mouth was very close. She felt the stream of breath flare from his nostrils in ribbons of trembling air. He seemed more devil than human, as though his mind were made of some strange machinery that exhaled cold fumes, having used flesh for its fuel.

He was managing, despite the cramped quarters, to thoroughly maul her breasts. She couldn't stop the drift of her steamy anger from rising with a panting passion of its own, a passion that must display itself but in garb that no one would recognize. The fury of the insult to her, that she could possibly enjoy these four hands and their faces crawling about, sent showers of perspiration to her skin. She twisted in her seat and rose to bite Ralph's ear, but lightly. As she did so, Tom cried, "Can we fling the skirts up over her head, d'you suppose?" He laughed and laughed with his head caught and straining between her thighs.

Ralph slipped backward, crushing into the boot tips of Humbert's extended legs. Victor, pressed to the wall, yelped uneasily.

"How many hours have we t'go?" bubbled Humbert while he snored.

"Rest easy. Rest easy," Tom called.

The words, meant to soothe, served to frighten him. His eyelids popped open with a start. "We'll miss it," he barked. "We'll be late. This damn blasted carriage is lumbering like an old crumpet. We'll miss the pickings altogether." He leaned over, and hanging on to the door, stuck his head out the window. "Ned? Get on with it, Ned! Whip up those blasted nags or we're done for."

"We're flying as fast as their legs can go," drifted down from the outside seat. "If you don't like my driving, take the reins yourself."

"I bloody well will do that," Humbert shouted back. "Stop this hay cart and let me up there."

"No, don't stop," yelled Victor with urgent seriousness. "The ship won't wait for us very long, the captain warned me. Go on with it, Ned. Go and don't mind anything else."

Humbert fell across Victor and grasped his lapels. "That's a good boy, keep the bloody bastard on his toes. But I can drive faster, you know that. Who won the race?"

"You won because you cheated," replied Victor solemnly. "You didn't go around the town but through it on the final stage—was I not with you?"

"I cheated nothing. You cheated. 'Twas you who went through the town, and now y'r throwing it off on me. French minds are always making something out of nothing. I'd slap you down if you were an Englishman."

"Don't touch my coat. I could kill you in a moment,

mon ami, and not think a word about it. Sit back and close your mouth tight. We will get there in plenty of time if you don't sag the carriage so much with your weight."

Bodies pulled and pushed in every direction, and suddenly the inside of the coach was alive with arms and legs, twisting, socking, biting, and kissing. Hands feeling, fingers pinching, nails scratching and clawing, mouth slobbering, cursing . . . and outside the horses galloped on, slipping and jerking forward through the mire. Ned swung the ship over the whites of their eyeballs, touching it to the stretch of a nostril or sometimes cracking it over hindquarters where tails flew up in the stiffening wind.

The city was long gone behind them. Shadows of fields were all the company that sped them from crossing to crossing. Ned, leaning into the wind, yanked the felt hat down over his ears and stretched his neck out from the high stiff collar turned askew. He gripped the reins lightly or pulled them back, working the horses skillfully with patience and a passionate love for the driving. The seat box rocked him mercilessly and he balanced himself between two muscular legs, sniffing the air as its smells changed, growing rank from the town sewages and sweeter through the fields and finally pungent with the rising salt tides of water.

Inside, Meg also caught a whiff of the freshened salty breeze. She tilted her head out to inhale it again, then spread her arms overhead in exultation as Ned called, "Ramsgate Harbor ahead!"

Chapter Twelve

"RAMSGATE?"

"Ramsgate!"

"Where!" Humbert thumped the carriage. "I don't ee it."

"Shut up, you fool, and be quiet. We're coming in ike gentlemen. The army's about. You want them urning back your papers of passage?"

"We're at peace, Victor, don't lose your nerve," said Ralph.

"It is not my nerve. It is my sense."

"Where d'you suppose the smuggler's boat is?"

"They won't print it in the dailies. Be quiet. A few niles west of the harbor, they told me." Tom slipped is head out the window as the horses slowed to a rot. "Do you know where, Ned?"

"We'll try all the coastline for the next couple of niles," Ned called down.

"What time is it?" asked Victor edgily.

"There's plenty of time for the boat, I say. Now rest asy."

"I can't miss it."

Meg glanced at Victor with tense sympathy but kept ilent.

"Neither can I, friend," said Ralph, hugging Meg to im and smoothing her hair.

Five horses appeared, cantering beside the carriage. hadows of uniformed men, with swords clicking at heir sides, kept apace.

"I say there, sir," the leader called in.

"This is the Earl of Eggleston here," Ralph answered in the haughty, hollow voice of his accustome position.

"Begging pardon, your Lordship. There's been smuggler's barque intercepted at Bridport. We're in structed to close off the passage."

"Yes, is that so? Where is your Captain Nor mande?"

"At the head, m'lord. With the boat."

"He's to speak with me about this, Sergeant. Tur your men aside."

"Yes, m'lord."

The carriage leaped forward as Ned took quick ad vantage of the opening.

"Damme it," groaned Humbert impatiently. "The got the goods."

"We don't know that yet," soothed Tom. "Mayb they're only waiting for the ship. Maybe they hav the news just as we have and nothing else has hap pened."

"Even so," blubbered Humbert, bereft. "Even so.

Tom, hanging out the window, cried, "I see some thing ahead. A knot of people. Lots of people."

"Merde," Victor flung at his bad luck, rolling a wil gaze around the walls and ceiling.

"Something's happened?" Meg repeated uneasil caught up, as Victor was, by the menace of delay.

"Looks like it, m'girl," grinned Tom with anticipa tion. "Looks mighty like something."

Ned pulled hard back on the reins and forced th frothy horses to a walk, guiding them to one side the roadway, where they panted fretfully and ner ously kicked up stones.

As the carriage shivered to a halt, Humbert had th door open and fell out. Tom skittered after him an Ralph ambled forward. Meg was ignored as Ralp scanned the sight of country people huddled abo and jabbering amongst themselves, laughing, shakin their heads, the women clapping with excitement.

"Where is Captain Normande?" demanded Ralp of a stocky Cornwall farmer standing away from th others with a comparatively stolid calm.

"Cap'n's up front with the casks."

"Oh, it's all over," Humbert cried disconsolately, ushing ahead into the crowd as fast as his legs would obble.

A vast milling of gleeful voices along the shore uided his direction. Meg followed after him with alph beside her. They trotted down a pebbly slope oward the long, low-rolling swell of an incoming tide. he closer they came to the water, the louder and more runken were the human sounds. A handful of sol-iers rode among them on horseback, trying vainly ith their shouts and orders to disperse the group that nored them in their unbridled romp. They dashed round the high-stepping horses, splashed beside the ooves and away into the waves, to catch and steer shore the bobbing casks that were floating in, one af-r another, in great abundance.

"Captain Normande, there you are. What's going n here, Captain?"

The captain recognized Ralph and saluted. "Yes, our Lordship. A French vessel laden with wine has un aground on the coast four miles out. As you can ee, they carried a smuggled cargo that dispersed when he hull hit the rocks."

"Have you secured the ringleader?"

"Not as yet, m'lord."

"Well, you must do that first."

"We're about it, m'lord, to our best ability."

"Not quick enough!" Ralph drawled with com-anding disdain. "And you must order your men to revent these good people from collecting and carry-g off the wine . . . and from drinking it."

"Yes, m'lord," he replied with continuing valiance.

"Clear a course and place a guard over the casks as ey drift ashore."

"We've been trying to do that for three hours."

"No excuse, Captain. Keep at it."

As Ralph idly took charge, Humbert waddled for-ard, crying out with joyous tears in his eyes and join-g the masses of men in the water. In the confusion, eg lost sight of him for a while. Then he appeared again with his sleeves dripping, huge arms lugging an pushing one of the casks on the waves as he staggere after it.

The wind had whipped up the water to a chopp tide, but no one seemed to mind the chill in the firs faint indigo lights of dawn. Long shreds of clou loomed, torn upward from the horizon and lowerin overhead. The wind whirled and shifted direction, tak ing a firmer tack with the tide. But Humbert in hi soaking coat seemed oblivious, hugging the barrel t him and pushing it ahead by turns as he struggle with but faint success to bring it ashore. Another bar rel bobbled close by. When it touched his arm, h swung his head, saw it, and shrieked in rapture, the tried to collect that one along with its mate. Now h hung his huge bloated body between the pair of cask and draped an arm over each, attempting to flo himself ashore supported by the twin pontoon Around him others of the same mind called and whis tled to each other in the wild merriment of their heav enly find. The shouts of poor country folk hailed a opportunity never to be repeated. Humbert's giggle proclaimed an orgy not to be controlled and gave hin in the midst of his waterlogged labors, continuin thrills and expectations of the glorious indulgence t come.

Victor's shoulders hung low as he stood disconso lately beside Meg, silently watching the proceedings.

"It is half after four," he muttered. "Half afte four."

"How much time does that leave us?" she replied her voice jittery as she watched Humbert flailin about.

"Less than an hour, mademoiselle. And he wi drink that whole cask, you shall see him do it."

Meg turned to Ralph and squeezed his arm. "Yo can't let him," she pleaded. "He'll kill himself."

"So much the worse for Humbert," laughed Ralph "But think of his happiness at the point of demise."

She held her breath and bit her lip by turns a

Humbert swung round and round, fighting the current for his booty.

The soldiers worked among the mob, walking their hesitant horses through the waves with no pleasure at all in the undertaking. Leaning over, their sabers drawn, they succeeded in intimidating a few of the meeker sort, but even flashing steel could not compete with puncheons of fine French wine.

Two soldiers came at Humbert from either side, calling, "Release your hold, sir. That is stolen property!" Whereupon Humbert, with a crazed shriek, bit into the front leg of one of the horses and continued, oblivious to all threat, on his journey shoreward.

With mountainous determination he finally stumbled up the violet sheen of slope, pushing the casks before him on the sand. But without water for buoyancy, the job was too much for one man, and a cask got away from him, rolling lopsidedly back toward the waves. He let go the first and dashed for the second, whereupon the first began its jolly topple backward as he reached and cornered the other. For some minutes he continued thus, wrestling with one and then the other and always failing to catch both together in the circumference of his embrace. The girth of the barrel staves was simply beyond him. At last, with a tormented cry, he flung both his arms around one and pressed his cheek to it as the other took off forever, sliding away on the bouncing, choppy tide.

Still, he did have the first, and he turned it to stand on end, finally at rest.

"He intends to drink it," Victor said in profound despair.

"Don't let him," implored Meg, thinking of the time required for that quantity.

"This is Humbert's moment," Ralph said with a cool chortle of vicarious ecstasy. "Would I could have such a pinnacle of joy in my short life."

With a terrible growl of impending deliverance, Humbert jumped upon the cask, and his plummeting weight stove in the head of the puncheon.

Clinging to the sides, he hung there, kicking his

feet to keep himself from slipping back down to the sand. He soon seemed to discover a way of balancing himself and gradually wiggled upward, clinging to the sides with both hands and ducking his head down in.

"There's eight gallons in that damn thing," said Tom, appearing from the dark. "He'll be drunk until Christmastide."

Ralph stood quietly watching, arms folded across his chest, drinking in the proceedings in fine sympathy with Humbert guzzling his way deeper and deeper into the barrel. With each passing moment, less of Humbert could be seen on the outside, his body slowly sinking further and further into the evidently receding surface as he stowed the wine into his belly.

They heard a faint gurgling sound. It grew suddenly sharp as Humbert's legs shot stiffly straight into the air and his body sank with a sigh, utterly out of sight inside the rim.

"Let's go to him." Tom started off at a run.

Victor hesitated on the bank but then joined the others, trotting after Meg, who was anxious to reach Humbert in his orgy and have an end to it.

"He's sunk in over his shoulders," Tom squealed. "Grab his leg."

With Ralph at one knee and Tom at the other, they hoisted out the limp, inanimate body, its closed eyes and open mouth dripping purple liquid. A great vapor of alcoholic fumes swirled in waves around his head, which hung limply on its thick neck. The neckcloth dripped wine. Wine leaked from his coat lapels and sighed soggily in the bloated shoulder cloth.

"I say, Corporal," Tom called from where he bent in the mud before his comrade. "Corporal! Over here!"

A horseman approached, saluting and asking what was required of him.

"We must get this man to a hotel, and immediately," demanded Ralph.

Victor said, "You see what comes of this?" He waved his hand, despairing. "There goes the hour. There goes the boat."

The soldier leaped from his horse and knelt beside

the inert, sodden body. He put his ear close to the chest.

"Is this man living?" he said.

"Who knows?" replied Ralph matter-of-factly. "That is what we have to find out. Take him over your pommel back to Weymouth, if you must. But get him medical attention."

He made a gesture that directed Tom and the corporal to haul Humbert over the horse in front of the saddle, which they accomplished after much pushing and pulling that left them both breathless.

"Away you go, Corporal."

"Either drowned in the wine or killed by the fumes," Tom said. "God spare his life."

Ralph, watching the horseman disappear with his swaying bundle, replied, "For what purpose?"—and led Meg, with his hand upon her elbow, back to the carriage where Ned waited, as they had left him, seated high and stoically, with the reins wound around his leather gloves.

"Mon Dieu, Ned, make those horses move!" Victor yelled, beside himself.

"Have we time?" whispered Meg to the Frenchman.

"Who knows?" He shrugged, embittered.

"And if you miss this boat?" laughed Ralph.

"I'll have no money for the next; you know my gambling."

"And I probably shall never go at all," Ralph replied casually.

Meg closed her eyes and prayed haltingly, as she had sometimes heard people do from the steps of a church she had passed when a child, with her basket of watercresses. The God she prayed to had Dick's face, with the same scar across his eyebrow but a more lenient look in the eye. He was the kind of God who would actually hear her and pay attention, as though what she had to say was important enough and sensible enough to warrant response on behalf of the plea.

With her eyes shut and her lips pursed, she pressed

her face into the sleeve of Ralph's arm, thereby guaranteeing herself a moment of absolute privacy from the madness floating around her and from the position she had accepted as all-around servant girl to the whims of her supposed protector.

She felt Ralph play with strands of her hair, twisting them and commenting upon the fiery color as though they were jewels that amused and attracted him. He worked down to her neck and massaged it intimately, teasingly, for he knew the power that lay in his fingers . . . as she had felt it many a time. The bruises from those hands had healed and supposedly were forgotten as he kneaded her flesh with aching, voluptuous caresses. If she did not know Ralph, if he were a stranger, she might, on this occasion, fall under his spell, believing that he hovered over her in sympathy and adoration of the female sex.

"You are exhausted," he said to her in breathy, insinuating demand.

She then recalled what Ralph liked to do to very young girls in their sleep.

"Utterly exhausted," she replied. "If only I could be safely stowed on that boat."

Ralph peered at her with narrow, appraising looks that slowly broke into satisfied yet hungry smiles. He ducked his head out the window.

"Ned. Whip up those horses."

"They're already half dead."

"I said, whip 'em up."

"You bloody bastard, they won't go."

"Do as I say!"

When Ralph commanded, even friends had second thoughts about defying him.

The whip cracked and the horses exploded into galloping spasms, stretching their ribs and their steaming flanks over the narrow pass.

"They will drop dead and we will be stranded here," muttered Victor. "Else we shall be late."

"It will be neither," Ralph shouted. "Now be quiet and stay where you like to be, in your gloom."

Meg took heart at this. It was true that Victor

looked as yellow as fog and only steps away from a suicidal spleen.

Tom stretched himself out flat on the seat that was all his now and propped his heels up along the carriage walls. "I hope we can hide the wench," he yawned. "These Frenchmen are peculiar, I hear. They think that everyone without a passport is a spy."

"I will go to Paris this night," Ralph said. "And nothing shall stop me, I say. Nothing."

Meg nuzzled her mouth along the underside of his chin, not knowing whom to believe about her chances, but placing bets upon this tyrant who could allow nothing to oppose his will.

"The boat must wait for us," she said urgently. "Does the captain know who is coming? I mean, darling Ralph, is he also expecting *you?*"

Ralph blazed a look at Tom. "You heard the girl," he said. "Does the captain expect *me,* along with all of you?"

"We made room, I told you, for four places."

"And now four are present," Ralph noted with a triumphant cackle, Humbert having so conveniently served him by dropping out. "Meg, we shall get you across, never fear."

"We mentioned no names," said Victor encouragingly. "Nor even *noms de plume.*"

"Ramsgate Harbor," Ned called as he had before, but now there was a different, meditative tone in his voice.

The wheels skittered to a halt beside the low, straggling wharf. Victor was the first one out, scrambling away in a thrust of long legs and aggravation. He raced ahead of the others, arrowing directly toward the prow of a small British cutter lying at harbor and pulling hard on the anchoring lines.

With daybreak, the weather had worsened. A bright green glitter hung back in the sky where normally a golden sun would be dawning. The wind howled and banged smaller craft. Masts swayed. Rigging had all been battened down. Hulls rocked giddily on whitecapped chop.

Ned leaped down from his box and led the horses forward.

"We mustn't leave these fellas behind," he said with loyal feeling. "They are much too valuable."

It was Ned, rather than Victor, who found the captain of the *Queen Charlotte* and dickered with him about making space aboard for his prize-running horseflesh.

"It's going to be a wild trip across, my lad," said the captain within Meg's hearing. "See that sky? We've got no room for good horseflesh."

Then Ned began talking money. Half crowns climbed to crowns. Silver changed to gold. The team of six was unhitched and hauled aboard.

"But who cares about it?" said Victor to himself. "We have at least made it to the ship. And soon . . . soon I shall be home."

Meg felt Ralph pushing her covertly toward the planks. "But Paris is exactly the place for my Meg, papers or none," he muttered cheerily. "A limitless refuge, dear, for every kind of hunted quarry."

Chapter Thirteen

As Meg climbed aboard the cutter, she heard sailors muttering that it was folly to put out in such weather, but an agent for transport, who overheard them and was anxious to get home, stifled the grumbling. Ned's horses and some valuable chargers from the disbanded cavalry were stowed together in slings and a family of Irish women, soldiers' wives and their children, herded on deck.

"No need to stand about and be battered," said

Ralph, edging Meg below decks as the prow turned into the choppy tides.

It seemed a miracle that Ned and Victor could disappear in such narrow confines, leaving her alone with Ralph and Tom trailing behind. She could almost sense the conspiracy of friends in this until she saw Ned amidships, motioning them on with a smear of eager triumph across his face. Evidently he had found something important.

Picking her way along the planks, banging a shoulder or wristbone against the wall as the ship rolled, Meg could only hope that he had found and stolen a pail of grog, which they would all swallow in a gulp and fall asleep over. Such was her one prospect of rest that day. But it was not to be.

"Lookee here. Lookee here!" Ned urged them into a sour-smelling room with an expansive gesture of his gloved hand. "I dickered the captain out of these quarters for the trip. What d'you say to it, boys?"

The four stood in enough space for two, most of it taken up by piles of canvas and tarry-smelling rope in coils.

"This is for a stowaway without hope," Ralph sniffed. "Go back and do better."

"Better?" exploded Tom, jumping and bouncing on the canvas. "Soft as Mamma's breast and a fine sight more private than anything we're likely to get, next to all those Irishers."

A whinny resounded and a kick thumped on the far side of some planks.

Where the hell are we, anyway? Meg thought, wondering if the horses could get angry enough to put a hole in the hull.

"I want an ordinary cabin," Ralph said smoothly. "Nothing special. No king's ballroom. Just a cabin." He spoke with exaggerated patience, a fine princeling expecting honest and suitable arrangements.

"This is what there is," Ned concluded simply, and flopped down beside Tom. "If you want better, go and try for yourself."

"Ned," Ralph said softly, feeling the walls. "If I

have to go upstairs and look at those sickening sea faces one time more, there will be a neck or two twisted and you'll have to sail this ship all the way to Calais yourself."

Ned blinked at the threat. A film of utter belief floated over his eyes.

"Don't rile yourself, Ralph," Tom said with pacifying advice, and scrambled rapidly to his feet. "I'll go. We'll both go, Ned and I. You make yourself comfortable, meanwhile . . . comfortable as you can, for a fine gentleman with his whore."

They were humoring him, and Meg knew it to be the smartest move. Ralph, hearing the attention being paid to his desires, subsided, came up behind Meg, and slipped both arms around her waist.

"I don't want a fine lady being discommoded," he said, putting his lips upon her ear.

They were out of the room and glad to go, Meg suspected, as Ralph laughed softly against her neck. "Those filthy buggers will settle for anything." He turned her in his arms. "*We* know there's better comforts to be had if they speak out. Now look at me, sweet. Are you happy? I don't like the way your hair is blown . . . the wind has tossed it all awry." He began to smooth the curls, concentrating on every strand with a burst of intensity out of place in the circumstances, his pale eyes glittering in the shifting swinging light of a lantern. "Kiss me . . . If we had water for a bath . . . Those horses will never settle . . . Did you know my uncle well? . . . Did you sleep with him? . . . Can he get it up?"

She muttered some inaudible answer to every question as though the jumble of intertwining thoughts made sense to her, while she considered how he was going to get her safely off the boat at Calais. But she needed to do more than merely placate him as the others did. She needed to draw him on and somehow take part in his imaginative fancies. Her fingers played upward from the damp collar into the limp wisps that hung from the salt-air dew. He seemed to have no idea of his own unsettled appearance and could only ocus on criticizing what had happened to her during he hardships of travel, such as how her dress hem was vet from wading in after Humbert. Of course she had lone no such thing, but she didn't dare correct im. She kissed the side of his neck, running her tongue ver the soft, unprotected throat with its rash of tiny, nflamed pimples, imagining how someone could press humbs right there and easily throttle him, meanwhile rooning love patter at his cheek, the edge of his ose bridge, his eyelids.

The unhinged door to a storage area swung and reaked, crying out as the ship's prow dug deeper into engthening swells. On one roll to starboard, they both ost their footing and together slid over the slimy lanks, tumbling onto the piled canvas, which was, as Tom had said, surprisingly soft.

While Ralph cursed, Meg purred and continued issing his mouth, undeterred by the goings-on around hem and intent on preventing Ralph from falling into vile temper, which could only be vented on her.

"Sweetheart, *mon cher,*" she said, practicing her French. "What can it matter where we are?"

Ralph, sunk in the canvas and fearful of being mothered, struggled to get his footing in some shrouds nd grappled a throw line that smeared his palms lack. "Ughhhhh." His throat clicked with disgust.

She lifted her skirt, quickly wiped his hands with it, nd kissed each finger, sucking the tips and peering p at him longingly through lowered lashes.

"I must be sensible," she said, "and not be done in y my surroundings. Not waste my time with these esser matters."

"You *are* a bright star," he sighed, suddenly relieved f his annoyances. "Now tell me, Meg, what do you eally want from me?"

The question threw her into speechless confusion. "How can you be so distracted at a time like this?" Her eyelids fluttered with the seeming shock of embarassment, as though annoyed by something else entirely.

"I'd like to know," Ralph said coldly. "I'd like to

know *why* I'm being taken advantage of . . . and the I can decide whether or not it's worth the trouble."

"I have no answer," she blurted, and trembled o the edge of tears. "I've run away from my father t the one person who understands what life is about and now *he,* too, disappoints me. Oh. Oh." She flun her hands over her face. "I'll get out at Calais an disappear. The guards will take me. You'll never se me again. Here I thought you wanted to make love t me. I thought *you* knew what a woman needs . . . bu you can't care less about my . . . desires. Oh, an they're so . . . so . . . insistent. You'll never understan the suffering. Yes. I've tried men. Many men. Bu that isn't the answer. Men are mostly . . . well, quic about it. Too quick for me. I need to take my tim To *feel* things. *Fondle* things. I like to find differen ways." She paused long enough to hear that his breat had increased its pace. He was listening to her, caugh up, enraptured by what he was adding to her speec from the twisted depths of his own imagination.

"Tell me more details," he said hoarsely.

She slid closer and lay beside him, playing with hi fingers, stroking his palm in slow circles. His hanc were as soft as a child's, pink and yellow and exudin perfume, as though the skin had died and were cov ered with petals.

"My darling Ralph," she said gently. "Don't mak me go through hell for you."

"Hell for me?" he said, enticed. "What kind c hell?"

"Oh, you know." She recalled the bear-baiting cor tests, the blood-lust, the stomping and thumpin "Don't make me chew myself to pieces over yo Don't make me tear my belly out with feelings . . . a sorts of feelings."

"Do you dream?"

"Of course I dream."

"About what? Tell me everything."

She flung herself half upon him so that one brea lay in the curve of his throat and he could sniff th musky aroma of her flesh. Where was Dick this day he wondered. Was the weather sunny in Paris? Was e in some boulevard, sketching?

A heavy footstep paused at the swinging door. Tom oked his head in.

"Here, Ralph. The captain doesn't *have* any quar- rs to give us. He's handed everything over to the hildren."

"Never mind," Ralph said rapturously. "Come in nd listen to this."

"I left Victor and Ned forward."

"Let them stay. Come in yourself. And be quiet bout it." He stroked Meg in the small of her back. Meg has confessions to make that you should witness. it down. Sit down."

Meg swallowed hard and summoned up a new vave of courage. She must think of something, any- hing, to keep them madly aroused. Yes, both. There vas no point in hoping that she would have only Ralph to contend with. He had let Tom get away with nuch, too much, in the carriage. They were friends in strange relationship that she dared not dwell upon ill she had to deal with it. But whatever did she care? Beasts could only be beasts. And each moment was bringing her closer to France.

She lay on her belly and didn't move when Tom opped down behind her. She had already experi- nced his mouth in her crotch, and now his hands on er behind weren't half as bad.

A thundering bang of water on the deck resounded round them. Then came women's frightened screams nd sailors' gruff voices reassuring them with talk about nean weather and not to worry on so tight a ship.

Another wave landed with a ponderous thud. The oat shivered and flung Tom on top of her back. A fit f heavy kicking began among the horses.

Tom sprawled, kissing her neck. "Yo-ho-ho and a ottle o' grog," he sang at a tiny, childish pitch. He lipped his arms around her ribs and squeezed her reasts together with the insides of his biceps.

"Tom says that a real woman can't be satisfied by ne man at a time. A woman with red blood in her veins wants a stick in her mouth while she's sitting on another. What do you make of it, Meg? Is that so?"

It was not Tom's idea at all, Meg knew, watching the hot glow in Ralph's eyes as he barely contained himself, waiting for her reply. She smiled slowly, as though reluctant to admit the truth, and remembering at the same time how Dick was enough for one woman ten women . . . as long as they all were herself! "Tom has the secret," she replied. "Where did he find it out? Who was so brazen to admit it?"

"Well, not every woman," Tom bragged. "Just some. I once knew a brothelkeeper in Seven Dials who had a girl working there by the name of Lu. Yes. Lu Lu, it was. A foreign type. From Genoa or Spain. She had one eyebrow that ran straight across the top of her nose. And the hair on her lip curled around like a set of cat's whiskers. But she wasn't the kind of girl you wasted your time looking at. You jumped into the bed on her with the candles snuffed . . . and she was already there, humping with a boy friend, you see. They were going at it like Whistlejacket siring the next champion filly. You had to make a place for yourself carefully so you didn't get cracked in the teeth by her arse. The bedstead was rocking like this ship."

While Tom rattled on, Meg began to massage Ralph steadily up along the inside of one thigh where the rumpled breeches were already pulling tight. He lifted his knee to make room for the movement of her hand groaning slightly as she began to touch him.

"Well. This Lu-Lu had her eyes shut tight as an owl in the daytime and her mouth wide open . . . and the thing was for me to creep around and up the pillows which I did like a skivvy in the shrouds, clambering sky-high. It was no mean trick, I tell you, getting around, keeping my arms and legs caught between and not broken."

The prow lifted suddenly and seemed to hang suspended over the crest of a huge wave. Then it dropped with a roaring slap. There came a tearing sound of leather and a scramble among the horses. They had evidently pulled loose from their slings and were ımping around now, kicking violently and biting each her. A howl of wind mingled with the terrified howl the animals flung free by the hurricane, but without ough room in their close quarters to find footing.

A voice cried, "We've got to get in there!" It was ɛd, furious, concerned, and horror-stricken for the te of the animals.

Ralph suddenly fingered his breeches open and ɔped up Meg's skirt to her hips. He floundered to- ard her from underneath and she grabbed the hard, 'ollen pole, holding it steady long enough to thrust rself down upon it with a will. The backs of her ighs met the fronts of his and the boat took a dive, unging nose downward, at the same time pitching to rt, so that she spun around where she sat.

"Don't be crazy, mister," called a seaman's voice. mpossible to get in to them horses now. The space too confined, don't you see."

"Got to," shrieked Ned in desperate agitation. They'll stifle in there from the hatches being battened ɔwn. Let me pass!"

"No, sir. We can't let yer fool with yer life. It's the ptain's responsibility. Not yours."

A scuffle of human feet kicked while horses gurgled the dread sound of their struggles for air.

"No decent girl licks the naked mast," Ralph ıghed. "Ask Bonaparte. Bonaparte says that a ɔman belongs to her husband just as his pigs do. And s houses." He was panting now, lifting his hips and rusting upward with a fury that raised her aloft while ɔm clutched her bottom cheeks tightly together to lp Ralph with his urgent mission. Clothes tumbling is way and that fell over Ralph's face, covering the ished or paling smiles that whipped across his mouth ever-changing expressions of mood. "But rare ɔmen . . . of an animal disposition . . . can't get . . . ough. Where are you, Tom? Tom?"

"You know where I am," gurgled Tom with wicked ustering.

Ralph ripped the cloth away from his eyes to devour

the sight of Meg, plugged orally, eyes shut fast, thrc working lustily.

The scene before his eyes, measuring up exactly his dreams, sent him into shivers of convulsive ecsta: His hair fell forward and matted into the sweat on l forehead wrinkled with mute urgency. His fing clutched at Meg, grabbing her neck, her breast, l waist, her hips, unable to hold all of her at once y wanting only that.

"Oh, lordee, lordee," mumbled Tom in tiny, glo ous shivers.

Meg hung on, feeling herself being torn in half a smothered, yet determined to be more than a mat for them both. The swordsmen galloped at her rele lessly. She outmatched them with her own attac swiveling her neck here, her hips there, gyrating, ma aging, somehow, to gulp air, to feel no pain, to reme ber Dick's face, his arms, the promise of their love.

The ship sank slightly to starboard and a topple inert horseflesh fell in that direction, remaining in heap as the hull struggled to right itself but could n altogether come around straight again. Above dec the howl of the hurricane had turned into a continuo driving whine that tore at the masts, which cracked a fell in horrendous crashes.

"Oh, Mither o'Mary protect us!!!" came a chorus stricken Irish accents with babies crying, followed a complicated jabbering of young women's vows.

The cutter limped into Calais, ghosting along on t dregs of an exhausted ebb.

A huddle of chastened humanity stood at the ra ing and peered gratefully at the sight of land, peace and glowing beneath a sky shading in the last rays sunlight to a russet sheen. Some birds overhe squawked and hung about in the yardarms, dippi and wheeling in quarrelsome search for food. No oth sound except the sailor calls at their work rent t clean-smelling air.

Meg, with her clothes smoothed as best they cou be, crawled topside, work and weariness forgotte Ralph had let her come up alone to survey the pro cts for getting ashore. He needed, he said, some vate conversation with Tom—exactly when she excted him to help her off the boat. Meg surmised t the talk had to do with their further adventures gether—or perhaps about dumping her at the port. ngrily she scanned the low notches of rooftops, ir outlines deepening at dusk. Which was the place customs? How could she tell it? She inhaled the eeze and a touch of chimney smoke, yearning to h through the crowds and be safely on land. Then e spied Ned standing by himself, not far from a sailor justing some instrument of navigation.

"Ned, hello. It won't be long now," she called, and nt to where he stood, dry-eyed and silent, staring the ripples curling away from the prow. Could Ned lp her in some way?

"Weather is a damned mysterious creature," Ned ered, more to himself than to her. "Thirteen horses ad. Thirteen."

The gloom was too much for Meg. She couldn't ar that people gave in to their melancholy and de things more difficult. It was easy, too easy, to go wn defeated, she thought, watching the lead lines own ashore and the hawsers fly after, pulling the ow in to the quay. And no help in that! No reward, her. She shuddered, shaking off the fury of Ralph's serting her in her need—and after what she had t gone through. "There'll be others, though," she d hopefully as the boat settled to berth.

"Horses are more precious and scarcer than mans," he answered tonelessly.

Victor, coming up behind them, added, "Humans ve no value at all. See if a human body would be rted ashore as fast as that horseflesh."

Meg turned swiftly at the rumble of wagon wheels aking up the plank. "That's how they take them ?" she said with a burst of light. "Victor, where all we meet?"

"At the Dessis Hotel." He smiled with a faint humor, quick comprehension.

She darted below decks, clambering down the narrow stairs and wending a way to where the commotic had started, of dead horseflesh being lugged, hoiste and pushed through the passageway. Quietly, wi gawking eyes and cold breath shallow at the lips, sl followed the expedition, watching how horse aft horse, not yet stiff and tails lightly fluttering in tl breeze, were raised and tugged with coils of rope, be either tossed into the wagon or overboard, depen ing on the mood of the men. In a moment of despa she thought that she, too, should leap and try to swir but she would only be dragged ashore by some intru ing gallant and turned over to the authorities. If on she could get into the wagon and hide there witho smothering. Or would she be squashed dead by tl weight? In either event, it would all be over in moment, one way or the other.

"Mademoiselle!"

She whirled into a splatter of French being hurl at her by an irate official in a flat black cap who w pointing at the same time to the herd of Irish childr disembarking with their mothers in the lead.

"Allez! Allez!" he demanded, pointing and poki a stubby finger.

"Oh, yes. Thank you, sir. I had nearly lost n family, were it not for you!" Off she raced, shuffli ashore with the girls and women passing by impatie and officious-looking faces that hardly glanced at he

The Dessis Hotel, a principal establishment in tl bustling port, was easy to find and surrounded by strange, nasal cackling of French that made an eer blanket of sound. Meg spotted Victor's tricorne ar raced for it, calling, *"Monsieur, monsieur,"* with a the accent she could muster.

Ralph, watching her arrive, said in a peevish ton "I intended to help you, but you were too quick fo me."

"Oh, but I wanted to try my French," she replie brightly, feeling peculiarly relieved to be back wi him. "My cousin Dick has taught me. Have you hear of Dick Fox? The painter?"

"No, dear, no," said Ralph, impatient at the sound of anyone's name but his own.

"I'm not surprised," she persisted gaily. "The dear, brilliant man is still aspiring. You must know how it is for artists, Ralph. You have such a sensitive heart."

"Artists work for money," Ralph replied in a bored drawl. "And I pay well for what I like."

The obscene notion of Dick working for Ralph had never crossed her mind. It sobered Meg now and made her quiet.

Victor set his hat straight across his brow in a style that gave him the look of a raffish eagle. "Now we are in my countree," he said. "I am the host. If you will kindly wait on this side of the hotel, I will go around and get four places for us on the diligence."

Ralph nodded, content to allow Victor to attend to the details. After a short meal of bread, tripe, and crumbling cheese washed down with a table wine, they were climbing inside a cumbrous vehicle of unwidely proportions, suspended on two leathern straps for springs. Behind it hung a basket as big as the coach itself, which rested on two hind wheels; it was expressly for passengers' luggage but was already filled with a quantity of various other merchandise, bundles, and strapped packages that did not weigh down the wheels at all, which were as broad as those of a London wagon. The seat in front contained a *conducteur* and two passengers who appeared not to know each other but were studiously engaged in conversation to make the best of things on outside passage. The postilion who rode the near wheel drove five horses, three abreast in front. He sat sharply in a short blue jacket with red facings and silver lace, proud powdered hair combed back and tied in a knot like a thick shaving brush.

"The French are a sturdy lot," said Victor, handing Meg inside. "And besides, we must be prepared against brigands."

"Brigands?" echoed Meg, settling herself across from Ned and Tom and wondering if she was ever to get to sleep unmolested. "What he can steal from me he can have!"

Ralph laughed heartily, and she realized the attraction to danger lurking in his bulging pockets.

"Remember," she said sturdily. "If it comes to that and you're facing a pistol, don't be brave, don't be daring. Give them the loot."

He looked at her coolly, with an unexpected grin that twisted in a moment to wry understanding. "So my life is precious to you, is it, Meg?"

"Very precious, my dear. You don't know how much."

The postilion leaned over and called, "We shall make good time. The Royal Road is in fine condition, they say. No broken carriages and the mud is hard."

Thank heaven for small blessings, thought Meg as the horses started up on the journey, pulling at the ropes that tied them and jogging off in a very independent manner.

"How long will it be?"

"If we are lucky," Victor said, "four days. We go by easy stages, you see."

"Yes. And how many tolls?" said Ralph, sarcastically amused. "Twenty-six?"

"It is a poor country," Victor replied, shrugging. "But *Maman* writes that the Consul is organizing everybody and good roads will be paid for."

Meg smiled. "You are so eager to see her."

Victor flushed, speechless.

"Yes, it is ten years," she said, repeating what was in his heart. Then, turning to Ralph, "And do you know the Comtesse du Beauharvais well?"

"Brava! You have remembered the name." Ralph smiled.

"Why, yes, I memorized it," Meg said with a haughty flip of her chin. "You see, Ralph, I will be nimble wherever you take me."

"A credit to me," he repeated with a baiting, wicked leer.

"A credit and more," she said, confidently drilling a level look into him. "You have told me that you come to Paris for fun. Well, I shall see to it that you enjoy yourself beyond your wildest expectations."

She spoke with such fire that Ralph seemed to burn up before her. Admiration for her independence turned into something more complex that flickered lasciviously across his eyes.

"I am particular in my pleasures," he said softly.

"And am I not?" she shot back, aware that in this conversation she must best him, dominate him. Now *she* must be challenger, daring Ralph to live up to what he thought was her real, though hidden, nature. He must learn to cling to her, because she dared not be alone in this hostile country.

She began, then, to see him come to life, a flutter of something dark and obsessive. It crossed his face like an illusion in a perfumed breeze, which he could only sniff at but not capture before it was gone. The impulse to run after and trap it remained, however, taunting and tempting and testing as it amused and interested Ralph, who watched her with growing excitement. He took her hand. His icy, clammy fingers told her she had won this time. Ralph was impatient for some mystery to be revealed, the mystery that was in her and that she alone controlled.

"My mother has been like a mother to Ralph," said Victor warmly. "And Ralph has been like a brother to me."

"There were so many Frenchmen in London, eh, Victor, that you could almost believe you were home."

"I understand there are many Londoners in Paris. We will have a good time. The French know how to make a good time with anything."

"I am sure your mother's heart has broken, missing you all these years," Meg said. "She will welcome you home with kisses, and Ralph with more kisses. I look forward to meeting her, too, for I feel that I am home already."

"*Maman* will find you charming," Victor replied with assurance.

Meg turned her face so that Ralph would not catch the flush of satisfaction warming her cheeks and temples. The plan of action seemed to unfurl itself before her eyes with no effort of strategy on her part. The comtesse must be a woman of social obligations. And she, Meg, would be invited to balls, salons, suppers. . . . Indirectly, she would make the connections worthy of Dick Fox, and since they were in France and not in England, so much the better. His reputation could travel before him back across the Channel and pave the way for distinctions at home.

She peered out the window at the monotonous scenery, watching row upon row of poplars guarding long, level tracts of farmland behind it.

"The French have such a long history of wars," explained Victor, watching her expression, "that it taught the peasants to build their cottages and their towns far from the main traveling routes."

"I don't mind," chirped Meg. "Grass is beautiful."

When they came to a stop for any reason, the horses kicked and bellowed and reared like wild beasts, flinging Meg across at Ned and Tom, who had fallen asleep upon each other. When Ralph pulled her back with her neck strained, she said, "I don't mind," with an impervious smile too sunny and sincere to be questioned.

The ropes that harnessed the horses broke frequently, delaying the trip. Meg turned her head the other way, trying also to distract Ned when the *garçons d'écurie* abused the horses and beat them with thick sticks to make them start again. But mostly they went along at a steady clip, doing five miles an hour in the middle of the road, where the coach followed well. Sometimes they met a train of carts with long axles that projected from the wheels, and the carriage slid sideways from the paving into the heavy mud road. Then the driver, with much cracking of the whip and hallooing of the horses, struggled to get them going. When they fell, the postilion in boots of iron and leather had nothing more to do than pull his leg free and leave the boot under the animal. Only at the crossroads was it nasty, where crowds of beggars alled for charity. "Just as in Ireland," Ralph muttered ith disgust.

Impulsively, Meg reached into his pocket and flung oins to them, "to see the riot," she explained to alph.

At night, at the inns, he dragged the mattress to e floor, away from the bedbugs, after a meal of ran- id sauces and red asparagus fried in something like arriage oil, so sour and miserable a bill of fare that 'om complained he could see them all growing thin- er hourly.

Thus they traveled, with Meg in a fit of quiet des- eration to hide the spirit leaping in her heart as she eached closer to Dick.

Chapter Fourteen

EYOND THE GATES lay Paris in April, afloat on sunny, ry air. Everywhere the colorful uniforms of soldiers loomed in a military flowering that opened Meg's yes wide to a splendor she could almost reach out nd touch. The glitter of gold braid and gold embroi- ery on white britches; high, swaying, plumed head- ear, sabers clanking proudly with debonair ease on unners, drum majors, and members of Napoleon's mperial Guard—all mingled with the *nouveaux riches* nd the female celebrities of fashion. Mustachioed hus- ars and color sergeants paraded the leafy, shaded oulevards. Crested helmets and decorated muskets leamed in the light. The dazzle of conquest and the all to further conquest hovered in the gold-painted agles of victory carved on every door. Was this e peace she had been led to expect? Meg hung out e window gaping at the strollers, the couples in cabriolets, the men on horseback, Frenchmen lookin English in their cutaway coats, English *touristes* at tempting to seem so very French, dawdling at café in lingering, sensual enjoyment, with fiddle music caper ing overhead. From some newly opened restaurar in the Rue Richelieu, where an artist in cooking ha been tempted away into self-employment, aromas (delicious spices tweaked Meg's nostrils. Opportunit seemed to lurk everywhere in the New Republic fo the quick and the brave.

"How wonderful," Meg said. "We will have a mar velous good time here, I know it!" But her hea quavered at the spread of this vast, jubilant curren Where had she got the nerve to believe that she coul find Dick all by herself? Her confidence was frigh ening because it was based, as she now could see, upo her ignorance. Yet there was no other way to procee She felt reduced to the simple, quite trifling expedie of scratching where she could for any leads.

Victor leaned forward in a suppressed tremble the diligence lumbered patiently on, then stopped the grand façade of a once-fashionable home poc marked with bullet holes and chipped from explosio of powder. The grillwork gate swung precariously o a single hinge.

"You must all come inside at once," he crie "*Maman* will welcome you with open arms, and w can have a bath and a delectable dinner . . . such there may be."

"But after ten years," Meg replied, "you shoul be alone with her for the first moments."

"Nonsense," cried Victor, already in tears. "Sh will be grateful, happy to meet my good friends wh have helped me through such an ordeal."

He shoveled them before him, and Meg amble curiously toward the astronomical street number 1,06 on the Rue du Bac.

"In my father's day," said Victor, eyeing the nu merals, "this gateway itself was of sufficient renow to need no other sign." He stumbled ahead, half hi its gone between hesitation and eagerness and fear f what he would find indoors.

Meg could not contain herself. She turned around nd stopped Ralph and Ned from following too closely fter him.

"He must go first, he must," she said hoarsely, and eld them back decisively while Victor, who did not otice, disappeared inside the two front portals open-ng to his knock.

"Well, you see, they do not miss us yet," she said ith a gentle smile as ten minutes passed. But when nother five had flown, Victor's voice called firmly, *Mes amis!"*

For one splitting instant of shock, Meg realized she asn't dressed for this meeting. Hugging close beside alph to bask in his illustrious company, she scolded erself with reminders that there were many ladylike ays she would have to acquire if she intended to go bout in fine circles and make the connections she eeded for Dick.

Yet the noblewoman who greeted them, Marie ecile Varéson, the Comtesse du Beauharvais, gave leg no cause for self-consciousness. A small but ivacious woman, grown too thin and obviously well ast her prime, greeted them in the French fashion, ith her hands on both their shoulders and a kiss on ach cheek, as Victor introduced Tom, Ned, and Meg. ven Ralph seemed subdued before her in his haughty ay, bending to the little face framed in its black vel-et hood fastened by a knot of ribbons at the chin nd with white frills of lace around the cheeks. A atching black velvet cape, protecting the narrow ut still straight shoulders from draft, opened into a uaint white dress trimmed with ruffles.

Meg thought that Madame la Comtesse would cry ad there been tears left in her to shed. Her once-arkling blue eyes had faded to a fainter hue. The lotches of red veins that crept through her cheeks vealed the stress of weary years she had endured id the changes in circumstance that had wasted her. ie could not be more than fifty.

"Mais non," she was laughing at Victor in respons to his question. "We do not inhabit the whole of th house any longer. The Consul would never agree t such a thing. Times are very different, my son. W have now what is called the egalitarian style, and a sorts of social classes live in the same building t gether. Even this, that used to be your father's . . . Her voice trailed away with memory but returne instantly to the present. "The tradesmen occupy sho on the street level. The rich, as we used to be, on th *premier*. The well-to-do, one flight over us on the se ond. Then those who have a salary, on the thir Working people are on the fourth. And, oh, the poo They are in the upper stories. Come. We will go up t your home, Victor." She turned and smiled at th others. "To all of your homes."

Meg, learning that most of the houses had no ba steps, climbed a staircase as dirty as the one she h left at home, for everyone went up and down this san way, which no one bothered to keep in good repai The littered steps were like an alley, a filthy stre that went vertically instead of horizontally. She beg to feel a certain ease with everything, for it was n so different, certainly not regal as she had expecte

The landing passed directly into a large roo flagged in black and white with a carved table set that might have been for dining. Yet the room, wi its pillars and nooks and gilded chairs and huge mi rors, seemed more of an antechamber, which, in tur opened into a drawing room beyond.

"You have done it over very differently," sa Victor, his voice hollow, face vacant in this shock meeting. His eyes shone with the longing to ask f news of times gone by, but the strength to form th words could not be rallied, and he settled, from tin to time, for merely gazing at the old lady in her clo whom he hardly seemed to recognize as the san woman he had left.

She, in her turn, would spontaneously hug her s with a sigh, yielding to the indulgence, staring at h hair and his shoulders and his lanky legs as thou taking inventory of all the pieces she had sent away to see if they were still in good repair. Satisfied with this, she would yet return to it again and again, to check one more time, unable to believe or trust that fate had been this good to her at last.

"You must understand, my son, that we are living in times of pure classical confusions." She laughed slightly at the absurd state of affairs but was content to demonstrate she was one of the modern faithful.

They followed her invitation to view the lion heads and griffins with clenched talons that supported tables, the gilt motifs of Victory with crowns and trophies, the mythic animals glowering over swollen, proud, defiant breasts.

"This is the furniture of fashion," said the comtesse, "and even the poorest have it in some way. Walk yourself into the home of any *cocotte* and there you shall see it, too. But you must be starving and quite worn from your journey. And here I stand talking." She shook her peppery ringlets, which bounced on a brow of transparent skin. "But, of course, cooking, too, has degenerated terribly."

No one wanted to interrupt Madame or Victor in their intimate verbal forays that must take the place of heartfelt worlds they had lost, never to regain. Yet Ralph, growing restless under the veils of sentimentality, said in his mildest manner, "Madame la Comtesse, shall we dine out at one of the new places, Beauvillers perhaps?"

"Ah, Ralph. Dear Ralph," she replied with a kindly smile. "It is *citizeness,* no longer *comtesse.* And shall I not give you a cup of strawberry coffee before we go anywhere? I will send it to your rooms while you change. And do not think of telling me you intend to stay at a hotel. I won't hear of it. We have ample wardrobes of clothing for all. To begin with, there is my daughter's husband, le chevalier, who left dozens of fine costumes behind him that will fit and, I can assure you, are in the height of fashion."

"But where has he gone?" said Victor. "You wrote me nothing of it."

"America. Yes, America," she said to his surprise. "One hesitates to write of political matters in these times, but nevertheless it is so. The chevalier has some diplomatic involvement concerning the Louisiana Purchase. You know that Napoleon is the *bête noire* of Americans, and one needs to handle them with care." She turned to Meg. "As for you, my darling child, since my own Elise has gone off to New York, heaven defend her, you must take her place in my heart." She squeezed Meg's hand with warm affection for Ralph's chosen love. "Pretty thing. So very pretty. I can see that Ralph will never part from you, and he has good cause! Come. We will go together to Elise's bedroom, and I shall show you how young Parisian ladies turn themselves out."

Meg's heart pounded with elation at this strange good fortune coming her way, as though the powers of fate were massing to give her the allies and opportunities she needed for finding and helping Dick. She touched the woman's wrists and kissed the fingers impulsively with the heat of sincere affection. "My own mother is gone these many years," she whispered fetchingly. "Since I was a child, I have known no maternal love."

"Dear me." The comtesse smiled, flattered, and patted Meg's cheek. "But let us try to find some hot water in this dreadful situation. Napoleon is frugal and doesn't seem to mind the lack of amenities so long as there are logs for his fire. Whenever one sees him at home, he is standing there handling the tongs. But we will have a roar aglow in my daughter's room for you. And yes, you shall be my second child always." She stood then, her limpid eyes radiating affection for young people, and indicated that everyone would be accommodated likewise. "Victor, you know where your room is. That much I have kept safe for you, thank heaven. Take your friends along. The servants, what remains of them at any rate, will give you everything." Then, touching Meg's elbow, "Child, you come with me."

Without flashing so much as a glance at Ralph for

ermission, Meg went along with her new mentor, onfident that Ralph could not challenge the hier-rchy in this house. Later he might complain that she ad deserted him, but she could defend herself at at time. Building in her heart was another, more owerful strategy that she could not resist attempting. the old woman could be won over totally, as it emed, then there were other supports, other friends f this noble relic whom she could also charm and se-ure to her side. No longer would she have to cajole alph for entree into the social circle she sought. Here was, in the hands of this lovely and generous *maman,* ho seemed delighted to please where she could.

The bedrooms lay at the rear of the apartment, nd with a ripple of annoyance Meg saw that they ere interdependent. While the comtesse chattered way about her daughter, the comforts of a draped ondola bed, politics, the United States, the marble replace and neo-Greek cornices, she listened to hear ho was directly next door to her room.

"But you young folk have come to Paris for a good me, and I am going on about world affairs! Believe e, you will find entertainments and amusements to our heart's desire. Napoleon himself is a veritable partan, but the rest of us manage. Here. Let me show ou the bathroom. A horrible little cubbyhole, to be ire. The lighting and water supply are not the most xurious, I am sorry to say. This is the basin and the ater jug." She smiled at Meg dutifully peeking behind e wall press. "And as for that other place, it is on e half-landing outside. But my Elise was too delicate d could not withstand such a lack of intimacy for at operation. And so we have, for emergencies, put this chair."

Meg took rapid inventory of her surroundings, so nate and inefficient. *This is how the French live in eir grand, revolutionized condition.* She felt certain at Dick had laughed to himself about it, too.

"I am delighted with everything, *Maman,*" she said eerily. "Is that Ralph you have placed next door?"

The velvet bonnet nodded and the eyelids crinkled

with the mischievous remnants of a gay and dissipate youth. "Should not lovers be close enough to hol hands when they wish? In my time we had no restric tions upon love. The king understood human natur and himself led the way. But Josephine and Napoleon What a couple! She agrees to everything as though sh had no mind of her own, and *he* is only too pleased t advise men that their wives are chattel. Females hav less and less to say about their own destiny and ar turned into brood mares." She twinkled and waved he narrow fingers. "What goes on behind closed door however, Napoleon need never hear of." She was a the closet, feeling through a line of diaphanous dresse "I see you do not paint your face very much. It is th fashion in this country to go at it heavily. And i Ralph looks at other women—I mean for the novelty my dear—why, you can bring him right back in lin with your new, French vermeil cheeks. I have every thing to help you."

"Ralph may need a rest from me," Meg sighe roundly, hoping to keep the woman's passion for in trigue at bay and to steer her in another direction en tirely.

"Heavens, child. What an idea!"

"But he is so easily amused by others, *Maman.* fear hanging on to his coattails and becoming a borin lump of baggage."

The comtesse laughed affectionately as though at baby's first steps. "You do not see him with the eye of an observer. I have watched him all the while w were in the drawing room. He does not take his eye from you. He *devours* you with every breath. I swea to you, with the heart of an old woman who has see many *amours* in her time, that your Ralph is secured.

"You know him so much better than I. I must be lieve you," Meg continued with reluctant submissio "Still, if he cares for me so dearly as you say, wh does he not want to help me?" She went quickly to th woman's side and squeezed her arm. "People who car for each other *do* help each other, isn't that so?"

"Well, certainly. Certainly." She kissed Meg's fore

head with puzzled reassurance. "In what way is he blameworthy?"

"Oh, it may sound foolish to you and trivial, but there it is. I have a cousin. An artist. A fine painter, truly. His name is Dick Fox, and I am *very* ambitious for his career, you see. Our mothers were so close, I feel that Dick is my very own brother."

"Your mothers were close?"

"Before they died, that is."

"I see."

"He is in Paris now."

"Fox? I have never heard of him. Do you know whose salon he attends?"

"Have artists entree to salons in Paris?" Meg quivered, coming alive.

"Mais oui. Certainement. Whoever has a particular merit or métier is actively sought after. You have lost track of him, I take it?"

"That is my problem exactly," Meg said with the resonance of actual fact. "And I can see in your kind face that you will ask your friends about him?"

The comtesse studied her for a long moment from the distance of years and experience. Meg felt something more intelligent, something less easily beguiled, than she had realized. What responded to her was no blundering victim of deception but a silent *conspiratrice* in the deepest, most feminine sense. Without a word of explanation on the subject passing between them, Madame understood the complete truth. And seemed relieved! As if to say; Never refuse any man; though nine out of ten should care nothing for you, that tenth may prove to be a useful friend.

Footsteps in the room next door moved quickly, reminding them that they dawdled.

"Ralph's mother and I were like two sisters, too, before the war," the comtesse continued, changing her tack as she extracted, in a more businesslike fashion, a pale green dress with a gold-edged train and held it up to Meg for approval. "This color becomes you. My daughter's hair is black, and she has blue eyes just like Victor. Would you like to see? Here is her miniature portrait."

Meg examined a tiny oval painting, a replica of the comtesse in charming, open sweetness and simple beauty, but unlined and unscathed still. "Why, this is you!"

"My sweet Elise is very like me, but she has more the winning disposition of her father. And yours is not unlike hers. This gown goes so beautifully with your hair, too. Once you have bathed and changed, I am sure you will find her wardrobe to your liking."

In less than two hours, Meg stood before one of the room's huge mirrors, admiring herself freely and with awe. The woman reflected back at her had grace and real taste for the first time in her life, as though she had taken on Elise's style along with the clothes. The waist, very high up beneath her breasts, fell in an easy line, and the short puffed sleeves revealed the rounded youthfulness of her arms. She had never been aware of youth or age, for in her harsh world they had both seemed equally dismal. Now, clean and dressed, the differences were astonishing. The tunic behind, falling straight, outlined and shaped her slender form without brashly emphasizing the charms and promise beneath. Her skin, flushed from a beguiling sense of power, was toned down by the application of white substance and the lips heightened with cherry red. At the same moment, the comtesse was fussing with the hair style, fixing small ringlets over the forehead and holding them in place with a ribbon of dark sea-green that brought Meg's gray eyes forward with dazzling lights.

"What a pleasure the new styles are," said the comtesse. "In my day dancing was a form of torture with the narrow heels we wore, three inches high that kept the foot always stiff on tiptoe, as though reaching for a book on the highest shelf in the library. And there was a stiff pannier of heavy whalebone spreading out on either side. The hair was dressed at least a foot tall and sprinkled with a pound of powder and pomade, which the slightest movement shook down upon the shoulders, and on top of that, a pouf on which we piled feathers, flowers, and diamonds pell-mell. But today it is so different, so beautiful. I would like you to wear this little dagger in your curls," she said with bland expertise. "It has just a few tiny gem-stones that will give you the right *je ne sais quoi* to balance that interesting red sash you seem attached to." She fixed the diamond pin into the crown of Meg's shining hair.

"Will I do?" breathed Meg.

"It seems yes."

For all the finesse and modesty of the understatement, both women explored the results of their combined handiwork and stood transfixed by the result.

"You shall go into the salons, my dear, and meet everyone." The comtesse nodded with delight. "They will take you into their hearts and love you instantly. And if Ralph looks jealous at your celebrity, you will have that to cope with, but not to blame your old *maman*, eh?"

Speechless, Meg swung around and hugged her dear, understanding friend, rapidly blinking away any moisture from touching the delicate old neck.

Chapter Fifteen

NED AND TOM HAD COME TO DANCE, gamble at *biribiri*, walk abroad with the *girls of joy*, and lose themselves in the rakehell sports of the new Paris. After some days of paying their dues to Madame's hospitality, they went off with Victor as their host. Soon they were seen no more in the household but only heard floundering up the staircase in the early hours of the morning. No comment passed upon their behavior. The comtesse, who was urbanely beyond taking notice, merely continued to have their rooms always ready when they returned.

Meg soon discovered, however, that the Comtesse du Beauharvais was distinguished not only by a love for youth but also by an infirmity of forgetfulness the results of which were sometimes bizarre. It would often happen that promises to attend a Wednesday afternoon at-home with the Marchionesse de B. would become, in the old lady's mind, an invitation to the Monday supper at Madame L.'s. Of course, everyone welcomed the comtesse wherever she arrived, with or without an invitation, and Meg herself soon became a source of notoriety as the companion taking the place of the daughter, Elise. Curious eyes turned to her. The benevolent despots in their transparent tunics tried to uncover her habits and past life. Some took seriously this competition from across the Channel and cast a dim view upon inviting a mere girl to serious dinners mostly comprised of men, wherein the danger lay that the conversation could be diverted from political topics to herself. Meg realized where her sole source of support rested and remained close to Madame's side when she could, but inevitably, there was dancing in the drawing rooms. The long minuet and gavotte were rising beyond the level of an art form, addling the brains of her transported partners, while Ralph watched moodily from his chair, sulking over what she could not hope to guess, and steadfastly refusing to participate.

During chatty interludes, she would make certain to smile at him encouragingly, signaling with her eyes that she yearned to have him join her in the dance. A new, partnered affair called the valtz had just been imported from Germany, and especially then, as she whirled with a man's arm around her waist, did she glimpse Ralph's dark look, as though uncovering her in some disgusting tryst. *If I am fortunate, he will kill himself with jealousy,* she thought, but could not really spend too much time upon the matter when French men were so busy impressing her with their bbons from the wars. They were a strange lot, these w citizens, in their rumpled, ill-fitting jackets with ge mutton sleeves and many creases down the back; e rage of fashion. They seemed deranged characters ho had slept in their clothes, yet were men of sub-ance, wealth, and connection.

"And are you interested in art, monsieur?" would her opening to communication while the *chef 'orchestre* raised his baton for the bolero.

Thus she drifted from man to man as they said s or no, wending an intricate path to those who ight lead her to Dick.

Then Ralph would come trotting like a wolf from is corner at just the wrong moment and dance her off a hard, possessive embrace.

"You are smiling too much at too many strangers." is voice was gentle as a snake, and as poisonous.

"I am being friendly to the friends of la comtesse," e objected with offended innocence. "I can't see hat troubles you."

"No, dear. You are acting like a whore."

"I haven't touched a soul."

"But who *hasn't* touched you!"

"That is because *you* do not dress me and *you* do ot take me about. You leave it all to Madame. Why, am reduced to wearing a second-hand wardrobe every ight of the week. I look to *you* to take care of me and onor me . . . as I do you. This is not London, after l. Social barriers are gone. You can be proud to be en with me, as others are."

"Others? These financiers in control of all the money e scum. They may occupy the finest houses, but they rtainly don't know how to bring people together. hese so-called parties are pigpens. Look at those fat llies gorging themselves. *Nouveaux riches.* They ink luxury is good taste and high living is *savoir-vre.*"

Meg saw the bluish veins pulsing in his temple and alized she had overstepped the mark by doing noth-g more than having allowed herself to be attentive others.

"I tell you, everyone thinks you are a whore," h repeated, burning with humiliation.

Suddenly frightened that he might act upon a whin to betray her to the legal authorities or perhaps some thing even worse, Meg raised herself onto the tiptoe of her buskins. "But, darling," she whispered into hi ear, "so I am. And don't you love me for it? Wha prudish woman of *this* regime would allow hersel to be tongue-lashed by anyone save her husband, an perhaps not even he?" Then, smiling discreetly at couple dancing past, "Good evening, Madame T. . . How are you this evening, Monsieur Y."

"You ruin me," Ralph growled with helpless lus "You explode my brain. I don't know what to mak of you. Other women fall madly in love with the me of their choice or with wealth. But you seem entirel free from either vice. Still, you are not cold. You passion for love is as inexhaustible as my own. Me Meg. You *will* love me. I will *make* you love me. Ye I will force it from you. . . . Does that sound lik madness? Perhaps. But then I am mad. And my wi is stronger than yours, count on it."

His softly spoken words were like underground ex plosions that rocked her with a deafening threat th she knew he must fulfill. Ralph had no other cours than to keep what he wanted enslaved. She dance easily with him, pretending not to be shaken by th crazed creature who had finally come out of th shadow and declared his intent. Too late, she realize she had gone too far, stretching his preoccupatio with her to the breaking point.

"But yet," he murmured, "you *are* ravishing. Ra ishing and mine. It is no fun to lock you away whe other men cannot see you and lust for you. Yes. will buy you the gowns you want. And jewels to g with the costumes. I shall take you to every ball th is given and show you off. You will flirt with th others. You will turn them into jelly while I watc The frustration of strange men amuses me. Perhap if there are one or two lurking about whom I thin sensitive and sympathetic, we shall have a merry g t it all together. I have brought you here for fun, ınd fun we shall have, eh, Meg? Eh?"

His arm jerked around her waist, squeezing the reath from her ribs in a violent assertion of his su-remacy. She looked up to see that spittle had gathered t the corners of his mouth and hung there in bubbles. he felt a flush of revulsion at what he could do if hurned up. Then above that fear rose her expectation f socializing at many different events. She had so ttle time, after all. How long before this unsteady nind would decide he had had enough of Paris and vant to return home?

"Can you really show me fun, Ralph?" she whee-dled.

Immediately challenged, he arranged for la comtesse o be escorted and left early with Meg, haranguing er in the carriage, for once begun he could not control imself to stop. "Every night I have lain in my bed and stened to you breathing. I sent you messages through he wall to come to me, but you disobeyed them."

"Messages," she said, wondering what fantasy she vould have to deal with now.

"Messages from my brain to yours. Of *course* you eard. How could you resist them? But then again, ou were probably thinking about your *cousin*." His oice curled acidly. "Whenever I hear you talking with a comtesse in the privacy of your room, you are jab-ering about art. *Art*. And what do you know about rt, my sweet mongrel?"

She had to calm him, stop him before the words red into something more violent. She lifted the tunic f her dress and draped it lightly, with flagrant dis-nissal of his ravings, over his hands.

"Now hush!" she commanded. "You are my little oy and you must stop being naughty!" She spoke and cted without a plan but from a strange, fresh instinct or what to do, even though a relationship of this na-ure with Ralph had never occurred between them efore.

His eyes narrowed and the lids began to quiver. Little boy? Little boy?"

She watched him wrestling to resist her. "Litt boy," she repeated, pursing her lips and extendin them to kiss the smirk on his mouth. The moment sh touched him he gave way before her, and she kne she had the magic secret! This fiend, this possessi and sadistic madman, craved domination. Like a chil he needed to be reassured of the safety of his cradl And her bosom was that very cradle. She pulled hi to her and held him in her arms, rocking him with t sway of the carriage.

"You must be good, you must be good, Ralphie she cooed. "It is late and we have both had a goo deal too much of the rack punch. When we get hom I will change my clothing and come into your roor Then I will lie beside you on your bed and hug yo and we'll make love. Won't you like that?" She strok his damp forehead and paused to let the rascal drea in the dark, solitary depths of his imagination. B she could feel him waiting upon her, demanding her go on. "And while we hug each other I will slowly ki you. Kiss you all over. Everywhere. And my body w dance on yours, exotically, as no man has ever felt before."

He began to chortle with satisfaction. She felt t tension ease from his embrace. He lay more quietl his head heavy between her breasts, twisting fro time to time to thrust a lick of his rough, hot tong into her cleavage. She glanced down at the swell of h tender flesh, wondering with a wistful ache how long would be before the *one* beloved head would lie upo her. When would the raven-haired pirate come to h and hold her and kiss her . . . when?

The carriage drew up to the house, bathed in sliver of moonlight, dark-windowed, the cannon-fi holes from the Reign of Terror resembling shadow scars. She had to force Ralph, unwilling to sit up, o and toward the hallway, each step he took hesitati and swaying, drugged not by liquor but by the va drain of his endless mania. She went behind him, pus ing him when need be, supporting him, playing moth to the vagrant child, hating it and at the same time a nost happy that she had found some workable chink n his amazing armor. Tonight, face it, she would have o give him his money's worth if she intended to con- inue, unconfined, her own searches. How strange it vas, being the aggressor, and yet she had always cnown that with Ralph it would come to this.

He had fallen asleep before she entered his room. Yet as she came to him she sensed that it was the sleep of a convict waiting for the guillotine; a light, nervous leep that saw what went on around him. She stood over him in a shaft of moonlight paling through a space n the ample drapery and listened to his riffling snore. A dank coldness lay upon the air, for the thick walls effectively kept out any touch of springtime. On the bed table, the mess of his bottles and creams lay in heir usual confusion. To one who did not know better, t would seem she had the choice of remaining or walking out.

"So, Meg, are you eager?" he asked directly out of his sleep, sensing her presence and instantly awaken- ing.

His hand sprang out and grabbed her around the knees. She buckled and fell forward, twisting to land on top of him, and heard the breath huff out of his lungs.

She ran her fingers through his sticky hair growing thinner by the day from the health applications he rubbed into his scalp. The smell of wine hung in the olds of his long nightshirt that had crept above his oins.

She snuggled beside him, wondering how a mother nakes love to her child. She recalled the crowded beds of her own childhood, the multitude of wretched hands groping and feeling, the starving, frigid bodies squirm- ng like coils of worms to find warmth in the heap. All he desperate ploys to survive, which she had learned before her thirteenth year, now came to her aid. From he necessity of this moment, she became efficient in her recall, wiggling against him, turning him to face her with the strength of arm equal to a man's. She was confident of her game, and her single-minded advances convinced him totally as he crept to her bosom and cuddled down, suckling first at one breast and then the other with tiny, happy burbles.

"I didn't do it," he snuffled suddenly against he flesh. "I didn't! Even though I wanted to!" he cried i the voice of confession.

"Of course you didn't, my baby. Tell me about it."

"I didn't pray God they should die. Only once o twice. And I didn't know that God would answer me."

"Of course you didn't," she repeated soothingly, an cradled his grieving shoulders. "Everything's fine. N one wants to punish you. You're not responsible. I isn't your fault."

"No, it isn't my fault," he sobbed, "that God obey me. *You* understand." He settled down lower, pressin his cheek to her belly and kissing it passionately. "N one else understands me as you do. Because you, too are wicked, wicked, wicked." He sucked joy from th word and kept repeating it as his mouth searche lower along the curve of her stomach into the fin fringe of damp curls below.

She had to pretend that she loved what he did, tha she desired him tangled in his sweaty nightshirt an shaking like a beaten calf. He might be playing th child, but the adult side of his mind would quickl know, when he found her dry, that she wasn't partic pating in the proper spirit. *Oh, Dick. Dick.* The ol supports, the standby recollections came rushing up a her summons. It seemed to her years had passed when it was only weeks. A month or two. How coul she keep track? Then she wondered if Mrs. Bannis had got some word from him. Did she sit with a lette . . . not knowing where to find her? Had Dick ser home pictures to Feargus with directions and explana tions for *her,* not knowing that this very night only few miles separated them? The tortured agony c frustration, the need to cry out, to grind her teeth she released at the same time that Ralph dived. Sh felt the press of his cold ears against her thighs.

He blubbered there, still talking, still admitting al while he swayed and clung to her hips, digging hi nails into her flesh and kicking his toes into the mattress, driven by his painful, drudging passion that could not say quits.

Dismissing him, it was easy now to imagine herself elsewhere, blown by the wind over the Paris rooftops and fluttering down into some garret, some hectic apartment surrounded by papers and sketch things and that strong, pungent scent of turpentine mixes.

"Oh . . . oh . . . you must find me," she cried hoarsely to Dick. "Here I am . . . here . . ."

Gurgling sounds were her only reply as hunching hindquarters loomed in the darkness tinged by the ruddy glow of the fire.

Starved, insatiable, Ralph played with his own wicked memories as much as with her, dragging out scenes of other days, reliving, through desire and those bewildered, childish imaginings, all the haunted, unanswered questions that pursued him still.

He did not need to penetrate her tonight but merely to slip his maleness between her legs and have her close them upon him. There were syllables mumbled about not making someone with child, and of spilling his semen upon the waters . . . a further confusion of adventures in his tumbled bag of recollections. Yet even after she felt the spill of his hot seed, he did not want her to leave him. She remained there patiently while he whimpered and called out names she had never heard of and suckled her earlobe; finally he lay quiet while she rocked him to sleep.

Meg knew she would live to regret it.

She had wanted no part, really, of any intimacy with Ralph that was meaningful. But too late. The episode of mother with son released a sluice of guilty secrets that made him her ardent slave. He did not show this openly, of course, but his obvious tricks to brush away the night's occurrence were rendered too intensely.

"You shall have your gowns," he said at coffee the next morning. "And you shall have hats and baubles. You shall have cloaks of lynx and silk-embroidered

shawls. And I shall buy you garnets for a king's ran
som."

Even the Comtesse, who was accustomed to ever
sort of outburst, looked at him askance. "This sound
to me like love in the old style." She beamed throug
a fringe of gray ringlets.

"Render to Caesar that which is Caesar's," boome
Ralph, aglow with mystery and hidden meaning.

"And what is Caesar's?" said Meg later on as the
sauntered near the Palais Royal among the *incroyable*
in their long-footed boots, strangling cravats, and coif
fures springing skyward in disarray.

"Meg is Caesar's," replied Ralph sunnily, bowin
to a *merveille* simpering along with a waistline up t
her armpits and the rest revealed by a dusting of gauz

In daylight, on foot, the society of Paris was a fan
tastic sideshow of strange disguises in which th
beaux of fashion shuffled, bent over, chests caving i
and shoulders sunken, intent on looking older, every
thing contrary to the wigs and youthful elegance o
the king's time gone by. The incoherence and ec
centricities that passed for beauty were here and ther
relieved by elegant Britons or by those Frenchme
seized by an Anglomania that made them dress lik
rich London aldermen. Meg, gazing upon the crow
hearing herself talked of as Ralph's *possession,* fe
herself spinning upside down in the center of som
mad dream.

"We will set Meg upon a pedestal, for all men t
yearn after . . . and none to possess."

"None shall have me, indeed," Meg replied as the
turned into a milliner's shop and then a jeweler's. Sh
was already thinking ahead to the aristocratic drawin
room where they were invited this evening for
private supper given by Denis Honoré Clermont, th
Duc de Beauclew—Ralph's uncle, and a very dea
friend to the Comtesse.

The dainty hat with its high feather swayed roma
tically, and the treasure of garnets twinkled in a circl
around her arm as Meg climbed the steps to the smal

select gathering on the Faubourg Saint-Germain, the last stronghold of the Royalist elite. A stooped-over servant, dressed in livery forbidden since the revolution, opened the door with a rickety hand, but Meg somehow felt he must be respected, since he had lived so many years in such fine company. A dozen gentle souls were playing charades, and others had organized a tussle between two pug dogs chasing each other around a pie baked in the shape of a castle. The room seemed a model of virtue and the ancient, slender duc who kissed her hand its standard bearer, well kept, sane, and very old France in black shoes, black silk stockings, black velvet suit, and trim, curled white wig. It was all quite charming, brilliant in a quiet way, certainly exclusive. At another time she would consider this the conquest of her life.

The duc, in turn, seemed taken by her, as though they already knew each other well. Meg surmised that he had had an advance report, and she hoped it was from the comtesse, rather than Ralph; she felt upon her the surveillance of intelligent but retiring brown eyes that held honor in graver esteem than mere aristocracy. The nobleman's face, with its frank but polite expression, seemed ready to praise grandeur of spirit as well as the good or the beautiful. He strolled beside her with a certainty of breeding and education that fortified him against changes of estate, setting him apart from human vicissitudes of fallen fortunes.

Meg, impelled to trust him with her secrets, responded by looking around the walls, expecting to discover there the reflection of the highest taste and culture that would lead to important conversation. But finding them strikingly bare of ornament, she blurted, "Monsieur le Duc, do you not care for art?"

Behind her Ralph coughed nervously, which she ignored.

"Ah. You are looking at my naked habitation," he said, aware of both merits and defects. "The pure fact is, my dear, I love art. But these houses have been cannibalized, as you know. The furniture has been taken and sold, the pictures have been sold, the footpaths have been sold, the trees and the Church and the property of the *commune* have all been sold." He spoke half laughingly, with an elegant sadness of *noblesse*. "But wine we still have aplenty. May I offer you a glass?"

When she had settled beside a vase of daisies in the anteroom, the old man seemed intent on pursuing her in conversation. "Are you not the young Englishwoman who has come home with Victor? La comtesse has told us some marvelous stories about you." He twinkled with the undercurrent of a silent message. "I understand you have a great passion for painting, but that you may need means other than social connections to find what you seek."

"Yes, that is certainly so," Meg replied with enthusiasm and an optimistic tilt to her chin. The comtesse had been as good as her word, somehow remembering to inquire for Dick and at the same time cautioning people not to approach that part of the subject directly, at least not in public.

"In that case, my dear, you must allow me to introduce you to Citoyen Murier."

A flotilla of bellies jiggled toward her at the mention of the name, all wrapped in citron-colored sashes.

"Ah, there you are, Hugo. You must tell Mademoiselle Watkins about the new Louvre, eh, *mon ami?*"

"And so I shall," replied Murier kindly, wiggling his fine mustachios beneath a mobile lump of nose and wheezing down close beside Meg on the iron settee.

"You are obviously a man of the people," Meg began, watching the duc retire, not quite certain how to approach this vast creature in his silks and medals, yet aware of how important it was to speak directly but beyond Ralph's hearing. Such a thing looked nigh impossible with Ralph right there, posing near the hearth, legs akimbo, gazing alternately from the flame to her while apparently in conversation with some deposed *princesse* who enjoyed the company of suave British peers.

"Yes. A man of the people," replied Murier with gusto. "A man of the army, of celebrations, of ceremonies. A man who knows things and can find out more. A man who has chronicled the works of art that the Consul carries home with him from all over the world. What can I tell you, my dear?" He spoke in a soft, raspy voice, as though afraid a more normal register would shatter the fragile thing entrusted to his care.

"It is so warm this close to the fire. Shall we stroll a bit?" Meg asked innocently, blinking into his round, gullible-seeming eyes that shone like a deer.

"It would delight me."

The apartment, though harshly bereft of its former possessions, rambled from room to room, and Meg kept going until she found a corner in which she could pause safely and also peer out behind Murier for Ralph's approach.

"My dear *citoyen,"* she began, not knowing how else to address him. "I am in dire need of friends." She spoke, part smiling, part serious, part flirtatious, vibrating her silk fan tremulously at her cheek.

"Am I not your friend?"

"Indeed. The duc recommends you and I trust you with all my heart . . . would trust you with more if only you could help me."

Murier's soft jaw slid open. He dared not believe what was obliquely being offered to him. "How can I help you? You who have everyone as your ally, la comtesse, le duc . . ."

"I am looking for my cousin," she replied hastily, touching his hand with the closed fan tip and tracing a line to the thumb. "My cousin Dick Fox. He is a painter. A painter of fine, fine pictures."

"Do you not have his address?"

"No word of him at all."

"But that is not so unusual in these times. Things are confusing in Paris. What you need, perhaps, is le prefect of police. I know him well."

"Oh, no, no. It must not come to that! And besides, my privacy would be violated. Privacy is everything, you understand."

A search for a lover, his eyes confirmed. "Yes." He

patted her fan lingeringly. "We Frenchmen understand the heart."

"If you could think over how you might help me, I would find a way to come to your apartment and talk about it at length." She spoke hastily but huskily, so that he could not mistake what she was prepared to pay for the information.

Murier rose and backed off, shaken, determined, and astounded by the sudden appearance of such fortune. "I shall certainly see what can be done for your assistance, mademoiselle."

At that instant, Ralph appeared in the doorway. He rapidly took them in but found no evidence from which to conclude betrayal.

"What are you doing to these creatures?" Ralph laughed with a serious edge, watching the rear of Murier depart.

"Dazzling them," she replied airily. "Just as you said I would."

"And that is all?"

"What can I do standing up," she replied snippishly, "and with six feet of space between us?"

She proceeded from party to party, from field marshals to highnesses, from concerts to pastoral ballets, meeting members of the *ancien régime,* officers of Napoleon's entourage, and vulgar, successful bourgeoisie. She danced in the drawing rooms and dawdled continually, wherever there was some possible protection of shadow, always asking the same question while touching a palm provocatively or pressing a silken sleeve. Week after week she sprinkled her inquiries, only to watch them sink beneath a surface of silence from eager men who would have slain themselves to help her. On nights when Ralph in his drunkenness left her alone, or after she had consoled him in some weary, demented fashion, she peered at herself in the mirror, unable to sleep, and asked herself, "What else can I do? To whom can I turn?" And finally was forced to conclude: "He has disappeared."

Chapter Sixteen

MEG STOOD listlessly at the dressmaker's, 89 Rue de la Loi, examining a length of sequined tulle. The comtesse had come with her in place of Ralph, who lay home sleeping, and together they were attempting to decide upon the evolution of a summer style that would be eye-catching in the balcony box of the Opéra. The fitter, one of a numerous, well-paid staff, was just approaching with fresh instructions from the couturier, and Meg, feeling the weighty depression of her futile double life, took up a copy of the *Gazette* while the other two ladies lost themselves in swamps of detail about the gown. She read French just well enough to scan the news, but even she, an observer with no great political call, could see that the peace with England had developed into a flimsy, well-armed truce in the throes of being ruptured by one side or another every day. Flinging the paper open to see what the theater had to offer, she turned page after page until her eyes fell at random upon a cartoon of no great size or importance that caught her and shook her to the base of her spine and sent her tottering a few steps backward.

She carried the paper directly to the sunlit window and folded it to the drawing, bending her head down and drinking in the penciled profiles leering at each other with threats—a French hog and a British boar, the faces of Bonaparte and King George drawn in cleverly with a biting hand. Her eye for the sketch was unerring. Almost afraid to believe what she stared at, she searched the picture for the artist's name and found: REYNARD.

A familiar, scorching heat lifted into her cheeks and forehead. She closed the paper protectively to hide what she had discovered and stumbled over to the others, clearing her throat in an agitation that turned them immediately to face her with questioning glances of concern.

"Where is this newspaper printed?" she demanded of both startled women. "I must know and quickly."

"Let us look into it," said the comtesse anxiously, without intruding any questions of her own.

The address was simply arrived at by reading an inside column, and had Meg been calmer, she could have reached the offices of the publication in less than half an hour. The fumbling, however, took up an extra fifteen minutes, and then she insisted upon traveling by herself in a hired cabriolet.

"You mustn't go about alone in this city. It is forbidden. I, as your guardian here, will accompany you."

"Oh, *Maman!* I cannot have it," she cried. "This is such a struggle for me, and I must do it myself, in my way." She begged openly, forgetting the lack of visa in her bag, thoughts already leaping ahead to uncover the fox in his lair, some cluttered hovel that would shock the comtesse to the bone.

She left the woman hastily without having gained her permission, and holding the tulle for the forgotten dress to attend the forgotten play.

The inky smell of the *Gazette* offices reminded Meg of Feargus in his attic, but she had the confidence now of a real lady in society as she stormed in, shockingly direct, proceeding to the first man she saw who seemed to be in authority behind a desk.

"But, mademoiselle, how can you insist?" He rattled the newspaper thrust at him. "How can I know who he is if I do not know who he is? There are many hack artists who send their work to us in hope of earning a few francs. Times are difficult. Newspapers are shut down every day by the Consul. *Oui*. I see his name is Reynard. Fox. Whatever you say." He squinted at the paper. "Well, this Reynard is lucky, that's all. I tell you he is no regular here."

Meg, colder now and steady, brushed past him, calling, "Who is really in charge? Where do I find the gentleman in charge? The publisher."

"The publisher will not know these things," whined the man behind her. "The publisher knows less than I, the editor, about journalists."

At a worktable at the far end of the room stood a man in a leathern apron with tousled hair and small spectacles, cheeks faded from lack of daylight, bent over and wiping on his shirt sleeve inky prints from his fingers. He approached Meg with a deliberate step.

"Pardon, pardon, mademoiselle. I could not help overhearing your problem. This Reynard. May I see the picture, please?"

"Of *course* you know him," she encouraged, thrusting the paper under his nose. "I am sure you know him. He is an Englishman. Very tall and lean. Blue-black hair. Dark-complected. A scar that goes across his left eyebrow like this." She moved her forefinger through her own brow. "Dick Fox. Dick Fox. Fox. *Reynard.* You understand?"

The pale man breathed heavily a few times and stared blankly off into space. "Reynard . . . Fox . . ." He studied the picture again. "Perhaps he is the one in the English coat?" he suggested to the editor. "Yes. The one in the short black coat."

"I'm sorry. I don't believe so," replied the other impatiently. "Besides, I don't remember him at all."

"I am sure of it now, I think." He hummed contemplatively a few times, each more strongly than the last. "Would you like to try, mademoiselle? I am not truly certain. But I can find his address for you, and you can call there and see if I am right."

"You would not forget him once you saw him, I know it," Meg cried eagerly.

He lowered his spectacles and smiled over them with a pleasant, subtle understanding. "I am sure I do not forget him."

He scribbled the address. Meg snatched it from his hand, dropping some coins of gratitude into his palm, and raced back to the cabriolet, singing to herself nervously, staring at the scrawled number almost incomprehensible on the dirty scrap, yet shining out clear as night stars.

In the cab she still clutched the paper, as though already clutching the man, unconcerned that she would have to take a ferry across the Seine. The horse seemed desperately slow, the traffic unusually thick. She called up to the driver once, then twice, to warn him that she was in a hurry and would pay double for rapid service.

The driver, acknowledging her fine appearance and her distress, tipped his hat to her and pointed with his whip to the acres of carriages crossing before them, the alleyways and narrow streets, the pedestrians, the carts, the men on horseback, and every other obstacle that she had never noticed, which had fallen from heaven just five minutes before expressly to hinder her passage!

Meg pressed her fingers to her eyelids and then to her mouth, but there was no screaming fit inside. Only happiness springing up, and thankfulness and many swallows to keep her heart down inside the lofty *décolletage*. She could feel that it was summer already, and everything perfect in its heaven. *He will be home . . . he will be home,* she told herself with absolute rock-steady confidence, feeling that fate would not have given her this lead if it were not to be consummated.

She lived half her life over in the cab and finally arrived at another of the once-grand houses, gutted and gashed with cannon shot, the ironwork gate swinging off its hinges. She dashed down the dirt path, reminding herself with a sudden stab of harassing memory that Dick's habit on sunny days was *not* to be at home working but to be out of doors.

In the dirty hallway, she paused upon this thought, yet could not keep herself from flinging herself against this sudden prospect of defeat. With despair as high now as her spirits had been happy in the cab, she picked her way through the rubbish to the third story, ntent upon inquiring there where Citizen Reynard ived.

On the third floor, a little woman made a fist and ointed her thumb skyward.

On the fourth floor, another, smaller lady did the ame, but with less dignity and a certain amount of eproach.

Meg confronted the narrow, vertical alley of a stairvell. Somewhere here where she climbed lurked a eries of pigeonhole garrets with Dick in one of them. Vorking now on sheer intuition, pulled by an invisible ord that linked her to the source of her life, she chose scarred and ill-fitted door to rap upon with all her eart delivered through the sound of her knuckles.

For a breathless beat she hung suspended over a ottomless chasm of silence.

"No one is home. Go away!"

A great, collapsing relief weakened her. All smiles, he banged again urgently, with both fists now, calling ack at the familiar, irritable voice, "Dick! Dick, it's Meg!"

Another silence, longer than the first.

The door pulled swiftly inward. There he stood filling the space, skeptical, still irritated by the apparent ffect of some coincidence, a flannel cloth smeared vith paint colors hanging around his neck, and from here, naked to the stained gray trousers. Tousled, disracted as always, his gaze nevertheless cut down her vith its fine, bladelike edge.

"By God! It *is* you!" his voice crackled, delighted nd amazed.

"Darling. Yes. Yes," she cried, flinging herself at im, her arms around his waist, pressing her cheek to is chest. She had nothing more to say, nothing she vanted him to do, and hung on with all her might, earing that he would find a way to slither out no mater how tightly she held him, and content to die right ow at the peak of her excitement.

"Meg . . . You in Paris? . . . How did you manage t?" He pulled her into the room, shut the door, and tood her away from him, studying every inch of her, swiftly taking in the extensive lace trimmings, th fashionably painted mouth, the carefully coiffed ringlets with their jewels sparkling above the ribbons. "An aren't you grand?" he added, amused now with a pleasure that came to him easily, sweeping away his personal concerns while he concentrated on her pampered perfumed shoulders, her revealed bosom, her self possessed way of moving. "Well earned, I do no doubt," he concluded with a mischievous smirk tha took in the sash at her waist.

"You see, I brought your luck back to you," sh said, following his gaze. She ran her fingers through hi thick, damp hair, lifting the curls from his neck, watching them twist and twine, unkempt, around her nail Impulsively she kissed his chest again and laughed a the repeated imprint of her lips. "I don't want to hea anything," she murmured breathlessly. "Not a wor from you about me. Are *you* all right? Are you fed? She began to look around her at the cluttered garre with its tiny window flung wide, letting in a patch o bluish light but little air. Stacks and stacks of drawing in various stages of completion were piled everywhere standing up against the peeling walls near the fusilier' rifle and a pair of high French boots, on the tops o dressing tables, stored vertically behind a washbasi filled with brushes soaking in a muddy orange wate One limp shirt and a waistcoat lay across the lump unmade bed, and on the wall peg hung a voluminou skirt, gray and worn. *Of course he has a mistress,* sh thought instantly, without disapproval. Then, recallin how he had run away, she sprang at him in a fit o pique and started again covering his face and nec with persistent kisses until they were both breathles and had toppled onto the bed.

"Sweetheart," she fluttered, needing to live a lifetime in this one moment. "Tell me everything that' happened to you. Tell me about your work. Is coming well? Are you happy? Do you go to th museum every day? Is *she* good to you?"

He lay on his back and lifted her over him, holdin her up in his hands like the world. "That Corsica aniac has brought home to this city all the genius at has ever lived. I am surrounded with it. I bathe it. It feeds me every day."

His voice was glorious. She began to rise on the ings of its enchantment while she blinked down at is sharp, dark face lighted by an interior lamp that urned through them both. "Tell me," she urged. "Tell ne everything."

"I will show them to you, Meg. The Italians, the lemish, the Dutch. There is so much in the Louvre ne can hardly step over it all."

"And as for you?" She lowered her face slowly to is mouth. "And as for you?"

She let her lips brush his and he kissed her back. uddenly art and talk of paintings were gone. His arms lipped around her, holding her tightly, the muscles umping with an eager compulsion that told her how nuch he missed her. *I will never let him get away gain,* she promised herself, looking down at him, vatching the gossamer folds of her dress undulating cross his face and tinting the fine profile with a ea-rose-colored shadow. The mossy musk of her perume disappeared into the heated scent of their skin nd sank into the deeply held aroma of the rough edclothes. She lost sense of time and place, not caring vhere she was, floating, blending into the iron-willed, ron-bodied creature beneath her, then beside her, then bove her . . . who was the other half and necessity of er life.

He entered her in a fine start at gentleness but, vith her clutching gasp, drove wildly deep. She cried ut ecstatically for her salvation, an animal finding tself saved, a pained body laved at its deepest hurt. Iow she needed him! Her gnashing teeth found his houlder and nipped the salty flesh. She spread her ongue flat over the bulging tendons to swallow him vhole if only she could. The prickles of beard scraped er bosom and the swell beneath the nipples as he issed her. She felt the open, galloping joy in him peeding, lifting and taking her along, traveling to over the earth in giant, godlike strides. Even in his love she felt his defiance and his triumph. The com plete creature, perfectly made, that loved its own lif and would live! *Take me, too. Take me, too!* She mus go along regardless. Having found him, having cap tured and possessed him, she tasted a triumph an defiance of her own. She, too, had dared the world an won her portion of it. Her fingers spread over hi sweated back, slipping lower, pressing him, guidin him, holding him steady, with the heels of her palm digging into his hips. The adventurous ship of her lov she held cradled between her thighs, and they wer traveling together, full sail before the freshening win of their desire.

"Darling . . . my sweetheart," she murmure "Faster! I want to . . . go . . . go . . ." Exhilarate she tasted his mouth, his hot brow, the top of h head. "Kiss me. All over. Yes . . ." The crush of hi pressed her into the bed, then lifted her from it b turns. Some garment caught around her wrist and to as she pulled viciously away from any threat of e tanglement that would restrain her. They swayed ont their sides, legs locked in an odd, balanced positio The channel of her filled with the swelling waters life, filling her entirely; completing her.

"Little fox," he grunted. "My vixen."

And the tide rushed in, exploding with wild co vulsions that rolled up through her gut, her belly, h chest, swelling in her throat, her ears. It consume her brain . . . and rested, finally, in a gentle, lingerin kiss upon her mouth.

They lay gazing at each other, exhausted, draine yet sleepless. The blue light had gone behind a clou and returned a deeper hue and tawny, slipping in coo ing wisps over her nakedness. She held him at arm length and then crawled closer.

"You ought to go home now," he said. "This is n place for you to stay."

Meg sighed. "You are always sending me off." Sh smiled with her newly learned patience, with th strength of persistence that had rewarded her, thu ar, so well. "But I won't listen to you, you see. I have more important things to think about."

"I don't doubt it." He smiled, humoring her. "Seeing as how you've risen so rapidly and so well."

"Perhaps I have," she said tartly, yet with serious intention. "Wouldn't you like to? You can keep this garret if you love it. But why not come and meet some of my new friends and rise a bit more rapidly yourself?"

"Oh, oh." Dick grinned. "Same old Meg."

"And that's not so terrible as you say! You used to intimidate me, but not any longer. I have learned too much about the world, and everyone in it agrees with *me,* not you."

"Not terrible at all," he replied with appreciation, ignoring her argument and stroking her hip, the side of her thigh. "Less than terrible. Better then good. Way above marvelous." He drew her again into his arms. "You can't know how I've missed you," he whispered against her neck.

She lay silent, content, happy in the truth of his confession, and stared at the gray skirt on the wall.

"I won't let you go again. I won't," she promised matter-of-factly. "I can't take the torture."

"But you don't know how I live."

"Don't I?" she replied acidly. "Have you changed either? Who is the skirt that comes to visit you here?"

"You see, you're wrong. This is Augustine's apartment."

"Augustine? Poor dear Augustine. How was she so unfortunate as to find you?"

"You're quite right about that," he laughed. "But she did and I'm here."

"Living off a lonely widow's pension?"

"Something of the sort."

"And roulette at night?"

"Mm."

"And the whores at the Palais Royal?"

"Vixen, I say!"

"And the dice box? And swindling royal intriguers? And sketching at the Tuilleries and the Louvre and storing away in your brain all the foreign faces th clutter this filthy city day and night? And sellin cartoons from time to time to a newspaper. And buy ing your poor widow a bauble with the money, f solace in her misfortunes with you!"

They were laughing together and kissing each oth wildly, kicking and screeching and bouncing and pun meling and hugging and biting, tumbling about in mad, giggling tangle.

The door had opened. The woman stood there f long minutes, not hiding but unseen, her pale, straine face appalled and frozen, eyes on fire, rough han twisted in the tattered edges of a modest shawl. S stretched fingers to her throat and began to clutch as though in an attempt to stifle the incredible pa rising in a slow vapor to darken her cheeks. She trie to wet her lips once with a parched tongue. Staring a the while at the happiness and excitement on the be she reached along the wall without looking at it. H creeping fingers found and grasped the long barr of the gold-encrusted fusilier's rifle.

The barrel came easily, steadily, into her horn fingers. It seemed to raise itself just high enough alignment with the bed. She fumbled with latches ar fixed upon the trigger, moving as though in a drear Dick seemed to catch something out of the corner his eye and leaped at it as the report and a billowi cloud of burned smoke filled the room.

Meg's body jerked sideways. A short, astonish rasp escaped her. The next moment a froth of bloo bubbled up from the area of her stomach.

Dick, risen to his knees over the woman, hurle the rifle like a lance to the wall, where it dug an stuck into the plaster. He turned to Meg and spran back to the side of the bed, grabbing up the sash an pressing it into the ooze. The red cloth was instant soaked through and turning darker. Sticky liqu seeped over his knuckles.

"A doctor. Get a doctor," he yelled, panting.

The woman stood, grasping her thighs and starin down at the floorboards, strands of faded hair fallin 'er her blank eyes. "You will not be unfaithful to me ;ain," she said woodenly.

"Get a doctor. For God's sake, hurry!"

She leaned limply against the wall. "You have ıamed the memory of a patriot."

Dick wrapped his coat around Meg's waist and tried cover her nakedness with her crumpled tunic. He ılled on his breeches and swept her into his arms.

"Get me a doctor!!!" His voice resounded into the ıllway as he stumbled with Meg's limp body to the p of the stairs.

Chapter Seventeen

OORS REMAINED CLOSED to him as he staggered from ıe fourth floor down to the third, for people had seen ıuch violence in their time and were not easily ɔused.

Dick clambered down as far as the second, prepared go straight out onto the street, but the doorway ɔened here, an inch and then another.

"Is it murder?" called a hesitating voice, trying to ɔund officious.

"Yes, if I don't get help," shouted Dick, distracted ıd elbowing his way into the apartment before he ɔuld be refused.

"Heavens! The woman's half gone!" A limp hand ›se to the sympathetic mouth of a middle-aged, wil-wy gentleman with gold-leaf decorations about his ›lvet lapels.

"Where's a bed?" Dick shouted, unable to control s voice.

"My bed is all there is. In there." The bony, blue-hite finger pointed hesitantly.

"A doctor, dammit!"

"Yes. Yes. Who? Dr. Colombe." He scratched som frizzled, powdered, fine hair the color of apricots. "I fetch him instantly. Put her down. Take care. That it, man. Don't fret! He's only three buildings fro here and probably home with his wine."

"Oh, God, Meg," groaned Dick, setting her car fully among the cushions and toying with the coa gauze, not knowing what else to do. "Fight for m Fight!" he gasped. "Hear me, you vixen? Help m Fight!"

He knelt beside her and put his ear to her boso Her face was as drained as the sheets she lay upo but the heartbeat went on.

"Fight," he begged again, close to her mouth wi his cheek lying pressed beside hers on the pillow. H stared at her for a long while, watching the way s breathed, straining to see the air going in and out her lungs. "It's only one blasted little rifle ball," whispered. "You're stronger than that."

Hours crept on until the doctor hustled in. He ca ried a knapsack with things inside that clinked.

"Shot?" he said from a distance, eyeing Meg wi experienced though young, deep chestnut eyes.

"Shot," said Dick.

"Not a woman with royal blood in her, I hope."

"No," replied Dick strongly.

"If she is, I will have to write an official report."

"I tell you not!"

The doctor flicked a cold, testing look upon Dic He nodded, opened his napkin, and set out tools top of a painted iron bed table with some books on "Let us see this." He lifted the coat away. "Yes. Clo Very close."

Dick hovered beside him, then behind him, swa ing to peer over his shoulder and see where he look and touched. "Not too close," Dick encouraged. "Not ing ripped away."

Dr. Colombe swung around. "Will you get o please? Julien, take him away from me if I am to anything."

Julien's fingers wrapped like tendrils around Dick's arm. "Come, my friend, let us find you another shirt." He pulled Dick gradually backward out of the room. "Do you know I am a linen draper? I can make you a fine, fine shirt for that broad chest. Please. Come away. Come."

A torch roared and flamed in her belly. She tried to inhale and the fire rose into her lungs, where it turned to smoke and she coughed. The pain broke into shivering, sparking bits, piercing her lungs from the back along her spine. She swallowed. Her throat was scraped raw. She could not tell whether her eyes were open or closed. No matter what she did with them, she could see nothing but a whirling, many-colored darkness. Cannon fire exploded over and over against the inside screen of her lids. She remembered. Heard it again. The blast. A mad blast from nowhere that burst over her, trampling her with the hooves of a thousand horses. Her gut, smashed by the hooves, caved in. She sniffed without breathing deeply and thought she could smell a reeking river. A sickly odor was rising from somewhere. Different from anything she knew. A putrid stench. Burned flesh. Rotting meat. Was she lying on the wharves of an embankment? *Dick. Where are you?* She knew she could not form the words or make them sound aloud. Yet even of this she was not always certain. Something ebbed and flowed. Was it strength? When strength left her, she felt strangely deserted and seemed poised on the very edge of a black abyss. She didn't want to look where she was called to the brink. Yet, peering over, she teetered, staring down, down, down into an endless, dizzying whirl. A wind blew, as though to lift her and drop her into the chasm. But then it subsided and another, different kind of rush poured through her, dragging her back from the cliff and giving her some semblance of feeling, of a body . . . and its pain. The all-consuming pain was what made it difficult to breathe. She heard a horrible struggle and gasping. Was this she herself?

Sometimes she felt a movement down where her

hips were. A weight was lifted and then replaced in torturous pressure.

A buzz of sound. Voices? She tried to concentrate and hear what they were saying. A tinkling, melodious voice, neither male nor female. Then a more responsible reply, definitely male.

"Dick?"

"Lie still there. You can't see anyone."

The struggle to say the name exhausted her. And the reply was curious. She did not understand it. She tried to say his name again, but it wouldn't reach her throat.

Wetness to her lips.

"Drink this." The tinkling voice. "Try to take a tiny sip, won't you? Here. You can smell it, can't you? It's marvelous Burgundy wine. Very good for the blood. Excellent. I drink it myself every morning at eleven with my eggs. And I'll live to be a hundred, you know. Here. Try. Try a bit."

The airy, soothing voice was exactly right. Not too light, not too heavy. A tonic of itself. She couldn't lift her head. There was no use in trying. She felt warm fingers creeping round behind her neck. Her head tilted ever so slightly, and at the movement the pain broke her in half down below. Sound came out of her in a long, low moan.

"Of course it hurts. Of course."

Yet, despite it, she found herself tasting wine at the edges of her lips and tongue.

"Dick?" Had she said it? Could he hear?

"Oh, him. Yes. He's right here, m'girl. I'll get him instantly. Dick? She's awake this day. She's calling for you."

Footsteps, eager but heavy with fatigue. She could count them. *One. Two. One.*

"Meg? I'm here. Right here. You don't have to open your eyes. I'm pulling up a stool to sit beside you. Now. Here I am. And here I'll stay. You can take your time and get yourself better at your own pace."

She let out an exhausted groan meant to be delight. She tried to smile and felt it was a grimace on her features. She formed his name, but no sound was behind it. She could move a finger. Two fingers. Then she felt the calloused touch of his fingers twining with hers. Instantly she was asleep, afloat in thick, colorful darkness.

Chaos at the level of her stomach. Rumbling of a deep volcano there, spewing lava and searing, unspeakable pain. Herself crying out.

"Get you drunk if you can't take it," growled the Spartan, practical voice. "But you're alive and that's to be thankful for." Further digging and scrubbing deep down in the very bottom of her gut, it seemed. "Julien. Bring here that damned Burgundy and pour it into her. Either she lies still and I do this properly, or she kicks me through the roof and that's the end of her dressings."

Shuffling, and the sharp scent of wine around her head. "You've been such a good, brave girl. Drink this right down, all the way. That's it. That's it, nicely."

Her brain began to spin. The voices and confusion faded. . . .

"Dick? Dick, is that you?"

"Yes. Altogether me."

"If I open my eyes there's a blinding light. I tried it once, earlier."

"Then don't try."

"Where's your hand?"

"Here."

"Your fingers are icy cold."

"Those are your own."

"Don't make me laugh, please. Hurts too much."

"You're resting easier. I must say, Meg, you're a tough thing. You're coming round nicely."

"Yes. I feel it. How long?"

"Twelve days."

"Twelve days? You were watching me? Twelve days?"

She smiled and drifted off into a sleep of velvet blackness, this time with Dick's face in it and none of the colors.

The sleep felt better than anything. Sleep surrounded her with warmth, feeding her, holding her close, nourishing the marrow and the spirit.

When it passed she opened her eyes. The lids fluttered faintly, and through their haze she saw him sitting on the stool beside her, as he had said, with his long legs bent up slightly at the knees. She put her hand out and rested it on one of the tilted thighs.

"You look uncomfortable." She smiled.

"How in hell do you think you look?"

"I'm permitted."

"Mmm. And you're permitted to take some food today. There's warm gruel here. I've been waiting to give it to you. Maybe it's not so warm," he mused, sniffing it, tasting it with a wooden spoon.

"No, not that," she said.

"Why not that?"

"It's garbage," she said.

"I know. And garbage is good for you sometimes. Try it. Just a taste. Make Dr. Colombe happy."

"You're afraid of him."

"Terrified. He fixed you up and nearly killed me in the process."

"I said, don't make me laugh."

"You can laugh a little today. I have permission from Dr. Colombe."

She turned her head from the spoon, spitting out the mess on her tongue. "Someone gave me Burgundy. I like that better."

"You old sot. You can't have wine exclusively. Try some of this muck again."

"Ucccch," she said after she sniffed it. Then, dutifully, she opened her mouth and swallowed.

"Good girl. It will make Julien happy, too."

"What about you?"

"I'm thrilled to death."

"Here beside me for twelve days and *you're* thrilled to death?" she squeaked, smiling.

"Fifteen now."

"Fifteen days," she repeated.

"See how strong you are?"

She reached down and touched the huge lump on her belly. "What happened to me?" she inquired slowly.

"Jealousy shot you in the gut."

"With a cannon."

"Her dead husband's rifle. Rather a pretty-looking instrument, too. I was the one who kept it filled and ready, wouldn't you know," he said glumly.

"Who wouldn't do the same?" she replied reasonably with a wan smile. "They'll steal anything right out from under you in this city, I understand. Don't aggravate yourself about that. Things have turned out for the best, after all. We're together, and that's what matters."

"Yes, together," Dick said ruefully, lifting her hand and kissing fingertips one at a time. "First I run away from you. Then I almost get you killed. And now we're together at last."

"But we really are."

"Yes. You can believe it."

A sprightly knock at the door and Julien stepped in without waiting to be invited. His jacket swung away from a narrow length of lace shirt ruffles. Over his arm hung two scarlet sash pieces obviously cut from the original.

"How did you take to your dinner, dear?"

"Very tasty. Thank you."

Julien smiled with appreciation for her tact. "Awful, yes, I know. Everyone always hates what's good for them when they need it most. Isn't that the way."

"I'm Meg Watkins."

"Yes. Your reputation flies before you." He bowed with a worldly grace. "And I'm Julien Grandeville, at your service." He laid the sashes across the foot of the bed. "I rescued what I could of this."

"This is Julien's apartment," Dick put in quickly, watching Meg's eyes fill as she saw the cloth. "He saved us from God knows what rotten fate."

"Tut, man. I'm off to the shop now." He swung a blue-jeweled watch onto a white palm. "For all I know, our most respected and enchanting Josephine may need some ball gowns for a fête this very week. I must be *en pointe* every moment. See you in a while."

When he had gone Dick said gently, "You see? Luck has returned. For each of us now."

"Yes. You said it would always come back." Her smile clouded with pain. "How much longer do you suppose before I can get up?"

"Have you tried to move at all?"

"Can't."

They looked at each other.

"Then there's your answer." He bent over and kissed her on the bridge of her nose. "But take it easy. I'm not going any place."

"My brave, loyal lover," she whispered. "Fifteen days! More than a fortnight! That's almost forever for you. I'm so content just looking at your face, but how can I stay here?"

"Julien doesn't mind at all. He can afford us, fortunately. And he likes the company, poor soul."

"That's not what I mean, Dick," she said with a growing agitation that knifed in the wound.

"Well, what?"

She turned away, not wanting to tell him, loath to admit her fear of losing her connections with a way of life he despised. "Look at it this way," she said finally. "I am in this country under the courteous protection of some . . . very fine people . . ."

"I've gathered that," he said, coldly poised.

"Now listen to me. Lying here these weeks, I've dropped out of their lives as though fallen through a hole into hell, and believe me, it feels like it. You know what I mean. Yes, you do. I've made those friends, those attachments, for a reason. How can I lie here and let it all slide? Destroy everything I've worked so carefully to build?"

"Like it or not, you must have done so already, anyhow. It wouldn't make much difference if you sat up this instant and ran all the way home. You've been gone fifteen days and that's that. You've been shot through your middle, which is plain enough to see with all your bandages. How do you intend to explain it away? Or would you put your cards on the table and tell the truth?"

"Sssss . . . sometimes Dick, you try my patience to the core. You really do that. And I don't have to explain every move I make to anyone," she stammered, struggling for some point of vantage. "You know, I think you *like* the fact that I'm in trouble. Then you won't have to show anyone your work here in this country, either. You can continue selling those cartoon things for a couple of sous each and go merrily whoring away. Wasting your life and mine."

They then fell into a frigid silence while Dick stalked around the room, tapping the tops of raspberry velvet chairs or carefully fixing messes for her to eat and drink in close keeping with a schedule that Dr. Colombe had prepared, now that he had stopped coming to visit every day.

Regardless of Dick's opinions, however, and her own bravado, Meg wondered if she still had time to quiet Ralph Carstip with suitable explanations that he would swallow. She lay in depressed reverie with hands folded over the bandage and considered how long it would be before she could do more than merely totter a few steps and fall back to bed. Some exciting sight she was like this! Inside the canopied bed curtains, lifted and pinned back like the tent entrance over Cleopatra's barge, she thought about the Duc de Beauclew and yearned to confide in him. Seek his advice concerning the best way to handle his nephew. There was no use in saying another word about any of this to Dick, and she discreetly refrained, grateful for his love and loyalty and intent to stay by her side. He had not invited her to Augustine's apartment, after all. She had gone there herself, against good advice to the contrary, and met the fate that she deserved. Or that Augustine thought she deserved, poor shattered woman. Who else except herself could have the strength of passion to accept Dick for what he was? Who else could understand him and let him *be?*

There were days when she could not bear the sight

of Dick prowling around the furniture, and she would send him out with his sketch pad, pilfered from upstairs while Augustine was away. Sometimes Julien would sit and chat with her in the mornings over a cup of good, strong coffee, which they drank alternately with wine.

It was Julien who opened the conversation on an altogether new tack she had not thought of.

"Now that our countries are at war again," he said, "I have been worried about my two young English friends."

"Is it war?" she repeated with tense concern.

"I'm afraid so. And there are ten thousand of you or more penned up here in Paris alone. But what has that to do with us, eh? Or your love troubles? Oh, don't be embarrassed. An old-timer can tell about these things without overhearing very much. What I am suggesting, or wish to suggest in any event, is that the pair of you agree to stay here with me. You see, the conscription will again drain us of our young men. The city will be impoverished . . . and I will pine for good company."

"Julien . . . Julien." She put out her hand and squeezed his narrow wrist hidden by ruffles. "Pray say no more. If I could please you, I would be more than delighted, I would feel it my duty. I love you for your generosity. I love you for your humanity. You saved my life! But what am I to do with this horrible state of affairs that surrounds me? May I unburden myself to you? I must tell someone. And you have the sense, the feeling. Perhaps we can exchange some ideas."

With halting difficulty, she was able to filter out the mainstreams of her dilemma and present them in an orderly manner for Julien's contemplation. He seemed to listen casually, strolling about the bedroom and removing a porcelain box of rings from an ornate drawer, rings carved in the shapes of animal heads with diamonds for eyes, which he slipped on and off his little finger.

"I can agree with you perfectly," he said when she had concluded. "If Dick is perverse, as you say, and have every reason to believe it true, then you *must* ıke the reins and run things. A man such as he is can ever be expected to cooperate. And with that in mind, can see how to solve it. Let Dick remain here while ɔu return to Madame la Comtesse and Ralph. At east you will know Dick is safe and not falling into ther, treacherous arms like those up there." He rolled is eyes ceilingward. "Now, la comtesse loves you like daughter. Write to Ralph for the sake of domestic eace, but it is really to Madame that you return. She wise enough to understand the tactic and approve of our finesse. She will be easily soothed and satisfied y any explanation that is halfway sincere. But the ıain problem is . . . what *are* you going to tell that ealous maniac, your earl, to keep him from seeking nasty revenge? Yes, it *is* possible that he could—or as—sent Tom to betray you to the police and reveal our illegal entry here. But I feel he's the sort who vould rather play his games face to face with you. es. I am convinced he is more interested in finding nd dealing with you directly. Once he has you, then e might threaten to turn you in." Julien speculated uietly, changing ring after ring, tying and untying the npeccably white cravat beneath a black waistcoat vith carefully wadded lapels. He posed at the mirror nd observed the full-length impression, concentrating n it and something deeper. "To forestall that, I beeve you should tell Carstip the truth . . . partially. es. Say that you were shot. And badly so. That will bsolve you of not having sent a message around to im all this while."

"I must do that at once, mustn't I?" Meg said, reeved to hear her own thoughts seconded, and with an ager anxiety to have it done with. Motioning him to ring her pen and ink, she said, "I am writing in the rst instant I can think clearly, which this honestly is —and am sending it to have him come for me?"

"Splendid! He will call and collect you right here my presence. Seeing me and knowing my profeson, for I shall be sure to tell him that, he will acept your story. How could you be deceiving him with a lover when you are lying helpless as a wounded doe?" He smiled with a velvet look in his shrewd eyes.

"Ralph will come for me while Dick is out sketching," she continued in a dejected falter. "Why do I do all this?" she sighed. "Why don't I give up and live the vagrant life with Dick?"

"You don't give up for the same reason that Dick refuses. It is not in the blood, my sweet. You are condemned to play out this game till the end of your very last strength."

Chapter Eighteen

No doubt a return to Carstip would be filled with unimaginable sadisms, yet Meg felt confident that in his twisted mind he had dreamed and yearned for her these weeks simply because she had run away. As she waited for Carstip like the vixen she was, alert to the hunter, she felt determined to give him a chase. The dependence she had felt all the way to Paris had ended with the rifle shot. Facing Carstip had an altogether different aspect now. She would cajole him only enough to keep him docile while she revived her friendship with the comtesse, Monsieur le Duc, and Citoyen Murier, whose connections rose directly to Bonaparte.

Dick would certainly have a fit about her plan. From his point of view Meg could not blame him. What reasonable argument had she for dropping back into that turmoil? She had pulled herself out by the threads of her very existence. Dick could call her a fool and be justified. Yet what had foolishness or sensibility to do with life? Life was superior to logic, she had learned. Life drove one before its irresistible winds and when those winds stopped blowing, so did th st. She could close her eyes and see all his pictures, ose gorgeous renderings of Parisian life, framed and onored with their own special place in a museum—erhaps the Louvre!

"You are not going to desert me, are you?" Meg sked softly.

They were both standing between the heavy curtains f the drawing-room window, gazing without interest t the never-ending stream of merrymakers trampling e earth-packed street, bent upon a first sight of the onsul at a reception or some tête-à-tête in a park, rotected from the August swelter by leafy bowers of lm.

"We are long past the notion of leaving one an-ther," Dick replied, linking her hand through the rook of his arm. "Perhaps you knew it sooner than I at we were destined to be together and remain to-ether regardless of the catastrophes we create." He huckled softly. "I do not deserve a woman of your trength and ambition. My luck is beyond understand-g. But there it is."

"You must do something for me, then." She pressed er cheek to his shoulder.

"Do I hear it coming?" he asked, quickly suspicious.

"Yes, you do." She grinned at him mischievously.

"I can't!"

"You can try. They all want so very much to help s. Won't you give me the satisfaction of at least show-g me your attempt? Maybe if I see you fail at pleas-g these people, I'll be so miserable at the sight of you at I'll never bother you with it again."

"I won't have that luck," he replied decidedly. "You re stubbornly blind. Just as I am. Both of us dumb, owerful animals, each one pulling a good cart but in pposite directions."

"Try!" she said earnestly. "Didn't I *live* to see it?"

Meg didn't care that she played upon his guilty con-cience; she didn't care *how* she won as long as she on!

"Meg, you have worn me down." He smiled, let-ng go of her arm and returning to the tray of decanters in a shadow of the farthest wall. Julien ha purchased some new gilded chairs with eagles an Egyptian mummy faces carved in their corners. "Th is what I'll look like when you've finished with me, he said, pointing to one of them.

"Eagles of Victory," she boomed. "How handsome!

She would not give an inch and felt no sympathy fo his weaknesses. Weren't strength and weakness real the same thing? Only pointed at different goals. "That how I looked at it, finally," she said, "all those da when I was lying there wondering what was to becon of us."

"Even in your pain you were thinking about m career," he sighed, shaking his head, incredulous.

"Don't play innocent. You, too, are obsessed."

"All right. I said I would do what you ask . . once."

She came to him, still with careful steps, and toc a glass of the heartening Burgundy that Julien kept fo her in good supply. "And I really don't ask much."

"Get on with it, then. Tell me."

She was all smiles and dimples of pleasure becau of her triumph, but soon the high seriousness of h intention prevailed. "I mean to return and live wi Madame la Comtesse in her household. I have to Carstip about you. In fact, I have told them all abo my genius cousin for whom I have been searching ar have finally found."

"Genius cousin, eh?" he said sourly. "They wor swallow that tripe."

"No one has to, except Ralph. And he will." Me was confident she could deceive him.

"Why must he?" Dick's face was dubious wi distaste.

"I'll force him to it," she said airily. "You've neve seen me when I get going. Especially with Ralph. understand that devil. I've been next to him when h insides were bared. I know where to touch him so he jump."

"As one flicks a whip at a horse, eh? But I'm no

ting you return. That's not part of our bargain. You ıy with me."

Meg could hardly believe it! She had lived only hear those words on his lips, but the irony of his ›rds coming now, when she could least afford to ten, caused her to swallow back a trembling tear of y. Yet in her heart she felt driven to a higher, better ward for which she must sacrifice this pleasure, a ward that strengthened her to go on.

"Darling, now listen," she said, grasping his bulky rearms and forcing herself to talk calmly from her tional conviction. "I'll return. Tell them that I was ot accidentally in some political intrigue and was lpless till this very moment. Ralph will believe me. l show him the wound."

"I said no. No more of that."

"The others will applaud," she continued deafly. 'hese pure-bred nobles are really thirsting with bore-m behind their doors. They'll be glad for a new lventure when I bring you on the scene."

"And on I'll come. Decked out like a fop in kersey-ere trousers. But only if you stay here and we go gether."

How could she survive this? "Dress any way you ease, dear, so long as it's fashionable." She smiled, th a peck on his lips. "And that much I can leave to lien. When they meet you, they'll next want to see ur paintings. They're dying to see your paintings ter all I've raved."

"I can't believe that anyone gives much of a damn out art," he said. "Except the characters who paint."

"But they care about the prestige. The coup of being st to discover new talent."

Dick nodded, reddening visibly. "You're making me ghty sick of it already."

"You *promised,*" she said, clawing at him gently.

"Yes, I promised." His eyes flashed stubbornly. "But t if you leave."

"Miss me." She kissed him firmly with longing. "To-rrow go out into the boulevard and paint, knowing that when you come back home at sunset I'll alread be gone."

"You mustn't. It won't work, Meg. You know can't."

"I'll get a message to you very soon."

She dared not respond to the turmoil of her feelin and rushed away to dress. Meg concentrated on crea ing the effect of a stricken princess for her return the Rue de Bac. She wanted to hurry while momentu and sympathy were still tipped in her favor.

After much heated discussion with Julien abo strategy, it was concluded that he should ride for Ral without delay, carrying a proper message written Meg's faint hand.

"He'll want to come back with you instantly, t suspicious bastard."

"And I shall bring him. To find you lying on r sofa, just as you are now, with some pale lavender si around you like this." He fluffed some folds arou her as she reclined. "One of the cherubim descende There." He crossed his arms, stood back, and studi the effect. "It breaks the heart beautifully."

The next morning Julien took away the breakf things, hugged her, and shook out the broad lapels his purple coat. "Rest easy, love. It'll be just fine, y shall see."

Through the window, she watched him mount dappled horse and disappear into the crowd, her fle prickling with anxiety but her jaw set. A flash memo of Dick sauntering off in the opposite direction earli shook her with tremors—how she missed him alread —but she chased that away, aware that her nerv were still weak and her body raw from the woun She needed all the strength she could rally to stri the right note of pride and independence before Ralp and at the same time have him suspect that in her o secret place she still desired him.

An hour passed and she heard him on the stair, h footfall hasty as a poacher darting after its prey. S flung a contemptuous glance at the sofa with its r morocco cover that was to be her theater prop a ecided to face Ralph as normally as she could. Let im find her standing. For she must stand up to him ltogether if he were not to ride roughshod over her esh and soul.

"My dearest girl, Meg! You have worried us all to eath. What have they done to you?"

He rang very true, rushing toward her with great overlike strides, arms outstretched, cravat bobbing, ıin hair tousled over a wretchedly drawn brow.

Behind him Julien winked at her and quietly withrew to eavesdrop from the adjoining bedroom.

"I can't begin to tell you everything at once." Her yelids fluttered as she fell upon his bosom and heard ıere the steady ticking of a new French watch.

"Don't try, my darling. Don't. Simply come home ith me and we will bring you around properly." His oice was breathy and stiff against her hair, a snake aiting patiently in the reeds. He stroked her head, xamining askance the bloodlessness of her cheeks, ıe faint lines straining at her mouth. He seemed ırprised and satisfied, yet reluctant. "I don't need xplanations," he said after a while. "It's obvious ıere's been a horrible thing come to pass. You can ll me about it in your own good time. Or never, if ou so choose."

Meg couldn't believe her ears, and she didn't. This mpathetic display was for Julien's benefit and to wer her own guard. "Yes. Sometimes I need kindss," she said in a smothered voice. "Let us go home. want to sleep in my own bed."

With dragging, regretful steps that passed for weakss, she went down to the waiting cab, with Julien ıttering behind and waving her good-bye. Then the b door closed, and she was alone again with the llow eyes upon her growing visibly colder, paler, the oulders tighter, the attention more severe. Ralph, ıo was sitting next to her, suddenly jumped over to e seat opposite, leaned back, and put his feet up on r lap in his familiar, contemptuous style. She winced d pulled her lap away, whipping him with a flashing gaze. "Must I show you the hole in my stomach f you to believe me?"

"Oh, I believe you, darling," he replied with horrible mildness. "I believe that impotent little ma too. I believe your suffering . . . that is what you very well, Meg, suffer." He licked his lips in a catli fashion. "But that is not what charms me. It's t *reason* why you suffer that brings me back again a again. The driving force inside you. I'd like to rip out right through your belly wound and gobble it dow do you see, and understand it with my digestion." I laughed softly to himself. "But I don't suppose y know what I mean."

"I know I am not well," she replied stoically. "A that you should have some consideration."

"Yes, Duchess," he replied affably, gazing out t window at a cordon of stragglers being herded throu the crowd by shouting soldiers on horseback. A gua riding behind them flung a rock that glanced off t side of a man's head and hit the carriage wheel. thud echoed inside.

"What the devil's that?" cried Ralph.

"Other people suffering, no doubt," she spat acid

"Miserable conscripts. This city is going to the do No fun here. Not a bit of it." He babbled pettish "What have we done since we arrived? Stupid ba Stupid dinners. Stupid salons. I look to you for f and what do I find?"

"What you seek."

"At first I thought the police got to you. You we smuggled in, and it is not good to be a criminal Napoleon's France. For if you are taken, you are l forever. That guillotine has not become famous f nothing," he said with a deep, warning knell. "Tell what really happened, Meg. Or can I guess?"

She played with the sapphire rings he had bou her, breathing on the high oval stars and wiping th with the back of a glove in careless, self-confid gestures. "Julien gave you my note. As for the detai I can add them quickly. You *know* I have been loc ing for my cousin."

"Cousin?" he muttered.

"Dick Fox."

"You've told me the name a thousand times. When you are not pouring it into my ears, it goes into others'. Have you found him, finally?"

"That is my story," she said with a sunshine smile, and bouncing across to where he sat, hung her arms around his neck in her favorite gesture of confidence. "Yes, I did find him," she said. "But he lives on the far side of the Seine. An editor at the *Gazette* led me to him, and when I was returning to you in a ferry, some madman broke into a fight. It was so fierce. With guns and knives. One cannot predict what will happen on the streets these days, you said so yourself, since France is at war with us. People explode in all sorts of furies. Which is what happened. And I, I was caught in the middle."

He leaned his face slowly toward hers. A shaft of light seemed to pass through his transparent skin. His lips touched the tip of her nose. The kiss was cold, dry as dust. It seemed to come from a mummy's face that she could breathe on and blow away. She pressed her mouth harder to his, exploring to find what he really wanted from her.

"You are a pretty liar," he said idly. "A very pretty liar, indeed. The gunpowder must have gone to your brain to make you think I would believe such a tale. But never mind. I have plans. You will make it up to me."

It was the satisfaction sitting in those drained eyes that terrified her. She could feel the fury lowering far back, a gale storm at the horizon coming slowly up, slowly up, blackening overhead. He tweaked her ear lobe. His nails pinched deep into both sides of the flesh, purposely vicious. She sat still for it, pretending not to feel, not to notice. She had lost the habit of giving him satisfaction, and it was difficult to regain it.

"There is nothing to make up," she persisted, innocently open. "But I want you to please me . . . I need for you to please me."

One fine eyebrow twitched with his nervous attrac tion to her. When she spoke like this, insinuating he dominance, recalling memories to him of her insati able physical hunger, he became pliable. She coul twist him, fold him into any shape she desired. Sh could direct him to a point, but not completely. It wa that no-man's-land beyond her control that lurked threatening her safety every moment, causing her t be watchful, defensive, alert, despite the pain startin to throb in her belly from the jostling carriage.

She sighed with relief when they reached the Ru du Bac. With a clenched effort she tottered towar the door, in a greater state of weakness than she ha expected.

The comtesse, waiting in the anteroom, met her im mediately. She held her face steadily by both cheek and peered with deep, motherly concern into her eyes searching further than the limits of pain for somethin more important. Her mute face said: Did you fin him? Is he all right? Are you?

How Meg longed to confide in this woman wh loved her but whose erratic forgetfulness was not t be trusted. "Oh, *Maman, Maman,*" she cried with min gled emotions of regret at having to return and c genuine affection for this lady. "It has been terrible.

"Never mind. Never mind." A faint aroma of vi olet perfume exuded from her breath. "Do not strai yourself so. You need rest. We shall make it all bet ter. Come, you must lie down this instant, and I sha bring you good things to eat that I made with m own hands. A tartlet? The summer asparagus is in."

They held each other and went with tiny step through the bleak, gold-encrusted rooms till the reached the round bed that was Meg's.

"Undress and lie down right now before the ai turns cold. Ralph, you must leave us for a few min utes, and do not follow after like a mother hen. I won't do! I wish you would see to Victor," she muse with sudden, remembered worry. "He, too, goes off an stays away so long. So long! I fear for him so! He mus not enlist in the army. He is all I have left. Child, wha is that on you? Such a bulky bandage. I am not sure you have had proper care. We must call our own physician immediately."

Meg collapsed onto the mattress with a sudden rush of helpless torpor that infuriated her. She had not intended to be the faint, sick thing before Ralph's eyes.

"Perhaps I should examine the wound," he said softly. "I, too, was an army captain and know about these things."

"Were you in service, Ralph?" the comtesse asked unhappily.

"But of course," he replied with crisp distaste. "The peers of our realm always lead the way to battle in service of our king. And I, for one, have done duty up to the eyes." He ranted on with a will while bending over Meg's bandage, eyeing it as he would a good fish on his dinner plate. "Now don't be shy. I won't hurt you."

"Don't touch it at all, since you *must* look," blurted the comtesse, hovering at a distance. "And I think you brazen and irresponsible for going this far."

Ralph, accustomed in his spoiled way to ignoring women's desires, picked at the edge of the gauze with a forefinger. His inspection caught a black crust of something underneath, and he smiled with a small, satisfied nod, reassured for the first time that she had indeed been wounded.

"You see, it is as I say," Meg said, taking advantage of the opportunity to lash him with a self-satisfaction of her own.

"Mm. But I still don't know who shot you."

"Neither do I," she replied, vehemently truthful.

They stared at each other, poised at the ends of their barbs.

"Don't be a fool, tell me everything," he said intensely.

"Dear, dear, dear," cried the comtesse, clasping her hands and turning to leave the room. "How will she ever get well in this atmosphere!"

Alone with her now, Ralph began to unleash a bit more of himself, pacing with his hands beneath his coattails, then growing flushed and flinging the coat from him. "How long do you suppose you must lie there mooing like a pathetic cow?"

"I feel more like a rebel than a cow, shot in battle as I was," she replied staunchly, ignoring his attempt to undercut her morale. "And I shall be up in a day or two at the latest, you can trust me. I have learned so many fine manners from you, my darling, that even my body would not dare to linger so long as to discommode the loving presence." She had picked up the knack of speaking with a certain court formality and enjoyed using it now as a fire screen that covered her from him. She longed for a cup of tea and Dick beside her, railing at her in a different style.

Ralph studied her from a distance, hearing little of what she said, distracted by his own driving considerations. His eyelids lowered, stiff and sharp-edged as the shell of an oyster. "Who shot you? Who shot you?" he repeated, beaten down again and again by the allure of some sordid, compelling mystery that evaded him.

Meg lifted her hands and lowered them silently to the embroidered coverlet, smoothing her fingers over the fleur-de-lis pattern, taking what solace she could from these surroundings that belonged to the comtesse.

"You *will* tell me," he flung out, and stalked from the room, leaving her debilitated brain to wonder whether or not she now had the peace to dare take a nap.

Sleep came of its own accord, without her permission, and with it returned the burning heat of a fever. For all her high purpose, she could not get on immediately with her social intentions as she had planned. Yet from day to day visitors came and sat with her in kindly concern and camaraderie. A curled, powdered wig and sensible face shimmered and floated around her. The Duc de Beauclew. To him she could talk! To him she could tell everything. Yet a restraining hand rose, even in her delirium, and held her silent.

"I am such a burden to everyone," was all she could muster.

"No. Never mind it." He took her fingertips in his soft palm and sat down beside the bed. "You are doing la comtesse a service by staying here. It takes her mind off that wild Victor and Elise."

"I don't see Ralph."

"He is out. He has been out since noontide with Tom, arranging passage for you all to return to London."

A lightning stab shot through her. She sat bolt upright, clutching the duc's silk sleeve. He pushed her down gently by the shoulder.

"The war worries him, but there is nothing to be concerned about yet, of course. I have property in both countries, as you know, and *quand les rats prenderont les chats, les Français prendent Arras.*"

"When the rats and cats together shall play, then the French into London will force their way." Meg smiled at the reassurance. "But we are here such a little while. I have hardly had time to enjoy myself with so many wonderful people. You know, monsieur, I have found my cousin—and I want so very much for you to meet him!" she cried impassionedly.

"Yes. I have heard so from Murier."

"Murier?"

"We knew where you were from Dr. Colombe, who reported into the prefect that eventually reached up to Murier, whose men were out looking for you. We were afraid you had been abducted—and killed as a spy. Mistaken for a loyalist intriguer. It happens every day."

A swirl of enlightenment washed through her. What a fool she had been to think she had gone off unobserved. These people knew her every move. They watched her when Ralph was not about. Murier on behalf of the duc. Tom and Ned, no doubt, at Ralph's demand. "I am a woman of importance in Paris," she said bitterly. "I am news."

"You are interesting and English, and Ralph is troublesome," the duc replied blandly. "And for your own protection we keep an eye upon you. Look what has happened nevertheless."

"It is my own doing."

"I am aware. Still. We feel our obligations . . . *noblesse oblige,* if you will, in these confusing times. Men and women are being kidnapped every day by the army. Murier tells me that Dick Fox has quite a reputation of sorts, too. You stare at me in surprise? But I have to help you, do I not, since I like you so very much? And it would break the heart of la comtesse if you were not cared for and advanced."

She lay weakly, unsure of what to say, how much to reveal, hoping the duc would go on. "Dick Fox has a reputation?" she urged without committing herself.

"As a rascal. As a scoundrel." He laughed. "And yes, as a painter. They say he works with the passion of cannon fire, when he does work. Some of his best pictures are lying about in the homes of the bourgeoisie, who haven't a spare franc with which to pay him a decent price. And good paintings can command three thousand livres."

"What can Murier do about that?"

"Danger foreseen is half averted, as a famous general once told us. Murier can bribe his admission to one of the Consul's receptions, if you like, and perhaps Josephine herself would take an interest. If your *cousin* has any conversational ability to speak of."

"But he has! In his own style."

"I am certain of it." The duc gently stroked her hand. "And so you must hurry and get well."

She fell back on the small pillow, watching him with a rise of mute thankfulness. He was so willing, so helpful. It was really out in the open to everybody. Her guile had charmed and won the sympathy of these worldly souls but fooled not one of them.

"You know, Ralph has come to Paris to seek my help in straightening out some of his American affairs," the duc continued. "In his own way he, too, is irresponsible. The difference is that from a wealthy man the world accepts much and excuses more. Wealth blankets folly in countless, clever ways."

"He told me he was coming to the continent to play."

"And so he has," the duc laughed. "Letting the work fall upon my shoulders, which is not unusual for him. I do it for the sake of the property itself and for his mother's memory. Among us, we manage to look after Ralph. But we don't take his lack of manliness to heart. That would be futile."

She felt in the duc more commiseration for his sister than love for his nephew. "I am sorry for Ralph," she said in this confiding moment of closeness with her mentor.

He leaned over and kissed her forehead with warm, damp lips. "How generous of you," he said. "How wise . . . and how brave."

Chapter Nineteen

THE STRONGER SHE GREW, the less generous, wise, and brave she felt in Ralph's needling company. The stronger she grew, the longer he hovered, the closer he lingered, studying her, impatient to get on with the sport brewing and bubbling in his mind. He spoke not a direct word of returning to London, hinting only that he would sail if he became too bored or frustrated here. Frustrated, indeed! What could he know of it? Meg burned while she placated and nurtured him as she waited every day for Murier to make connections for Dick. Then Murier sent her an invitation to the salon of the boldest, most dominant patroness in the city, but somehow the note disappeared from the silver tray and was later uncovered by accident, torn to bits and hidden under a decanter.

"But what am I to do, *Maman?* He will intercept everything and taunt me with it later."

The comtesse brushed the incident aside, saying that in storms of uncertainty only acts of good faith represented permanence. She then mentioned a dinner party for artists in a *maréchale's* salon. "I'm sure this will be your opportunity, my dear. Madame is a natural leader and the most important thermometer of artistic opinion; her Wednesdays are not to be missed." But this became confused in her mind with a banquet for archeological research. There were so many interests to be remembered. So many people to bring together. So many others to be kept apart.

Meg, not knowing from which direction fortune would finally come, took to hovering at her door with each sound of the knocker downstairs, and was rewarded with a second notice from Murier, which she acted upon instantly, firing off a secret letter to Dick and sending it on by the servant's hand.

The very next morning Ralph sat staring into the ashes and said with a dangerous edge, "I don't know what delays us in Paris when there is so little here to amuse."

Meg felt the cold ripples of warning. "That is because we have seen nothing and done nothing, I am sure." She complained heartily, aware that he was alerted, yet not quite certain, this time, of how much or exactly to what. But he must be kept in harness and led from the trail that would take her irrevocably away from this hellish, double-faced existence any day now. Any day. There was only one way to keep ahead of his growing suspicions.

"Every tourist in Paris comes to see the reviews on the Carrousel by the emperor, and the prostitutes of the Palais Royal. But what have I seen of that debauch? Clearly nothing. Lying here in the midst of this unique city and rotting with boredom. Ralph, I am *itching* with boredom. You must take me out."

He swung around from the dank hearth and came to her sofa, falling beside where she reclined and pressing his mouth to the side of her bosom. "My ear, you redeem yourself. Dress. We will go today."

Meg struggled up, aware now of what she was bout and how to cook the brew of his dark soul. With nough of her strength regained, she could stroll for s long as required to show him sights that would oil him over.

"What shall I wear to please you most?"

"Anything. The white tunic with the sky-blue trim. nd the garnets. I love you in my garnets. Satan ould have the color of your hair, were he to wear nose garnets."

"And you aspire to that throne?" She stroked his heek confidently. "Let me help you to reach it."

"How?" His eyes glittered.

As he hugged her to him impulsively, she felt him eaping to the state of readiness that had been forcibly eld in check this past week with smoldering groans of ortured abstinence. "Must I tell you everything and poil the surprises?" she flitted, lording her secret over im as she knew he loved her to do. "Take me to the rcades, and we shall not want for interesting company o give us a new turn with each other."

He could hardly believe the promised joy of what e heard. He flushed with a pleasure that spread to his ars, which seemed to stand away slightly from his ead, the sandy hair, carefully groomed, brushing over heir tips. He had spent some hours, for want of anything better to do, at his toilette, fumbling alone among is combs and lotions, sniffing his musky perfumes and assaging astringent solutions into his cheeks. The ockmarks always concerned him, and he sometimes omplained that they marred an otherwise smooth and eautiful complexion. Never before had she studied m so carefully as she did this day, using her previously hoarded vitality to keep him unsuspecting and eer him, as she must, in harness and on *her* road.

What she needed, but could not admit to him, of ourse, was someone to help her with him in bed. She as in no condition yet to move about for very long. very sway of her hips was stiff and still rather pain-l. The galloping violence needed to amuse and satisfy Ralph's nature was still far beyond her capa bilities, despite all determination to the contrary. Ar sewn up as she was, she felt a queasy horror of pulli stitches. To mask this from him required an ingenui and the assistance of other, more capable force Along the Palais Royal strolled the kind of wome who, unwittingly, could be her aides and salvation.

"Let us go before sundown," he suggested in happ impatience.

They arrived at the long rows of hovels purporti to sell lavender water, toothbrushes, sealing wax, ga ters, and thread at the hour when the street was begi ning to assume its evening character. Already gatheri in the shadowed corners, full-bellied gentlemen li gered with scantily clad girls whose youth lay hidde beneath very white face paint and dark lip colo Young black women mingling with those more fai complexioned shared among them a style of tunic c very low at the top and high at the bottom, reveali to any casual passerby the curves and dimpled hin quarters offered for pleasure. Daytime female shoppe were for the most part gone, and Meg, strolling arm arm with Ralph, gazing as he did at the display of a dently aggressive humanity, presented an unusual sig to those with their wares for sale. Some, who took for a challenge, winked at Meg and her escort, motio ing with unmistakable gestures to floors upstairs, whe private lodgings awaited the convenience of those i terested. One or two ventured over and shook the breasts so close that Ralph had to brush them to g by.

"Help a hungry girl in the cold?" cried one, panti in the swelter of steamy air.

Meg looked her swiftly up and down, found her to skinny in the ribs, not tractable at all, and with u imaginative, flat eyes. "No, mademoiselle!" she replie firmly, pulling Ralph past.

Ralph tittered and giggled while Meg kept testi and judging, issuing her "No, mademoiselle" as a go erness would to her failing charges.

"What will please you, I wonder?" he drawled even-ally, breathless.

"I know our type better than you do," Meg an-ered with decision. "It is a quality of fire."

Speechless, he nodded in awe of her inspired search. e felt his arm grow limp as he allowed himself to be lled along through the shadows and shady walks of e *fête galante*.

One young girl with springy, lemon-blonde ringlets ew herself away from a huddle of others and came urrying after them, bouncing along behind and call-g small-voiced, obscene names calculated not to ir-ate so much as to stun them with recognition of her pabilities. At first Meg would not turn. She listened the caressing tone of the voice and concluded that re, at last, sounded the call of a woman with the ght ideas and perseverance. The girl continued to amper behind, dashing into all the nooks and cran-es as they appeared, whistling up and down to the ezzanine floors and in front of the theater, bawling ally for her own amusement, "But then is it *tooth wder* that you want to buy? *A ball of thread?*"

Meg held Ralph in tow so that the girl could swing ound in front of them and exhibit herself in the full oom of her juicy flesh, presented with a brassy, for-ard thrusting of her curves beneath the weak, flaring slights.

"A fine appetizer, don't you agree?" Meg said, ob-quely watching Ralph toy with the notion of what, to-ther, they could do here.

"An entree," he responded enthusiastically.

"What is your name, child?" Meg offered, thus let-g the girl know she had been chosen.

"Florinda. Florie, they call me. I am like a flower. ou see this?" She lifted her breasts on her palms. ee the petals? And cherry blossoms down below, I omise it!"

"No, don't promise what you cannot deliver," Meg vised from experience, aware of how many times e, too, had played the virgin, hopeful thereby of me extra change.

"I can delivair. I can do eet!" Her brash blue ey sparkled behind a mask of self-confidence. "Come t my apartment. I have beautiful rooms. A general use to live there and has left me everything. He died c the battlefield of love, you know, and now it is a mine." She sidled up to Ralph and took hold of h arm.

Meg said, "You like her, don't you?" and hea Ralph clicking his teeth in that slow concentration th revealed the unbridling rise of his desire.

"Yes, we shall go to your place," Meg said.

"You may have no fear of it there, Englishman Florie said with a boastful smile. "It is large and clea You shall see." Ralph, fired into action, hailed one the multitude of cabs waiting close by and wiggled between the two women, who sat pressed against h thighs.

"You will watch what I do to her," he ordered M with jittery impatience. "And you will see for the fi time the real nature of my interest."

The girl in her horrible innocence pinched Ralph flesh at the level of his white piqué waistcoat. "It is a hard muscle here," she observed happily. "And how the rest, I wonder?"

Ralph kept his eyes fixed on Meg as Florie's finge searched lower along his trousers. "You enjoy watc ing, is that your secret, Meg? You are a voyeur and am your subject," he continued with relish, decidi that he understood now the reason for this threesom "But I never knew you were perverse. How delect ble." His hand slipped down to the back of Florie and moved it rapidly lower, squeezing her finge quickly as he created heated conversation with Meg.

"I have many aspects to my nature," Meg rambl with ease.

"And I will find them all!" he whispered growlish "How fascinating that you are made like this. Wh other woman would not be threatened by the ministr tions of a prostitute going on before her very eyes?"

"They do it behind our backs," she smiled. "An are we not the wiser?"

'Darling. I love you!" He leaned over and kissed g with a feverish, biting nip.

She sent her fingers up into the soft roots of his hair ove the neck nape and clutched and held his skull. ou are fascinating to me, never forget it. Men stly burn themselves out in their youth. They drown ir maleness in wine and fall into bed besotted and less. But not you. Not my dearest, most lascivious lph."

"No, not I," he echoed with satisfaction and pride. live for love. And so shall I die, I hope. Between a man's legs and her breasts. That's the place for it. the crest of one final, roaring—"

Meg closed the word off with her mouth, needing silence for a moment in which to conjure up other, re bearable pictures, soon to be fulfilled with Dick. e total image of their last embrace, the flight sky-rd, the shuddering, trembling ecstasy . . . all of it scended upon her while she carefully held her unded stomach away from Ralph and let little orie do the more energetic work.

The carriage seemed to sway on forever. Ralph ght have been satisfied half a dozen times if he did t willfully resist Florie's offer to fall down before n on her knees.

"You see," she said when they finally arrived before lingy pile of houses surrounded by scraggly trees t creaked their flowered branches in the night wind. will have something very interesting for you. Only elve francs the couple, if you want it."

"What are you talking of?" said Ralph, his brows wing together.

"*Oui*. For twelve francs the couple, you can go tairs." She pointed to the blackened middle-floor dows. "Inside you will find . . ." She grabbed his d. "Come, I go with you. I show you. And I enter self."

"What about our arrangement?" Meg said, pulling back by her dress ribbons.

"What about it? Here is something you will like n better."

"We pay for *you,"* Meg insisted coldly, clinging the girl's wrist with an iron grip in case she deci to bolt.

"But here, I am trying to do you a favor," Fl complained, desperately misunderstood. "A parte

"A *parteee* is not what we want. Only you."

The girl glanced from Meg to Ralph and b again. "Only *me?"* she repeated in amazement. "W you can have twentee or fortee othairs? All at onc

"Is that what you are paid for? To bring pe here to a free-for-all?"

The girl sighed, defeated. "My place is on *quatrième.* Come, I will show you where we can alone, *à trois."*

"Exactly," Meg said, relaxing but still follow close behind Florie, who went ahead at a noncha skip as though suddenly she couldn't care less ab the fleshy tussle to come.

The apartment was exactly as she had promi the flags scrubbed and shining in the glow of candles. A collection of spare furniture such as m belong to a general's aide-de-camp, made from li colored fruitwood with brass corner fittings, had b placed about the white-washed walls, lending an of transience to the place, as though no one actu lived here or had time to express the warm touc of a personality.

"We have French wine and English porter. W ever you like." Florie wiggled her fingers, telling Ra to help himself while she danced over to the place and jiggled the low embers into a brassy ange radiance. The Seine seeped through the th folds of draperies, a pall of humid, rancid sten They were very close to the river on its far side.

The trip and the stairs had taken too much out Meg. Ralph put a glass of some dark, fruity-scen liquid into her grasp, and she drank it off with a si quaff while he watched her. This habit he had of specting her every movement began to unnerve She turned away so that she would not see his slop shoulder jacket and the idling stance of his hip. Flo lding a large bumper of wine in both palms, stood rectly in front of Ralph, drinking and saying "Ahhh" er every swallow and rubbing her behind against the ont of his thin thighs.

"Whatever you want to do," she said faintly. Whenever you want to do it . . ."

Beneath them reverberated the squeaks and guttral laughter of a party going on in the dark. Ralph anced down every so often between the stance of s boots, as though to burn a hole through the ceiling. Whatever is happening there?" he said, distracted.

"I tell you it is wonderful," trilled Florie with the llow, overinflated enthusiasm of a circus barker. From eight o'clock till midnight, ladies and gentlemen ter the drawing room and nobody knows who anyody else may be. It is entirely pitch-black down ere. And whatever else goes on, one *must not* atmpt to discover the identity of the others. It is a olic. Ooooh, yes! Ladies and gentlemen from all asses of society meet and do as they wish. Of course, ne's reputation is preserved. The ladies are expected leave fifteen minutes before the gentlemen . . . and "—she blew kisses around the room—"the folly reains a private matter. Would you care to join them? is hardly ten o'clock. Not too late." Her voice, r eyes, beamed with enticements. "And what is elve francs to a gentleman of your estate?"

She had hardly ended her speech when Ralph, inamed by her manner and gestures, swung her and abbed her so hard to him that the glass she held ttled against her front teeth. The tunic rumpled and d up, revealing the naked behind as she kicked her et back and dropped her entire weight into the care his embrace.

Meg, admiring the technique of this aggressive little ench, only wished that she could shuffle Ralph downairs into the anonymous mass below them. But it ould not be wise to allow him the attraction of such personal pleasures, free from his fixations upon her. hile he held Florie, rubbing her breasts against his ffles, he spread his other hand, palm upward, in the air and beckoned to Meg. She walked toward aware of what those fingers would search for, a lifted her own bosom into his grasp but stood just enough away so that he could not get a solid hold flesh. Opposite the hearth, a long sofa covered w red and orange stitched draperies seemed a suita place for the three of them, if they would fit. I Ralph evidently had his own ideas of how to approa pleasure. With Florie still in his arms, he dropp down to the floor, dragging her close to the fire, wh waves of crackling heat warmed them on the spread before its light. Meg, sensing that she ought keep herself busy with him, sat down and began undo the front buttons of his breeches, reaching arou his waist from the back and murmuring fiercely, "W an animal you are!"

Florie, beneath him, echoed the very same wor taking inspiration from the woman who knew h better. Already she was naked, the pitiable bit tunic flung like a handkerchief to the winds. Her am globular breasts, flattened by the pressure of Ralp chest, rolled outward as he brushed himself along h Hiking up on his knees or dropping prone, he dragg her closer and closer to the heat, as though intend to force her to lie upon the coals.

Thank God not I, Meg thought anxiously, surv ing the tangled sight before her, yet poised to spr in at any moment if Ralph should call.

Outside, couples hobbling about on the stairc were yawping and whistling to each other, their voi all the while reaching closer to Florie's door. M alone seemed to hear them and waited for th drunken, stumbling bodies to fall in on them. T glass that had rolled from Florie's hand wobbled a clinked. Her foot kicked out and one toe accidenta hit it and sent it skittering along the flags to the w where it bounced but miraculously held togeth Ralph, with one leg in his breeches and one o presented to Meg the pale-fleshed, thin-haunch hairy-bottomed sight that had, in her younger, m innocent days, sent her into nasty hysterics at the m opportune times. But she didn't find Ralph funny ow as her stomach contracted, asking her to change r squatting position to one more stretched out. The fa was too far away and therefore out of the ques- on.

Ralph lifted his head from between Florie's breasts d croaked, "I'll do this to you, Meg. To you. Come er here. Hold me. Kiss me. Pull this tart out from der me and give me—"

Florie, cast aside, erupted with indignant screeches at shattered the eardrums with every blast.

"Shut up. Shut up," Ralph muttered in his mur- rous tone.

Florie swallowed and became starkly quiet as two umbs pressed to her throat. He flung her aside and e sailed off as light as a kitten.

"Come to me, bitch," Ralph shot at Meg. He unded drunk or in a fever, totally out of control. ut Meg knew this was his normal self, as he behaved, disciplined, in private. Immediately she obeyed the mmons and slid into his grasp.

"You know how to please me better than any of ese damned quims that walk the streets for money." e held her by the arm above the elbow, dragged her ound in front of the flames, and flung her to her ck so that her head thudded to the carpet. The light ught in her vision. Her eyeballs felt made of red e. A shadow from his nose slashed a dark triangle to the hollow of one cheek. He was smiling with ticipation, but his widespread, pointed teeth glinted e tiny daggers. Between the spaces she saw the ngue pressing into the shapes of prickly pillows. ine had spilled onto his chin and cravat, giving him blood-spattered look of violence.

Meg twisted her body protectively so that his weight l on her hipbone and along her left side. From the rner of her eye she saw Florie creeping toward the or with a malicious grin.

"Feel me?" Ralph blubbered in a crazy rapture of lf-adoration. "Feel how big it is? You'll get to learn how good I am for women like you. Take it in your hand and shove it in. Go ahead now. Now!"

She was not even undressed and he didn't care. Didn't notice, probably, so long as her clothes were hiked up high enough for him to get at what he wanted.

A log fell, knocking up a shower of sparks that blazed brilliantly and were gone. In the flare of light she glimpsed Florie picking at the door and working it quietly ajar.

"Kiss me, spicy girl. The things I'm going to do to you!"

From Dick she had learned to make love on her side, cradling their bodies head to foot, one into the other. Finding that position now, she was instantly reminded of him, so that Ralph disappeared for a few seconds and she was holding her true lover, fondling, caressing, kissing with her tongue the only maleness in the world that could ever mean anything to her.

Ralph, flaunting his size, thrust it at her with a sudden jab that burned her gullet as though he were spewing acid. He continued to bore into her with brutal, thoughtless onslaughts, pounding at her until her head was forced backward for air and her body twisted and arched, pulling taut the tender, wounded belly flesh until it threatened to be rent anew. She clasped her hands together and pressed them upon the small bandage that still protected a swollen wound, holding the stomach muscles to give them support as she began to swivel and undulate her way toward a safer position.

"Hey! hey! hey!" hiccuped a male voice at the door. "Here's another party, folks."

"A quiet little party, though. Where's the girr-uls? Och! Here's a one. Sweetheart!"

Meg lay with her back to the merrymakers who had finally stumbled in, guided by Florie's muffled calls. For a moment Meg hoped that the intrusion would anger Ralph and delay him.

"Hear voices?" Ralph muttered uncertainly as though they might be in his head, and daring her to errupt the thrust and stroke of him to look around.

"What care I?" she grunted back.

"My darling love."

His fingers sought her thighs and were caught in eir trap. She put her own hands over his, urging em upward. Her tender flesh had begun to respond his direct pressure. Better to feel something sexual, ything rather than this rude molestation. What a rden it was to be ignorant no longer, nor insensitive the true sensation of love! In one instant she wished the old days when this gummy, raspy intrusion on her body was all she knew. But her experience uld never be the same since Dick, and she suffered re from the comparison.

She murmured Ralph's name inaudibly, at the same ne cursing the pompous pirating of her body. Yet o had she to blame when she was doing this herf, had come to this herself, for a particular and very purpose? She became aware, then, that Ralph's vement had stopped with the abrupt whiplash action a horse reined in before a wall.

"What? What is it?" she said, raising her head.

She saw Ralph blinking up while he trembled in curve of her fingers.

Then she looked and saw half a dozen men in htshirts down to their ankles. They had not come m the party below but from neighboring apartnts, drawn by the noise and their curiosity into the ong quarters, guided by Florie.

"Never mind them, never mind," Meg whispered, tling desperately against the disrupted climax and swell of Ralph's violent outrage. "Don't stop now. n't leave me." She had to keep him going, had to p him with her or there could be murder. "Kiss . Forget them. I don't care who's watching. I need u."

"Do you, my pet? Do you?" Distracted finally, he arded her and flew apart into different kinds of ns, the mouth leering, eyes smirking, cheeks wrinng with the nervous force of his own torturous sexlity.

"Gentlemun, gentlemun, leave that loving cou
there and come to me. Don't you see I'm lonesome
Florie slithered over and rubbed her breasts agai
each in turn, dragging their attention back to hers

Ralph shifted himself around beside Meg. She f
the edge of his front teeth slicing into her ear lobe
he hung suspended, forcing himself inside her, pryi
her thighs wide in preparation for his release. She dr
breath and thought, *It will all be over soon.*

"Meg, Meg. What must I think of to satisfy you
Ralph muttered, with savage call to battle.

Meg stared at him in the flickering hearth light. H
intuition had picked up something, but he could n
catch its essence. "Perhaps I cannot *be* satisfied," s
murmured with a tantalizing laugh that danced beyo
him.

"There is no such thing. Not with me. Not in r
arms," he replied confidently, stroking his wet fing
tips over her mouth, and moving restlessly within h
"I will think of things. Bulldogs? Horses? Who c
tell? But rest easy, my very own darling. Your fate
safe in my hands."

He chuckled with a queasy-sounding pleasure, gra
pled inside a pocket, and fluttered a note onto her th
he watched her read in the hearth glow.

*Dick will not honor any engagements until you r
turn—Julien.*

As he spilled his seed triumphantly, Meg murmur
not a word, not an excuse. What was there to s
now that Ralph knew all?

Chapter Twenty

CITOYEN MURIER LUMBERED across the dainty carpet of the duc's drawing room while Meg sat demurely on the edge of a wide-striped cushion chair, waiting for his decision.

"My dear Mademoiselle Watkins," said Murier, bouncing Meg's garnets in his white-gloved hand and exploding in a tiny, calculated fit of exasperation that masked his blighted hope. "Why should you want to leave for America when you are only beginning to love France?" His gaze shifted quickly to the sparkle in his palm before he drank off a swallow of claret and continued pacing. "There are still thousands of Englishmen enjoying themselves here wholeheartedly, and did I not arrange for you to visit the salon of Madame Recamier? But you disappointed me. And then the Académie Royale de Musique, and again you and your cousin did not arrive." He waggled one forefinger stiffly with regret. "I could have introduced him to everyone."

"Unfortunately, Citoyen Murier, I was indisposed," Meg replied wearily, aware that she need not expose the half of her reasons. "You are an ex-cleric, an ex-Terrorist, and an uncommonly subtle man. I should not have to tell you my troubles. Will you sell those jewels for me and arrange passage for two? Or must I look elsewhere for that gallant assistance?" The ability to bubble and to flirt with him was utterly drained. She spoke forthrightly from the depths of resignation to her entrapment by Ralph, combined with Dick's stubborn refusal to cooperate. Vanquished, she depended on the value of the garnets to do their wor on her behalf.

"Yes. These are very, very precious," he replied i solemn calculation of their worth and assessing Me now with a different, businesslike shrewdness. H strode around a low marquetry table gleaming wit inserts of Napoleon's profile and lowered the pendant ear pieces, necklace, and armband into a glitterin pile. "There are not many men in these strained time who could fetch any figure approximating their value.'

"And yourself?"

"Yes, I can do it," he sighed modestly. "That i perhaps not the most difficult part. The tickets. You *billets de passage* . . ."

"But many are leaving. Why should it be difficul for me?"

"Many are leaving, that is true. But not many ar leaving safely now that the oceans are aflame wit war. Travelers are all hoping for passage on a American ship. The Stars and Stripes is still neutra and everyone reaches for its protection on the waters England has swept all her merchantmen from the seas France and Holland no longer carry cargoes beneat their own ensigns. Even Spain is afraid to send he galleons to Mexico. So, you see, all the ports are beg ging for American ships to transport their wares."

"Then I, too, shall accept Yankee sail. It will d very nicely, thank you."

"If it can be arranged. They are altogether involve with the sugar trade in Cuba and their holds fille with Brazilian coffee. So busy are they, traveling be tween Manila and ports hostile to Britain, that you country has condemned American vessels for aidin the enemy. And our French privateers are not lyin idle in that quarter, I can assure you. There is no suc thing, in actuality, as a neutral ship. You would p yourself in great danger to try for a crossing."

"Nevertheless," Meg said without hesitation, "suc must be the case. I rely on you."

Murier secreted the garnets inside his expansive si jacket. "I will do my best."

Murier's best had much to recommend it. In less han a week they met in the arbors of the Tuilleries nd he showed her the tip of a bulky blue package f papers.

"It is not the most luxurious," he said. "But we have nanaged something. A French ship, *Le Lourrier de Orient*. Once a naval vessel, now supposedly a mail arrier but really owned by Paris bankers, with its ervices subsidized by the French government."

"I do not care if it is an Indian canoe!" She grasped is arm, thrilled. "How can I thank you, monsieur? But ere. One good turn deserves another. You must de- ver a message for me this very hour."

Murier glanced at the name and Julien's address. Mademoiselle," he said, squeezing her fingers with ympathy. "You are running away. And all I can say you is, good luck. One must have short stories and arry long knives."

She sprang on tiptoe and kissed him full on the soft ushion of lips, rubbing herself up along his bulk and nanking him ardently with her body and mute gaze. hen she pushed him off to contact Dick, so that when ne went to him this very night, he would be waiting or her in the apartment. . . .

The cabriolet had barely reached Julien's door and opped when Meg jumped down and ran inside, care- ss of her own safety, of being followed by spies for alph. She raced up the stairs, into the rooms and ulien's arms, tumbling a bolt of puce-colored silk om his grasp.

"Is he here? Is he?" she cried breathlessly as they oth bent to recover the upset silk.

"In his bedroom, waiting." Julien chuckled. "You ook very rosy and well."

"Yes, I am." Her voice trailed behind her while ne raced into the large rear room that Dick had taken ver, its pristine neatness undone by the domination f brushes, colors, chalks, and papers. But Julien's aste had prevailed in another way. Dick's careless, olor-splattered breeches were replaced by clean, fawn- olored trousers and polished boots of soft leather, somewhat elegant, surely French, and, Meg realized totally becoming.

She fled into his arms. He caught her, lifted he into the air, and alternately kissed her mouth and he eyelids, saying, "What's happened to you, darling What's going on? Sit down. Catch your breath and tel me."

"Dick, I have the most marvelous news," sh gasped, the words catching in her dry throat. Too ex cited, she could not sit, but pulled out the passage pa pers and waved them.

"What's that?" he said, laughing.

She thrust the packet straight at him and pressed it into his palm. "Passage to America!" she sang a she turned the parcel over. "You don't have to open it if you don't wish to. You can believe me."

Julien had set out a little tray of tea things fo them. Dick, eyeing her with careful reserve, began to pour tea into the porcelain cups and transferred some triangles of watercress sandwiches from their pile to a separate plate. "Is that so?" he replied noncommit tally.

"For us both," she added, pressing on with he cheer.

"I would think it," he commented dryly. "Now eat this. How is the wound doing? You seem much improved."

"Oh, bother the wound! Listen to me, my sweet Don't you *see* what I'm telling you?"

"Yes." He sat down close to another small, iron back chair.

She plopped into hers and pulled it forward till thei knees touched, then reached over and pinched hi thigh hard. "Well, answer me. Say something. Aren you alive?"

He threw back his head and laughed, the long, mus cled neck relaxing as though she had merely told hin a good joke.

"You make me furious!" she spat. "You are th most argumentative, difficult, obstreperous . . . *thing,* she stuttered. "First you promise me the simplest ac of cooperation. Then you refuse as though I were dragging you to the guillotine. And I forgive you! I forgive you everything, though I can't say why. Now here comes this." She shook the packet close to his face and hit him on the shoulder with it. *"This chance!* And you laugh at me. Laugh! Why do you laugh, you imbecile? I hate you." She leaned her weight forward and stepped as hard as she could on his boot toe, grinding her teeth in exasperation as she felt that she could barely make a dent upon him. "I am at a loss for words."

"Loss for words? You?" The laughter suddenly stopped. "Oh, Meg. My sweetest darling." He lifted her hand free of the papers and stroked and kissed each finger. "How can I go anywhere when the navy will press me into service the minute I step out the door? I have been sitting here these past days thinking that I shall go back to serve in the Dragoons. It is inevitable. One must fight for one's freedom and not let the job fall to others."

"Tush and bother," she said in a dark, distressed tone. "I don't believe a word of you. You've served your time already. Enough for six men. Look at you, cut up in the face and almost clear across your belly. How many more slashes can you take before you topple over in two? Just show them you're used up and they'll let you be."

"We both have a country to serve, Meg."

"And will you serve it by dying?" Her eyeballs burned with vexation. She felt them standing clear out of her head. "You were meant to do one thing and one thing only in the service of your country." She snatched up some newly dried watercolors and rattled them in his face. "Remember?"

"Dying is inescapable," he replied soothingly. "Why fear it?"

"Yes." She bounced back undeterred. "But what if you *don't* die? What if you only lose an arm? Both arms? What shall I do with you then, for the rest of our lives together? Would you not curse yourself for being too eager a fool, destroying yourself thus and of no good use to your country?"

Dick shook his head and carefully took the paintings from her impassioned grip. "Careful. Careful," he said. "I just finished those this morning."

"Oh, listen to me, do!"

"I am listening. And when I hear reason I shall listen the more closely, my dearest."

"Reason? America is a fine, fine reason, don't you think so?" she said, changing to a tone of enticement. "Haven't you heard things? *I* certainly have. La comtesse has a daughter who went off to America and writes home how unique and picturesque a place it is," she continued, making it up as she went. "There are monkeys in New Jersey the likes of which we have never seen at Pidcock's. And tigers in Carolina. Won't you be pleased to see them with your own two eyes? Think of the drawings. Think of the paintings. Think of the . . . the *dissections!*"

Dick had leaned back in the chair, his eyes beginning to sparkle with fascination for her. Meg, sensing that she was making a dent, already saw the name he could build for himself in the new country. She had a hefty supply of louis left over from the sale of Ralph's jewels that would buy them fine, American-style clothing and take them everywhere. A reputation in America would carry well, back to England. Make him the talked-of man there, too, when eventually they returned.

Building on her advantage, she flung herself on him quietly now, letting all she had said sink in, allowing her body to go limp as she settled down, snuggling comfortably on his broad lap as though leaving the ultimate decision to him of the stronger sex and mind. But she could feel him breathing with a new animation. The unsettled conditions of Paris, the threat of more blood spilled in a futile clash of powerful nations, the promise of new adventure in an exotic, beautiful world, were all working on him deep down. She could bide her time and let Dick put the official seal on what she knew was already decided.

"You know what I think," he said. "I think it would be a good idea to get you far away from Ralph Carstip. Why I allowed you to return to him . . ."

". . . is water under the bridge. And I shall never go back. So let us erase his name forever."

Dick turned his head and peered down at the top of her curls. "Do you think you will like America?" he asked teasingly. "I hear the men there wear feathers in their hair and stripes across their cheeks."

Meg smiled and closed her eyes, thinking: *Darling, darling, thank you!*

She was never one to fuss about possessions. She had grown up with nothing to preserve and had learned to concentrate her efforts upon the protection of life and limb, which came in handy now against Julien's protestations that she pack dozens of articles aboard, especially pink bottles and green bottles for the prevention of mal de mer.

But Meg, in her usual practical way, replied, "If my stomach rises, I am sure the railing will never be far from reach."

The date for the passage was two days hence, September 14th, and they studiously avoided talking of the North Atlantic at this time of year. Occasionally Julien noted aloud how unusually mild the weather remained, and on the day of departure they rode off in the sweltering heat of a sunny noon.

The coach trip, uneventful except for an occasional mire knee-deep at crossroads, passed beside cavalry regiments massing in villages and strings of army horses stabled at quiet farms. Meg knew in her heart that she was right to take Dick far from all this bloodlust madness. A retired priest sitting opposite them in the coach observed that if one power could move large armies by sea, so could another, and as the days were not come when the lion and the lamb were to lie down quietly side by side, there would have to be a headlong collision. "And besides, the forage is becoming scarce."

"We were betrayed," replied a woman passenger,

hefting and hugging the bundle fuming with garlic on her ample lap.

"Perhaps so," muttered Dick. "It is the way the French explain every disaster." Thus he ended abruptly, in his natural style, the intercourse of friendly conversation.

They stood quayside before the long, trim bow of a foreign-looking frigate, her hull painted black. Meg, peering up into the sails and rigging, saw no sign of the French tricolors. Behind them a gaggle of restless men, women, and children shuffled around the wharf, fussing with baggage and packages preciously gripped tightly, and seeming to take this unexpected turn of events with aplomb.

"That's an American ship o' war," muttered Dick.

Behind him a burly man interceded with, "What of it, lad, we're going home," in a strange, drawling accent that Meg found delightful.

"Ask me no questions, I'll tell you no lies," piped a child from beneath a black leather bonnet and clung to his father's knee breeches.

The gentleman, well decked out in a blue cutaway with bright gold buttons and an enormous powdered wig trimly tied behind, pushed the boy to his mother, and leaning toward Dick, advised, "Listen to me son; be circumspect."

A collection of midshipmen and crew bustled aboard, ignoring the passengers staring up at them in fascination. At last a senior officer appeared beneath the spars and worked his way down the plank. He stood stiffly on land before the spindly group of ten refugees and surveyed them with a mixture of distaste and pity that took in the lot with a sharp, round glance.

"Hear me a minute and I'll be done with you," he said, poking a cigar in the air. "My ship is not equipped to carry passengers, and I have already refused a dozen others. Lieutenant Neeps will show you where to stow aboard and will make you comfortable as can be expected considering our present condition.

I make no bones about it. We are a fighting ship as has limped away from Tripoli and those damned Turks and have put in to port here at the request of certain authorities who must, perforce, remain nameless. That you were expecting a French vessel is none of my concern. I can assure you, however, we have no prisoners in the lower hold and no sentinels at the hatchways. But as for actual comforts, I hope I will find you all sensible, and we shall maintain a constant vigilance against privateers at all times between here and New York. I expect to cross in thirty to thirty-three days, depending on wind and weather. I bid you all fair journey."

With one raw-boned, final stare that brooked no questions, he turned his back to the group, shoved his cigar into the venomous hole of a mouth, and proceeded to wave the crew to prepare for boarding.

"Nothing marvelous in that one to trust," muttered the woman with the bag from inside the protective confines of a large bonnet.

The gentleman standing behind Dick noted, "Our sail looks much like a privateer herself."

Meg glanced inquiringly at Dick, watching him survey the stepped-back masts. When they boarded, she quietly studied the surly nature of the crew hanging about in blue jackets and white duck trousers, some with tarpaulin hats pulled down to their eyebrows, others bareheaded, all with a rascally animal glare pondering at the feet of every passenger.

"Don't take it amiss, my sweet," Dick muttered. "These men have seen miserable action, I warrant, and are hungry for home."

"They can look as they please," quipped Meg, "for all I care. Where do we bunk? Where do they stow us?"

Lieutenant Neeps, a white-skinned, yellow-haired youth who seemed to have toddled from the cradle to shipboard, was directing families and couples to various quarters below decks. Meg and Dick arrived at a cabin very comfortably laid out with a looking-glass and mahogany furniture not at all in keeping with the austerity of a navy vessel.

"Seems like the admiral's cabin itself," Dick chuckled, examining the fittings with mingled interest and disbelief. "I dare say those papers of yours brought us to this."

"If it's the only one of a kind, perhaps the family with the boy should have it."

"I wouldn't interfere just yet with our captain's arrangements." He unrolled a bag and removed some small bottles of pink tonic. "Julien did manage to send these after all."

But Meg heard and saw nothing beyond the thrill of waiting to depart. "How long before we leave?" she sighed over and over, opening the chest of drawers, walking about the small quarters, touching everything while imagining the shores of a far-distant country.

"The tide is coming in now," Dick answered. "A few hours at most."

He had given up trying to calm her impatience, which had stretched thin by the time darkness arrived and the ship actually cast off, with sailors hanging overboard and holding out lanterns into the night.

September blows gusted day after day and filled the crowded sail that sent the prow slipping over high whitecaps. Above decks, her cheeks whipped by the wind, Meg hung on to one of the bronze carronades mounted forward as though to drive fire into a fleeing vessel. Sometimes before noon she watched the sextants brought up to take the sun and listened to the calculations of the second officer verifying the course in reference to the ship's speed. Great blue swells rose to foam across the surface and pounded each other crosswise, only to disappear in booming gurgles of froth. Not a bird. Not a gull. Air without scent, neither rank nor sweet, as though it had disappeared except for its constant flap always lifting and pulling at her skirts.

The lady in the poke bonnet appeared one afternoon in a voluminous flowered dress and black shawl, standing amidships and gazing off to where an unusually serene surface caught the liquid bronze spill of westerly sunlight fading gradually into violet. She looked around with a guarded arrogance against the sailors, who could pop up from behind a hatchway or drop down from a shroud to be found standing and staring soundlessly. When she spied only Meg returning the glance, she smiled and began to approach, grasping the rail and going with a roll of a stride, in keeping with the keel's unsteady toss. "Good day to you, Mrs. . . ."

"Fox," Meg said importantly. She felt herself thrill as the name came out of her unexpectedly, but in so natural a voice that she wondered she had never thought this before.

"I am Mrs. Weddiweather. Annabella Weddiweather of Boston. You are not an American lady, nor French, I don't think?"

"British."

"Oh, yes, I should have guessed it." She nodded with a square, friendly face, young but hard-worked into bunches of wrinkles at the eyes and mouth.

Her son appeared from behind a sailor who had just dropped down from the lines. The boy came dashing at her to throw himself against her knees, retching with his head buried in her skirts.

"Poor bird is suffering so," murmured his mother, stroking the back of his fine tow hair. "Some never become accustomed to water travel," she added with a regretful sigh. "I must take him below."

"Wait and I shall go with you," said Meg cheerily. "I have a bottle of calming medicine among my things, if you would like him to try some."

A slanting drizzle began and no one appeared for days, except the crew, who ignored Meg and Dick as they strolled, stretching their legs and inhaling the fine, clean air.

"Everyone is downstairs heaving." Dick smiled.

"I'd never do it." Meg grimaced valiantly. "You can take *me* anywhere."

The rain dried and the wind turned baffling that night, slowing and rocking the ship. Then a placid sea settled out ahead with a light, steady breeze taking the topsails. The little boy appeared above decks again, this time hanging on to his father's wrist. The gentleman was accompanied by another in a black suit with a gray felt hat and small gold spectacles, looking as though he had been demoted from a fine merchant to a poor practitioner of medicine.

"You know, sir," he said to Dick, "we carry a cargo of cognac in the hold. And I have persuaded the captain that I can cure his crew of any fever for the price of some few glasses."

"An enterprising approach," Dick replied with approval. "And have you both completed the bargain?"

"Not while the crew is well, unfortunately. But I hear there may be someone with tertiary fever hiding aboard. An older man and I must find him. Perhaps I can lure out some word of him at the gambling table."

"Do you play whist, sir?" intruded Mr. Weddiweather hopefully to Dick.

"Once or twice in my time," Dick admitted with reluctance. "Can't say I have the knack."

With misgivings Meg watched Dick go off protestingly in company with the other two. Oddly, she had supposed that he had left the old ways in the old countries. But since he had no other source of livelihood, how could she begrudge him the opportunity that forced its way into his hand?

After twenty days a number of the women had gradually ventured back upon deck, more settled and sure of themselves against the ship's erratic motion and able to stroll with a scrupulous conscience away from the railing. But they carefully kept to themselves, as though fearful of conversation with strangers. Mrs. Weddiweather returned, her son with her but independent now, dashing from one set of ropes to the next and forgetting his mother completely.

"This is more than a decent journey," she commented to Meg. "And I am grateful for the boy's sake. Before I was married to Mr. Weddiweather, I traveled a great deal, but mainly at home."

"A single lady traveled a great deal?" Meg said th wonder.

"Before marriage one can play about," she ex-ained. "After the vows comes the settling down and ending to the business of household."

"How very opposite from our style," Meg replied. ingle, respectable girls are kept indoors." Privately e mused how sly the English were to hide behind e married title as an opportunity to enjoy whatever ison the heart desired.

"Your husband is English, too, I expect. Well, then, u must visit Boston. It is the most English of Ameri-n cities."

"And are the chances favorable in Boston for art-s?"

"Why, Mrs. Fox," replied Mrs. Weddiweather oudly. "It is the center of a flourishing artistic com-unity the likes of which you will not see out in the lderness places. Mr. Gilbert Stuart, who painted esident Washington, God rest his soul, lives among . The circle of artists is a very lively one, I guarantee u."

"I'll remember it," Meg said, intently grateful.

"You should. You must, if that is your husband's terprise. Mr. Weddiweather has an eye for business, at's his line. And he plans to do something further the cloth trade when we arrive back home."

Meg hardly heard one word out of seven that fired om the confiding lips of her companion. She gazed t across the waves, feeling the rise of her own dependent nature, and saw herself steering Dick's ture away from New York up to Boston. She ex-sed herself after a while and sauntered off in search Dick. She found him leaning against some ratlines, etching the curl of foam as it eddied away from the ip's stern.

"You know, I have been thinking, Meg, as I look these free-wheeling Americans, that my way of life s not produced much to show for itself." He uinted across deep green currents drifting into dark cesses of blue. The lines around his mouth were less taut than she remembered them. He seemed actu ally sunny in a covert way, as though he had bee going over his life and finding ways to change th things that bothered him. "I am in the habit of work ing hard enough. No one can call me a slacker. Bu I see that I have not directed my efforts in an o ganized fashion. You were quick enough to recogniz the defect, ignorant though you were at first, whe you stole my pictures away thinking I would neve miss them."

"But you did!" she said, pleased and disconcerted

"And I didn't care. For I lost interest in a pictur once I conquered its subject. Feargus tried to mak something of me after his own style. So did Jame Dufferin in Maldon. No one could succeed. No things are shifting direction. I feel somehow that th whims of the soul have stopped blowing me about an I can go forward straight on, pulled along altogethe where I want to go as though by a team of twent mules."

"Mules?"

"They use mules in America as much as horses, understand. In fact, I could have won a team fron a merchant very careless at the card table, but I didn' see any sense to taking them while we're drifting a sea."

"Strange for a gambler not to think ahead to othe times," Meg said with quiet delight.

Dick shrugged as though tossing off an old, heav cloak. "I may not be much of a gambler, either, whe it comes down to that." He smiled at her studie interest. "I could be finding a few new gaits in thi old horse."

"Never mind it, Dick," she said, comforting hi unspoken questions. "Whatever you are, whatever yo do, will only help you to paint better."

"I do feel a restlessness for work, that's true Twenty-eight days, and all I've accomplished are thes few chalks."

"Not the best circumstances for drawing, my dear Don't be too hard."

They passed a Bermuda brig the following after-
on, and two days later a lookout hanging skyward
the crosstrees set up his telescope and scanned the
tance. The next morning the deck became littered
th cases, trunks, and barrels organized in a serious
le that none of the passengers could make sense
Some thought the captain had done a bit of pri-
teering on his own and had foundered on a barrier
f, but not wishing to admit the breach of ethics,
d conspired with government officials to settle the
ares out with his crew and turn the cognac cargo
er in some private trade-off.

"We shall never be the wiser," intoned Mr. Weddi-
ather.

Then all concern with cargo or the captain's ad-
ntures was forgotten as the lookout's voice rang
ar through the midday spectacle of glittering sun-
ht:

"Land ho!"

Chapter Twenty-one

HERE IT LIES, Mrs. Fox, the finest commercial city
our continent." Mr. Weddiweather caught his son
in his arms. "I wish you well in it. And in our
untry."

With a throbbing mixture of nameless, wordless
notions, Meg lifted her gaze to the heights of The
arrows slowly rising in a green curve from the dap-
ed water as the boat drifted into a silver bay sprin-
ed with islands capped by turreted forts, their colors
apping high upon flagstaffs in breezy gestures of wel-
me. Light, sharp-keeled vessels of many shapes and
zes flitted cheerfully within the circular band of the

Hudson's bay, some traveling with the boat past t shores of Staten Island and Long Island. For ma uninterrupted miles she could see hundreds, perha thousands, of thriving farmlands in the spectacle pure air.

While the ship glided toward the city, little bo powered by active rowers sprang away from the va ous shores to approach and call up to the vessel, "A well?" thus beginning conversations between row and seafaring passengers. All manner of questions f lowed concerning the weather, the length of the voya and the latest war news from Europe. Mr. Wed weather, in his turn, shouted down questions concer ing the health of the locals and the condition of t harvest, only to be drowned out by the calls of oth passengers regarding a conglomeration of trifling m ters of interest to them. Finally, one or two boatm inquired offhandedly if passengers wished to landed, asking this in the most civil style, more as common courtesy than from a desire to gain emplo ment. To Meg the tall rowers seemed uncommon agile and foreign-looking, their sunburned faces h den beneath light hats. As they floated around t southernmost point of the city, where the Hudson a East rivers flowed together, she pulled Dick to her admire the panorama of New York, its compact fo standing straight out beside the public walkways lin by autumn-colored trees that bent toward the wat where well-dressed strollers paused to admire the a proaching vessel. Behind the shores, white-paint houses disappeared into the distant rolling hills, w poplar branches appearing above rooftops and marking the line of the streets.

The city, expanding and widening from the Batte traveled northward alongside the Hudson. On its side, the coast of Jersey was a scattering of villag and villas. White walls gleamed through the tre Here and there woods gave way to sheer walls rock. Over to the right flowed the more winding w ters of the East River with its wooded heights Brooklyn and busy quays and warehouses peepi rough the forests of masts. At last the ship reached s dock and the crowd of vessels, where tars leaped om the yards and rigging to assist in clearing a passage. Then came the first touch of land planks laid assist the passengers, to support unsteady feet, and take charge of bundles.

Meg, so eager to arrive after all the weeks she had een dreaming aboard ship, felt the smother of hesitation that was her heartbeat as her eyes took in the rowded, bustling city going about its business in the risp October air. Her mind sought for some familiar yle, French or English, among the buildings and inhabitants while she hurried, beside Dick, over the ound, paving stones, along streets going every which ay, some straight, some forming half-circles, others ossing through and forking to make a triangular area or houses. The brick and clapboard had a sturdy, neven set to them, with green gardens and slender ees dropping deep russet leaves at this season. ven the wide thoroughfare of Broadway had someing irregular about it, so that her eye could not take all in at once, but unfolded the vista bit by bit. ripping Dick's hand, she pulled him hither and yon round the water pumps in the center of the street, to e everything she could before losing all her breath.

"Where is the governor's house? Dick, can you find out? I must see that first." After a few inquiries, ey found themselves at the lowest end of Broadway, ear the Battery, where, overlooking the spread of ater ahead and placed, to her mind, upon a handome elevation, there stood an elegant abode with n elliptical approach, built on about an acre of ground nd enclosed with an iron railing. In the midst rose n ornamental building two stories high with a portico efore it and a carved bas-relief of the state arms, istice and liberty, as large as life, everything white pon a blue field, and supported by four white pillars he height of the two stories.

"Why, how pretty it is," Meg breathed. "But nothng as large as a palace."

"And when do you expect to meet the governor?" Dick chided.

"Oh, soon. As soon as we are settled," Meg replie seriously. "This is a free country, is it not? With n social classes to speak of? I shall have a card of in vitation to a ball before you can snap your finger and say Yankee boy dandy."

"So you probably shall. Though he lives in Albany.

"And what is that to me? I shall find him whereve he is." Meg smiled slyly, not revealing just yet th horde of letters that filled her purse. When she ha first hit upon the idea of coming to America, th comtesse had instantly offered her a note of introduc tion to Elise, and then, as an afterthought, had writ ten a host of others to various dignitaries who migh lead her to Elise in case she missed or lost the girl i her travels.

They picked their cumbersome way through th lively neighborhoods, drinking in the brilliancy of th pure air and watching the never-ending play of ves sels shooting off in every direction, up the Hudso Bay or around the quays and wharfs into the Eas River. For the first time in her life, she thought sh could draw a free breath, so clean and free from chimney smoke was the air, so white and neat th prospect uninterrupted for miles.

"While you were planning our social schedule," said Dick, "I have taken from Mr. Weddiweather th name of a tolerable boarding house where we ca meet an example of every type of citizen who inhabit the country, as he puts it . . . let us see if I remembe it . . . adventurers, artists, statesmen, grafters, smug glers, merrymakers, mariners, pirates, guzzlers, In dians, thieves, stuffed shirts, turncoats, millionaire inventors, poets, heroes, soldiers, harlots, bootlick nobles, nonentities, burghers, martyrs, murderers. . . Now here we are arrived. Shall we go inside?"

Meg leaned against an iron newel post, laughin and holding her bosom. "I am not at all certain th I care to be confined to such distinguished compan this early in our travels." On second thought, howeve e famished, empty feeling inside her did its convinc-g work.

They climbed a stoop of three steps and passed rough a polished doorway into a reception room. A acard above a mahogany drop-leaf table read: *ohnathan and Emily Briggs, a comfortable and mod-n boarding house for the sojourner.* Beside it hung modern banjo clock in a mahogany case with a brass-riven weight that swung to and fro, telling the hour nd the minute on a white metal face with delicate on hands pointing to slender numerals in black. Arm hairs, also of mahogany, with curved backs and legs ood in the corners of the large, light room.

Mrs. Briggs entered immediately and introduced erself in a deep, handsome voice. She smiled at em from a face surrounded by short, dark hair and white muslin cap. Her dress fell to the ankles in ant but modest folds over her burly shape. "You ust be right off the boat that's come in this day. Why, I am sure you are starved. Let me bring some uit and tea to your room, and dinner will be shortly."

Gratefully Meg climbed the last steps behind the urdy woman and finally stood, alone with Dick, on floor that neither swayed nor creaked, gazing hap-ily at a canopied trundle bed comfortably placed eside a window hardly covered by draperies that ung to either side. A chest of drawers with a round irror, a chair here and there on a colorful carpet, ave a cozy feel of rest to the atmosphere and induced Meg to collapse, aware of excitement in abeyance, of nergies drained by the novelty of every sight that he looked upon.

Quietly, without a thought in her head now, she alked to the bed and lingered beside it for some oments, bleakly aware of her fatigue. Then, drop-ing face forward upon the coverlet, she stretched ut, arms above her head, and with one cheek press-ng into the horsehair mattress, watched Dick standing t the window gazing out upon the mob milling below.

"What do you see out there?" she murmured. "Come o me. There is a painting of President Jefferson hanging on the wall that I can see from here, behind yo One day, my darling, I should like to see the portra of a president hanging on my bedroom wall painte by yourself."

Dick, enthralled where he stood, made no answe for a long while. "I tell you, Meg," he said finall "The smartest thing you've done was convincing m to come here. This country is teeming with life. An the way the light falls on the subjects! I can actuall see things that in London were always hidden in yellow pea soup, to be more imagined by the ey than visualized. Yes, I love it here already. I will d great things."

"I know you will, darling. It is like breathing fo you, to do great things."

He turned from the window and smiled at he "How do I deserve a woman with such continuin faith?"

Meg smiled, half asleep in her heaven. She wiggle her fingers, motioning Dick to come to her. When h approached and she could feel his leg, everything els that she dreamed of seemed already fulfilled. In he imagination, they were talking in the bedroom of thei own mansion built somewhere on the Bowery o Grosvenor Square. Dick's world filled with commissions for portraits for two years ahead of time, and h worked joyously from morning till dark while she entertained the wives of the famous. King George himsel had to use the royal prerogative to gain a sitting. The it was October, only a few months after the latest exhibition at the Royal Academy, and Dick's reputatio had taken a terrific leap, an exotic twist that buzze his name about in the morning dailies. She had all t do to convince him that health demanded a shor vacation at their great house in the north country. Fo holidays they would ride together or entertain som visiting diplomat from Russia. Of course, the war ha been won and Napoleon was long since sunk down t defeat, so that she looked ahead with relish to Dick' plans to drive through Northern Italy the followin spring.

"Feels good to be on land, eh?" he whispered, leaning over and kissing her cheek.

"I can't tell where we are," she sighed with her eyes closed.

"You nap while I go downstairs and chat with Johnathan Briggs about how best to proceed."

"No. Not without me," she yelped, and struggled to sit up, touching her hair in a half-dream state and ready to walk out again.

"You can't take five steps," he laughed, "without falling asleep on your feet. Now come lie down and I'll stay with you."

"You won't leave me when I've drifted off?" Her voice held more concern than she realized.

"And if I do leave, where will I go to?" he replied sensibly. "If I know you, you'll turn me up wherever I might wander in this fair city. You tracked me from London to Paris. You certainly can find me from Broadway to Wall Street."

But Meg didn't consider it funny, and she felt none of the nonchalance that sounded in Dick's voice. So much to be done. And all among strangers. "Lie beside me a while, so I don't have to think. Will you do that?" Her voice in its sleepy state was almost childish, but demandingly so. She clung to his wrist and his knuckles till he collapsed beside her, stroking her head and neck tenderly. To make certain he would go nowhere while she slept, she flung a leg over his hip and anchored him thus, then, feeling that she had to trust him or die of fatigue, she drifted off to the faint street cries of "Here's clams . . . here's clams."

"But what did they tell you, my dear?" said Mrs. Briggs with a stark, scandalized look. "The old governor's manse is now a custom house, and the American Academy of Art is to occupy the top floor. You must believe no one. Folly, credulity, and ignorance are surely rife, and hoaxability is catching. But your man can find everything he wants in New York and earn his living as he chooses." She leaned over to pat Meg's knee reassuringly, biting down at the same time into a ball of butter in her palm and chewing it slowl "And so can you." She gave Meg a long, confidir wink. "This is a free country, Lord be praised. M Johnathan eats well, drinks well, and is a good Presby terian. But we ladies must keep an eye out for ou selves."

They sat in the drawing room with Mrs. Brigg near the doorway, into which she leaned over occa sionally to keep watch on the hall, where rogues wer known to sneak in and steal the coats from the wa pegs. The windows stood open half a dozen inche bringing in the bleat of an angry pig being chase down the middle of the road, and calls of "Hot cor lily-white hot corn," came from a Negro woman carry ing a pail. It was another sunny day. Five days c light and clear air in a row. Meg could feel her dis position easing because of the weather. She didn't seer to worry so much that Dick stayed, day after day down at the harbor sketching, without a care in th world about what would happen to them on the mor row. Somehow it would all turn right.

"I have an introduction to a lady in America," Me said brightly, taking out the letter from the comtesse "I think I shall travel around there this morning. Ca you tell me where it is?"

"An elegant handwriting," said Mrs. Briggs, pursin her lips. "To Madame Philippe Arbut Chevalier d Vievelorain. Why, this is away in the country. I d not know the address, but we have a map somewhere I keep it folded in between my nephew's books. Here Here it is. The rewards of neatness." She carefull unfolded a crisp square of heavy paper and stretche it out on a table, holding down the ends with tw pewter candlesticks. "Ah. There. You see. She i somewhat north out of the city, in a little village calle Greenwich. A fashionable resort and very pretty, hear tell. The ladies go there summers to escape th threat of yellow fever. If you want to make the trip Johnathan will take you in his wagon. Or the publi stage runs through. Husband going with you, I sup pose?"

"I don't care to bother him and take him from his work just now."

Again Mrs. Briggs winked shrewdly, wrinkling her rough-skinned face. She folded the map and pressed it under Meg's arm. "Since you don't take the man, take the map. I shall wrap a chicken for you and pure tea water. New York has all things good in it but water, what a trial. And take your necessaries, dear. You'll be gone two or three days, I should think. Who is to say what conveniences these French have neglected? They don't live as clean as us, I know for a fact. You'll see the revolutionary characters wandering around the streets plenty. They look like they've been pulled from a ditch and stood up backward in a gale. And some of our fanciful young men think it a style to copy."

"Two or three *days?*"

"Why, that's not long for so far." Mrs. Briggs stared at her, perplexed. Then the bright brown eyes understood. "Take him with you if you must. A good woman should convince her man of what's right."

"Thank you, Mrs. Briggs. Thank you for everything." Meg backed distractedly from the room and ran upstairs, steeling herself to compose a suitable note for Dick. But what would she tell him? She wandered around the room, shaking out the new dresses and the silk sandals she had bought during the week, berating herself for the useless plans she had made to slip out of an afternoon to Elise and return home again by sundown. Now her intention was developing into a major strategy. She dared not go without him for so long. Would he join her? And if he did agree, would he be gallant? And if he could not be a gentleman for a simple visit, how would he behave at the governor's ball when she finally managed them an invitation? Meg shuddered at the thought of Dick let loose in society. For all his good intentions, he was still . . . himself.

"But this is America!" she cried aloud. "Manners here, at best, are peculiar. They will find Dick a novelty. And charming at that. Especially the ladies. He is a foreigner and an artist. They will make excuses for him on every count." Giggling with encouragement, she danced over to the mirror and said to her reflection, "We are saved!"

Her instinct was to run down to Coenties Slip, find Dick, and tell him to pack his chalks and paper for the journey, as though she could go straight to him midst the thirty thousand people in New York. To stay cooped up in the room and wait was unbearable. She should spend the time dispatching a letter to Elise to warn her they were coming. Warn her Dick was coming!

My dear Madame,

Through your mother's kindness, I have the pleasure of introducing myself to you, and my cousin Dick Fox, the painter . . .

How terribly stupid it sounded. How obvious. She tore up the paper and started again. But no matter how many different ways she phrased it, the truth stared out from between the lines. "Cousin Dick" simply did not ring on the ear. "I am such a good liar, usually. But not in this case, why is that?"

By sundown she was still pondering that very same problem, and Dick solved it for her quickly. "You are mistaken, love. You are not a very good liar at all."

"But look at you," she trilled, suddenly caught by his appearance. "You have cut your hair and bought yourself a pair of duck trousers. How marvelous! Why, you look completely *American.* I'm impressed." She came up to him, fondling the cravat and running her fingers through his windblown crop.

"Is this American?" he repeated, disappointed. "I meant it to announce my revolutionary sympathies."

"Oh, you can't mean that."

"But I do." He smiled. "Why so pale suddenly?"

Meg clapped her hands together with chagrin. "Isn't this inevitable? Isn't it just my luck? Here we are going to visit the daughter of a true French Royalist, ınd there you stand blazing with your love for their leepest enemy."

"Again we are at sword's points." Dick laughed vith a rollicking burst. He lifted her from the ground, swung her around, then slowly let her down while their ips touched caressingly. "What are you getting us into his time, eh, vixen?"

"The good graces of a French diplomat and his vife." She sighed with resignation at her troubles to ome.

"I should have known." He toyed with her ringlets, ntranced by their color in the candlelight. "President efferson would not approve of your sympathies, you ealize. America is on *my* side."

"America is on its own side. Dick, listen to me with n open mind. You know you owe me a favor."

"I owe you many." He smiled. "And I shall always be behind, never catching up. Which one is it his time?"

She took his hands and kissed them, sat down on iis lap and settled herself into her safest, permanent erth, put her arms around his neck, and pressed her heek to his. His skin smelled crisply of sea air, and is clothes were still cool from walking outdoors. Meg losed her eyes for a moment, wishing they could imply be together like this, quietly, and not always vorking out some major difference of opinion. Things ad run so smoothly these past days because of the xtra money she had, courtesy of Ralph Carstip's ewels. But she had no more garnets to sell. What vould they do when her little horde was entirely pent? Elise might be able to arrange some commisions for Dick, if only he would agree and manage to ooperate for a while. As casually as possible, she old him about her letters of introduction from the omtesse.

"Sounds like a very wise approach," Dick said when he had finished. "Efficient and foresighted. Quite the pposite of my rambling ways."

"Will you do it, then?" she asked, careful not to

press. "Will you come with me? And will you simply be yourself without getting upset? I mean, will you meet these nice people and accept that they're ordinary folks like the ones you draw every day on the Battery, and that no one is stepping on you or trying to control you? And that it's a free country, as Mrs. Briggs says? And you can live and be happy in it . . . and so can I?"

"How impassioned you are," Dick replied with a quirk of sympathy in his voice. "Why shouldn't I do all of that? Of course I will. I would like to see some of the inland villages," he said, nuzzling into her neck. "But your cousin Dick Fox might look at you peculiarly from time to time in the company of strangers. What will your fine friends think?" He smiled with amusement. "But if we are to go, we must do it properly. You will write Elise a letter and wait for her invitation, not barge in there like some traveling peddler of pots."

Meg placed a long, grateful kiss upon his ear, then stole from his lap without a word and returned to her writing desk, eager to get it over with and out before Dick should change his mood. "Will you tell me what I should say?" Her tone was small, almost humble.

"Yes." His eyebrows drew together with an effort. He clasped his hands behind his back and walked about on the flowered carpet.

By the time one tallow candle had burned low, the letter was written, sealed, and put to post.

Chapter Twenty-two

VITHIN A WEEK they had an answer from an appeal-ng, girlish hand, eager to hear news of her family, specially Victor, and requesting Miss Watkins and Ir. Fox to visit as soon as they could, to stay for as ong as they wished.

Meg read the letter a few times to herself, once to Irs. Briggs, and quoted parts of it to a brown and vhite cow on the road as she ran over to the coffee ouse behind the wharves where successful merchants vith Republican ideas made good subjects for Dick's en. She found him halfway inside, where the voices f privateersmen and bookkeepers and prosperous raders of international fame sent up a smoky din hat curled around the gruff, unusual profiles Dick vas rapidly noting by the light of a whale oil lamp.

She stood at his arm, waiting for him to pause ong enough to notice her presence. After what seemed ike hours, he did, saying absently, "Well, what is it?" Then, catching her controlled yet buoyant grin, "You ave an answer."

"Yes. Yes. Yes." She waved the letter at him. "We an leave any time. We can go today!"

"I'm glad. I'm glad for you," he cried enthusias-ically.

"Glad for *us,*" she corrected, clenching her teeth in jaw that opened again instantly with laughter well-ng in throaty burbles.

Dick folded his pad and seemed willing enough to eave the day's work. He led her back to the boarding ouse via a roundabout continuation of crooked streets rowded with ship chandlers' shops, sailmakers' lofts, and weary, satisfied travelers returned from the China trade, their spirits alive with stories of tea and silk and ventures around Cape Horn.

Mrs. Briggs had ready the box of chicken she had promised, and journey cakes and pure tea water. She took them outside to a lively black horse that had a cushion behind its saddle for Meg to ride on. "You'll get there quicker and safer this way. Horseback is the best for our roads, you'll find."

"But this is how I best like to travel." Dick patted and stroked the neck, mane, and flanks, sizing up the stance and legs with a practiced eye.

"Thank you, Mrs. Briggs," Meg sparkled. She would have gone on foot if need be, but could not think of a better way than this, with Dick to hang on to. When they were employed together, she wanted for nothing, had nothing more to dream of or ask for.

They bounded off at a canter with no pack mule behind to slow them, their capes whipping in the wind, full sail behind, as they posted northward from the center of civilization. Soon, leaving the cluster of houses, shops, and traffic, they passed from streets to countryside.

She kept a lookout for bears, but the tales of wild animals proved much exaggerated. Some raccoons with masked faces waddled out of the way of hoof-beats, but except for these and small rabbits, the flashing black eyes of deer, and the occasional call of a turkey-cock, they had little for company beyond the circling birds and the clumsy wagon travelers they by-passed.

The mansion stood by itself at the outskirts of the village of Greenwich, white and shining in the middle of a long field. It rose from deep, waving grasses turned wheaten at the tips and amply sprinkled with the crinkling leaves of poplars borne down by cross-country winds. A dark dirt path led them directly from the trail-road to the door where a gold-painted eagle spread its wings, caught in the center of light blue scrolls. Meg, who had felt neither tired nor achy nor stiff till this moment, observed the even dis-ay of shuttered windows and felt reluctant to come own off the horse. From this vantage she could see e stables behind and the seed drills standing idle, here some Negro lads in curly white perukes and arlet livery with coffee-colored lapels stood squint-g at the newly arrived disheveled sojourners.

One of the boys broke into a run, chasing three ng-haired sheep as he went, and disappeared around e back as though warning of a fire. Meg forlornly ped a smear of dust caked on her lip and prayed at she could have a bath, a nap, and a meal before e met Elise. Then, remembering the dirty city upon dirty ditch that was Paris, she consoled herself that ise might not notice, and if she did, wouldn't mind. ck, meanwhile, tramped to the front door and opped the knocker once with a thundering an-uncement of their arrival.

The young Negro who had run around the back w peeped out from behind the neat brown breeches a manservant who opened the front door, releasing din of partying voices, easy laughter, truculent, unken calls, fawning chatter, strung through by mu-al notes of womanly cheer.

Dick glanced around to look at Meg, who leaned er on the horse and peered into the interior, where e glimpsed the finery of New York and continental ciety crammed into a rambling yet orderly estab-hment.

"We have come at the wrong time," Dick an-unced, turning on his heel and striding back to her. e slipped his toe into the stirrup, ready to remount d gallop away.

As he grasped the reins, a very slender young oman with silver-blonde curls bouncing on a smooth rehead, large, clear blue eyes, and a creamy, pam-ered complexion appeared at the doorstep, to spring ithout a moment's hesitation toward the horse and so grasp the reins.

"Oh, *mais non!* You must not leave us!" she cried vaciously but with genuine concern, her body bend-g in its white Empire gown more modestly cut than the Paris version, a higher bodice protecting ter der breasts and a hemline lowered to the small blac slippers. "Do stay! Do!"

"I think not, Madame," Dick replied, his coolne melted by the mannered French breeding.

"But you must stay." She made a piquant, dimple grimace and pulled at the reins. "I know you are Dic Fox. And you, *mademoiselle,* are Meg Watkins. have *so* looked forward to meeting the dear friend my family. Come inside, won't you please? It is crowded part-ee, yes. But I cannot help that, you se We are political. And my husband *lives* in the middl of politics. What am I, a poor wife, to do, except help him? Oh, please, please." She glanced imploringl sweetly, at Meg and slipped a warm hand over her "You have come so far. And I will be too sad."

There was something so sincere, urgent, and charm ing in the plea as she waited, ignoring the cold, th it seemed almost tragic to refuse her. Dick loosene his grasp upon the reins. Meg, who had been yearnin to throw her arms around this woman and embra her as a sister, slid from the horse, instantly yieldin to that impulse.

Dick stood with his hands folded across his che and watched with interest the exchange betwee them, until Meg, noticing his weary mouth, laughe pulling him close while Elise lifted up on tiptoe, plan ing a kiss on Dick's cheek, to also include him.

"Why, you shall be my cousin, too," she cried, ey shining with friendship.

Meg saw Dick soften, unable to resist the simpl elegant honesty from this woman of breeding.

"Come inside. Please. I myself will show you to yo rooms, which I have been keeping ever since I ha your letter."

Impassioned by the warmth of her new friend, Me stepped boldly into the hall, where a crush of ma different accents intermingled, the dress of every pe son radically different from his neighbor. Cheek cheek were clean-shaven chins, long, trimmed beard plain blue wool suits of the Benjamin Franklin sty ɩomen in the high, powdered hair of a different, more onservative generation, the flow of Grecian tunics unulating on younger girls behind them. The scent of in floated from hiccuping breaths that expelled the ames of Livingston, Governor Clinton, and Colonel urr.

Elise glided up a broad, carpeted staircase, with leg and Dick following gladly. On the second story e roaring voices became somewhat muffled. Elise, rning to her guests, put her fingers to her ears and ughed with helpless relief. "I will not even find my usband today, I can assure you. He is lost in there ith the Democratic leaders of the state. You underand, we cannot sell good will to your country any nger. Napoleon has ruined everything. But we try. 'e can only try. Mr. Fox. Shall I call you Dick? lease. Here is your room. You will find everything esh, clean, and, I hope, to your liking. I will send a an to you immediately. Meg, dear. Come. We must lk."

She pulled Meg away and the two women entered large room with windows that faced in a westerly rection. A silver ribbon of the winding Hudson River as visible not many miles distant at the horizon. dian summer had gone. A first trial of frost glittered ith the fading of the afternoon sun. Pure white ouds, windswept and ragged, blew in long curves ver the deep sky. Meg felt the exhaustion disappear om her limbs with every word uttered by her new iend. Such warmth and earnestness gave her a tangie sense of the future. Elise would help them, as her other had. She would help anyone of ardor and erit. Most of all, she was a woman who understood nd loved people.

"You are so very much like your mother," Meg id at a pause in the chatter.

"How I miss her. And miss my home." Elise smiled ddenly with a lonesome look. "I make a good show t these fêtes, but in truth, I am not a woman to run ight and day, which my husband needs. I am grateful meet a person like myself who is not politically inclined. Everything in this country is politics—mor so than in France. The carpenters and the shoe peddlers and the winemakers and the milk sellers, the all talk politics and know what it means. At first did not believe it. Then I discovered that everyone i this country, with and without an education, is engage in protecting his freedom. Everyone has a say in th government and makes sure that his voice is hear Incredible! Such a noise day and night, you woul think they are preserving the very gates of heaven! She sat down carefully on the edge of Meg's bed an folded her hands in her lap. "But you are different. She smiled with appreciation, showing pearly-whit teeth. "You are a companion."

Meg untied her cape and dropped it onto a chai rubbing the soreness in her arms.

"Here I sit talking about myself!" Elise leaped u "When you have had such a tedious trip."

"Not so very wearing as I expected."

"But on horseback."

"It was enough for one day, truly." Meg smiled t herself, recalling the physical pleasures of riding wit her arms around Dick.

"You shall have a good bath right away. There i hot water in the kettle. And we have a tub."

Surely enough, in a separate, adjoining little roo a hearth crackled away, warming the air pleasantl and bubbling up the water in a large black bucket.

"I must do this for you," protested Elise, all dimple "I must help you." She hefted the pot with surprisin agility and poured its steaming contents into a sma lead tub.

Meg needed no further encouragement. She pulle the stiff, dirt-caked clothing from her skin, then folde her weary body down while Elise added the wat carefully around her.

"Who wrote that letter to me?" Elise aske twinkling. "Not you, I dare say." She smiled mischievously. "Dick, I suppose? I thought so. The har is yours, but not the working of the mind. He is yo cousin?" She stared deeply, dubiously, into Meg's eye

Meg saw in this blossoming friendship her first op-•ortunity to unburden and speak the truth. "He is sup-osed to be my cousin," she replied, sinking back eneath the water's warmth.

"I understand that," Elise said without surprise. But why? In this country there is no such thing as rotocol, you understand me. Women do get married arly, but there is no need for . . . special effects. If e is not your cousin, why not say he is your . . . our . . ."

"Lover?" Meg grinned. "I suppose we will get mar-ied one day," she mused, not daring to rely upon it. But you must suspect I have come here to ask you great favor. Perhaps the greatest favor you will ver do for anyone in all your life."

"Ah. Is that so? What can it be?" said Elise eagerly, npatient to confer whatever would be asked.

As Elise stood there, utterly attentive and with the otal commitment of her heart given beforehand, Meg egan to tremble with the unfathomable joy of her hanged fortune. All the kept secrets, the hidden tribu-ations, her rows with Dick, crumbled and fell away. he prospect before her of facing social necessities eemed already accomplished. Even as she told Elise f the entree she needed, the words seemed trite, as hough the ocean voyage had turned everything upside own and brought them indeed to a new world, where fe was revealed to be a simple matter of *living*.

"But of course. If he is a painter he must meet veryone. We do it the same way at home. You have ome *exactly* to the right person to help you!" Elise impled further, delighted with her own usefulness. Why, this very night, everyone who is anyone will e at the dinner table; you and Dick among them will aise the *ton*. Do say what you like. There is no for-nality, no class of society. Men here are completely ndependent, and your Dick shall have a great success, for one can assure it."

Meg nodded in grateful compliance. For once she ould say nothing as a tear stood brightly at the edges of her lashes. She stepped out of the tub, clean an refreshed, and dried herself off with a thick towel.

"You, too, shall have a fine success," Elise adde with a husky shadow in her voice that quickly change to pleasure. "Come and look at all my dresses. W are the same size, I see. You shall wear somethin most beautiful. Something magnificent for the men t stop their talking and look at."

At these words Meg carefully searched her ne friend and saw that they understood each other.

"Yes, of course. It is the same the world over. Elise smiled with light philosophy. "Your Dick Fox i a mule about his career, eh? So *you* must be th diplomat. It falls to the woman every time." Me smiled and nodded her head in agreement as Elis held out a gossamer, dove-gray gown that moved wit silky whispers. "We perhaps never dreamed of bein courtesans when we were children. But one sees i every day of the week in every line of business. Th woman must be, to some extent, the *cocotte,* and s her husband flourishes, never the wiser."

Meg flushed at such an open limning of the positio of a French diplomat's wife, but she was quick t appreciate the advantages of honesty and to ask abou American salons.

"There are no salons that I know of in New York, Elise said thoughtfully while Meg carefully donned th gown and shiny black kid slippers. "It is all politi cal, as I have said. What your *cousin* must do is tak commissions for portraits of the governor and othe nobles of the state. He will not set up a painting roor right away. It is not done. He must travel first an make a name for himself as he goes. Then, whe there is enough money, the patrons will come to hin But look at you! You will *destroy* the gentlemen. The will fall in love with you and wish to have thei portraits just so you will never forget them." Sh winked at Meg. "I am naughty, eh? But a woma must take care of herself!"

By the time Meg descended the stairs, the form dining table had been set with a long row of porcelai lates, with pale bone centers and delicate fringe decrations in robin's-egg blue. Silver spoons, saved from nelting during the revolution, lay in a row of three t the head of every plate, and elegant knives and orks of silver-handled steel bordered either side. The nen were already pulling themselves up to the cloth vith much scuffling noise of chair legs. Some, tottering ideways from drink, knocked into their neighbors laced too close at the elbow. Much slapping of backs nd interchanges of private confidences developed into urther backslapping and intimate laughter. Meg lanced from one red-cheeked face to the next, blearyyed row upon lengthy row of robust gentlemen who adn't the least notion of art, it would seem, and less notive to discover it.

Searching for Dick, she found him standing in an nteroom with a large glass of whiskey and water, vhich he had learned to drink upon rising in the norning. His face seemed altogether calm. It occurred o her that Dick must have managed a nice, long nap vhile she had been bathing and dressing. He had aken care with his appearance, too. His dark hair leamed in the evening light that flickered brilliantly rom a cut-glass chandelier obviously brought from 'aris. His riding clothes had been exchanged for a lark blue cutaway with double-breasted plate buttons nd a striped waistcoat beneath. A white cravat astened in a small knot dropped its two short ends o touch the ruffled top of a white cambric shirt. White reeches displayed his muscular legs as he stood very traight and surprisingly at ease in the elegant evening ttire. Meg had never seen such a contrast in him efore. It made her observe with thoughtful appreciation the strength and cut of his solid physique, like a ine animal well groomed but not yet broken completely.

She could not see, at first, the woman he talked to, nly a wide expanse of backside covered by folds ipon folds of gold-embroidered wine silk. The gorgeous aura of Dick's shining eyes reflected, however, a edium in her company that said she could be neither pretty nor bright. He had ceased to wave his glass about, as conversation petered to its lowest ebb, and was given over to drinking in large drafts, escaping the woman, if not physically, at least by means of the alcohol. Meg's impulse was to go to him and save him. Then a gentleman appeared at her elbow and yet another, each one saying at the same time, "You shall do me the honor, Miss Watkins, of sitting with me at table, since you are a close friend of the chevalier."

Her sleek, foreign appearance had beguiled them into a show of manners. Meg, caught up by the attention and delighted with the instant, high-toned impression she would make, allowed each of them to lead her in on a hand. Apparently Elise had started the movement of her social flow. Taking the opportunity offered, Meg glided into the dining room with enchanting looks that turned her companions utterly docile.

Expecting conversation at the meal that she would lead into something more material, Meg was outdone by the clatter of dishes and dinner things as course after course after course appeared of terrapin cooked in its own broth, roasted, spitted turkeys, puddings, pickled watermelon rind, pork ends, corn, deer steaks, pigeon, canvasback . . . the endless procession handed around hour after hour. She watched the food being shoveled into gaping mouths on the backsides of forks in continental fashion or on the blade ends of round knives in the American style. Everything felt cramped, dismal, disgusting, and the room was growing hotter from the masses of human flesh mingling with the miasma of cooking odors and wine, cider, beer, and more mash whiskey. Polite conversation had deteriorated into drunken chaos.

All the while Meg kept a weather eye for Dick but never saw him at table for longer than ten minutes, when he sat sullenly and silently filling his plate, cutting the contents, then rapidly pushing food into his mouth. After this was accomplished, he rose again and wheedled out of the ruckus. While Meg boiled at his lack of good grace, she also envied him his practical sense.

After midnight, the men began dragging themselves away from the litter and rubble with much bilious puffing, clinging to their whiskey glasses with pained and suffocating looks.

"Miss Watkins, I say."

The distinctly British accent made her swing around with an eager, welcoming smile, almost straight into the arms of a handsome gentleman in his thirties, elegantly dressed in a coat with black velvet facings, white silk stockings, and black pumps. He was extremely tall but lanky, almost fragile-boned. She had a long way to look up into a marble-white complexion, nut-brown hair, and changeable hazel eyes sparkling at her openly but with a spoiled consciousness of their own charm. She wanted to like the man and struggled ardently against her own intuitions of danger.

"I've been trying to catch up with you all evening," he said chattily, bending his head to her, taking her arm and leading her into a more quiet reception room. "I am Philippe, husband of your new but very good friend."

"Chevalier. But you are British."

"Very British." He laughed, showing a row of large, clear white teeth. "Very French, too, depending upon which side of the family you talk of. My education is therefore complete. But politically I am awfully split in half. It is all so embarrassing. So tiresome."

Philippe was trying to make light of a matter very serious and troublesome to him, trying, in deference to her female sex and appearance, to maintain the charm of an attractive presentation. "But I am delighted to meet you at last. Come. Let us have some brandy together and chat. La comtesse has written of Miss Watkins to us and has said so many appealing things about her. Do I understand that you are a friend of the Earl of Eggleston?"

The name, so unexpected in America, cut like a saber's edge through her heart. Her spirit, rushing along in a lively way all evening, became heavy and sluggish. For a while she let the echoes drag, hoping they would disappear. But when she looked up into the swaying face, its smile seemed to grow chill around the mouth, the fine nostrils flared slightly, and she recognized shades of other days reflected here, as in the depths of a bottomless dream.

"The Earl of Eggleston?" he repeated, smiling broadly, in case she hadn't heard.

"Yes. Yes, I know him slightly," she replied in a low, faltering voice.

"He is a very great friend of mine. He and Victor and I . . . we are like brothers."

He led her through the reception room and out its other door into a very long and narrow room also empty of people, where gorgeous embroidered rugs shone with a silken luster. Two horsehair chairs done in striped upholstery were near the fire, but he steered her around them and walked her to the wall. There he stretched his arm out above her shoulder and pressed his palm to the plaster molding.

She felt trapped where she stood and sipped her brandy, aware that someone else would surely walk in here very soon. The house was so crowded with humanity wandering every which way, it could not be private anywhere on the first floor for very long at a time.

"The comtesse mentioned that you came to Paris with Ralph. I dare say you two must know each other well?"

Meg heard something persistent and exploratory in his tone. He must find nothing. She lowered her eyelids to her drink and watched the reflections of light dance on its amber surface. Had Elise really married this soft fop? A twinge of sorrow passed from her. "We were friends in London long before Paris," she replied with crisp defiance.

"Yes, I supposed so. I know his tastes well. And whom are you with tonight? I didn't see Ralph, did I?"

"Oh, no, no. He isn't in America," she replied quickly, unnerved by the thought.

"Paris still?" he inquired with satisfaction, leaning in slightly closer to her.

"Or London. He may have gone home by now."

"To the war? I doubt it. Ralph has no more fondness for battles than a sensible man should. But who are you with? What did Elise say? Something about your cousin?"

He was playing with her in a too-familiar style. She recognized the rank breeze of sadism blowing beneath his words. It was necessary to handle this, for the sake of Elise, poor thing. How could she have come to such misfortune as marriage with Philippe?

"Yes. My cousin. Dick Fox. A famous painter in some quarters. We expect you will all get to hear of him, too, before long. *If* you are staying."

"Oh, yes. We plan to remain. As long as Napoleon is in power there will be nothing but wars for France. So we cannot go home. Not to Paris. Nor to London. America is by far the best and most interesting refuge, don't you think so?" He talked politics but closely examined her hair, the curve of her ear lobe, her lips.

"I suppose it is a refuge," she answered coldly, hesitant to conciliate this man or amuse him in any way.

"You seem tired," he remarked after some moments of her silence. He shook his thick brown curls as though trying to arouse her interest.

"Do I?" She sipped her drink, waiting for him to become bored with her lack of response and release her.

The long arm moved on the wall, approaching closer to the side of her face. She glanced at it, shifting her eyeballs without turning her head. "Dick might come walking in any time, you know," she said flatly, without a care.

"He might. And he might not. There are many amusing women at this party. Bored ladies who enjoy the entertainment of a fine young man such as your *cousin.*"

"You've seen him, then," she replied with a complaisant smile.

"I have seen a stranger in this house tonight, and there is only one, yes."

"Good. I want you to recognize him. I want his face to become popular. Quite popular. As popular as that of any politician."

"If that is the case, this is the house in which to do it," he replied slowly, as though engraving the thought upon her mind. "You must have looked around you and seen many famous faces tonight. Roger Morris. Robert Murray. General Armstrong. De Witt Clinton. Half the Democratic ascendancy is being entertained by me and my wife. France has dropped a generous parcel of land into the hands of the American government, which has amazed even President Jefferson. No one can understand the mind of the Frenchman or imagine what is coming next. So they are all pleased to attend our parties. In return, we dine at the governor's ball two Fridays hence. And from there to Washington. What more could an up-and-coming artist want in the way of friends?"

"Nothing more."

"You are a fine, beautiful young woman, and very full of brains."

"Does that mean you are inviting me to the governor's ball with my cousin?"

"That is entirely possible."

"I wonder, then, why you do not offer it to me directly now, without further conversation on the matter?"

"I *am* offering it to you."

"And I accept." She smiled slowly into her glass. "*We* accept. At that time, you will introduce me more personally, in the youth of the evening, to these gentlemen who don't seem very capable now of interest in anything beyond the bottle."

"I am eager to do whatever your heart desires."

"I shall be eternally grateful."

"Are you grateful this minute?"

He was grinning at her directly, his face brazen and bold as the sun with a self-congratulation that reminded her so eerily of Ralph Carstip that she traightened her shoulders against the wall for support. he could barely speak, but not wishing for him to ee the rush of irrational terror, she nodded and smiled ack with a mute nonchalance that she hoped passed or icy control. His fingers moved again. She felt them ouch the side of her neck and tilted her head slightly way. The fingers followed her, walking like a spider long the wall.

"Impossible now," she said with decision.

"Not impossible," he replied. "Improbable, but not mpossible."

"Completely impossible."

"How can you be so destructive," he mused, "when verything you want is in my power to give you? I m sure I do not astonish you by my request. I am ure I do not trespass on the delicate green grasses of nnocence. What has become of that fine brain you xhibited only moments ago?"

"Impossible now," she repeated. "There is no guarntee of privacy."

Philippe sighed. He continued to smile as though othing in her words could change what he knew nust come to pass.

"Especially not with you," she added with sudden nspired retaliation.

One fine, arched eyebrow lifted in astonishment. His narrow face became lined with helpless puzzlenent. "Especially?" he repeated.

"You are the husband of my friend."

"Yes. And I, too, am your friend." He glittered with nthusiasm and the easy, gliding habit of betrayal.

"I have met her family. I am indebted to them all."

"You could be indebted to me even more. And so ou shall be. Why don't you think it over? In the neanwhile, a kiss to show you I am not the ogre you eem to fear."

He leaned his face down. Meg drew hers aside.

"You are stubborn," he said, opening his eyes.

"I do not betray Elise," she replied, glad for the eason, a reason he might conceivably understand.

"But I don't believe you at all," he burst out with

an angry will. "I have met women like you before Ambitious, beautiful women. Cunning women. Wome whose hearts are forever loyal to . . . whatever th ambition is. In your case, it is this Dick Fox. Thi painter. But what is there so engaging about painter to keep you faithful?" he said, growing heated. "Pain ers, particularly face painters, are in the same clas with hairdressers, tavernkeepers, musicians, stag players, buffoons, and exhibitors of birds and puppets They are, as the gentlemen say, unprofitable la borers."

Then he grabbed her face with both hands, an holding it rigid, pressed his mouth to hers so hard tha her upper lip curled back.

She tore away. With the same hand that held th glass, she smacked him swiftly and sharply. The liqui flew out, arcing over the rim. It slapped into his ea and over his cheek.

"I have told you impossible!"

He took a step away and removed a handkerchie from an inside pocket. Dazedly he sopped the wet ness and sponged what he could while the whites o his eyes grew large and bluish and luminous wit rage.

"Itinerant painters are unprofitable laborers," h repeated stiffly with smoldering fire. "To make end meet one has to be a really industrious fellow, fo there is no honor in the work. He will have to be pre pared to paint in general, which means everythin from the back of a house to the decoration of a ti coffeepot. Even then he will not earn a living fit fo one single person to survive upon. He will have t paint miniatures and make lockets, rings, and hai pins. He will engrave and perhaps run a dancing schoc or teach reading, writing, and needlework. A ma with no reputation, such as a painter is, will now an then have to paint on glass. He will create tavern, shop and post signs. This poor, lonely, itinerant artist wi have to grind colors for his bread and decorat coaches."

The voice droned on and on, spelling out for Me

all the actualities that indeed faced Dick if he did not come to his senses and somehow learn to get along with other men.

"In the meanwhile," Meg flaunted, with the same assurance as a child reading lessons from a Bible, "you have met in my cousin Dick Fox a painter equal to Joshua Reynolds and above Benjamin West. The next time you look Mr. Fox in the face, tip your hat to him."

He began to offer her one sweeping, mocking bow before he left the room. As his arm swung back it brushed the sleeve of someone behind him. He paused in mid-gesture, the smile freezing on the surface of his eyes. Alert, sobered, he turned his head slightly and saw what Meg was also looking at.

Dick caught him above the elbow and spun him around. "One profession you have forgotten to add, Chevalier—a painter can also be a boxer to earn his bread."

Meg clapped her hands to her mouth, stifling the mute cry of her mortification as Dick lifted Philippe into the air by his rib cage and held him high, walking around the room with him, saying, "And a dentist and a wheelwright and an acrobat."

His voice rang, bringing in stragglers from the adjoining room. Catching sight of an aristocrat being jostled, they began to laugh and clap at the unusual festivity, egging Dick on with calls and looks that considered the chevalier fortunate to have escaped a death in his own country fully merited for past tyrannies.

"No, don't! Don't!" Meg rasped, purple in shame, shaking with humiliation and fear for Philippe as Dick ignored her. "Put him down," she implored, rushing to Dick. "He is a *nobleman.*"

"In America, Madame, there *are* no noblemen," burped a large-boned Democrat expansively, from above his rumpled cravat.

Squealing with disgrace, Meg dashed from the room, leaving the fate of the men behind her in their own hands.

Chapter Twenty-three

THE GOLD AND ENAMEL CLOCK tinkled four in the morning. Elise sauntered from the bedroom hearth where she had poked some embers into flame, and sat on the edge of the window seat, folding her fingers demurely on one knee. With her blonde ringlets, pure face, and blue night dress, she looked to Meg like an angel descended. "No, my darling friend! I do not wish it. Please. You must not run away from this house on my account. I know about Philippe, and your words do not embarrass me as you might fear. He was born with the blood of a mouse in his veins. Nothing he can do can hurt my feelings any longer."

Meg heard the reassurance as a hollow echo at the very bottom of her aching heart. She had talked herself dry to expiate Dick and forestall repercussions from his impulsive defense of her. But to do so without revealing the cause had been impossible. Elise, dear, sweet thing, was taking it in stride.

"But Philippe. What about his pride?" Meg persisted, still appalled. "And his position with the others?" She could not stop herself from tracking the carpet border, measuring it over and over with a nervous, exhausted stride.

"Nonsense. There is nothing to it," Elise replied with good nature. "You do not know how easily they forget. In the morning it will be gone. Drowned in the wines."

Meg shook her head in dubious, persisting objection. Her restless fingers drummed the top of an embroidered fire screen, and she stared down at the ashen coals. "The politicians, yes. Your husband, no."

"Don't you think I understand his nature best of all?" Elise spoke with an honest, regretful sigh. '*Maman* warned me, on the eve of my marriage night, not to expect love from this alliance. And I didn't. It is quite bearable to me, I assure you."

Meg gazed at her friend with pity.

"Your problem," continued Elise with an immediate rise of animation, "is certainly greater and *much* more important. Where mine is a matter of honor, perhaps, yours is a matter of life. But come," she said, laughing again with the irrepressible good sense of her breeding. "Nothing can really hurt us, can it? And to show you how smooth everything will be, you must return to New York with us."

"Elise, I can't. I don't know what I shall do with Dick."

"Oh, yes, you can. And you will. And the *reason* you shall come is not a social one but a matter of business. I myself will be the first subject for a portrait done by Dick Fox. Yes. You look at me strangely? A woman of my position should have a fine, enduring picture for the grandchildren to come, should she not? And once the wives of these famous senators and the daughters of these congressmen see that I am onto something . . . Well. *Mon Dieu!* Not one of them will rest until *her* portrait is also painted . . . and by the same hand."

"Oh, Elise," Meg cried. "You're a friend! More than a friend, indeed. I would give my life for you. Never fail to ask it of me, or anything else." She flung herself down on the sill beside Elise and hugged her.

"You are like a sister to me," Elise replied with endearment. "I have had only a brother." She patted Meg's trembling shoulder with a gentle, philosophical wisdom. "You understand Philippe instinctively, I can tell. You know him as well as I do."

"How do you bear it?" Meg groaned with a stifled cry against the woman's shoulder. "Why don't you leave him? You have your independence. He cannot harm you."

"I could explain, but what does it matter, really?

Philippe is the stronghold of my family heritage. He is its final resource. Victor, as you know, is undone. Ruined by the wars. In his unhappiness he has squandered much of the family interest, what was left of it. Very little. For my mother's sake I wanted to make a new start. Philippe is excellent at diplomacy. Already he has begun to build my fortune over in America. And besides," she added with a small, girlish laugh, "I promised in my marriage vows."

Meg sat back and looked at her, amazed. "I have never known women of honor before meeting your family."

"Oh, there are plenty enough in England." Elise patted her cheek. "I see one sitting before me this moment. But Dick, your Dick, there's the thing. There's the *provocateur,* eh? No diplomacy in that man. I knew it the instant he spied me in the doorway. I thought: Now there is a savage for you. And I envied you instantly! But see. It is getting daylight. At the end of October there is a false dawn that glitters at the horizon. I think it comes up from the starlight on the river. We must take a beauty rest so that our men will admire us and think we do nothing all day but inspect ourselves in the looking-glass. And tomorrow, or the day after that, depending upon what Philippe has arranged with the others, we shall all return to New York."

Meg, tempted to acquiesce, still hesitated. "Philippe could never bear the sight of Dick Fox in his home, much less have him paint your portrait."

"You are gloomy because you are tired. Philippe will agree to whatever I wish for the sake of peace. And perhaps this time he may learn a little lesson from his follies. Now truly, we must go to bed."

Meg wandered along the landing toward her room, her numb brain dazzled, flabbergasted, and spinning from the sudden turn in Dick's career. One horrible evening had been transmuted by the alchemy of a friend into a mine of golden happiness. If Dick would only agree. With eyes half shut, she pushed up the iron latch and stumbled toward her bed, needing to all upon it, to bury her face in the pillow and cry out gainst the confusing demands of her destiny.

"Eh, what's this?" Dick said, catching her on the attress. "Where have you been so late?"

She dropped prone onto his chest, wrapped her arms round his waist, and let hot tears roll, feeling no immediate need to explain herself. "What are you doing ere?" she sniffled after a while. "Why aren't you in our own room where you belong?"

"Once in a while I have to apologize to you," he aid, patting and stroking her head languidly, yet with oncern for her heavy in his voice. "I think tonight is s good a time as any."

"Apologize for what?" She blew her nose into the it of cloth he offered.

"For what? Well. I didn't kill him, did I? Suppose begin by apologizing for that."

"I could kill *you,"* she responded grumpily, membering. Still it seemed to have happened ages go. And for a while she had a secret to keep her arm that made her benevolent toward Dick. "Only I on't," she said, abruptly lighthearted. "I'm giving you nother chance. Just one, and only one, mind you."

"Thank you very much," he said with mock civility, uddling her into his arms. "But I *am* sorry that I essed up his curls and his waistcoat in front of you."

"Dick, please. Let's just forget the entire episode." he began steeling herself now for what she had to tell im. "You can make amends to me more easily than ou suspect. And to Elise, which I'm sure you want to o."

"Elise? Why, yes. I hadn't thought of her. Tomorrow shall offer my profoundest regrets and hope she acepts them."

"Yes. A woman suffers for her husband. That's omething you'll never know about, I suppose. Take ay word for it. Elise likes you very much, neverthe-ss. Her perceptions tell her there's something in you respect, though I can't say *I* know why," Meg dded, unable to resist.

Dick lifted his head from the pillow and studied

her. "You're getting at something, Meg. I always kno that tone. Out with it."

She reached a hand up and caressed his lips, hi eyes, his ear lobe, and hung on to that. "Yes, I am And it's marvelous." She sighed and he lay quite stil She rose and fell with his rhythmic breathing as h lay waiting for her to reveal the precious secret. "Elis wants you to paint her portrait," Meg said finall trembling with the thrill of her news while attemptin to hide the joy of the miracle that would occur as th result of such an easy accomplishment.

"She . . . what?"

"Yes. Paint her portrait."

"Does she know what happened?"

"Mmm. I told her myself. Everything. She says has nothing to do with the case. She wants you paint her portrait."

For a long while she felt Dick continuing to breath in his easy, relaxed manner, as though nothing mo mentous had occurred. Then energy began to floo through him and his heartbeat echoed resounding against her. Meg thought: *My God. All is lost. He going to tear this very roof down on my head.* Sh clung to him with her face ducked against his nec waiting for the explosion.

"Good girl!" Dick bellowed. "Good for her! Inde pendent. Intelligent. I knew it the first moment I sa her!"

Meg hung on for a while in the silence, waitin for some aftermath to spoil the ecstasy. Nothing cam

"Then you'll do it?" she said, her voice growin stronger with confidence. "You'll do it? You promis you'll do it?" She clutched his ears and kissed hin

"Of course I will." Dick bolted upright. "She ha such marvelous color. Against a backdrop of blue, think."

"In her home?"

"What do you mean, in her home?"

"She invited us to stay with her in New York City.

"That's perfectly fine," Dick replied instantly, Ph lippe obviously forgotten. "I'm sure the house is larg iough to furnish us with a painting room. Yes. Iarvelous. I couldn't be more content."

And I couldn't be happier, Meg thought, beginning giggle in giddy release of tension. Her mind, open-g now, started to absorb the marvel of this leap om despair and destitution into a world of fame and rtune for Dick. It would happen as surely as night llowed day.

Then his lips touched hers and the laughter sub-ded. In the early, golden twinges of dawn she saw s profile sharply defined against the blur of curtains ginning to stir. He had lifted a window to let the noky air out. Now clear streams of freshness were ishing in, washing over her hot flesh. Her skin quiv-ed where he touched and caressed her. The aching iots of apprehension were gone. She felt easy, limber, ght, as though she could live on forever in this mad, er-changing world as long as Dick was beside her.

His lips pressed hers open. Their heads lay close gether, sunk deep in the pillow. Everything around r was cool, making a halo of their hot, mingling eath. Carefully, he was removing her dress with stures that sculpted her body as they touched her. lready he possessed her, in his fingertips and with s understanding mind. She slid the heel of her palm rough the tufts of his chest hair, her thoughts float-g down from fluffy clouds to survey calm and beau-ful love.

Soon his touch upon her breasts transported her to ore stirring, active sensations, as she pictured him ngrily taking her. Her hands reached to grasp his aleness, already risen, waiting, offered in its insistent ll to her femininity. She let her stroking pass from at silky pole over to one tight, hollow flank, herself conqueror now, proud as her escort, defiant as life it-lf. Her flesh streaked with flame, parts of her hard, irts of her soft, parts of her growing damp. The idened cave of her private place beckoned. She abbed Dick's hand and placed it there upon her. is fondling became greedy as she urged him on with ooing sounds and pinches and little nips. He was her warrior, her defender, her life within life. She kicked out and the coverlet tangled between her legs. Nothing could stop her. She flung it off, freeing her ankles, bringing her hips up close to his thighs where she pressed herself, clinging.

"Love me, love," she whispered.

His lips crept from her bosom down to the palpitating curve of her belly, absorbing and gathering her into herself, turning her breasts, stomach, thighs into a single point of living rapture. They seemed to be rising together airlessly, wings spread, eagling out over endless, whistling chasms. The height was dizzying. She sucked his lower lip into her hot mouth, then dug her teeth into his shoulder. Her nails scraped down the sides of his back through the grooved, satin flesh till she reached the bony hollow. His supple spine undulated and he flowed into her easily, mingling there with the tide of her welling desire.

"Are you all right?" he said.

"Yes. Yes. Yes. Love me!" She kissed his face with a longing, animal drive. "Take me harder. Oh! Love you!"

"Dearest," he groaned as she beat her hips upward, matching his force with her own storms. A patch of light suddenly rose over the windowsill, streaming pale blue, violet, and bronze. Rocking on their tide of ardor they sailed into a gradual spread of warming, roseate sun.

"Oh. How beautiful we are," she whispered, not t Dick but to destiny. *Oh, thank you . . . thank you . . thank you . . .*

Her words of gratefulness filtered off, spreading in to an even higher blue-white splendor of the spiri that shimmered with a fanatical, all-consuming powe to grip her convulsively, shatter her thoughts, and sen her flying out into a gorgeous forever as dawn broke bringing the promise of the fufillment of their lov

The pristine Greenwich farmhouse grew smaller be hind them. Meg glanced back once, quickly, to mak a picture of it in her mind, for she must never forg this stopping-off place in Dick's career. The coach rattled around a twist of road, then behind a grove of thick tree trunks, and the vision was gone, perhaps forever. Meg snuggled underneath the lap robe and shifted her gaze ahead, already looking toward the smoky ribbons of New York City chimneys clustering somewhere beyond the next few hills.

Democrats and diplomats had gone on ahead of them with Philippe to take possession of his fashionable house on Cherry Street, more convenient to local festivities than their own country seats on Harlem Heights, Inchberg, and the Bloomingdale Road. Dick, absorbed by the study of Elise's face, sat opposite her in an open coat, hat pulled down to his brows, staring at the bone structure of nose and cheeks, commenting to himself inaudibly with every shift of light.

"I have the very room for you to work in," Elise offered with a smile of enjoyment at his preoccupation. "On the top floor, facing north and the East River. The light is excellent and steady there. You will appreciate it."

"I see you have a feeling for art, Madame," he said with a tender respect that encouraged her to talk.

Meg saw he was altogether a different man with her, considerate and interested, an unself-conscious gentleman. If only there were others like Elise to stimulate Dick thus, his future would be assured.

"Believe it or not," Elise said, "I visited your famous Mr. Turner. In his studio on Harley Street." She nodded sweetly, preparing herself to share a precious recollection. "We were escorted into an enormous gallery cluttered with pictures of every size, hanging on the walls, standing on the floors. My memory is one of being dazzled by light and more light. At first I could not tell where it was coming from, and then I realized—the pictures themselves! He had captured the very sun in his canvases. That little man with his protruding paunch and shaggy, reticent face was a magician. *Maman* wanted to purchase something for me, but by the time I had quite made up my mind as to which I should have, Mr. Turner had decided not to part with any of them that day, as though was more than he could bear to do." She laugh with a telling sound of wistfulness. "And so I promis myself to be quicker about it next time." Her smi fell flatteringly upon Dick's attentive gaze.

Under the robe, Meg squeezed Dick's cool finge as she said to Elise, "Have you heard from yo mother?"

"Not recently, as you know. But the duc has se word that he is leaving for England. Everything el is as well as can be expected. Victor's friends ha become harassed by the war situation and are sca tered, he says, over the four corners of the earth. N one, it seems, wants to take part in the conflagratic to come. The men fear it will be a massacre now th Napoleon is so happily returned to his muskets." S sighed with a sad glow of resignation. "And here v sit, so very far away. So safe. I sometimes feel like traitor."

"What else can you do about it?" Meg put in se sibly as a word of comfort.

"Of course, there is nothing for a woman to do Elise replied with calm intelligence. "But look. V have already come to Harrison Street while we we talking."

They had reached the northernmost point of t city proper and soon were crossing over hilly countr sides of fields and orchards, over an arched bridge a a sluggish stream between the Hudson River and Fre Water Pond, around Lispenard's oozy meadows to picket fence across the road at Astor Place, t southern boundary of Captain Randall's farm. T horses picked their way around the swampy Washin ton Square, along the new Potter's Field and do beyond the Jews' burial ground near Chatham Squa then the Negro burial ground at the northeast corn of Broadway and Chambers Street, proceeding in zigzagging, easterly direction to the river and Che Street, where a row of fine houses stood at ample d tances from each other, built in the style of the b townhouse homes of London.

"We are very English here, you see," Elise noted wryly. "It is a sign of elegance. Especially now that he United States and France are growing cooler toward each other. Look. We are arrived."

Dick was listening now with the barest show of poite attention, his mind obviously employed with other, nore pressing matters as he approached the red brick ouse and eyed it in relation to the slanting sun.

Once indoors, he was all business and almost gruff. Yet Elise went along with him easily, understanding he goal of his concentrations and approving of them.

"Let us look at every room on the second story," he said. "You can choose the one that suits you most."

They went up the stone steps into rooms of unsually calm and restrained appearance, with nothing f the Greek revival apparent. The drawing room was imply furnished, its flowered wallpaper design carried ut again in the carpet in front of the fireplace. A mall painting of George Washington hung over the nantel and was framed on either side by two pewter andlesticks. A small settee in deep yellow silk stood erpendicular to the hearth. A scatter of curved-leg ables and chairs left room for many people to conregate at their ease.

"How very quiet it is in here," said Elise appreiatively. "They must have all gone off to Fraunces 'avern for a bite to eat and some of the very fine nadeira." Her smile beamed charmingly. "Shall we tarve because we are neglected? There must be some urkey roasting on the spit downstairs, I promise you."

But Dick's preoccupation threw its pall over the ffair. The meal became a hasty matter, gotten rid of n half an hour so that they might return to a tour of he rooms and find the one most suitable for painting.

The room Elise had mentioned, at the top of the tairs and facing the East River, proved the best with s ample spaces, long clock near the curtained winow, and businesslike pair of crossed swords susended above a mantling eagle on the fireplace. This ad once been used as a general's office, and the goose uill still stood in its pewter well, with an old revolutionary tricorne and some other war relics placed on a leather-faced table.

"Whatever you wish to preserve of these," Dick said with a knowing smile, "please take them from here before I begin."

"You must heed him," Meg added with concern.

"Oh, but of course. We must not clutter you."

Elise immediately began dragging things away, with Meg and Dick helping her pile them behind a clothes curtain where space was plentiful.

In the next few days Dick set to work buying and arranging his easel, palette, and brushes, grinding colors and setting them; at the same time, the diplomats' wives began arriving in an incessant stream downstairs, setting up their clutter of embroidered gowns, capes, shawls, colored kidskin gloves, necklaces, imported perfumes, all with a steady, excited babble that climbed the walls and the stairs, driving Dick to quarantine himself behind his door. Meg would sometimes go to him, peep in, wink, and say, "Aren't you glad to have a place indoors where the light is?" And he would motion her out for interrupting some sketch just then forming in passionately rapid strokes on the preliminary ground.

"Your *cousin* is an oddly single-minded man."

She had not heard Philippe's voice for days. Now its ill wind blew after her in the hall with a smell o gin upon it. He curved overhead, poised, followin rather too closely, and by the tilt of his face seeme rife for some scandalous amusement with her. Wha was there to reply? She wanted only peace with Phi lippe, and distance between them. Yet her instinct told her that Elise was wrong, that Philippe had hardl forgotten the insult of their country encounter and wa biding his time to find some nasty means of retaliatio Thank heaven the house was so crowded! He woul not be able to corner her, since with every three ste they tripped over ample-bosomed ladies bedecked flowers and pearls wandering about or seated in formal circle with others exactly like themselves. Th house was a nesting place that waited for the greater interest of the coming ball.

"Don't hurry away from me, Meg. I want to speak with you."

The skittish voice drew people's curious attention. Philippe's diplomatic finesse had nothing to do with his personal social sense or lack of it. Meg, glancing at the women, found eager eyes devouring the spectacle of this married foreigner chasing someone else's woman. It made her worry for Elise. She would not want that lovely name bandied from one hen's tongue to the next.

"And I want to speak with *you,*" Meg replied. "Elise has charged me with a message for your ear alone."

The gaggle of observers relaxed. Disappointed, they looked away while Meg, touching Philippe's arm as though in confidence, walked him out of earshot.

Philippe wet his lips with interest and swung a fob that ticked loudly. She drew him into a rather antiquated music room with an inlaid mahogany spinet from London and an old violoncello leaning against a stool, wondering what she was to do with him.

"Yes?" Philippe demanded. "Yes?" His long, supple fingers curled around the carved throat of a violin and plucked its strings discordantly. "What is the game we are playing today?"

Meg lowered her eyelids and glanced at him sideways, stalling for time as she realized that here was no fool. He had not believed her fib but had purposely allowed her to entrap him, trapping herself. Alone with Meg, Philippe seemed very serious. He closed the door behind him and stood, waiting sternly, tapping the fiddle against his palm and his boot heel against the plank floor.

The best idea was to stay away from him, remain at arm's length, on guard against some burst of animosity bridling in his angered soul. "I have been intending to apologize to you," she began.

Before the sentence was out, he stalked toward her and tilted her chin up to look directly into her eyes.

She saw the telltale bright red rims that reminded her instantly of Ralph Carstip.

"Apologize? For what?"

He was leading her on. Tossing oysters to the pussycat. She wondered what it would take to swing around him and propel herself back outside to a safe corridor and the company of other women. Yet, supposing he lost his temper and came after her? She could not humiliate Elise twice. Not with the same company!

"You are such a lonely soul," he continued on an unexpected tack. "I know my wife has introduced you to the ladies, and they admire your style. But I never see you much engaged in conversation with them. Are you not egalitarian, my dear? Do their manners appall you? Are you less content to stuff cheese and fruit tarts endlessly into your face, as they do? Yes," he said, eyeing her bosom openly, "I believe that must be the cause of your lonely state. You have a certain delicacy of the figure. Here. Let me see."

His hand shot out. The fingers clawed, grabbing her breast and hooking it painfully.

Without thinking, she responded, slapping his hand away with a wicked cut from the side of her palm. She had learned early to fight well. The habit returned in a flash, taking command of her and unleashing its power in the safe and private dominion of the elegant room.

"Ah! Wildcat!" he called happily, tongue flicking the words.

"No. I shan't fight with you." She leaped back as he lunged for her. "I shall be your friend. Despite both of us and our human natures, I must declare a truce with you, Philippe. I must, I will, be your ally. Now be good. Behave yourself with me. Let us shake hands and try to be kind with each other." She spoke desperately in a low voice that would not drift past the door.

"I *am* your ally," he replied, puzzled by her forbearance. "I shall take you on my arm to the ball, yes, I shall."

"No. Elise will be on your arm."

"And you on the other."

"I have an escort of my own," she retorted, flash-ɪg pride.

"We will find someone to occupy him amply."

"If you can, then yes, I will go along with you." he saw him instantly take up her defiance, and just ; quickly, she regretted the foray. "You mustn't fight ith Dick, either."

"If I do again, this time it shall be properly."

"No fighting at all."

"For gentlemen's honor? That is a different matter. hat is demanded, you see."

"We are neither in France nor in England. Nothing ere is demanded except survival. No duels, Philippe. o ambushes. No bloodshed. You must promise me." ie kept thinking of Dick's disadvantage, alone with-ıt friends or seconds, pitted against this strange mind at could rally dozens of perverse and wily plotters to s cause. "No revenge," she pleaded. "No revenge,) you hear?"

Philippe became suddenly calm, his tongue moving oughtfully around behind his teeth. "Is there a price r such a promise?" He smiled.

"Of course. Certainly," she answered without sur-ise. Did she think she could evade it when Philippe ıd promised himself to bed her that very first night Greenwich village? Perhaps the sooner she sub-itted, the better. But still. In this crowded house. ɔw dangerous. "I shall meet you somewhere else," e replied softly. "Where shall it be?"

Philippe swayed above her, suspicion casting a dark cker across his eyes. "You don't mean it, my sweet. hat cooks inside that foxy brain? Your lover's ca-er? Yes, you must preserve *that* at all costs, even the omise of your body. Well! Do you hold your body so eap, then? Or *his* so dear? I must ask Ralph, one ıy when I see him next, what your secret is."

"You must do that. I trust it will be in London," eg flipped, praying the door would open and some waggle-tongued missus would fall in and put an end to this annoyance.

"Well," drawled Philippe. "The price is not so light as you suppose. I can see you have been through the jungle in your time, and one more lion upon your person would make precious little difference. I, for myself, would care for a higher novelty than the mere spread of your warm thighs, which I don't doubt are round and beautiful. Nevertheless, I have my fill of lovely women, as you may suppose."

"Yes. Female society must be enchanted by you." She spat these words so venomously that he jerked forward and flicked a finger under her chin in a sniping attack that could not find words fast enough.

The door burst open. A white, curly-topped head peeped in, all piled about with yellow pearls. "Why, Philippe, darling angel. I thought you were with my husband." The dark, popping eyes rolled about wickedly. "Why, Miss Watkins. Is that you? Where is your mysterious gentleman? One hears that he is painting the most famous portrait ever to be done in these parts."

Meg half turned her back to the woman as a scorching heat seeped along her throat. They had been spied upon behind the door and now were being dangled. Yet she was hearing Dick's fame already on the rise and turned a sunny smile of pleasure upon the eavesdropping witch.

"Your husband is with General Alby," Philippe offered with a charmingly controlled turn and bow, reminiscent of Versailles manners. "I have seen them in the morning room but ten minutes past, discussing the matter of financing a Lewis and Clarke expedition. Of course, they would have nothing whatever do with me, poor Frenchman that I am, with all interest in that territory relinquished."

"But not relinquished in *every* territory, I trust she chirped, swinging a sly smile at Meg and wiping her mouth with her tongue tip as though a film cherry-flavored ice lingered upon it.

Philippe pointed a finger at the pink, splayed nc

"You are a naughty, naughty woman, Mrs. Granit. I must dance with you every dance at the ball two weeks hence. You have an amazing quadrille step in your repertoire that quite eludes me."

"Oh dear, dear yes," she tittered. "I shall be glad to teach it to you. They say it began with Josayphine and an unnamed lover before Bonaparte."

"Shall we say eleven o'clock, to meet in the old drawing room?"

"And dance away till dawn."

"And dance," he corrected her with a lascivious smile dredged up from the bottom of an overflowing heart, "till the dancing rooms of the new governor's mansion in Albany are complete and ready for us to begin there again."

"Ah. How enchanting." She flung up two chubby hands and patted both his cheeks with glee. "You are a charmer." She recollected something and sighed regretfully. "Why do American women marry so young? Think of the fun one could have, and all the dancing missed by these seventeen-year-olds already betrothed."

"Don't think about them," moaned Philippe lustfully. "Think about . . ." He put up his hand to shield his mouth from Meg's hearing. "*. . . us.*"

The door crept shut. With the woman gone, Philippe burst out in a low howl of disgust. He fell upon the chair at the pianoforte and began to ripple off a religious Bach prelude.

On and on he played, laughing in contempt and grunting as he went, humming, puffing out his chest grandly, rolling his eyes to heaven, altogether absorbed in ideas Meg hardly dared imagine. She stole quietly out the door, not thinking of what he would confront her with upon their next meeting.

Outside and safe, she was caught by the ache of a dark, lonesome hollow in her chest and, from habit, directed her steps up to Dick's room. On the stairwell a tangle of four well-dressed children flinging paper dolls at each other, taunting, kicking, and pulling each other's hair, soothed her nerves as they made evident all that she felt inside. Working past them, she wave to Elise, who was crossing the corridor after hours modeling for Dick. An aura of enchantment lingere around her as she disappeared inside her bedroo with a bright knit shawl swinging from one hand, an Meg tasted again the sweet reminder of Dick's increa ing fame so well deserved.

She let herself into his room and found a chair ne one corner, settling herself with careful movemen so that he would not be interrupted by her presenc He glanced at her but said nothing as he attacke with a flat bristled brush the scenery of sky and clou forming around the new outlines of Elise's life-si image. The huge canvas, mounted and stretche on a heavy wood frame, was beginning to come life. It leaned obliquely away from the windov where a receding light had begun to steal away th brilliance of blue and aqua tints.

Dick put the brush down reluctantly and wiped h hands. "What have you done with my sunshine, Meg It goes behind clouds."

"Yes, I have it in my pocket," she replied, peerin out the window with him. "I suppose we are spoile expecting sunshine every day."

"Mm. Looks very like rain."

With forehead ruffled, he leaned on the sill an surveyed the dark, muddy wash rising behind th crowd of masts on the East River.

"It may blow over soon," she encouraged valiantl "Besides, nothing can stop you now." She hugged h arm, watching the wind whip and twist the sapling newly dug in around scraps of fenced land. A shortag of firewood had resulted from all the trees bei hacked down. Now people, too late in the day, we hoping to rectify matters with an occasional plantin of small arboreal clusters.

"November," he said in contemplation. "I unde stand New York winters are drab."

"You've worked in worse," she said with sparklin confidence. "Remember London? And Elise is an e cellent subject, is she not?"

"Yes. It's going well," he admitted, placated. "Might as well soak these brushes and hope for better light tomorrow."

By nightfall the skies had lowered to the rooftops. Hard gusts tore away at the branches, bending them in loops and threatening to turn out the less firmly secured roots of the youngest. At coffee time the following day, a slanted drive of rain battered the tiny windowpanes and made a crackling, pebbly noise as he first hard pellets of sleet pattered and bounded rom glass to windowsills. The street pump stood abanloned with a muddy pool filling up around it that vould threaten to contaminate the water below. Iorses, racing with desolate riders, flung their manes ip and whinnied into the freshening frost air. Women uddled with their shawls over their heads, battling gainst the bone chill, clutching their packages and alling irritably to the older children playing like colts ı the nastiness while the younger ones clung and hid ıeir faces in billowing skirts.

Indoors as the days passed, Elise's protected comany poured out an endless stream of tea, coffee, ine, cider, and gossip about the art going on in the rbidden cave upstairs. Talk of the portrait superded news of the shipping schedules carried in on the ind and dispersed by the merchantmen arriving from eir warm coffee houses, where they had read their ipers at ease and were now philosophical about the als of their captains on the ocean. Meg, accosted in ery corner by husbands prodding to have their wives ne before any other, beamed contentedly and prosted that she had no influence upon the artist's owded schedule, but promised to see what she could , at the same time hearing behind her Dick's rassed reply to some lady's dull, demanding question out art. Once Meg saw him cornered between a volving bookcase and three stout matrons discussing relative merits of yellow versus wine-red ribbons a painted subject. When she caught Dick's eye er the babble, his drowned face accused her of ng to blame for this. Dutifully she hurried over and redirected the conversation to herself, while Dick, with a perfunctory bow and a leap, disappeared, to prowl the house elsewhere in another cranny or peer out the window, helplessly cursing at the greenish, metallic thicket of dark skies.

"If one cannot paint a picture in this weather," said one lady, catching him in a doorway and gobbling a fruit tart while she spoke, wiping the drip from her chin with a kidskin glove, "cannot one cut out a portrait silhouette? I have seen them do it, and many's the pretty likeness can be had with paper and scissors."

"So it may be, Madame," mumbled Dick, smothering his temper and backing off like a tiger before flame, then darting away to a card room where men were taking solace from their wives.

Meg glimpsed him next at another window, with a tall glass of whiskey fast disappearing as he walloped the drink back, scowled blankly, and drank some more. She could almost hear the chains of the caged animal rattling as she came up beside him and whispered, "Has my love so little patience against an act of God?"

"The only acts of God are birth and death. The rest is society."

"What shall we do about society, then?" she replied hopelessly content with his fame.

"Don't fool with me, Meg. I'm up to here with it," he muttered, drawing a finger across his throat.

There was no humor left in the man these days. He worked through the endless gray hours, but there was no relief, no escape from the endless gray people who preyed on him relentlessly. She dared not tell him, however, what a curious, intriguing couple they seemed to these Americans. Men to whom she had hardly been introduced were confiding impassioned braggart lies to her, eyes sparkling large with lust and seduction. While Dick brooded and slunk away from harmless ladies who wanted only to praise and p him and make an appointment to be painted first, she found herself slipping from admirers who looked upon her as a prized animal to be caught and conquered.

"But it is everywhere the same," objected Elise, the only one with whom Meg could share the situation. "Men are king of beasts and women must run the show quietly from the high grasses."

"How do you do it?" Meg dared to ask. "I am not subtle that way."

"Oh, you are more subtle than you know," laughed her friend. "I have seen you save him many times. He *survives* because of you, don't you know it?"

"It is the painting he lives for, not me."

"Ah, *oui*. My picture is exquisite and almost complete, I believe, despite the grim weather. But you are too modest, *ma chère.*"

"No. His passion is all in the work."

"Do you really believe it?" Elise asked incredulously.

"Why, of course," Meg answered sincerely. "I have no reason to think otherwise. No evidence, surely."

"He paints to impress *you.*"

"Never!" Meg said firmly, delighted nevertheless. That shows you do not know him. He loves me, but he does not need me."

"I bet otherwise. I bet my life on it."

"If you only had proof," she said intensely. "I worry that when he has finished painting you, there is nowhere else for him to turn."

"But yes, I have proof. How he looks at you. How he listens to your opinions. What he thinks behind those dark, steely eyes. How he . . . holds you at night, I would venture."

"As you say, my sweet," Meg replied lightly, unimpressed. "If not this one, then another woman. I am sure that he loves me. But painting is what he needs to survive. He will seek it out, with me or without."

"Has he told you that?"

"And has done it often."

"But you are together!" Elise laughed softly, with the convincing evidence all on her side. "Let us not talk such foolishness. The day grows old. We have a magnificent fête tomorrow. The women will flock to him and he shall have work for a year. Come. Let us see to our dresses. I fear, Meg, I have neglected you these past weeks for the others. But believe me, my dearest, I have missed the pleasure of your confidence."

Chapter Twenty-four

MEG COULD NOT PULL Dick from his room. He stood immobile, iron legs placed in a wide stance, rooted like a tree in his last-ditch effort against the inevitable

"It's only one party," she pleaded. "I won't ask you ever again. At least not for a while."

"You press me too far," he muttered ominously.

She gave up tugging and stood beside him, leanin against his arm in its dark dress coat and gazing dow at society streaming over the cobbles to Mr. Franklin' mansion looming sedately in the nippy nine o'cloc dark.

"Show your face for an hour," she coaxed. "Is tha so very much to ask?"

"There's nothing for me there."

"Nothing?" She pushed him with disgusted strengt that hid her anxiety. "Now, you smile and go in ther like a gentleman, for once. The women are falling o their knees in front of you. You don't have to do thing except agree to take commissions."

"Take orders is more like it."

"Spoiled child." She shook him, her shattere frustrated wits rattling in her head. "Your whole futu has turned a corner, thanks to Elise. Don't you ov it to her, at least? Doesn't her hospitality to us me anything? Aren't you grateful? Aren't you human She glared up at him while he remained unshakab distant to all her efforts, his face frozen in the withdrawn mood that she had learned to fear.

"I don't owe anybody anything." He peeled her fingers from his arm and set her at a distance.

"You have to escort me," she persisted defiantly. "It's only manners."

"Philippe has those manners, if that's what you want. And Mr. Morris. And Mr. Granit. And how many others? All those prosperous gentlemen, those financiers of the revolution, waiting on you."

Meg stamped her foot in hearty outrage. "Why can't you at least be *jealous!*"

The first grin of the evening broke through from behind his eyes as he suddenly noticed the white silks and satins, the star sapphires that flashed upon her heaving bosom. Reaching for her cape tossed over a chair, he swung it around her shoulders, fastened it carefully at the throat, and pulled the dark fur trim close to cover the bare flesh lifting from her bodice.

"Come along, then," he said. "I'll walk over with you."

Placated, Meg kissed him, but she did not fool herself into thinking she had won any important concessions. "How is the portrait coming?" she asked to soothe him and, hopefully, to distract him from the mob gathered at the famous door they were approaching.

"Almost finished," he said enthusiastically. "A coat of varnish and she'll have it for her great room."

"I think that's marvelous."

The words were sucked from her mouth and drowned in a monstrous uproar, her body drawn into a vortex of circumnavigating human beings who separated her from Dick. People whom she had seen but an hour before leaped past her as though she were a stranger, to grab up tarts and ices and fruits and coffee cups and teacups, all teetering and sliding on japanned trays precariously carried around by angry little black boys smothered underneath them. The women hardly glanced at what spilled upon their gowns in the general rush to push into their mouths as much food as they could and bolt it quickly without chewing. Behind them, the drawing room provided musicians and a maestro zestfully waving a baton for couples capering, leaping, spinning, sliding through the dance in a space the size of a pie plate.

Looking nervously around for Dick, Meg found that he had been swallowed by an ocean of curled, bobbed, greased, and decorated headdresses. Despairing, she went for the refreshment room, which she knew must be to the left from whence came the wafting stench of alcohol. As she wiggled and elbowed and sidled through, hands of all sizes slid over her covertly, above and below the waist, some no doubt accidentally, others taking the opportunistic gall to pinch, probe, and quickly search out the charms protected beneath lacy folds. She paid no attention but pressed on into the miasma of gin-punch fumes where sedate ladies were licking piles of ices from iron knives, women who just yesterday she had heard boasting of their French or English manners. No Dick here. The whist room? Meg smiled with renewed expectation as she passed through the dining quarters, laid out with uncovered dishes of duck, mutton, and a variety of soft-boiled vegetables surrounded by plenty of good French wine. Those still hungry came and went, attacking courses that appeared all at once without design. A portion of the tribe had drifted to the second floor, but it was quieter upstairs. Except for muffled, clandestine squeaks behind tall fire screens, one could hear oneself think.

Waves of cigar smoke drew her to the card room, where a circle of men sat vying contentedly with each other, snapping down cards to meet disappointment or triumph. Spying Dick in the middle, gently flipping cards as though they were his children, she watched an interested, concentrated frown ebbing and flowing; it caused her to pause and observe him, unseen, in his happiness, thanking heaven that he had found a refuge acceptable to them both. The men, attentive to him runting, cackling, cursing, laughing behind their bluff 'hiskers, admired him as a gambler. Rogue Fox, in is way, was something of a land shark, which gentle-ien of enterprise found familiar and worthwhile.

She stole backward out of the doorway, satisfied nd secure that they would somehow get through the st of the night and then plan for the days to come.

A hand darted out from a circle of women and rabbed her wrist to stay her progress. Philippe merged from the center and toasted her with his wine lass high. "Congratulations, my dear. I understand my 'ife's portrait dazzles the eye with its beauty. The idies are all talking about Mr. Fox with an envious ompetition that means your future is assured."

Meg strolled slowly along as he followed after. She ould take him tonight, somehow, and was glad for ie cowardice in him that had avoided further confron-ition with Dick.

"Where do you go from here?" he pursued. "A lace of your own, no doubt? In the very heart of this aming center for the arts? Copley himself was not immediately successful in Boston. Your luck is a ing of beauty, and I admire it."

"Not luck, Philippe." Meg smiled.

"Of course not luck. Forgive me. I mean work, and edication." He was tugging her toward a narrow de door. "The dedication of Mr. Fox to his painting id myself to the honor of Elise."

Meg flung him a black but forbearing look. She nderstood his insinuation. Of course it was true. 'ithout the protection of Philippe's roof, without s singular hospitality, she could never have cracked to his social circle—not this soon. What appeared n the surface as Dick's miraculous triumph was ostly the result of her own evasive promise of prom-cuity in the right places, covered by a fine veil, the irage of social status and acceptability. Had she been aive instead of a wench, the whole matter could not ave been so smoothly contrived. All of this came at er in a flash from Philippe's penetrating smile.

"Now it is time to pay your debt," Philippe grunte pushing her into the room and swiftly closing the doo

"I owe you nothing," Meg flung at him, remembe ing these words on Dick's defiant lips. She lifted poker from beside the hearth, dipped it in flame, an swung it casually in front of her skirts. "But yes, w shall soon have our own place, to which I hope I ma invite you and Elise for tea. I am good friends wit your wife. I should enjoy being an equal, though di ferent, friend with you."

"How unwise," Philippe commented, eyeing th weapon, "for you not to appreciate my talents as we as your *cousin's*. I begin to believe that you wish discriminate against me. I know, for instance, th Mr. Granit and Mr. Talsam are your *admirers*."

"You are mistaken in their meaning," she flare "Either they are liars or you have an insufferab mind."

"Yes, insufferable." Philippe laughed with deep en joyment, as though the ridiculous word was a compl ment. He took a small step closer that blocked h way to the door.

"You shall let me pass from this room now, an we will try our friendship again another day." Me came steadily at him, the poker still glowing. Sh watched him with a level look that said she would n be afraid to use the tong.

"You are indeed a pretty picture in your regal gow and your rascally weapon," he said, backing o "You can be sure we are not yet finished with ea other, Miss Watkins."

She had no need for the last word and float past him flaunting another weapon that reinforc the first, her natural strength of pride and intent live as a lady, which had always been with her a was openly, irrevocably, declared the day she h fallen from the carriage at St. Catherine's docks.

Pulling the door shut behind her, she could feel t threat of Philippe and his kind vanish into her p as she strode to rejoin the tide of current events which she yearned to do her part generously.

By two in the morning, the card players in the game room had changed seats for luck, and some had left and were replaced by others. All had moved except Dick, who seemed eternal in his position.

"Why, Madame, he is a genius at the game," said one gentleman beneath his mustache, laughing affably.

"I have gotten away scot-free," cried another to his companions, as though that in itself were fortune.

"He has taken my horse and wagon. That's when I knew to leave the table."

"Why does he paint, when *here* lies his talent."

Meg smiled with yielding femininity and replied nothing, offering only protesting murmurs from time to time or "You shall win it back again next time"—rather enjoying, in a new light, the idea of gambling, and certainly approving of Dick's ability to make friends in his own peculiar style, a successful one at that, certain to increase his popularity as a sought-after confrere.

Then in an eyeblink he was gone from the room. She thought he must have gone outside to renew himself in the frosty night.

By daybreak, she had scoured the mansion in all its varied corners, confided in Elise, and prevailed upon her to help. A fierce recognition of the inevitable mingled with a wash of equally fierce hostility toward the only man she could ever love.

"But don't condemn him so soon," Elise cried, trying futilely to calm Meg's distraction. "Perhaps he was unwell and has gone back to my house. Come. We will walk over together and see."

By turns listless, by turns enraged, Meg proceeded unsteadily toward the spread of dim stories that she knew beforehand would not yield her prize.

They ran immediately to the top floor and his painting room in the hope that he would be sprawled asleep on the mat.

"See?" Meg cried. "Your picture is not on the easel."

"Is that a note up there, tacked to the frame?"

Meg snatched the paper down and read aloud: "Elise, my dear friend. Your portrait is in the keeping room and still drying. Please take care not to handle the varnish."

Meg exploded with the fulfillment of a bitter premonition. She flew down the staircase to find the picture, as though Dick himself were hidden somewhere inside it.

"There it is!" Elise called.

The huge, completed portrait startled them with its immensity and brilliance, as the face and grace of Elise, as her spirit with its high flamboyance and genteel wit, radiated into the atmosphere, charged by the first long rays of daylight. A genius of life emanated at them little by little, as though they were in another flesh-and-blood presence that spoke in gesture and color, moved in some mysterious fashion of life, touching the furniture and the carpet, pulling the room together as Elise herself could do with her charm, an enlarging its effect in concentric circles like a pebbl tossed into a pool, infinitely outward beyond the con fines of the frame.

"I could never repay him for this," Elise breathed "It is dazzling. It is a privilege."

Meg, struggling out from beneath the influence o distance, crept to the picture and let her gaze slid up and down it at closer range. She worked her sou into the brush strokes, as though she could touch the with her eyes, feeling the day-to-day spirit of her ma spending itself here, in his thought, in his passion in his driven search for enduring ecstasy, for his nee to discover some pressing, throbbing secret hidden i the universe and meant for his hand alone to revea As she gazed at the colors glistening beneath the varnish, she relived his arms around her and his pro ing mouth, shuddering while the vision quickly tran formed itself into recalled memory of their interlock and rocking bliss. The painting's passion drew upon h own, in a form that was her own but which could evoked only by Dick, shared only with him.

After a while she became aware of Elise's waiting silence and pulled herself together with an enormous force of will.

"Perhaps we should try his bedroom?" Elise ventured, aware that she was again permitted to speak.

"He is not in this house." Meg shuddered. "I know it."

"He may be asleep. It would be natural after the food and liquor."

"He neither ate nor drank very much," Meg replied. "I watched him."

Nevertheless, she had to search on, follow the trail as best she could.

His bedroom, as she had expected, lay empty and hollow to her gaze. "You see? His chalks are gone. That's the proof. He always keeps something to sketch with, even beside his bed."

"And his clothing," Elise added, pulling back the curtains of the hanging wardrobe. "Look on the dresser. Is that another note?"

"He would not leave one for me," Meg replied, boiling and bitter. "I am the last one he thinks of, always."

When she did not move, Elise went over instead. "But you are wrong." She thrust a bit of paper happily at Meg.

Meg blinked at the scribble, afraid to discover that everything they had built so far in these past weeks had fallen to rubble at her feet, leaving her the ruin presented in a few sentences of brooding scrawl.

"Darling," she read to herself, "you don't believe me, but there's nothing here. I have gone toward Albany, where the landscape is unspoiled, and perhaps I will find an Indian face or two. From there to Boston for a while. Elise will give you the money for the portrait, which will keep you till I return."

"See how I've come up in the world," she mumbled with a vitriolic chuckle. "At least now he tells me where he has gone." She crumpled the paper and flung it with all her might into the fire. *What is it that I love in this man who always leaves me? Why am I condemned to follow him? I make a fool of myself, I dare say, not only in my own eyes but in others', talking forever about art like a trained dog at a fair.* "That bloody, insufferable brute will be my death," she spat, destroyed, from between gritted teeth.

"What has he done?" Elise asked without understanding, staring helplessly after the note curling in the fire.

"Gone off. That's his style, didn't I tell you? Not reformed at all. Leaving me with these women to face and make excuses to. What reasons can I give them? He has a fortune waiting and turns his back on it."

"But gone where?"

"Albany. What is particular in Albany?"

"An antique city, I understand," Elise replied reasonably. "With Dutchmen."

"Dutchmen! Painting Dutchmen! Have they influence with the governor?"

Elise shook her head with a tinge of sadness. "I am afraid not, my dear. Perhaps he will see the governor by himself," she added brightly.

"Not my Dick," Meg said from the depths of her gloom. "He'll stay with the Dutchmen if they have interesting faces."

Elise came up to her and rested her hands on Meg's shoulders. "And you. You shall stay here with us till he returns. He will soon tire of the wilderness. It's a very hard place, I hear. And he will pine for you very soon, I should think. And come galloping back thankful to have returned to his senses."

"A pretty dream." Meg smiled. "If you knew him you would realize I don't have a second to spare for dreaming."

"No, you aren't . . ."

"Going after him? Yes. I must. He won't forget me but he could become so embroiled in other things that . . . that . . . that I don't know what he may do or where else he may go."

She spun, dazed, around the room, beside herself with fury and confusion. Only one thing was certain. "I heard last night that he won a horse and wagon

That must have turned his head to get going. Now he has a fine start. How am I to catch up with him?"

"You can't. Don't try."

"I must. I will," rang Meg's voice.

"Innocent. How shall you do it?"

"The Post Road."

"That goes to Boston. To Albany, you will need a boat up the Hudson, which will take you there directly in a few days."

"With a boat I cannot overtake him."

"Overtake him? I have gone many times to Albany for conventions and such. It is an uncomfortable trip at this season. Oh, if I could only travel with you. But I shall give you our houseman, Jonah. He knows the trails like an Indian."

"Can I go on horseback? Is it possible? He is only in a wagon. How I should like to get ahead of him and greet him as he arrives!" Meg's eyes flashed. "I shall get to Boston first and meet him there."

"You are wicked. Wicked. Very wicked."

"Yes." Meg clasped her friend to her bosom. "And shall use my wickedness to forward Dick, whether e helps me or not. You have given us a perfect tart. Shall I let his poor sense stifle everything even s it begins?"

"Truly, as I look at it through your eyes, I undertand . . . so many things."

Meg heard the suddenly wistful note. For a fleeting nstant she felt pity for Elise, who had never known ove as she herself was living through it now.

"Come, we must hurry." Elise pulled Meg from the oom. "We must get your things together. I will send our trunks after you, one to each city. You must have oney to take. Oh! Where is Jonah when I need him? t the wheelwright's shop, early. I shall send a boy ound to fetch him home. You must have patience ith the inns on the roadside. They have very fine *ctuals,* as they call food. But the beds are high and bominable. Of course you won't feel a thing. Meg. eg. Meg. How fortunate you are! Take care, darling. ost me letters if you can spare the time. One only. To let me know you are arrived safe and have found him."

In her excitement Elise seemed to drain Meg of hers. In place of the dizzy spin came a vibrating sure-headedness, for Meg could not forget that Dick had made gains of friendship and reputation that must continue to work in his favor and add to his fame wherever he went. "Will you write me a letter of introduction to Governor Clinton?"

"Why, yes, I am already doing it. George Clinton is a shaggy, benevolent man. You will find him much to your liking."

When all was done, the two women hugged each other dearly.

"We will let no grass grow on the path of friendship," Meg said. "Let us promise."

Chapter Twenty-five

THE DAPPLED ROAN, Hickory, waited with springy hooves that kicked up dust as Jonah rose easily into the saddle, his long, gray-flecked whiskers flapping in the brisk noon air. He had suggested, for Meg's sake, to go with a pack mule behind, but she had dismissed the measure arrogantly, insisting that they must not ride, they must *fly*. Jonah's sun-squinty eyes had sized her up from beneath a floppy brown hat that protected his wrinkled neck in all weather. He had found reason for confidence. Now he reined the horse backward toward her at the stoop, clasping and settling behind him the cushion she intended to sit on for the duration of their journey. *One day I will learn to ride,* Meg promised herself. *I will race Dick from*

London to our country home in one of the shires. She had no doubt of their future. Prosperity and happiness were assured.

Jonah reached down one broad arm and hoisted her aboard. She felt with her shins two small saddlebags that contained the few personal items she had elected to pack. Elise, bundled in a heavy woolen shawl, called, "Are you safe there? Feel comfortable?" and a thousand other questions, all beside the point, as Meg blew her kisses and signaled Jonah to be off with a pressure to his ribs.

Hickory needed no urging. He sprang away in a gallop, his black tail lifting and spreading in the wind that carried upon it the fading, haunted refrain of Elise's farewells.

They found the Post Road, leading up from the Custom House where it pressed along Park Row. She held lightly to Jonah's waist belt, the side of her gaze aking in clumps of stunted poplars and the skitter of nimals squabbling with indignation as Jonah hailed hem to be gone, his sturdy voice cheerful but full of usiness. His ribs moved with a supple, swaying mo-ion. She held him lightly, feeling in herself a natural ptitude for balance astride while the flanks stretched eneath her, pursuing the journey northward toward puyten Duyvil Creek. The farms had lost their green yellow November gorse. The trees had dropped ieir leaves. Weeping willows, which stood beside very house, draped soft, low branches, and from eneath the tips that trailed groundward burst spotted ogs, yapping in giddy excitement at a moving object.

A sense of time dissolved as they moved in a onstant, monotonous round without the respite of ap-ointed ritual mealtimes. How she had changed! She ho had starved most of her life now looked forward tea cakes! They galloped past Fort Independence d the Negro Fort, crossed Rattlesnake Brook, and tered the town of Eastchester.

She thought she could ride on for two days without opping. Jonah, with the good sense of experience, lted at an inn rudely built in the style of a log cabin but much larger, with a porch and pillars of squared-off wood from the forest not far behind it.

Inside, whiskey was everywhere, in small glasses and tall, glinting in bottles and dripping down the chins of chill travelers. Out beyond the city's protection, a rough, devil-may-care style brought Meg quickly to a new frontier. These were civilized men, of course, but not citified. Lusty, yet pale-faced and listless deep down, they seemed inured against starvation and difficult times. The innkeeper wore his felt hat over a mane of shaggy hair. His bearlike expression tried to smile gently at a lady and succeeded only in being masculine to a woman.

"How are y'finding the roads, missus? There's a public stage due in tomorrow at sunup. Y'might want to ride it a way."

"Doing fine," intruded Jonah, pushing up the sleeves of his jacket, slugging swallows of whiskey from a squat glass. "Is there beef tonight? Or turkey pie?"

"He could give you *biled* vegetables," laughed one of the locals from across the room.

"You can sit at the fire in the parlor," said the innkeeper. "We'll feed you good and full up. There's hog steaks if you like 'em. There's a nice bed waitin' with clean covers, how about that?" He leaned an arm on the counter and grinned a snaggle-toothed smile.

"Everything's fine," Meg replied. The luxury of sheets had come to be quite a common matter for the likes of herself, who had slept so long on bug-ridden straw!

The night passed in an eyeblink. She slept completely oblivious, relaxed and half drunk on the whiskey. She thought she would dream of Dick, but he mind was an endless black sky. She came awake suddenly before dawn, filled with energy to get going Jonah stood at the window downstairs, swallowin mouthfuls of cider while waiting for her. She gulpe some with a bite of waffles and catfish. Then the were off again, pacing through Eastchester beside dark, freezing stream called the Hutchinson Rive passing tumbledown sawmills and grist mills from b fore the war. Through Mt. Vernon the road crossed the Hutchinson River and the old Pelham Manor and led to New Rochelle, scattered with thrifty French farms along the shores of the Sound. Onward jogged Hickory in the cold, gray, endless daylight toward Mamaroneck line, beside stone Huguenot houses with weather-beaten shingles and tangled grass creeping up the front toward the carpenter's sign hanging on its street face.

"We'll rest here a bit," said Jonah laconically, eye-ng Hickory's right foreleg where veins stood out on he muscle. He walked him around the Huguenot irst Church, then they all walked awhile, traveling ast a hollow beside the road with Tom Paine's cot-age in it, covered by green blinds and with a vine-overed porch. Meg thought that if she looked around, he could see the old Quaker staymaker, which Paine ad been in England.

From there the road struck out toward the Sound. oon they were trotting beside the gray watery spread or much of the way and through the neat little Mamaroneck village and past the Jay House on the ay toward Rye, a long one-room structure of eighty et that gave the effect of a tunnel. In Rye they opped again. Jonah fed Hickory water with salt in and watched how he walked, tenderly favoring the ght foreleg. Then they were fed on a French fricassee f some odd concoction, contrary to any notions of aste Meg had ever experienced. At the next station, Haviland's Inn, all very neat and decently fixed, they at at last with mugs of beer and Jonah sucked slowly n a pipe.

On past the cattle roaming free on Manusing, they ped toward the orderly log-cabin homes of the old ttlers from Greenwich, then over the Byram River to the State of Connecticut, territory of General rael Putnam, along Cos Cob with its ample frame ouses and brittle lilac bushes that had survived both agoon and Yankee fire.

Jonah reined Hickory up beside the old settlers'

burying ground and walked him around near the headstones sinking into the grass.

"That's a lame horse we're riding," Meg called, her breath curling away on an icy vapor of wind.

"Mite finicky sometimes," Jonah replied, lifting the right front hoof and feeling its shoe.

"Now what do you say?" she asked an hour later, feeling Hickory begin to sway and wind along sideways.

"Mite finicky for sure."

They both stood silent for a while and watched the sun begin to slip slowly behind a web of branches. Jonah walked off, lit his pipe, and drew thoughtful puffs. Then he sauntered in a circle and finally came up to her.

"Missus Watkins, you're a sensible woman," he began slowly, pushing the felt hat back and scratching some of the stubble underneath his chin. "Here we are, caught exactly halfway between Boston and Albany."

They both eyed Hickory nuzzling down among some grasses, his weight resting off the questionable front hoof.

"Exactly halfway between?"

"Exactly half." Jonah leaned his back against the scruffy, grayish bark of a gnarled trunk and scratched a few times across from shoulder to shoulder. "I could put you on a stage to Boston, as it goes past in a mite. Or I could fetch us over to the Hudson River and push ahead straight north."

"Jonah," Meg said patiently, "this is my first time in your country, and you've been riding around here for thirty years?"

"Forty, ma'am."

"If you were in my position, Jonah, looking to meet with a person who'd started for Albany yesterday and was going on from there to Boston, which would you say is the likeliest route?"

"How long did you say he's staying in Albany, ma'am?"

"I didn't." Meg paused. She certainly had no idea

how to explain her predicament. Dick could become involved with any number or kinds of embroilments. If she went on ahead to Boston she might have to wait weeks for him, stranded there, her money running short while keeping up a face in social circles.

"You'll go to Albany," Jonah concluded, as though reading her thoughts. "Damned less irritation in the journey."

"How do we do that?"

"First we walk back to the inn for another horse."

"That's four miles behind us."

"Five miles."

"Let's get started before Hickory decides he doesn't want to get up."

The lolloping trip to Boston had started off too well to last. Now, with Hickory traded in for William, a coltish-seeming ten-year-old that shied miserably at every owl hoot or leap of a hare, they began the slogging cross-country trek where turnpike travel diminished into forest trails hardly wider than footpaths for Indians. Meg narrowed her eyes to a squint very much like Jonah's and gritted her teeth most of the way. Branches snapped at her ear, and the wintery forest breathed its dank breath in drab patches of twilight gray, tangled in wild vines. But Jonah, who himself seemed part Indian, guided William along with a steady, inside knowledge of how to soothe horses and found unexpected trails hidden beneath moss and bracken. Sometimes they met a sign on a planted post with a mailbox nailed fast, which was a town. In a week they had reached the Hudson River. Meg sat rough-skinned, lean and aching, to gaze across at its western shore.

"We are just about twenty miles above New York," Jonah said. "You can tell by that ridge with the valleys between it. If you look down you can see the tide ebbing. There'll be a boat coming ashore to cast anchor in a while. Mark me."

Trusting Jonah seemed the easiest, most natural course in the circumstances. Her mind kept harking back to Elise, who had depended on him for more than a year. With no spirit to spare for objections, even if she could think of any, Meg waited in an obedient slump for one or the other of them to be proved wrong. She would get to Albany somehow, in a sloop tonight or one tomorrow.

"There you are," yelped Jonah. "Here come one of them keelboats now. Hey, ahoy! Hey, ahoy!" He cupped his horny fingers around his beard and mustaches, hallooing at the top of his voice very much like the nighttime braying of cats.

A wide, rather lopsided vessel seemed headed in their direction even before Jonah's cry. In an hour Meg, Jonah, and William went aboard, to be greeted by a melee of warm-handed, aristocratic Federalists, a drunken Scotch Presbyterian minister and his wife, four raftsmen, a violent Democrat from Staten Island, and various free blacks acting as steward, cook, and cabin boy, all eager to bring their latest cargo below decks in the face of some jagged lightning streaks and rolls of thunder that brought in their wake a swift drive of freezing rain.

Below stairs there seemed scarcely a breath of air. From the waters, shad and sturgeons had been pulled aboard to make dinner, for which Meg had no stomach. She took a bit of gingerbread and some dark bluish preserve of swamp huckleberry, then said good night, intending to stay safely asleep in her cabin portion behind a curtain, oblivious both to coarse manners and to delicacy alike, until she should arrive at Albany.

Meg looked out at a vista of green hills and lovely thick-needled pine trees riding down the slopes to the water's edge.

"But, Captain, have we actually arrived in Albany in just twenty-one hours? I have been told it would take longer."

"Yes, in a flatboat, but not by sloop. Besides, it always faster passage *up* the river, winds being equally favorable, for we carry the flood tide with us and no need to outrun the ebb."

Jonah, who had turned unmanageably social, was now once again the taciturn guide, saddlebags hefted over his shoulders and a flinty eye cocked for Meg to follow after him with no dawdling. He seemed to know Albany like New York and easily discovered, at the ferry slip, news of some new tavern near West Pearl Street, which was, he told her as they rode, "where the aristocrats have set up housekeeping."

They passed through an antique town of no more than eight thousand residents, something fourth-rate, Meg thought, with pines everywhere, everything quiet and primitive, the margins of the river overhung in willows and nature hardly disturbed wherever she looked. Soon the ancient Dutch mynheers appeared in sharp-cocked hats, every one pipe-smoking, and every one in a red-ringed worsted cap pulled tight down over the head. They stood about and noted the weather in front of their compact, single-story houses with sharp-peaked rooftops, each surmounted by a wind vane in the shape of a rooster, the gable ends built to the street and huge iron numbers announcing the dates of erection. Long, wooden gutters projecting six or seven feet outward into the street discharged spills and drips of rain from the week's foul weather over the center of the wide walks. Foot passengers going beneath ducked around as best they could so as not to be doused.

They pressed on past the Dutch church in the middle of State Street and finally came to rest at a low-roofed, longish tavern in good repair, brightly lit behind its windows. In Meg's bag lay Elise's introductions that would lead to eight o'clock teas, evening parties, dinner at the governor's, and perhaps meetings with legislators in the House of Assembly and their important wives. She thought about this while she slowly washed the travel-weary sluggishness from her limbs over a basin of water in a comfortable bedroom. Then irrepressible cheer overcame her anger with Dick. There was nothing he could do to turn back the clock! His accomplishments in New York City must travel before him. With just a bit of steering from her he would float, never to be an obscure artist again. But she had learned a lesson or two without thinking about it directly, which had purely to do with business. She must not confront him eye to eye, never threaten him with social obligations. The wild horse must always be tempted back into the ring with sweets held out upon the palm, with smiles and kisses and . . . She hefted her tired breasts to the mirror and smiled. In some respects Dick was no different from other men, thank heaven.

She sat with Jonah before the huge fireplace, bolting down rump roast and thick chunks of bread in company with other hungry travelers seated around a long, oval table.

"In New York it might be a break-leg matter to find such a man," Jonah said with his mouth full. "But here? This is only a village. I could turn 'im up in a day, Missus Watkins. Rest easy."

"Jonah, you have come through in every crisis. I believe you now. You say you can do it in one day? One day only?" She peered at him earnestly, as though this last hour were the ultimate haunted hell to be lived through. The many days they had traveled were lost. Her eagerness had been forced to take second place to the physical hardships of transportation. Now, with nothing else to do but wait, a day seemed the most unbearable burden of time.

"I'll go with you," she concluded, dropping a mutton leg bone onto her plate with a clink.

"No, you won't neither."

"You have your secret ways, Jonah? They'll rest safe with me."

"Not secrets, missus." He scratched his head, eyeing her closely. "Not secrets."

Surveying his evasiveness, Meg wondered if, this once, Jonah was trying for more than he could accomplish, with no clear idea of how to go about it. "I want coffee," she said. "You?"

"Whiskey. Hardly got the dust clear from m'throat."

"Whiskey!" Meg called with a will.

A reedy man wrapped in flannels and a leathern apron began bringing the drinks that Meg intended to use to loosen Jonah's tongue. After the first three bolts, he drank slower, however, hesitating as she watched him and seeming to lose his spirit for the work.

"Jonah, you talked me into it." Meg stood to catch the waiter's attention and called for another glass.

Soon they were deep in mash liquor, leaning over the table, forehead to forehead, comparing notes about the goats in Washington and the sheep in London and the hogs in Paris all trying to run a world without the proper consent of their thoughtful, intelligent citizens. The Great Apostle in the White House was the planet's last hope. What use was it for fools to sit here in this old-fashioned town, criticizing the Postmaster General?

"We have big things to do," Jonah sighed, folding down against his ladder-back chair. "Thish is the New Hope, America." He brightened suddenly and pulled his hat down to his eyebrows. "But you want to know my way of finding ol' foxy Dick Fox, don't tell me different." He laughed softly. "And I'm not telling the li'l lady any of my ways 'n' means."

"Tell me nothing, Jonah. That's fine with me. But bring 'im 'ere. Tonight. There's a dollar for you. Two. Three. Anything you want."

"Tonight, eh? Think I *can't?*"

Meg leaned forward, chin upon her knuckles, fixing Jonah with one half-closed eye. "You can do it," she replied with a terrible, compelling grin. "You can do anything you say you can. Didn't you take me from New York into the forest and out again?"

"All on a dang lamed horse and a silly colt," he agreed with a violent nod.

"Then go on, Jonah. Get 'im now. Whatsa use of waiting till daybreak? Snow, most likely. Your ol' horse'll slip all over the roads and break 'is leg."

"Poor Hickory."

"Go get me Fox!"

"If I was you, missus, I wouldn't put Jonah to the test." He stood then, remarkably straight-backed, swaying slightly leftward.

"Go," she whispered, patting his fingers pressed to the table for balance, pursing her lips and furrowing her brow. "Go get him, man. Go."

Her words swished about him like a whip at the ear of a blooded, highly strung animal. Jonah seemed to quiver along the nape of his neck where the fine hairs stood on end. He swung on his heel and marched for the door, elbows straight, head facing forward, intent on the urgency of his mission.

Chapter Twenty-six

URGENCY! Two days gone and no sign of Jonah.

"Drunk, most likely, and dead asleep in the stable," the chambermaid assured her, blowing on the tips of her goosefeather duster. "Beneath a horse or a whore."

Skeptically, Meg turned away. She couldn't believe it of the man who had borne her safely this far.

"Couldn't be too many places a painter would go," said the innkeeper with expertise. "We'd uv heard of him hereabouts if he's as good as you say. Unless he's gone off trapping in the woods, as some do."

Meg gasped with recognition. That was it! Avoiding society to paint the tangled forest vines and wild creatures. "How long could he stay out in this cold?"

"If he took a pack with him, maybe weeks. These wilderness fellas don't feel weather."

Meg wandered outdoors to the wooden plank veranda, alone with a melancholy sense of her entrapment. *What a damn fool position you've got yoursel this time, missy. How can you stay in this traveler' prison, not knowing when or if Jonah can track him down in the woods? But should you go on to Governor Clinton's place? What can you accomplish there without Dick?* The leaden sky had turned brassy at the horizon, slowly rolling up a storm over the ravines and scattered spires. As she stood there with her arms folded, hugging her shawl close against the penetrating chill, the first hard-flung drops plummeted. She stepped back from the water, but the air itself was wet.

"Come inside and take a glass of rum," said the innkeeper, behind her. " 'Taint very interesting what you're looking at. 'Bout to grow mighty mean."

He made good sense. But how could she listen to him? "I've a man to find. There must be some way."

"Only if he's staying at a tavern, you see. Then Abe Traskit would know for sure. There's an old law in these parts that every newcomer to an ordinary is signed in and kept track of by a town selectman. Hereabouts, that's Traskit."

"Where will I find him?"

"Lives near the river, the cussed fool. When the pour stops, you'll find him in the round house beside the ferry."

As if in a dream, Meg lifted her shawl to cover her head and stepped out into the pummeling of icy, juicy drops the size of stones that battered her but which she felt only vaguely through the veil of a deeper, more driving intuition. In the distance the ferry slip hung behind a vaporous fog. She turned her steps in that direction, moving through the swamped streets where water was rising in eddies. She felt inclined not to run, not to become breathless, as though her movements were timed to some larger clock, to some broader schedule written by a mightier hand than her own. What she had to do was merely walk while she held her face straight ahead, squinting against the driving rain. Her cheeks burned from the cold even as steamy breath poured before her. How strangely close was fate. Close and true. Her instincts stood out on stalks, alive, sure, aimed directly as a snowbird migrating through the seasons. She had no time for pain or questions, as though she had lifted clear of her own body and were traveling lightly, without substance and invulnerable.

She covered ground in what felt like a sweeping flight that carried her past the swaying willow branches, leading her to the edge of the city where sloops and flatboats swung violently in the center of the river. At quayside, smaller, narrow-keeled ferry boats rocked, oars or poles crossed lengthwise in the bottom, knocking together when the small vessels spun about in contrary tides. Her gaze flew over the iron-colored waters with its boiling yellow caps that grappled a fish occasionally and tossed it up, wiggling, into its enemy element. The larger craft farther out were fast becoming ghosts in the thickening mist. Somewhere behind her a dog howled and subsided into mournful yelping. She was soaked through but paced the riverbank, searching, driven beyond reason, catching her toe and tripping over a patch of wild-growing briar.

She heard sloshing footsteps becoming louder.

"No one's t'stay down here, missus. The wind'll blow you straight into the river."

A short, barrel-shaped creature, dripping from the brim of a green felt hat, from the point of a short bushy beard, and from the sleeves of a hide jacket buckled, like Jonah's, by a wide leathern belt, pushed his formidable bulk between herself and the tides. "Now you stand back," he called, "or come with me if you care." He had the rough, sufficient look of a frontiersman used to travel and weather. His thick soled boots were supple, gripping like fingers into th mud.

"Where do you stay?" she asked, the voice insid her speaking out of its own volition.

"Thar." He lifted the beard slightly and pointed toward a makeshift hut near the ferry station built mud thatch walls with an overhanging wattle roo rather queer-seeming and solitary.

"Abe Traskit?"

"Yep."

"I'll go with you," she said, starting across the incline toward the door. "Is anyone inside?"

"I'm alone," he told her simply. "You can go or stay."

She was right behind him as he lifted the creaking wooden latch. They entered a room warmed by cooking smoke mixed with the raw smell of apple whiskey. A straw bed with blankets stood near the fire and a squat chair set beside a hewn table against the wall. There was a full tinderbox and stores of dried-meat strips neatly piled, everything simple and oddly inviting. She pulled off the soaked-through shawl, wiped her palm over her hair. He tipped his dripping hat far back on his head so that water from the brim sluiced down the back of his jacket while he stomped over to the fire and shook himself out all over like a dog or a bear.

"Mighty miserable night," he said with an easy look of acceptance. A black pot hanging over the fire bubbled with something brackish. He sniffed at it approvingly, then dipped a ladle in, transferring chunky contents to a deep iron plate. "I looked out the window and said to myself: there's a madwoman or an Indian squaw got astray." He grinned, revealing three teeth curved like claws, and handed her the plate. "Then I said: no, she's lost. Then I said: she's a furigner. Then you started walking like a damn fool down to the water." He motioned her to the chair. "That's good 'coon. Eat it up."

She couldn't bring herself to sit and started picking at the soup where she stood.

"What you doing in these parts?"

"Looking for a man, name of Dick Fox," she said, the spoon half to her mouth. "A painter. Paints pictures of bears, maybe. Or Indian squaws. Pictures you would like."

"Yep." He smiled with amusement. "Got a picture like that. Got a few. Painted them m'self as a matter of fact. Abe Traskit, painter. Come here 'n' I'll show you."

From the corner of the room he tossed aside boots, an ax, and five heavy leather gloves to lift out a bundle of rude sketches of deer antlers and the hindquarters of a raccoon, drawn with burned sticks.

"This ain't what you're looking for, though," he said, studying her with a twinkle of quiet expectation from where he knelt. "Then how about this?"

He hauled up two larger drawings, also done in the same burned sticks, of the same antlers and the same raccoon hindquarters, but with a difference that unleashed Meg's spirit as she stared at them, instantly alight and trembling with curiosity.

"When did you get those?" she said, pouncing on them greedily with both hands.

"Yestiddy."

"From the artist?"

"Sure. I gave him a good jackknife in trade."

"Where?"

"At Jack's Groat Tavern."

"Is he lodging there, do you know?"

"He was drinking there."

"How far is it?"

"Two miles, maybe. On the east side of town near the hills, but in a good, open place on the road."

"I want to go there right now."

"You ain't going anyplace afoot in this pour."

"How, then?" she pressed, heeding his shrewdness. "Is there a horse nearby that can take me?" She fumbled in her bag for gold coins. "Have you one?"

"I ain't owned a horse since Caleb died last June. But I can steal you a wagon."

"*Pay* for it, dammit. Here!" She flung the coin into his palm. "And hurry!"

Ten minutes later, Meg stared at the wobbly wagon waiting in the rain. It was less of a wagon and more of a dray cart for carrying muck or corn, with foot-wide wheels, two only, and a wooden box between for the cargo, which she was supposed to sit in. The black horses, wet, bony, and dreary, stood with hang ing heads while Meg surveyed the accommodations, pressed another coin into Abe's hand, and thus bargained for him to ride in the open wagon while she sat up front on the one good seat.

"Pint 'em to the big elm tree and whistle a bit," he called from behind, shading his face from the water. "They'll do the rest."

Keeping to the center of the cobbled roads, Meg had little to do than will her way forward. With half an hour's struggling. Jack's Groat Tavern came into view, a rambling, listing, white-painted inn shaped like a lean-to, glowing warmly orange at the windows, a welcoming beacon through the shifting fog. The reins were taken from her. She hurried toward the roar of voices inside, of travelers and local idlers gathered to comfort themselves with brew. When she reached the parlor, the crowd of faces in the tap room adjoining told her this was the most popular place in town. Wiping water from her lashes, tossing back cheery banter as she went, Meg worked her way inside to the bar.

"Is there a picture seller here?" called the frontiersman behind her. "Anyone seen the picture seller that took my knife?"

"Someone stole yor knife, Abe? The one with the chawed-off edges?"

Through the laughter and the smoke and the liquor fumes and the waiters maneuvering around chairs and tables with trays held high of leg mutton and humps of sliced roast meats, Dick was there, leaning at the counter, his dark head above the others, talking earnestly with someone she could not yet see.

The tension and compelling need drained from her as she stood inside a strange, unreal peace, watching him at a distance, herself unseen. It struck her how relaxed he was, how easy, how comfortable, how *affable* in company with the shorter man. Sometimes he smiled a bit, and it was a friendly, impulsive reaction of agreement. For once he was not forbidding but lounged slightly at an angle, with one leg propped on a foot rail, drinking casually from a wooden tankard and dressed in a new, belted leather jacket cut with the same fringe collar that Abe wore. She admitted that Dick had already become an American frontiersman without half trying. Obviously the rough-and-ready presence suited his mood. For a while she hesitated to go to him at all, fearing to spoil, with her appearance, whatever he was about. Abe offered to push a chair for her to one of the tables, but she dismissed it gruffly, preferring to lean against a wall and study the entrancing situation before her. What to do now? How to approach him? She wanted everything to work exactly right and with a sensitive feel for his need so that Dick would be glad she had come. Yet where and how did a woman fit into this life here? She thought, *What has it to do with me? How can I make myself useful?* The answer was plain enough. She couldn't. Then, with a sinking sadness, she wondered, *Am I wrong? Have I only been ruining him? Is he better off without me?* She had traveled miles to find him and now hesitated to close the distance of twenty feet.

"Well, missus, there's your man. What you going to do now?" Abe said.

She found some other coins in her bag and pressed them at him. "Please return the horses," she said. "I can do the rest alone, thank you."

But she didn't move. She stood balanced at a crossroads, swiftly reviewing the possibilities. She could not bear to greet him and see him shrink from her with involuntary distaste for the demands her presence would imply. Someone good-naturedly pressed a glass of cider into her hand. Absently she began to suck at the rim, never taking her eyes off Dick's back, as though able to send a message through the air to reach his brain saying that she was different now—that she promised always to be different—that she would do what he wanted, as long as he was happy and remained with her.

She expected to move forward, but something stopped her. She realized she was not yet ready, not all of the questions answered to her satisfaction. Could she honestly give up her ambitions for him? Could she? . . . No. The blushing fire of truth heaved pink anger into her face. *Then I must compromise. I will give up nothing, but I will treat him differently. I will go about things quietly, alone, in my own way.* Images of how she would proceed in Governor Clinton's house began to form. She would resign herself to a solitary social life and become the conveyor of Dick's paintings, not of the man. That's it. That's the ticket. *I will sell the pictures he has painted and avoid the clash of personalities.*

Now her feet began to wend a way through the crush. She came up on the left side of Dick and stood there, curious to overhear the subject of his easy banter and glimpse the amazing companion who pleased him so. Snatches of something to do with muscles and bone drifted to her while she drained her glass and slowly slid it along the side of his forearm where the elbow rested on the counter. On his far side a young, rosy-skinned gentleman had much to say about the human body, all very earnestly presented. The absorbing conversation held Dick's attention entirely. She could not compete without bluntly intruding. Would it never stop? She touched the glass to the edge of Dick's palm, then along the suntanned finger, moving the glass as he moved his hand, till finally he snapped his arm away and hooked his thumb in his belt. She then leaned lightly against his side, gradually increasing the press of her weight as he gradually edged away. After a few minutes he finally turned his head and looked down for the source of the annoyance.

"Well," he said, and waited within a pall of silence.

"Well?" she answered, smiling hopefully with a flicker and finding what she had come to dread but knew she had earned, nevertheless: his imperceptible shrinking away from her and the style of life her presence represented. A pain of remorse stabbed through her chest. She wanted to throw her arms around his neck and promise loudly in his ear that she was not the same woman. No. Never would be again.

"How's Albany treating you?" she said.

"Fine. Just fine." His gaze hung there, cool but not neutral.

She saw the ache in his eyes, the restraining of many different responses that leaped between them. "Are you staying here at the tavern?"

"It's the best hospitality in town."

"The liveliest, too, I hear," she replied with a smile. "I'm at the other end. The Hoof and Bottle."

"Elise and Philippe with you?"

"No. Of course not."

"I expected they'd be up for the electioneering."

"That has nothing to do with me. I've come alone. Your note didn't say to come, but I thought it might be fun, anyway. New town. New scenery."

"New people," he concluded for her.

She fell silent, deserving it, deserving everything he did to protect himself from her clawing ambitions.

"I'm not surprised to see you," he said quietly.

"Oh?"

He nodded at Jonah, slumped on a stool beside the wall, one ear pressed to the planks, drinking whiskey in stupefied, measured sips. Meg, seeing him, felt the scorch of degradation. Jonah had found Dick, given him her message, and Dick had refused to return with him!

"Is there someplace we can go to talk privately?" she said, mustering every ounce of balance, every inch of fairness, every urge not to revile either Dick or herself, that were still in her control.

"I have a room upstairs," he said simply, and excusing himself from his companion, began to guide her through the crowd.

She moved behind him, staying close, feeling he could go up in smoke and escape her if she wasn't careful. This was the tenderest, most delicate moment of their lives. She wondered if she possessed the power to turn a corner with him and start again down that different road which would keep him with her always.

He had bought new boots with thick leather and iron-bound soles that rang on the staircase. Nothing like the looks of an aristocratic gentleman remained. Nothing like an artist, either. She scurried along behind him, thinking that, like Philippe, she had mouse blood in her veins right now and was afraid to confront him with her deepest feelings. She wanted to kick and scream and force him to see things her way. But she had to be careful about it, very calm and adult. She had to allow him his right to make his own decisions about her, or else it was all no good.

His room was spacious, with a large, high bedstead and two plain chairs before the fire, cozy and quiet. He had been here only a week or so but had already made it a home, with detailed drawings of deer antlers propped on the windowsill between the curtains.

"Fascinating creatures," he said, following the direction of her glance. "Very different from the roe deer we have in England. Men hereabouts say I can find herds of them near the waterfalls a few miles northeast. I expect to go there when the weather clears."

"Would be beautiful to see them in the snow," she said with quiet appreciation. "Those cloven-hoofed racks, so very delicate. The black, shining noses. You night even run into some Indians."

"That *would* be luck," he laughed. "They've been cleared out of here a while, I understand. Maybe along the Mohawk River or in the Genesee Valley. Nothing on the pike to Boston, unless I wait for spring and actually live in the forest."

"You wouldn't want any of the *civilized* ones, of course."

"No."

"I bet you find some black bear, too. Might have o sketch them from up in a tree, though. But you do have Abe's knife."

"He brought you here?"

"Yes."

"How did you find *him?*"

"I was in luck." She smiled, strolling to the window nd watching the water twist into dozens of rapid vers frothing at the wheels of carts tied to the rail below. She had no idea if it was day or night. Nothing mattered but this conversation that must go on and on and never end. The very words themselves were her lifeline to Dick, to Dick's renewed confidence in her.

"Abe and you don't actually travel the same social circles." He grinned, taking her wet shawl and spreading it over a chair back, motioning her to approach the fire with a spontaneous, concerned gesture of which he was unaware.

She stood at the hearth, slightly in front of him, lifting bits of the wet material away from her dress with an easy, unself-conscious motion, as though she, too, were at home here. "I'll tell you how it was, if you'll believe me."

"I will," he replied gravely.

"I had to find you," she said simply, her voice very low. "I said to myself: I am going out to find Dick. Then I did just what I had to do, though it seemed unreasonable. Somehow it worked."

"It always works for you," he said with rueful acceptance.

She glanced up at him beseechingly. Her eyes said: *Is this going to be the last time between us? Does it have to end?*

"I'm not a nuisance, really." She plunged in abruptly as the pressure inside bubbled up too strenuously for her to bear. "I was not born to molest you and drag you away from your comforts. I want you to know right now that I haven't come here to convince you of anything. Not anything at all."

They were walking around the room, carefully not touching each other. She ached to brush against him, to stroke him, to fondle only the edges of his jacket. But she wouldn't make the first move. Wouldn't force her sex upon him. She knew she could have him in a minute if she wanted to attack him with their passion. But she was living through something greater now. A higher thrill of enlightenment. An understanding that her love for him stretched far and away beyond the throbbing demands of the flesh. She had to reach him on a different level this time. She had to touch him mind to mind. They had to be a special kind of friend for each other. A special kind of confidant. He had to be able to trust her with the care of that driving animal inside him that made him what he was, endearing and impossible both at once.

"You aren't saying a word to me," she said, tremulously inhaling a breath. "What are you thinking?"

He was rubbing the back of his neck slowly, gazing down into the fire. Shoulders hunched forward, he seemed shy and firm in a mixture that didn't sit easily. She knew what he was thinking, she supposed.

"It isn't fair for me to ask you to reveal your mind." She smiled. They hadn't been together, hadn't kissed in so long. And she wanted him to stand there and talk to her! But it had to be so. She couldn't let him believe that she seduced him for the purpose of softening him to agree with her about other, hidden matters.

"Why have you come here?" he asked. "What do you want from me?"

She took a step backward so she could not, would not, be tempted to reach out and touch him. "Nothing."

"Nothing?" his voice echoed, hollow with disbelief.

"Only to be close."

"Then what happens to us, Meg?" he said disconsolately.

"What happens to us? What can happen to us?" Her voice throbbed. "I don't know of any two people who love each other more than we do. We are the fortunates of the earth, Dick. Can't you see the gift that's been given us?" She felt the pulse beat in the side of her neck and yearned to tear herself open so that the inconsolable, stubborn creature watching her would be convinced.

"It seems to me that things are easier when we aren't so fortunate," he said wryly. "I've come away, not only to paint in the woods, but to think about us, too."

She stared at him, amazed that he actually considered it important. He saw and understood the look and shook his head.

"You make me out to be some maniac machine that does nothing and wants nothing more than to put a brush to canvas," he said. "Well, some part of that is true. Maybe . . . mostly it's true. And I don't expect any woman to sit by herself in a teepee while I'm working. Especially not a beautiful, wild thing like you, Meg. With all your brains and that mighty spirit, you were meant to be the center of every social set that gathers. Men adore you. Women envy you. You've shot up from the gutter and made a place for yourself. Not many women could do it. Not many would have the gumption. And I adore you for what you are. Do you understand that little difference? It's important, Meg. I adore you. Love you for yourself, not for what your wit can do on my behalf. I'd love you if I never met you but were only watching you from a distance. I would watch you forever, and never grow tired."

She heard the change and the crack in his voice. She began to cry silently, turning away from him so he would not see.

"Don't." He put his hands on her shoulders and squeezed them. "Two pig-headed people who love each other should not live to hurt each other. I don't think we could ever be together for any length of time, Meg, without locking into a fight on one subject or another. That's how we are. It's the way we mix."

"Or don't mix," she added, shakily truthful. "Bu I don't want it like that. We aren't chemicals. We'r people. We can change. I mean *I* can change . . . an I have. That's why I've come here to you, Dick. want you to see how I can be a different sort o woman from the one who gets in your way, pull and pushes you around, or tries to, anyhow. *Tried* to Oh, I am so different! Chastised. Mortified by my stu pidity and narrow-minded blindness. Worried tha you'll stop loving me. That you won't find anythin left to appreciate in me. I'm turned around in entirely different direction. You'll see. I have decided, completely and absolutely, to leave you alone."

"Leave me alone?"

"I mean about your work. In the area of your work. I've given up plotting out your career. No more portrait painting if you don't want it. Not of imbecile women, anyway. I won't ever introduce you to those silly bores again as long as I live. No more of those cows with ringlets and ribbons. Never."

She teetered and toppled into his arms. It happened as naturally as the tide, and he hugged her close.

"Oh my sweet, impetuous, imaginative woman." He breathed into the top of her hair. "How you do struggle. How willing you are. How virtuous and single-minded. Why, I wouldn't begin to believe all those promises. I don't want you to make them, either. You wouldn't be you."

"I don't want to be me," came muffled from against his shirt.

"Yes, you do," he soothed. "That's who you are, anyhow, so why fight?"

"But I want to be good for you. I want you happy with me around, can't you tell?"

"How is this going to be resolved?" he uttered with a low, miserable drone.

"Just try me. Try! Give me one last chance to show you I've learned what's important."

His hands began to move along her back. The broad palms radiated a smooth, controlling heat. The touch of him, his surrounding muscles, were doing their work upon her mind and her body. Resolutions to straighten things *first* were beginning to drift into another, stronger tide, taking her carefully, floating her gently but swiftly out into a dangerous sea.

"Then you have no plan?" he said skeptically. Hopefully. "You came here with no plans for us? No intention for us to sport a dancing toe at Governor Clinton's?"

"No plans except to love you," she sighed, "if you let me," and receded, with Dick holding her, into the sweet, yielding creature she wished she could always be.

The windows were rattling wildly in the storm. The small fire purred with a stretch of blue-pointed flame that drifted down into embers. She closed her eyes while he undressed her and dried her warm flesh with his own shirt. How docile she felt. How completely trusting and trustworthy. How confident that she could glide along on the even keel of her good intentions. She found his mouth with her own and clung to it, dissolving herself in his embraces, putting away the fighting spirit, that unprofitable, fighting spirit! *I am a woman for him. I am his woman.* What more could matter?

Wandering fiddlers had entered the crowd below. Music filtered through the floorboards along with the sharp, warm smell of rum. Meg sighed and lay back on the bed, stroking his neck while his head roamed her body. He knew the special responsive places of her womanhood and went straight to them, muscles rippling on his back, curving downward into the tight pattern of his flanks. The saber scars were strangely white and ghostlike today. She remarked how they changed color depending on the weather and the light. Living flesh. Breathing, changing, maturing, growing. Her own, too. The breasts that he clung to with his lips began to flutter with the motion of his tongue driving small rings of sensation into their points. He cradled her as though she were a child, yet treated her as a woman so that she came alive, flashing and glittering like the many sides of a precious jewel. Her fingers twitched, becoming curious and possessive. They reached out and downward for their rights with him. There was always something innocent about it, as though when she touched him it was the first time which always jolted her into a new, flaming heat of surprise. Shudders chased their feathery sensations downward along the insides of her thighs. She placed him there and squeezed her legs together.

Drowning in love.

His hips became steadily more brutal, forcing her

wide, taking her with greedy craving. He had been with no other woman, she could tell it! Now she wanted to kiss him all over, too, her body arching, rising, claiming ownership in return. No mere gentle, passive creature could be his for very long. She knew how he loved her to be strong in her way.

"Darling, let me. Let me," she whispered, moving her lips, even before he answered, along the shiny, sweaty ridges of his tight stomach.

Now she was upon him, a free-roaming mare, galloping upward and up to conquer the hill, to claim the mountain. She clung to his narrow waist, eyes wild, wide, and staring, nostrils broadened, loving the salt taste, the musky aroma that rose from the dark brush of his vigorous loins.

"I want you," he groaned.

She knew she possessed him by the agony vibrating in his voice that set into shivering response all the tiny, sensitive muscles beneath her touch. His stormy strength rose inch by inch, mile by mile. Her kisses seemed to find the very soul beneath the flesh. Then she could bear it no longer.

At the crest of her strength, he sensed her need and turned her over quickly where she lay, panting, open, calling to him.

He came down upon her in one long silken thrust, driving deeply to the hilt of her dark and throbbing scabbard.

"Ooooooooooooooooh." The haunted song rolled from her throat, lonesome and yearning, even as she possessed the very thing she cried out for. All her life's sadness and all its joy hung about her at once, as though she had never lived before and would never again, beyond these moments, flying her one after the other over the dark, arching chasm of endless mystery.

Together, it could never end, only pause for a while. They lay side by side, the one beneath the other, resting or kissing. Sleeping or kissing. Talking close together, mouth touching mouth. They held each other's fingers and nuzzled each other's fingers, listening to the end of the rainstorm dripping into the puddles. Horses began to run along the streets. Wagons resumed their arduous hauls. Night slipped away into morning. A pale sun filtered vaporous light through paler clouds. The first real touch of winter crackled upon earth, freezing the tops of puddles into thin, treacherous film.

"Tell me the complete truth, Meg," he said, biting into a thick slice of breakfast ham. "You have come to Albany with letters in your reticule. I know it."

"Yes, certainly," she replied with airy nonchalance. They were alone at the dining-room table watching the stream of Albany traffic gather force. A thousand inhabitants seemed on this one road alone, riding in the direction of the main street. "But what have my letters to do with you? Didn't I make you a promise?" Her eyes sparkled irrepressibly with assurance. "Which I intend to keep," she added firmly as an afterthought. "Yes. Every word." Then, squeezing his hand, "I really mean to."

"What about your social life?"

"We needn't even talk about it, Dick. It's something I intend to pursue alone."

He couldn't have cared less when I did it in England. Taking his pictures is not the same as disturbing the man himself. Meg, back in her own room, dove down into the leathern trunk with the brass nailhead fittings that Elise had sent after, filled with evening-dress clothes. She had been true to her word with Dick and tonight would be seen alone—yes, alone!—at the governor's to dine. Eight o'clock at night without an escort. *How can he mind if I promise to show Mrs. Clinton one little painting?* She had purposely kept her room at the other end of town to prove to Dick that he could maintain as much privacy as he wished, without her intrusion. And gradually during the past few days she had managed to filch three darling pictures of spotted wood fawns that Dick, in his prolific carelessness, would never begrudge her. They now lay safely hidden in the trunk between a blue and a lilac chemise.

The last pang of misgivings faded as she did up her curls and pinned a sprig of fern in with the tiny and unassuming pearls Elise had packed along for luck. She had one week left, Dick had warned her, before they were off to Boston. And the ladies in Mrs. Clinton's circle were so very busy with social matters relating to the meeting of the Legislature that she had had no chance to interest them in art.

She heard the familiar rapping of Jonah's knife ilt on her door. He had never forgiven himself for ailing to retrieve Dick. In penance, he had become er running footman, driver, and man-of-all-work, unil he would feel absolved.

"The carriage is ready to go, missus, if you're ready o ride," he called impatiently through the door.

"A moment, Jonah. I'm coming," she retorted to the oice of punctuality, and let him in. "First I want to iow you how to carry some pictures into the govern or's drawing room when the proper day arrives."

The governor's drawing room had become like a econd home. Tonight Meg felt an uncommon ease nong the ladies who sat crammed in a formidable rcle on straight-backed seats that they hardly ever ft. During the course of the evening, gentlemen venred in and began talking to one another. There was ever a chair vacant, and they stood juggling several iina plates with peaches and grapes upon them, and ter, pyramids of ice followed by preserved pineapple.

Mr. Grange and Mr. Pulinner from the House of ssembly spied Meg within five minutes of her arrival. iey descended on her before dinner, bearing blancange and red champagne which she gently juggled, sting daintily of one and sipping at the other.

"But no, I have never been inside the House of ommons, Mr. Grange." Then, smiling, "Yes, Mr. ılinner, I should love to meet General Van Rensser at his home."

"In that case, Madame, I hope you will come and ar me speak tomorrow," intruded Mr. Grange.

One had blue eyes and the other brown, but they th were stout and of pale complexion and generally taciturn at the dinner table itself. It could all be very confusing if she cared.

"Ours is a most satisfying form of government, Miss Watkins."

"I certainly think so," she agreed.

"Perhaps you do not know that each state in the Union has its own Legislature independent of the general Congress of the Government?"

"No. I see. How reasonable."

"The laws of each state are made by its Legislature but must not interfere with the general laws of the Constitution."

"Yes. That wonderful work. A work of art. Do you care for art, Mr. Grange? And you, Mr. Pulinner have you a taste for pictures?"

"Pictures?" said Mr. Grange dubiously.

"Pictures," Mr. Pulinner echoed. "Certainly. Wha kind of pictures?"

"I understand there are men of the artistic persuasion who slip into the House of Assembly and penc portraits of the various debates on the spot."

"How interesting, Miss Watkins."

"No one has done that of me."

"But it could happen, Mr. Pulinner, any day, that not so? Is not everything possible in America?

Tarts, fruit, and cheese kept going round the roo without a rest, as though the best way Mrs. Clinto had to amuse her guests was to keep them eating. The came Mrs. Clinton herself and her mother, Mrs. Jone both ladies smiling at Meg with admiration for her fi French gown. The two Miss Clintons appeared, daug ters of the governor by a former marriage, and M Clinton's niece, Miss Allen, all a formidable t friendly family.

"Another glass of wine, Miss Watkins?"

"Thank you, Mrs. Clinton." Fondling the cut gla quite an inch thick, Meg responded with good nat to the animated face.

"But, gentlemen, you must not let our British frie think that our manners are not aristocratic. Hand in to the table politely. That's it, boys. Are you go

:o the debate tomorrow, Miss Watkins? You'll hear a ine lot of interesting drivel if you do," she added, aughing with pleasure and pride in her own cul-ivation. "We are so very, very English, they say.)ther ladies of your country are always amazed to ee how we dress the same, so exactly to the stitch hat there's no telling us apart. Don't you think so, too, Aiss Watkins?" She patted her ample bosom with trong red fingers. "Don't you think we have the hang f the real *haut ton,* as they say in French?"

"Oh, indeed. I see it all around me, and especially ι you, Mrs. Clinton."

"Well. That's what the chevalier says, anyhow, henever we gets to see each other. Elise is such a ıarming girl. Pity they aren't American, but not ev-y soul can be. Are you staying in Albany through ıe elections?"

"No, I'm off to Boston in a very short week. I had ›ped to show you some very pretty paintings before eave."

"Paintings? Why, yes. Elise has written me of her arvelous portrait, and its painter, the rage of New ɔrk, I understand."

"The ones I would give you reflect your native ɯntryside, Mrs. Clinton. An aristocratic view of ɜ American scene, before things change, which they ɜ surely bound to do."

"Oh, yes. It will go quickly. They're hacking back : forests at such a rate. Well, that's very good to ar. Why don't you bring them to me before you ?"

"Thank you very much. I hope I can do that soon?"

'Is tomorrow soon enough for you? After the de-:es?"

'Splendid, Mrs. Clinton, yes. I thank you again."

Meg crowded into the gallery and looked down upon speakers. She was not much of a judge of public tory but felt sure she would never hear anything te so bad again. Yet it was a small price to pay for showing the pictures to the governor's wife and leav ing them with her, the name FOX clearly painted i one corner. The speakers, who were speaking o what she could not tell, wandered oddly into strang corners of discussion that she couldn't follow. Th principal speaker stood with his left hand in hi breeches pocket and poked the air with a pencil tha he held in his right, now and then shifting the lef hand from the favored pocket further back to clutc a less delicate place and position. From what she coul make of it, they occupied a complete hour in discuss ing whether or not there were sufficient number pre ent for business to be transacted at all that day. The someone else stood up to read a long paper whil most of his colleagues settled their legs across th table nearest them and spat openly all over the floo The senators seemed to spit wherever they please and frequently. She had never seen so much spittin in her life, particularly so close to government.

But soon it was got through, and Mr. Grange an Mr. Pulinner accosted her near the steps. Then off th three went to a smallish dinner at Mrs. Clinton's bread pudding, cauliflowers, mashed turnips, biscuit ducks, and plums, first and second courses flung t gether indistinguishably and handed round with mu fussing. The ladies, filled with boiled mutton and pot toes, continued, nevertheless, pressing upon the se vants for another helping of one thing or another. was a tiresome business, waiting for someone to qu but after three hours or so, greasy fingers and mout were wiped on the hem of the tablecloth and peo began straggling away for a rest.

While Meg was deciding to drift over to a chub woman with active eyes, seated in the corner of own social circle, Mrs. Clinton found her and lowe a glass of madeira into her hand. "Have you brou me my pictures?" she asked.

The lady with the active eyes heard it across room. Her gaze lifted over her companions and res upon Mrs. Clinton, listening carefully as she contin her own conversation.

"Indeed, yes," replied Meg loudly. "I brought the woodland scenes for you and some marvelous wild forestscapes. Mr. Fox does not paint for notoriety, I can assure you. But his genius has brought it to him in New York, as you have heard. Mrs. Clinton, you shall understand it when you see them for yourself. I have left them with my driver. Do you wish me to call him in?"

As she spoke, Meg became aware of other conversations falling to erratic syllables. All eyes were upon her while she directed a servant idling near the wall to go for Jonah.

Jonah, true to his training, paused in the doorway for a long dramatic minute, a single painting held before him so that only his squinty eyes, nose, and a bit of mustache showed over the frame. Slowly he approached Mrs. Clinton with the measured, army-style teps of a British sergeant, which allowed every eye n the room to take its fill.

For one fraction of an instant, Meg luxuriated in he thrilling glow of Dick's work radiating before its ublic. Then her mind snapped back to business, rapidly assessing which ladies possessed the greediest, most acquisitive-seeming faces.

"Yes, those are pretty animals, but I should like a ortrait of my son. . . . Alicia, I am older than you, e shall paint me first. . . . Is this the man who did e chevalier's wife? . . . The very one. . . . Well! Let e tell you something else he did! . . . Now that's the eling of an artist; he shall do my entire family ong with the ducks. What did you say his name is? 'olf? . . . Fox, my silly sweetie. Fox. . . ."

Meg basked in the sound of Dick's name *here* and the flurry of gossip that trailed after the pictures. e watched Mrs. Clinton glancing around the room ith good-humored appreciation for her own triumph.

"Yes," she said after drinking her fill of the chatter. 'his is a fine, sturdy present, and I accept it with easure. I'll have it hung up over the mantel in the ting room between the pewter candlesticks and the rmer jugs." She flicked a gaze of complacent satisfaction over the other female competition. "And when your Mr. Fox does a portrait of *me,* we'll see that it's hung in the new governor's mansion as soon as the building is ready."

Chapter Twenty-seven

WAS HER FATE always to be this? Watching Dick Fo stand on the mountaintop of his fame and turn hi back on the glory? Mrs. Clinton had asked her t bring him in for a dish of tea next Wednesday, an here they were instead, pushing about in a miserabl winter gloom, boarding the stage for Boston.

She climbed to a seat beside the window while Dic saw to the last-minute stowing of his packages an her trunk, assisted by their new traveling companio Allan Newall, the first friendship she had ever see Dick encourage. Newall was a Boston name so prom inent, she had heard it mentioned in New York, b Allan, she suspected, was returning home from som secret or personal matter that would never be talked in social circles.

She heard Allan bellowing genially up to the pc ter. "Keep the green bag on top, sir. That's it. Squa in the middle. Balance it properly, sir, and the dar thing will stay. That's it now. Square. Like a head its pair of shoulders."

Over the window shade she watched him swingi one arm with painstaking but cheerful direction, m like a prosperous merchant of crockery setting wares than a medical student returning to Harv College. She did not know whether to love or to h Allan for his effect upon Dick, especially when two men sat up till dawn, talking and arguing ab how muscles formed themselves on the bone, how bones articulated behind muscle.

"Is it got right at last?" she said, as they finally climbed aboard, beads of sleet melting in their hair.

Dick sat beside her, content in his damp jacket, Allan opposite, in a short woolen coat with an otter-skin collar, black and glossy and rich, turned up care-lessly to his ears. He had a smooth, sensitive face always on the verge of smiling and always interested in the troubles of his neighbor.

"Were there a jot of sense among us," Allan said in his animated voice, "we'd be sitting round a cozy fire instead of banging off to Boston in this ungodly trap."

"I heartily agree," Meg blurted, avoiding a look at Dick. She intended to stay in good humor if it killed her, ducking her chin down into the vapor of her breath caught inside her shawl and quietly choking on her resolution to behave.

"We'll be just fine," Allan concluded, turning his mile first on Meg, then Dick, then leaning over to the lderly gentleman beside him loosening his coat from ts buttons, and lastly the gentleman's wife on the other ide. "So long as we're a healthy bunch, which it eems we are."

"Amen," muttered the woman frigidly.

Allan settled back. Meg felt him studying her in is easy way, the serious brown eyes searching deeper han the playful glint on their surface would indicate. Meg, you are going to enjoy Boston tremendously," e offered, with exactly the encouragement Dick would ever think to give.

"I usually manage to enjoy wherever I am," she eplied in the willingness of her new spirit, and snug-led her hand down, unseen, to play with Dick's ngers. He seldom wore gloves and the hands were ured to the weather. Warm. Calloused in places. oft in others. She felt him stroking her knuckles with e slow intimacy that assured her he was in an open ame of mind and pleased with her.

"In that case, you shall enjoy Boston especially."

The elderly gentleman lifted his hat and wiped its brim on his sleeve. "I don't particularly recommend it to a lady," he said with brittle good sense.

"Why not, sir?" asked Meg, as though it could matter.

"Boston is a city of commerce above all," he explained. "For those who are not employed in the counting houses, there is precious little else to do."

"You are quite correct, sir," said Allan. A smile of secret knowledge passed from him to Dick. "My father himself is a merchant of the first water, and he says the very thing. We are all for trade and profit and good sense about government, are we not? I take it by your looks that you, too, are a proper Bostonian, though I haven't the honor of knowing you."

Meg could not tell how much playfulness lurked in Allan's statements, but probably a good deal more than the old man suspected.

The wife, caught by the sociability, added, "We go only as far as Worcester, where our daughter lives She has come down with the measles and there are five grandchildren to think of. Last year they had the good fortune to escape the epidemic, but here we have i in our family now."

"Oh, my, yes," responded Allan, his rosy feature straightening into a more earnest cast. "But you mus take heart. We would rather the measles, happily, tha the putrid sore throat."

"Yes, yes," continued the lady with warmth. "Tha has killed off much of New England this past year."

"Along with dysentery, diphtheria, and small po I hope you have allowed your doctor to inoculate yo for the cowpox?"

"There seems to be such disagreement whether kills or saves."

"It saves, decidedly," Allan replied with heat. "A everyone must take it. Thousands upon thousands ha come through."

"How do you know of this? Are you a magistra sir? Or a clergyman?"

"I am a doctor, Madame."

"Oh," she replied, pulling away, offended, disappointed, and now distrustful of his advice.

Meg felt Dick settling down, smirking inside himself at Allan for trying to communicate what people did not want to hear.

At Worcester, after the couple had gone, Allan said to Dick, "You cannot blame me for trying."

"I do not blame you, dear fellow," Dick replied aloofly, stretching out his legs. "I merely find it foolish and absurd to try to educate where no education is wanted."

"Do you agree with him, Meg? I can't believe that I am the only clown in this lot. Besides, if one does not stir up a fuss, there will be no advancements in medicine. European doctors, who have the jump on us as regards dissection and a knowledge of the human body, are no longer sailing to our shores. Medically, we founder in America."

"You do your part," Dick replied without passion. "And shall continue to do even more."

"We shall continue," Meg echoed. Hearing the dread word *dissection,* her heart began to flutter with the first glimpse of comprehension.

Allan said, "He hasn't told you? I shall."

"There is nothing to tell her," Dick warned. "She will only try to talk you out of it."

"Out of what?" Meg insisted, miffed. "I will certainly *not* try to talk anyone out of anything. That isn't my place," she concluded with her new, righteous indignation.

"The dissections are a vital part of anatomical instructions," Allan said in a level voice. "And they must proceed by actual demonstrations, popular opinion against it notwithstanding. At Harvard, we have something of the sort struggling on, in great privacy, mind you, attended only by a small number of medical students and practitioners, chiefly persons once attached to the army. Doctors who have a real education in the matter have learned their lessons from bodies culled on the battlefield."

Meg turned to Dick. "What has all this medical matter to do with you, painter friend?"

As Dick hesitated to reply, Allan folded his hands across his lap and added, "Mr. Fox seems to have a greater working knowledge of anatomy than most medical men I have encountered, at least so far as horses are concerned."

"Has he talked you into allowing him to attend some of your human studies?" Meg cried, working to keep a rein on her agitation.

"He has talked me into nothing at all," Allan replied, "but has offered his services to help us."

"And how can he do that?"

"We are quite short of bodies, you know. We must contrive to get whatever we can, in whichever way we can. Now, this has nothing to do with ladies, and I shouldn't be shocking you, my dear. But how can I resist your mettle? Dick, perhaps you should tell her."

"I don't want Dick to tell me anything. I want to know how I can help before I hear another word from either of you."

"Valiant lady!" Allan boomed.

She felt Dick's fingers squeezing hers, relieved and loving her.

"I don't see what you can do," Dick put in now. "I have agreed to go with Allan on some nights to pick up the dead cats and dogs we might find."

"Also, you see," Allan added softly, "there is the matter of the convicts. Those who are condemned to die."

Meg felt the breath catch in her throat, waiting to hear what was coming next. "What about them?" she said, facing Allan straight on.

"There are ways," he said, "of obtaining their bodies, too."

"Body snatching?"

"No. No. Nothing so vile. It is quite legal but requires a bit of doing. You see, we can obtain a warrant of possession from the governor, when he can be talked into giving one. Sometimes he does see fit to hand over a corpse to the medical institution when it comes down from the gallows. But, of course, there can be complications of another sort. Family and such. When there is a wife to deal with, we have no chance, except where money has changed hands. There are convicts who are in high glee to be given the opportunity to sell the corpses they will become, and to have the money to give over to their families. There are other poor devils who simply like to have it for themselves. Dick has offered his services to come help me with these matters as they arise."

"In return for a ticket of admission to the dissecting room," Dick added dryly.

All this was spoken with such vague hints that Meg shuddered in the effort of swallowing down her immediate revulsion. How like Dick. In the past they would have fought about it bitterly . . . and she would lose. Now she must prove to him that her promise to cooperate was good.

"Of course I can help," she said eagerly. "You just didn't think how, but *I* know a way. Obviously you go out at night when there is no one to see you. Do you go with barrows?"

"Barrows and bags and carts, whatever comes handy," Allan answered her with growing curiosity.

"Do you go into the poorer sections of town?"

"Usually to North Slope Ridge. The poorest, meanest, most tumbledown area in all of Boston."

"Now you see," Meg pressed on readily, as though she were talking about tarts and cheeses. "I can go ahead during the day while you are across at Cambridge. Yes, I can mark for you where the poor animals have fallen. And at night I can accompany you on the journey, to show you where."

"My God, Meg!" Dick's voice was a wall of objection. He would have none of it.

"But don't say no to me," Meg pleaded. "I have wished and prayed to help you in some little way. Allow me this. Let me do it! What a help I can be. It is a dangerous occupation, I understand well. But I know dirty streets and miserable quarters as much as you, Dick. Certainly better than this well-to-do physician with his fine coats. Yes! Hear the truth, Dr. Newall, and that will increase your confidence in my abilities with the low things of life. This fine dress you see me in is only a cover and a convenience. The real Meg Watkins can do more for you than you know."

Allan's glance shot to Dick for confirmation, and Dick nodded.

"Now don't *you* say no to me, Dick Fox. You are to learn to love my company in every condition, no matter where you go—and there's an end of it."

The journey proceeded with lighter talk and much silence. Both men looked relieved at the sight of Market Square coming up ahead. While Meg hung by the precarious end of her passionate intentions, flurries of disbanding and disembarking brought them into a bustling maze of narrow streets, Boston, where the first spires she saw were buildings of public worship.

She could smell the ocean everywhere, which whisked in from Massachusetts Bay. The vigorous air came up unbridled around the spires and clustered clapboard houses, so that the town felt to her something like a ship's figurehead, standing straight out into the sea. She glanced around her and saw a vista of three hills that held in their bosoms secret lanes, courts, and alleys more so than broad thoroughfares. Already she saw herself skulking, scavenging among them, while Dick studied the sky masses of clouds and the cast of light over the sloping fields that winter had denuded of rambling cows and children.

"We shall all stay in a fine, aristocratic boarding house on Tremont Street," Allan was saying as he directed the transfer of their luggage to a smaller cab. "You will approve of it heartily, Meg, for its interesting patronage and extraordinary fare. Then you shall come to dinner and meet my family, who hobnobs with only the cream of society. It may not bore you overmuch."

She saw Allan playing back at her in retaliation

for her fine speech about low beginnings. Did he suppose she was a social climber for the dubious thrill of it?

"Allan, I will take advantage of your connections," she said quietly out of Dick's hearing. "Perhaps one day soon you shall understand why."

"Don't you think I do already?" He winked at her while carrying the mysterious and important green bag to the cab.

She hurried after him with no time to pursue the hook he had so neatly baited. In just a few blocks they were dismantling and organizing themselves into the upstairs rooms of a respectable, white-painted clapboard house at the side of the road and behind a high hedge of scraggly bushes stunted from the broad blows of winter.

Instead of caring for her dresses, she went to watch Dick unpack and see what she could draw out of him about his own inclinations, socially, concerning Allan Newall's family.

"We could do with a bath and a long sleep," she sighed, coming into Dick's room with seemingly no ambition in the world.

He was standing at his favorite place, a window, gazing out with an appraising eye. The view faced in the direction of the wharves, but little could be seen except for a high mast or two beyond the Market House and Faneuil Hall, itself surrounded by carts, drays, wheelbarrows, trucks, and porters competing with pedestrians for the narrow cobbled paths.

"Would we were in Italy, eh?" she said, hugging his arm. "Lying with some wine. Sleeping under a tree. You could draw till nine o'clock at night without having to come indoors."

"I can draw till nine o'clock at night now," he replied with a greedy taste for it, the ringing thrill only half suppressed.

"I know you will, in the dissecting room with Allan. I'm so glad for you, Dick. This is what you want. You couldn't wish for better. What a stroke of luck that you ran into a man like Allan, after all."

"Yes, it is luck." Dick patted her hand and swung her around to stand in front of him.

The precious moment of themselves together, without Allan, stimulated her and made her generous. She began to imagine herself dining with the Newalls and their friends, carrying the name of Dick Fox like a banner while Dick happily supplied her with the paintings that came rapidly from his easel.

"I shall work like I have never done before." His eyes narrowed with concentration and the sharp cheekbones stood taut. He breathed deeply as though sniffing turpentine and paints. "The clue to art is nature. Now I shall have my deepest experience of it. Can you imagine, Meg? To see, to really see, how a human head is structured. How the limbs are held together. I shall paint as no man has painted since da Vinci." He spoke, not humbly, but true to himself, his voice resonating with passion.

"Then you will paint human beings at last," she murmured, unable to contain herself. "You will do portraits. Beautiful portraits, the equal and superior of Reynolds."

"Oh, yes," he laughed. "Easily." His humor was arrogant and sure and ecstatic as he swung her around in his arms and kissed her fully on the lips.

She pulled her head back, straining away just sufficiently to look him clear in the eye. "I meant what I said before, my darling. I wish to go with you, help you in your work. *That* has come to mean everything to me."

"I believe you, Meg."

"We shall be good for each other, you'll see. Without even trying, we will be hand in glove. No more arguments. No differences of philosophy. Oh. I am thankful for Allan Newall, too."

Dick threw back his head and chortled, letting rip the amusement he felt at her capricious responses and shifting conflicts regarding his new friend.

Meg stood in his arms, not minding his fun at her expense. She had what she wanted. To be part of his world. Part of him! And he would do portraits, too. What more could she ask of her world?

She flung her arms around his waist and began kissing his chest with the pent-up passion of all her worries transmuted into channels open for success. He sensed her agreement with him and lifted her up along his body. From above him she looked down upon his dear face and kissed the mouth while she hung suspended overhead, supported in his steel grip, made weightless, made immortal by her lover.

They heard Allan on the far side of the wall dropping his bags and pushing about his trunks, taking out his study books, no doubt, settling possessions around himself for a year of comfortable work and study. Meg smiled at Dick wordlessly while he carried her to the bed and lowered her to the coverlet, then dropped down beside her, stroking her hair, her eyebrows, her lashes, the curve of her upper lip. At these times she could lie still, her fears calmed that Dick could leave her. These moments of attention were his tribute to her as the curl and splash of playfulness intermingled before the onset and rise of carnal desire.

"I know how you feel about the Newalls," Dick whispered against her mouth. "I hope you do take Allan's invitation and go to dinner with him there."

She waited, not voicing the question she yearned to ask, but letting it vibrate silently through her being. Dick looked down into her soul through her eyes. The eaglelike, serious intensity softened as the minutes passed, and she did not speak the inevitable plea that he go with her, too. His arms went along her sides, then, and began to lift her so that her back arched, bringing her into the concave hollow of his stomach. She could feel his heart thumping like a huge fist. Her own pattered, keeping up with him as when they strode along the street and her footsteps rushed to stay abreast. Outside, the strange city, the new city with its enormous opportunities, could wait at the feet of their most personal and important ambitions with each other. For that was how she saw their love, as ambition satisfied, the utmost ambition to live with all the strength, faith, and shared trusting that two reckless human beings could command.

A howling, gusting wind blew night across the sky, snatching away daylight even as she embraced her love and held him, peering over his shoulder at the sky outdoors, yet seeing in her mind's eye only his face, only his body's nakedness aligned with her own. How far she had come to reach this moment of acceptance. Perhaps that was the answer: to *not* resist Dick's intentions for his art. To take what he gave and somehow work with that.

His mouth lusting for her kisses went at it with a will, prying those kisses loose in drawn-out probings of his tongue. There was no hurry between them, only the urgent, driving lift of their mutual flame, breathed upon ardently by each in turn and both together, the spell of love molding from liquid fire a new, single creature, larger, stronger, more passionate than they each could be alone.

His nose lay in the hollow of her throat while his hands fondled her breasts, touching each carefully as though he had never known them before. That amazing sense of *novelty* came upon her again and again. Love with Dick was always the first time, each mingling of their bodies a new adventure never explored before and never to be recaptured. She sensed the uniqueness, the irreplaceable moment, as though she stood on a point of destiny that was dissolving and creating itself anew, even as she balanced. Then the old pictures rose before her closed eyelids, of herself with Dick, home again in England, comfortably ensconced at court, popular, famous, receiving guests of world renown. Other images of lovemaking intruded. And there was Dick, descending upon her in the guise of a leopard, mounting her from behind, growling and gnawing on the back of her neck. She heard the hissing whip of his tail as sexual heat rose in him. Then the animal faded and he was a snake, insinuating himself completely to disappear within the deepening canal of her body.

"Oh, take me, take me," she moaned, compelling

Dick the snake, Dick the leopard, Dick the male body above her.

Her limbs spread wide, creating the beckoning chasm, the hungry, lusting place. She lowered one hand and grasped his sturdy thickness, guided into herself the ancient, pulsing, heated mystery of the difference between them . . . felt that difference blend with her, making of their two bodies the single unit that, she felt sure, Nature had meant at first to create.

"Yes . . . yes . . ." she breathed.

"Hold on to me," he muttered, bearlike, at her ear.

She clung to him with her knees, her ankles, her talons. As she gripped him, he began a longer, gliding motion than she had ever felt, a more forceful driving of himself deeper than he had ever gone, crying at her as though in pain, needing to know her in the very bowels of her soul. How she understood him! She lifted her hips gradually higher and higher, tilting herself to help him, balancing her weight on the straining wings of her shoulders. She was uncaged and rising in a musky flight of love, circling, spiraling upward, up and up, carried by him at her hips so that they soared together over the top of passion's highest peak of struggling. Free! . . . free!!! into a cloudless, never-ending sea of crystal blue.

They had long since left behind them the sick yellow glow of street lamps. She could barely hear the track of Allan's footfall ahead as they climbed beside a ive of shacks that gave out raucous cries of brawling ailors and the tinkle of lively music mixed with wom-n's voices bellowing in song.

"Where are we, Allan, for crissake?" called Dick ehind her.

"Mount Whoredom," Allan called back, hardly au-ible.

"How can you tell in this muck?"

"I can smell it, dammit, can't you?"

Meg had fought to ignore the stench. As Allan oke, it came to her in suffocating waves of garbage mes and putrifaction. They were going uphill, steeply climbing the back side of Tri-mountain, forested by tumbling dance halls and disorderly houses, all shacks of rotted wood. From behind slitted window holes drifted Negro accents, sometimes laughing in heavy delirium or cursing or crooning ancient melodies. There crept about Meg the familiar atmosphere of lonely hardships that flung her back to other times that swung her between past and present.

Dick had opted to carry the rough sacks in hopes they would fill all three. She heard him pause behind her, and kick something with a firm thump.

"What have you there?" Meg called back to him.

"Nothing. It's stiff," he uttered, scientifically factual. "Too long dead."

"Come on, then, we'll lose Allan."

She lunged for Dick's sleeve and brought him forward. Half the breath was gone from her already. They had been searching through the tangle of alleys for an hour and had come up with only starved and bony things no good for dissections. What they wanted were plump, recently deceased specimens, probably creatures with something broken who had died abruptly, unexpectedly, in the midst of healthy lives.

"Someone bring me a bag," called Allan.

Meg yanked one from Dick's shoulder and rushec headlong, eager to accomplish the first haul. "Here Where are you?" she called, plunging toward his voice

"Watch! Don't tumble over it."

"What have you found?"

"A cat, I think. Feels . . . long . . . enough." H probed around with his boot tip.

"Come along, then," Meg said swiftly. "Snatch up and be gone."

Allan laughed as he bent to his prize. "You kno where there are better, Meg?"

"We'll find them. We will."

Dead weight dropped inside, bulging in the lim sack. Allan quickly twisted the top closed and swu the bulk over his shoulder. "Damn things weigh li an anchor," he grunted. "Should have brought a ba row."

"And go creaking through these hills?" Dick offered. "Half an inch an hour? Hand it here."

He was bigger than Allan by half a foot at least in all directions. Merely having him along gave a certain active movement to the endeavor. Meg, pressing ahead of both men, thought, I've seen bigger, deader in my own home, and ran ahead with a renewed jolt of confidence in her capabilities.

What they needed was a night with a moon. Snow clouds obscured every glimmer reflected from the sky and enlarged every cry or scuffle that rose from the crowded hovels near where they walked.

"Here's something better," Meg called, feeling with her sandal the soft, swollen belly of a creature on its back. Her foot felt its way to find each of the four egs pointed skyward. There was a long sleek tail, tiffly quiet. She was bending to it as Dick came with a bag. "A plump dog," she told him.

"Let it go," Dick said, squatting beside her. "We lon't use this."

Meg, feeling more closely, said, disappointed, "Oh, t's a rat." *This is going to be one long night.*

They returned to the boarding house and crept past he snores of other guests up to Allan's room. They mptied their spoils on the floor beside the green bag rom which Allan handed out other creatures, deuded to the bone. It was a special bag, indeed; akproof, sewn with a number of linings hardened y cakes of blood.

"What a beautiful skeleton," Dick said, admiring a nall creature quite white-boned and arch-backed, eld together by bits of wood and metal pegs.

"A Cheshire cat," grinned Allan. "My prize. I alays take it with me. Want to draw it?"

"Dick has a book of unborn infants," Meg said.

"I'm sure he has." Allan sighed with envy. "You nglish are quite ahead of us in all directions. Here are supposed to learn about the human body from ulptures of the antique." He lined the corpses up the carpet and surveyed the night's catch. "Tomorrow I shall take these off to the medical institution, where Dick and I shall do a proper job upon them. Tomorrow evening, Meg, if you so desire it, I should like to escort you to dinner at my father's home. He has not seen me for the two weeks we have been back. But I have told him of the new, lovely lady in my acquaintance."

Meg glanced quickly at Dick, who did not seem to hear their conversation as he lay prone before the cat skeleton, chin propped on his knuckles, peering intently into its hollow eyes with that innocent smile of contentment that marked his most satisfied moments.

Chapter Twenty-eight

STILL THINKING of Dick's grisly expression, she rod off to the mansion on Bowdoin Square, built with classical European elegance for its prominent master. Sh sat at a table before a vast spread of roast meats an a profusion of root vegetables heaped about on beautiful china plates in no order whatsoever, served b one or another of the dozen lackeys who leaped awa from the walls upon command to assist Mr. or Mr Newall in service to their guests. Still arriving was sedate crew of gentlemen dressed as she had nev seen Americans dressed before. They were ol fashioned, pre-Revolutionary types as far as she cou tell, removing huge cocked hats as they came in th revealed queues reaching down to their backs, th swinging off cloaks of scarlet broadcloth lined wi silk and faced with velvet, all of them obviou wealthy, if not well-born. She had already met t directors of the Massachusetts Bank on State Stre constables, surveyors, and overseers of the poor; a I

Thomas Welsh, Visiting Physician at the Port, some variety of selectmen, the Hay-weigher and Weigher of Onions.

Presiding over the establishment sat Mr. Peleg Newall with his great, black Surinam walking cane leaning against his chair, its six-foot length protruding above his right shoulder as he leaned into the madeira that washed down every second swallow of roasted pig. His broad, soft face spoke out with its smallest movement that he had ample intentions and capacity for enjoying life if only the foolish Democrats would give way again to their Republican superiors; if the weather and native uprisings would allow his ship captains to find their way safely into Canton and home again; and if his son Allan would give up his unspeakable dedication to healing the sick and take on more serious, important interests such as commerce.

In this comfortable atmosphere there was speech that Meg recognized, long-lost voices and philosophy reminiscent of home, which put her quite at ease in a way very different from her friends in New York. From time to time she fired a look of appreciation at Mr. Peleg Newall, who had already digested a great portion of her admiring glances with the acknowledged acceptance that it was his due. "With every man is born a station in life," said his eyes, "but every woman makes her own."

After dinner, he seemed to enjoy crying to Meg about Allan. "If he wishes to do good with medicine, why does he not join the clergy? *There* he would learn something, and ah, the position. The position, my child. I myself have come up from humble beginnings, very humble. A dry-goods retailer, my father, who lost money twice over and cared nothing about public opinion."

"Do I hear you talking about your Allan?" said Lawyer Grigg, who had acquired wealth as a conveyancer, executor, and trustee, never again to be seen in court. "Have you spoken with him about the *word* on this matter of doctoring? 'No chirugeons, midwives, physicians, or others shall be allowed to practice medicine, except as he shall pass an examination and be approved of by a board of nonmedical officials such as judges, the attorney general, the mayor, and others . . . to throw a sufficient safeguard around the indiscriminate use of medicine.' I am with you, Peleg. Advise him strongly, never too strongly, to join the clergy."

"But he is now at the medical *institution,*" said Meg, hoping that Allan was in earshot and would take some solace from her aid to his cause.

"Institution!" spat Peleg Newall. "There are nineteen edifices for public worship in our town. Nine for Congregationalists. Three for Episcopalians. Two for Baptists. The Friends. Roman Catholics. Methodists. Sandemanians and Universalists. All of them ornamented with beautiful spires, clocks, and bells. It would please his mother much if he donned the cape and shovel hat and went forward thus. But here. I am putting you into a humor over your friend Allan. You must tell me of yourself, Miss Watkins, and how my English counterparts are faring."

"The war has sickened most people at home," Meg replied glibly, suddenly aware of how long she had been gone and of how little she knew of home affairs.

Talk drifted then into trading and commerce worldwide, which seemed a passion with these Boston gentlemen. For all their easygoing manners, they were intent on navigating the course of American affairs according to plans of their own trading interests, and Meg was hard put to get away from talk of cargoes to China.

At last, when she felt quite useless and disgusted not to get a word in edgewise about art, Allan strolled up to her and pulled her aside, a breathless secret spilling from his lips.

"Here, Meg," he whispered. "I have just spoken to the governor. Come away. Come with me." He beckoned her to follow him into an elegant drawin room, one of dozens, it seemed, that overlooked an ample garden tucked in by a fast-falling layer of snow.

"What is it, Allan? How am I to make headway with your father's friends? They don't give a farthing for the social graces. All I hear tell of are those damned otter skins they barter in Canton."

"Meg, listen," he said, quieting her with a squeeze of the arm. "I tell you I have spoken with the governor."

"What of it?" she said impatiently.

"He has given me a warrant."

"Warrant? I don't care for any warrant." She felt free to speak as she wished before Allan, with no pressure upon her to dissemble.

"It's a warrant for the corpse of Silas Peddle."

"If your father does not care for art, perhaps I can interest your mother in the cause."

"Silas Peddle, I say," burst Allan. "A man. A man!"

The words sank in then. She began to pale. "When for?" she asked quickly.

"He is to be hung tomorrow night."

"And then?" Fearing the worst, she merely stared at him, unable to prod him further.

"And . . . I must be off now to haggle with him about the price for himself. I understand there is to be a widow involved who does not weigh the money but prefers to bury her corpse in proper, ritual ground. We will be up to our ears in troubles collecting on our warrant, I am afraid, unless something can be arranged."

"But what is to be done?" cried Meg with wretched attention, pulling herself away from the door where people milled in harmless talk about trade.

"I suppose we must try to dicker with the wife."

"If she is afraid of the devil, you will get nowhere." Meg turned from him. "You would be a fool to try, warrant or no."

"Then we will have to come by him another way. He is rightfully ours."

"Oh, you sound fierce, Allan. I hate you like this."

"Remember Dick's painting," said Allan with a quick, thoughtless wave of complacency.

"Above all things, eh? As your father believes in his Chinese trade."

"Exactly it. But look, here comes Mother. Talk to her about Dick. She'll cheer you up."

Meg had no idea what could be going on behind Tabitha Newall's generous energy on behalf of keeping her guests well fed and happy. She had a simpler posture than the Albany set and kept herself more modestly employed after dinner with needlework done on a round frame, listening to others rather than forcing upon them what was best, in her opinion, about everything to do with politics.

"My dear Miss Watkins, will you look at that snow! I am quite surprised to see so much of it so fast. But, of course, our weather is quite unpredictable." She stood leaning her plump but compact body between the curtains, her genial expression quite reminiscent of Allan, the same shining brown hair straight and thick, held back discreetly by a velvet band.

"As it is in England," replied Meg, feeling the rise of an enthusiasm in Mrs. Newall, but for what she could not immediately discern.

"My husband watches the weather much more than I. The men do, generally." Her dark eyes shone as though at the antics of children. "But people come and go in this house from every country, and I am quite concerned that they do not leave us with the catch-cold. That, truly, is my main interest in the weather."

"I fear I do not think of it ever." Meg smiled. "Or I might stay indoors all winter with my knitting." She spoke with flowing conviction, hardly hearing how ludicrous she sounded to her own ears, as though she could care a fig for snow or fog or sun, much less knitting. Yet it sounded right in these surroundings and served to oil the wheels of conversation with this genteel woman, obviously of great influence, who commanded the attention of so many.

"You have such a interesting face," pursued Mrs

Newall. "You are British, but have, I hear, French connections in New York?"

"I am international," laughed Meg.

"That is the best course, certainly. These men, like my husband, give themselves headaches and attacks of gout day and night, talking, talking, talking about the evils of French democracy and the decline of British trade and the narrow-minded legacy now in the White House."

"If you wish to know the truth," Meg said, "I don't think of politics at all. I think of art."

"Art?" said Mrs. Newall, her voice rising with curiosity. "What a novel idea. Of course, you are British and have a considerable artistic heritage behind you. Our own Gilbert Stuart has studied and made a world-famous name for himself in England. Now that he has returned to us, he is enhanced by that connection."

"Returned to you? Here in Boston?"

"Why, yes. And quite recently. Our circle is all aflutter about him, poor dear man. Putting up with our questions and our admiration as though he had nothing better to do in the world." She adjusted two chairs at the fireplace and beckoned Meg to join her. "We should be sewing, I trust, if we were truly in the British fashion. But let us be quite at our ease in our own style. Sit near me. My legs feel rather knotty in wintertime. And I shall tell you about Gilbert Stuart since you are interested in art."

Meg, seeing no reason to hide her enthusiasm, let it shine unabashedly. "My cousin Dick Fox is a painter, you see. A fine painter at that, if I may be immodest and say so. He has done pictures for the chevalier in New York and Governor Clinton's wife. So I am quite delighted to hear as much as you will say about Mr. Gilbert Stuart." She paused, waiting on the edge of her chair for Mrs. Newall to read her mind and speak it aloud.

"Certainly you can meet him," burst Mrs. Newall, pouncing on the opportunity to oblige.

"And my cousin?"

"And your cousin. Why did you not bring him here tonight? I should love to have my portrait done by a man who has painted for the distinguished Mrs. Clinton."

Meg felt a flashing tightness in her throat that signaled the wild frustration she must on occasion grapple with. "I'm sure he will be honored to meet you," she answered softly, avoiding any talk of a specific date.

"I shall count on it," Mrs. Newall replied. "But tonight you must stay here with us. So shall Allan. I won't have you going outdoors at this late hour, in this weather. Now obey me, child. Not one word from you. We shall send a message round to whomever you wish, saying that you are here and quite safe."

"Yes. Quite safe." Meg looked at the woman quizzically, wondering what this was really about.

"You see, dear, I am counting on you for a favor in return, which I am sure you will oblige me." Her firmer, lowered note strung a bond between them. "Mr. Newall lives in hopes that Allan will see his way to a decent occupation and come down to the counting house with him. Mr. Newall asked me, very particularly, to invite you on a stroll with him to Long Whar tomorrow morning, for if *you* agree, Allan will b influenced to accompany you. Once there, in tha healthsome atmosphere, perhaps Allan will begin t glimpse the more serious matters of life and, wel think about things. I'm sure you follow me." She wave one plump hand limply. "It is a desperate plan, know. But I do so like to oblige my husband in h little wishes."

"Why, Mrs. Newall," said Meg, confident that long as Allan was with her, Dick would not be f removed. "Whatever you ask of me, I will with plea ure attempt."

The rich Bostonian merchants were late risers, least two hours later than their counterparts in N York. At ten in the morning, Peleg Newall sat in silk dressing gown, chin tilted ceilingward, while a N gro barber who had come down from North Slope Village drew a long razor tenderly over the soft cheeks. Meg, expecting a rush of activity, lolled about in this lackadaisical household, peering unhappily at the crisp, clear sky and wondering where Dick would go off to today. Impatiently she picked at her eggs and tea while Peleg puttered with messages and household notes, attempting everything other than walking off to work.

Allan, noting her darting, piercing looks masked by short, bored bursts of frivolity, leaned an elbow on the black marble mantel and said mockingly, "This is the life, eh?"

"I promised your mother."

"Mm. But *I* did not."

"You shall come with me, Allan. Or I will see to it Dick does not go with you tonight."

"You are a monster."

"Yes," she said decisively. "That is what saves me."

Within the hour, Mr. Peleg Newall had pulled his gouty legs under him, donned a heavy woolen coat vith his beloved tricorne, and the three strolled away rom Bowdoin Square, a Negro servant behind them winging a shopping basket on his arm.

The first stop had nothing to do with business and verything particular to Mr. Newall's two o'clock dinner, as they hauled into Nathaniel Scribbs's grocery tore on the corner of Tremont and Court streets. here they joined other merchants, their long queues winging as they bent and chose thoughtfully among he turnips, carrots, and potatoes, making, at last, the erious selections that were dropped into the basket eing held at their elbows.

"Fine day, Peleg."

"Good morning to you, Horace."

"What say you to this shoulder mutton?"

"I say, since you saw it first, take it and be amned!"

"Why, Peleg, you stole the ducks out from under y nose yesterday."

"And so I shall again tomorrow."

"Good luck to you, Peleg. Why, isn't that your boy, Allan? Haven't seen him for a year. Where are you keeping him?"

"Yes. He is exactly my image, don't you think so?"

"A handsome lad and a credit to you, Peleg. But the likeness is more toward Mrs. Newall. Are you coming in with us, Allan? I am glad to see it. Better late than never, eh, Peleg?"

Peleg Newall laughed self-consciously, a broad fortress with empty guns behind it. Soon Mr. Horace Apthorp had pulled Peleg aside into a confabulation with three others. Meg heard a buzz of ships' names mixed with grumbling about France.

Allan pinched her arm underneath the shawl. "Enjoying yourself?"

"What has all this hen's chatter to do with international trade?"

"Nothing and everything. They are one big family, these codfish millionaires, can't you see? Among them they own the commercial seas, or like to think they do. But their days are numbered because of the war. At any event, let us go ahead to the counting house and fulfill your bargain."

"We shall stay for an hour and run off," Meg replied. "I shall see to that."

"All you shall hear is more old-fashioned complaining, I can promise you."

In the great room of the counting house, Peleg beckoned his son to approach where he stood, warming his hindquarters in front of a huge hearth.

"Yes, Father?" said Allan with a profound show of respect.

"Old-fashioned, eh?" launched Peleg with paternal hurt. "Days numbered?"

"I should think so, Father," replied Allan calml[illegible]
"The time for British aristocracy in America is gone[illegible]

"Is that so? Who do you suppose *pays* for your fi[illegible] democratic government? Who shoulders the respon[illegible] bility for American debts, if not your men of property?" He turned his head slowly, painfully, to gaze upon the model of a three-master sail on the mantel, beneath a fine painting of George Washington who gazed candidly out over the room.

"Boston has led the way in Royalist times but will fall behind if she does not acknowledge the changes that are coming fast upon us."

"The changes that are coming are the China trade!" bellowed Peleg Newall.

"Here! Here!" echoed his colleagues, who had been listening, until this moment, in silence.

"Now, my lad, hear *me,*" called Horace, untying his spectacles from around his head and limping up to intercede on behalf of his sputtering friend Peleg. "You have come on a fine day to get yourself an education without moving a finger. Our young commander of the brig *Faithful* has berthed on Monday last. These are her papers of exchange. What do you say to it, Allan? Read. Go on, read it yourself. We have acquired ninety thousand dollars' worth of pelts from the Oregon Indians in exchange for a few thousand dollars' worth of trinkets—some shoe buckles, I believe they were—brass-headed canes, and a handful of snuff boxes. There is a rumor currently that the Northwest Indians are using ermine pelts for currency, which we can obtain at Leipzig for thirty cents apiece and trade *them* for one thousand dollars' worth of otter skins, worth in Canton, as you can see, fifty dollars each."

"Fine trading, indeed," Allan agreed candidly, but remained unimpressed. "There is nothing more for you to do except make yourselves comfortable before the fire and pass your workday hearing news of the rewarding activities of your men in exotic ports."

"Which will become *your* inheritance eventually," added Peleg Newall with bitter reproach. "But I see you are not to be persuaded this day or any other, I do believe. It is only coming out that we make Miss Watkins uncomfortable." He thumped his cane once as though calling an end to the conference. "I suppose you must run along home. It is eleven-thirty. We have some Englishmen arriving to discuss those matters of business which will never concern you, I fear. Be sure to present yourself at the dining table, two o'clock sharp, for dinner."

Meg drifted out with the least amount of display she could manage, watching the shipyards beyond the hall windows and waiting for Allan to make as swift an escape as he could.

Along the corridor came the lilt of approaching British accents that jarred her with nostalgic loneliness for the familiar way of life she missed. Then Allan appeared. She grabbed his arm, turned him to her, and said, "I regret this altogether. Truly I am sorry we came. You must know I thought it would be harmless, but here I have succeeded in helping to hurt everyone." The Englishmen passed. She glanced at them obliquely, out of habit. Her gaze passed in a disinterested blur over three bulbous, red-cheeked faces and fixed, widening, upon one pale, milky-skinned profile that in exactly the same instant turned, caught, and fixed upon her. The recognition was a thunderclap. Her heart seemed to stop, stopping time itself, as the other's eyelids froze and mouth drooped numbly. Then the trio passed off into the room where Peleg Newall and his associates waited, while Meg stood shaking, trying to absorb the horrible fact that she had just been staring at the presence of Ralph Carstip.

Chapter Twenty-nine

THE COLD, WINDLESS NOONTIME went powerfully through the bone, yet seemed to encourage the merchants appearing on State Street and Long Wharf to continue business outdoors, as they had always done, with no inclination to settle themselves comfortably inside the new coffee houses built for that purpose. The crowds were thickening on the streets but could not console Meg nor hide her in a world shrunk to the size of a thimble.

"Where are we going, Allan?"

"Home to Mother, like the dutiful son they wish I could be. There is nothing else for us, anyway, until tonight. Poor Silas Peddle is to die. And I am looking forward to his corpse. What an unthinkable world this is."

"Tell me," she said, squeezing his arm. "Does your father always bring his business people home to entertain them for dinner?"

"Hm? Yes, often, but not many at once. It will never be a party there in the daytime. He worships the family bosom, you see. It is a happy, Bostonian trait."

"I understand how he might bring home Horace." She spoke breathlessly. "Would he ever bring home, well, foreigners? An Englishman?"

"Why, those he loves most of all, like his own flesh and blood," Allan chirruped sourly. "For him it is tragic that the mother country has so lost affection for her prodigal son across the Atlantic."

"Don't fool with me, Allan, please. I am quite serious."

"So am I. Never more so," he protested. "What is the matter with you, Meg? You look as though your pulse has dropped. Are you ill?"

"No, not ill." She spoke in short words whipped from her mouth by the wind. "But I cannot go back to your house. Not today. Not ever."

"Of course you can!" Allan hugged her affectionately. "My father has no inclination to oppress *you,* dear girl. I am the jack rabbit he wishes to catch. You run free."

"Not ever," she repeated. "Let us move away from here now. I must."

"Meg. Stop. What is this?" he called after her as she tore loose and began to run, not knowing her direction, past the vessels in the yard. He caught up with her finally and grabbed her arm. "What's wrong? What are you doing?"

"I'll tell you later. Only take me away from here now," she pleaded.

"But you are hysterical."

As he tried to restrain her she slapped his face and dashed around him, eyes wild, hair streaming back in a gust that blew from across the water.

"Meg! Meg! Please! I mean to understand this. You must be in a fever."

They had got a few blocks inland along Court Street before Meg subsided and slowed to a rapid walk. "What am I to do?" she gasped, Allan quite forgotten beside her.

"What is this, and why must you run from my home? Besides," he soothed blindly, attempting to calm her with sense, "if we are not there for dinner, Mother will be terribly offended, and what will that do to your plans for Dick? How do you mean to sell his work if you abandon the very household you mean to impress?"

She heard the logic and stopped short, repeating "What *am* I to do?" dizzily aloud, yet resoundingly inside her throbbing head. No doubt but *he* had seen her. Was he in Boston purely by coincidence? What was he doing in America? Nor could she forget the riveting look, so brief yet so animal-like in its hungry, burning lust for vengeance. "Allan, you must do this for me," she burst, grasping both his elbows and squeezing them. "You must listen to me very carefully and then use the fine wits God has given you to help me. Will you do that?"

"Of course," he said, relieved. "Tell me everything. We will walk along the market stalls and then across to Tripp's Oyster House. No one will see us in the crowd or much care what we have to say to one another. You will tell me the trouble and I will surely help you."

The confident voice of friendship gave Meg something more solid to lean upon than her vicious memories. She obeyed Allan's advice and they went together to Union Street, taking refuge on the second floor of a fish ordinary, in a dark wooden booth away from the windows. As she unfolded in faltering fragments her involvement with Ralph Carstip, the horror returned with a new, deadlier threat.

"The reality is that I stole his jewels. Not only did I run away from him, but I took his belongings, too. I made a fool of him. I'm sure he must kill me to heal his pride."

"Well, he won't kill you under my father's roof," Allan assured her, facing up to a hearty pile of mussels, shrimp, and Cotuits on the platter between them. "He has come to America, no doubt, to see about his property here, not in search of you. He won't dare make a scandal of any sort while you are under the protection of the Newalls, I guarantee it."

There was something very clear-eyed and secure about Allan that allowed Meg to believe him. "Then will you play along with me, Allan, just for safekeeping? Will you pretend that we are . . . involved with each other?" She studied him earnestly. "A premonition sits on my shoulders that I cannot shake loose. I feel he is after Dick, too. And at all costs, I must keep him from that trail. He must never know Dick is here in Boston with us. He must, instead, be convinced that you and I are lovers. Will you do it?"

"He will never believe such a myth," Allan laughed, patting her arm. "Not the way you treat me. But if you care to try, I will certainly play the game out."

"In that case," she said, her voice sinking again with dread, "let us return to your home in Bowdoin Square. For dinner."

By the time they arrived at the huge, comfortable house, the smallest Newalls were dashing about the eating room in expectation of their father, the cloth laid pure and white on the table, the plate warmer resting by the fire; everything cozy, happy, and far from Meg's tense state of treacherous anticipations. Mrs. Newall's voice rang up from the kitchen, where, busy with two unmarried aunts and the female servants from close-by farms, she carried on with them the business of readying the great meal, one huge, blithesome family that could imagine no harm within its domain.

"You see," said Allan, taking her cloak. "You must meet things as they come. Today a lady of this respectable house, and tonight?" He lowered his voice and his eyes, leaning down close to her face, and said mischievously, "A dark snatcher of corpses. We must leave here nine o'clock sharp."

"If only Dick had some of your disposition." Meg smiled, cheered by his impregnable good nature. "He would have a huge social success already."

"You will take your Dick Fox home to England one day." Allan kissed her on the forehead. "He wil do you proud, mark my words. Dick and I have ha many a probing conversation. There is no force o earth can stop him from his goal. You may not agre with his methods exactly, because they are above re proach. It is difficult for mere mortals like you and m to understand how it is possible for anyone to live o this earth without compromise. But that is Dick's wa and though surely mysterious, it works for him ar will reflect in material rewards."

"I hope I live to see it," Meg sighed ruefully, h

lashes fluttering with unabashed pleasure at Dick's name spoken so favorably by an intelligent mind. "I am so glad he has you for a comrade," she whispered, accepting the glass of madeira that a younger brother spilled for her, half into the glass and half onto the flowered carpet.

Meg drank with the intention to become just a wee bit tippled and debonaire as she watched the clock hands approach searchingly close to the hour for Peleg Newall's appearance. Yet, though she polished down three full glassfuls and watching her became a game for the children, her brain stood aloof and unwilling to bend before the assault of mere alcohol. Meanwhile, Mrs. Newall and the servants dashed up to set piles of cut, cold delicacies in different corners, making an ample spread that hardly left room for the hot dishes by the time the master of the house arrived home.

She didn't have to strain for Ralph Carstip's voice. It came to her with gale force, blowing a destructive path, somewhat high-pitched and nasal in contrast with the American's longer accent. Before she saw him, her very fingernails seemed to be eaten away by the gnawing sound of him, her flesh riddled. Yet as he entered over the threshold, she turned to face him directly, with dazzling smiles and lifted chin, as though she herself were the mistress of this house and unassailable within its walls. She waited to see if Ralph would acknowledge their acquaintance before the Newalls, and didn't have long to wait before the listless face turned itself inside out in grimaces of mingled hatred, fury, satisfaction, and desire all aimed at her. She saw the desire unbelievably clear, flickering behind the nervous lowering of his flimsy, sandy lashes. He had changed alarmingly in a year, grown more gaunt in the throat, stringier in his hands. The fingers seemed to be hung together by wires tightening beneath the transparent flesh. They danced with jeweled rings too flashy for an American dinner table. His ruffles, exquisitely clean this day, exuded a dark, arresting perfume. Yet for all this barbarous glitter and costuming, the tailor had failed to bring alive the man inside. The bluish veins standing upon his temple could almost be seen pulsing like some ruthless creature that had shouldered its way up from below earth to walk upon the planet, endlessly separate from human beings.

"Meg Watkins?" His voice hooked into her with barbs. "Yes, I do believe it is Meg Watkins, the very one herself."

"You know the lady, do you?" said Peleg Newall, delighted but without surprise, as though he expected every Englishman to know every other one in the realm. "My son's dear friend."

Allan jumped forward, easing himself between Carstip and Meg. "Do I have the honor of your acquaintance, sir?" He leaned protectively close to Meg, as though barring her from the assault of a possibly attractive gentleman.

"Why, this is the Earl of Eggleston," said Mrs. Newall, pleased that she had some information that went beyond the bounds of her domestic realm. "My husband has spoken of you often, sir. We are pleased to have you at table."

Carstip, forced by conversation to avert his gaze from Meg, appeared to tolerate the Newalls with barest civility, his nostrils pinching in at every mentior of his name spoken with lack of grace and prope form.

"M'lord, how have you been faring since last w have seen each other?" trilled Meg cordially, innocently, and on the very best of terms with him.

"I do well," he replied, returning to her his long curved glance that drifted down like a sun frozen hig above in its heavens and intent on spoiling her wit cold. "And yourself?"

"I am flourishing, as you can see." She laughe with the faintest touch of a flighty, giddy satisfactic that imitated so many of the American women sh had met and that was calculated to fill Carstip wi loathing. She watched the soft, curling lip quiver at the edge of its madeira glass and knew how the pampered palette suffered without its customary port or claret, so rarely seen on American tables. "Yes. One is forced to flourish in this charming country," she added with a satisfied nod.

"You have seen much of it, have you?"

"I have been everywhere."

"Your Meg Watkins is an exciting personality," put in Mrs. Newall, handing round platters of potatoes as everyone walked to take a seat. "I understand that she has been to Governor Clinton in New York."

"Come a long way," Carstip said with an ironic searching of Meg's face. "I am glad to see you have made your fortune so quickly."

Meg felt the icicle stab. There it was. He had not forgotten the jewels and he must mention the circumstance immediately, to let her *know* he had not forgotten . . . certainly not forgiven, which was beyond his understanding.

"Fortune? Fortune?" Peleg Newall sniffed. "What fortune is there to be made in New York? Everything comes from Boston. From State Street. Perhaps Washington has fallen to the Republicans for a while, but our loyalist maritime supremacy is the thing, eh, Earl?"

Somehow the dinner went on and was concluded, the afternoon lived through beside a swiftly fallen sun that sank away from the windows and surrounded the house with darkness. Allan, true to his word, followed her around the rooms like a lovelorn pup, whispering, when he could, "It's getting on to seven. We must prepare to leave." But they could not shake off Carstip, who casually stalked and met up with her seemingly by accident, in a corridor, at a hearthside, near a curtain, never saying a sentence beyond "Made your fortune, eh? Made your fortune?" the rusted, bleary eyeballs peering out with a bulging look meant to grapple her conscience.

"We must talk about things closely one day and reminisce," Meg replied with the effect of scattered brains as she searched for a way to make her escape. "You must come to tea, just you, Allan, and myself."

At the voicing of Allan's name to make three, Carstip swayed. Meg could not tell whether he seethed or imagined some unholy threesome tangling in joy. She lifted an eyebrow slightly and moved one finger the barest inch toward the doorway, thus signaling Allan to take this opportunity to leave.

"Yes, we will meet, Meg Watkins. It will be you and I alone," Ralph told her quietly in one corner of a room filled with children, aunts, and harmless others who seemed so far removed and strange, with Allan gone. "I stay at the King's Tavern, Market Square."

"Yes, we will meet," Meg continued in her vacant style. "Let us hope it is at the White House."

"Among *Republicans?*" thundered Peleg Newall, who seemed to overhear all conversations with political undertones wherever they occurred.

For once, Meg felt grateful to this eavesdropping quality, until Mrs. Newall added, "And your painter friend will be at the White House, too, I suppose. Since he does not favor *us* with his company."

"He will quite soon," flung Meg, flabbergasted and blushing, torn on the rack of indecision about whether to hide from Carstip or flaunt for the Newalls. "I have promised you."

"Promises?" spat Carstip, eyes twinkling with venom at Meg's secret, revealed. "What mean promises to a lady?"

"Whatever are you talking of, your Lordship?" Meg smiled as emptily as a barrel rattling on.

She bowed out of the room as though merely intending to glide into another, easing a long, low, meaningful look at Carstip in her wake. Then, unseen in the hall, she turned and sprinted away on tiptoe, slipping out the door to where Allan and Dick waited for her, each on horseback.

Allan dropped her cloak around her shoulders. At the same moment Dick swept her up behind him on the prancing bay.

She clung, squeezing his waist in the circle of her arms, hugging as hard as she could, much harder than was necessary to stay in balance on the galloping horse. "Faster! Faster!" she called against Dick's ear. "This nag moves like a sow!"

He laughed with an uproarious sound flung to the dark sky and dug his heels into the flanks. The horse, responding, stretched long, sinuous muscles that seemed to shatter the cobblestones beneath sparking hooves. They flew between the slower, dreary movement of carriages crossing the long thoroughfare, going southwest toward Frog Lane and the gallows at the bottom of the common. No longer did she hold a fright of death, for the salty night air brought life to her, lifting her half from her seat to kiss Dick on his neck hunched inside the turned-up jacket collar. Half standing, her knees dug into the belly sides for support, she lifted herself and crooned to him, calling, "Faster, faster, my lover," till they plunged headlong across the town, the horse shivering its mane and jerking its head high to send back loud snufflings of glory, breath roaring out from a deep, fiery forge.

They reached the gibbet that the sheriff had built upon the sloping grass field. Allan took the lead and brought them to a shapeless huddle of shrieking, cackling voices erupting from the half-insane mortality that waited in the shadow of the noose.

They had almost arrived too late. The dreary tones of a clergyman's lament rose and fell in waves of admonition, crying out to the Lord for mercy upon sinners, then sinking to the facts of the devil's grip upon erring human flesh, rising again in holy supplication to the divine, sinking into the thrall of the hell that awaited transgressors. Perhaps some soul listened as he shook his open book at the heap of squirming flesh. Weeping female cries wailed skyward at a greenish, round-faced moon, aloof and unhearing as a skull, that rode high behind shrouds of fast-moving, brackish vapors. Already the stench of death lowered its putrid, smothering hand to claw open the terrified consciences of those gathered to watch the proceedings. But those condemned had their backs turned to the stark, makeshift post with its arm and dangling rope. They writhed together like snakes in a pit as Dick and Meg and Allan approached them.

"Who is Silas Peddle?" Dick called hoarsely. "Who among you is Silas Peddle?"

Meg, hanging on to him, clutched his trouser hip as though a stiff wind might rise at any time and tear her from his side.

"Peddle? . . . Hee, hee, hee. Where is Peddle?" squealed someone from the crawling mass.

"Peddle is gone to the devil," squawked another.

"Peddle? Who is Silas Peddle?" Dick repeated. "There's money for Peddle."

Three pairs of hands reached to him, croaking, "Here's Peddle. I'm Peddle."

Dick, surveying the confusion, added, "Peddle, I've a message from your wife, I have."

"Message from me wife?" A weak and quivering voice rose from the bottom of the heap. "Me wife?" A wondering face, half man, half starved dog, thrust its bony nose and then its gray cheeks upward. A frail body that had long since ceased to shiver stood stooped in its tatters, peering at Dick from beneath hanks of frozen, tangled hair. He leaned hunched forever into a curve that thrust the neck forward, the head dangling and waggling loosely. "This is Peddle," he croaked. "This is Peddle."

Allan pushed himself between Peddle and the others. "Peddle. We have money for you," he repeated, and drew out a handful of gold coins, holding them on his open palm.

"Money? Money? Why! That's real gold, it is!" He began coughing hoarsely and dancing around Allan's hand but would not touch what lay offered upon it.

"This is for your wife, Peddle," Meg continued. "Will you see she gets it?"

"Me missus? *Me* see she gets it? Hee, hee, hee." He bent over with a sudden jerk and bit the side o

Allan's palm. The hand pulled back instinctively and coins rolled onto the dirt. The clinking worked as a signal. Bodies flung themselves upon the gold, covering it with their scramble, while the clergyman called out from beneath his shovel hat, "The Lord giveth and the Lord taketh away . . ."

"Is the wife of Silas Peddle in this company?" Dick called into the small knot of spectators waiting for the proceedings to conclude.

Another, hoarser bawling of angry male voices yelled, "Who is it that wants with her?"

Thrusting Meg behind him, Dick approached the chorus. "We have a bargain to make with her."

"She wants no bargain," croaked the spokesman. "Her husband will be buried in God's hallowed ground. No bargain!"

Allan whispered to Meg, "The corpse is legally ours. If she refuses, we shall take it, anyhow."

"How can you?" Meg replied in an undertone. "She has sent an army for him."

"We can and we will," said Allan.

While they talked, a brawny silhouette dragged Silas Peddle from the swarm, pulling him toward the rope. Behind them tethered horses pawed the hard ground and banged restlessly into one another, anxious to be off and running and springing forth in lightning streaks of life.

"They are going to hang him now," Allan said. "I must see to him."

He strode across the grass, reaching Peddle as the black, greasy rope slipped down upon his skinny neck, straightening the loop so that it would not mar the larger arteries.

"I done nothing, y'r honor," cried Peddle, no longer laughing. "I'm an innocent man."

"You have stabbed a girl in her sleep," Allan muttered. "Your own daughter, they tell me."

" 'Twere another man that did it. Not me, your honor. Not me!"

". . . lift thy voice to the Lord . . . and for the mercy

of the Lord . . . for it is He who shall visit thee in thine iniquity!"

The thick shadow stepped to the platform and kicked something in the dark.

Meg saw the body jerk up and swing, legs kicking wildly in midair as a hollow, sickening, snapping sound crackled in a high wind.

"Is he dead?" called a gruff voice from the chorus.

"Dead," replied the servant of the Lord. "Lift up thy voice!"

The chorus shouted, "Sheriff, give it here!" The dozen men rose as one and shuffled to the now limp body, which the sheriff cut free to drop into a cart.

"He is ours!" Allan called firmly.

"Take him from us, then," replied the voices, as two of their number began rolling the cart slowly toward the riverbank.

There was nothing else to do but walk beside the cordon, Allan pulling money from every pocket and thrusting it as bribes that fell unfailingly on deaf o wooden ears.

"They are kin to the wife," Dick commented t Meg. "That is the only answer. They won't give u the body, for she has put the fear of God's vengeanc into them."

"What will they do with it finally?"

"Bury it in hallowed ground, as they say. But the will have a long haul to escape Allan. Allan has a wa rant. And Allan has a purpose. We will have th corpse."

"A corpse for the sake of life," murmured Me horses clip-clopping behind and cart wheels screechi ahead, surrounded by its tireless guard while All cajoled, threatened, and tempted, sprinkling gc vainly before the stony-faced crew.

Soon the rope walks appeared. River noises cre across on the night wind. One of the bodyguard calle "Where are the others?"

"Ten paces north of the crossing."

"With the boat?"

"There it be. Look."

At the water's edge waited a long barque with half a dozen oarsmen standing precariously balanced in the hull but scattered evenly along its full length. When the wheels rumbled down the steep-sloping dirt, the rowers each stretched one foot ashore and anchored there, while those with the cart waded into the frothing ripples and heaved the small body aboard.

"Got 'im?"

"He's here."

"Ain't gonna move none, neither."

"Mary's waiting for us at Dorchester Point."

"Let's get a-going. Heave oars, fellas. Row away."

Allan watched the proceedings, moaning low with remorse. "If we had come but an hour earlier, the governor himself would have cleared our possession."

"But we didn't and we haven't," replied Dick tonelessly. "The man said Dorchester Point. Do you know the whereabouts, Allan? If so, we'll ride around and see if there's a chance to intercept it there."

"Why, man, that's fine." Allan smiled with renewed hope. "The horses will carry us faster than the men can cross the tide."

Again they climbed astride and began the journey, ut soon the road became a slippery stew where the revious night and day's snowfall had melted, turning he earth to knee-deep muck in which horses slipped nd struggled, barely pulling themselves through without breaking legs. Where the road was higher, boulders ad been tossed up in defensive fortress walls during he Revolution and never taken apart.

The moon had drifted far beyond its zenith when llan finally called out, "There's the point, Dick. Fifty aces ahead."

They dropped from the saddles and ran to crouch n the spit of land, peering as far as they could see nto the blackness riding over the water.

"No sign," said Meg.

"No sound, either," Dick added softly. "Have they eaten us to it?"

Allan, groaning again with dismay, jumped into the ater, searching, hunting, splashing about up to his hips, and reaching out a hand in hopes of touching the boat. Finally, shivering, he dragged himself ashore, calling, "No sign. No sign. They have escaped us."

Then they heard a rhythmic poling offshore, and faint, trickling droplets. The three stood to one side, hidden by darkness, while the boat drifted in, preceded by a low whistling signal in imitation of a bird.

From some stunted copses a broad woman dashed out, calling, "Asher, 'ave you got him? Aye, Lucas? Jethro?"

"We got 'im, Mary. Have no fear."

"Lord be praised, the bloody sinner!"

She leaned across, catching the tip of the boat as i drew ashore, lifting one dead arm and then another inspecting the corpse generally, as though to make sur they had taken the right one.

"They wanted to buy him from us, Mary," on man told her with faint regret.

"Buying and selling souls is the work of the devil Yep. This here is Silas. I recognize the smell. Alway stank like he was dead, even when alive. Now h smells worse than ever. Never mind no gold, Jethro We're to stick him in the ground right over here an say our bloody prayers over the poor lost devil. An raise a marker for the Lord to know we done ou proper work."

"Why not to the burial ground, Mary?"

"Too far. Too far."

They were so busy hacking out a rectangle of fr zen ground, so intense, that there was neither time n inclination to turn and spy out the three watche waiting on the far side of two horses behind a tre everything hidden or revealed by turns in a sca moonlight spiraling down in circles of cold.

Meg stood for ages, it seemed, listening to the cli of metal scratching upon the stones it hit undergroun Beside her Allan wheezed in agony from the ch wrapping around his wet legs. Dick waited silen with his arms folded across his chest, like a great co quering eagle.

"Drop him in careful," said Mary.

"Ain't too deep," muttered another male voice.

"Dig deeper, then," Mary replied. "Don't want his toes sticking out."

Grunts of agreement sounded, and then a renewed hacking that chipped out hard-won bricks of frigid earth.

"Here. That'll do it fine."

"Set him in gentle, m'boys. Well, there y'are, Silas. Laid out in your own bed all to yourself. Hope you likes your sleep better than you liked your children."

He killed his child for sleeping in his bed, thought Meg, and wondered how many had done the same on St. Catherine's docks and not got such a decent burial afterward.

"Covered?" Mary said after a long but softer sound of shoveling. "Then here's the prayer—Silas would've done different, Lord, if he knew how."

Meg felt in Allan and Dick vibrations of movement even while the burial party gathered its tools and straggled away. The footfalls had hardly faded when the two men on either side of her shot forward and began clawing at the earth, struggling to reach their prize before the ground froze over again. She dropped beside them and dug her nails in with energy, flinging clods of grassy mud over her shoulder at a furious pace that pounded in her chest with the pressure of harsh breathing. But Silas proved to be only a foot and a half down and soon was raised by ankles and armpits, dragged out from the trough, and flung over the pommel of Allan's horse.

"Dammit, I'm freezing," he called in triumph. "We'll ride round to Brackett's on the Neck and knock him up to give us a dish of coffee. He'll keep our secret." Allan cantered off, and Meg saw him hunch over his horse, one hand protectively upon Silas.

They reached a tavern on a ledge of land over the water, and after a long labor of knocking and pounding, the keeper finally swung a door open, mumbling that it was close upon four in the morning.

At six they tumbled out, warmed but exhausted as

they walked into a gray light with stars fast fading at the horizon. Meg brushed some dirt from Silas's knee and said, "Whose bed does he sleep in now?"

"We must get him to Cambridge this instant," groaned Allan, squinting at the sky. "Or we are in jail."

The doors of the Harvard Medical Institution had never seen a woman behind them. Meg, pausing in the yard before the venerable portals, recalled the sight of Mr. Dufferin's horse dissections pulled up on tackles. Suddenly she felt no need to go further with Dick.

"Do what you have to do," she said, sending him ahead without her as the experience of eighteen years rallied into a first discreet wisdom of abstention.

Chapter Thirty

"WHY, SIR! The Louisiana Purchase means less to us than our own Thanksgiving!"

The imported chandeliers wafted a glorious ligh down upon old Peleg Newall stumping through his rooms, aglow with his patriotism and their proper festivities this evening. Everyone who was anyone had come through his high front doors, from the milliner on Prince Street to the district attorney. Periodically Meg felt a rush of misgiving that she had refrained from working out some scheme with Allan to have Dick here just this once. But when her glance passed acros the mottled countenance of Ralph Carstip, pumpin madeira into the white slit of mouth and spewing dis dain upon the ladies attempting to befriend him, Me knew with positive relief that by keeping two wil dogs apart she had made the only choice.

Yet Ralph's look became limpid with distraction and seemed most strangely at ease whenever their glances happened to meet above the decorated tresses of more innocent chatterers, as though Ralph were at home with some important bit of secret news to his particular advantage. When Meg wandered away into a different room or submerged herself in a circle of gossip or was cornered by Allan's heated humor on the subject of lazy, Federalist politicians, she would eventually be drawn to glance across the room and there find Carstip, as though connected to her by an invisible thread. Her annoyance had a biting edge of premonition, not from fear of Carstip, but for the unknown yet to come.

"Why, Meg Watkins, *there* you are, my dear." Mrs. Newall sailed over and possessed Meg's arm with a comfortable, smiling pride in her party, waving, greeting, kissing the fencing master, the stage comedian from Sheaf's Lane, behind him the chocolate maker, on the far side the clerk and inspector of the market, introducing to Meg reverends, honorables, and esquires with every new arrival. "You will know half of Boston by the time this evening is gone." Then, turning to her with a query of special importance, "Have you seen the lobster catch? We have had an abundance of fish fairly to equal what our forefathers took in at Plymouth. It is beyond believing, had I not seen it with my own eyes. The surf has piled them up upon the beaches two feet high, I understand, and the tide pools are full of crabs."

"Excuse me, Mother," intruded Allan, gently tugging Meg aside. "There is a sailcloth millionaire across the room who would feel honored to meet our fine Meg, if you will allow it." Dragging Meg away, he murmured, "You must thank me for saving you. Next you would be swamped in salmon swimming so thick with their heads above the water that out you would rush to catch them with a frying pan."

"I don't mind her a bit." Meg smiled. "She has befriended me well. I am indebted to her."

"Not to me?"

"You, Allan, have not arranged a meeting for Dick with Mr. Gilbert Stuart, and we have known each other longer."

"Oh, my poor fate, that we do not travel in the same social sphere. But I shall tell you that the dissection went beautifully. Dick has left a number of magnificent drawings of the human body with our surgeons. He will be famous, if not in the drawing rooms, then at the operating table. His work will certainly help to save lives."

"Bite your tongue! He will be a famous painter at the Royal Academy." Meg knifed him with words flung from between the clamlike edges of her teeth as they strolled and chatted and smiled at the deputy sheriff, who did not recognize them in the light, the bookseller of Marlboro Street, and Mrs. Newall's furrier, everyone turning to watch the train of high-piled trays pass along, replete with sea bass, cod, pale cold roe, and quarters of venison surrounded by tubs of condiments.

"What can be in that amazing giant tureen?" came a voice behind Meg.

"Oh, that?" Allan said, stepping aside to accommodate Mrs. Hunt, the apothecary's wife. "That is the remains of the sixty-pound turtle Mother kept tethered in the garden earlier today. Didn't you see it?"

"But turtle soup on Thanksgiving? What a difficult complicated, and very expensive dish it is. Of course your mother presides over a first-rate kitchen, an one would not expect her, of all people, to buy i from a turtle-soup house."

"Turtle-soup house? My mother? Let us not utte those words in the same sentence." With mock horro of such a consideration following after him, Allan le Meg along, informing her from the side of his mout "Friend Carstip was watching that show. Hope h liked it."

She did not have to move even an eyeball to fe Carstip forever watching her, till finally she said t

Allan, "Do you know what it feels like to be a hunted terrapin yourself? About to be caught, boiled, and brought to table? I will not go on this way a second longer. I will talk to him."

With the temper of her split-second decision, Meg drew her arm clear of Allan's protection and sailed to one side of the room near the double settees, gradually closing the circle between herself and Carstip, resignedly pleased that she was taking matters into her own hands. She floated to where he stood turning the fire logs, swallowing the sick dread of her revulsion behind an aristocratic, sunny smile.

"How do you enjoy this unique American holiday, Ralph?" She spoke with no preamble, gliding right into the talk as though they were old, dear friends.

"Thank heaven there is nothing like it in our country." He sniffed with distaste the half-glass of amber luid he held, then quaffed it with a quick, decisive gulp.

"An interesting place, however, these United States," she observed blithely. "One has great freedom here, if one wishes it."

"Yes. And to be a thief, too, do you suppose?" He gazed out blandly over the crowd as he spoke the urning accusation, his fury too great to face her irectly without release in some violent act. Deep, uspicious-looking pockets dug in beneath his eyelids, nd long rivulets of strain were drawn through his heeks. "Do you know," he continued softly, "people eldom get away with murder." He swung his head wiftly and knifed her with a look.

"I have committed no murder, Ralph." She laughed ith arrogant bite.

"But close enough." His fingers closed round her m above the elbow, immobilizing her as though she ere stung. "And would have murdered me in my d had it fit your purpose."

"Ralph, what a foolish idea. Let go of me. You're urting. Allan will see this and be very upset."

"You care nothing for Allan. Don't take me for

a fool. Come with me, and do it quietly if you fear to make a fuss. As far as I am concerned, you can cause all the row you wish. These people are nothing to me except as trustees of my estates here, and imbeciles at the job."

He moved her carefully through the crowd, never releasing or diminishing the pressure of his hold. Her wrist and then her palm began to pulse. As they moved, she struggled more with herself than with Carstip, suppressing the urge to swing upon him and kick herself free. Despite his rage, she felt certain Carstip would do nothing in front of these people, and to be forced to cause a scandal under Peleg Newall's roof would ruin her own gains.

"Will this drawing room do?" she said.

"No. There is a couple behind the fire screen."

So it went, from corner to nook to cranny, all of Boston cramped into the mansion on Bowdoin Square. Once they passed old Newall, who smiled upon them benignly from under his powdered wig. He was beaming at the cream of London that now graced his home as though matters soon would be tied up well again with the beloved mother country.

"This is a veritable circus," spat Ralph. "Monkeys everywhere. Or are they militiamen? I cannot tell the difference with their caved-in chests and bow legs. We'll try downstairs for privacy."

"Among the kitchen help?"

"If they do not run and leave us when we wish," said Ralph with cool ease, "we'll blow them into the fire."

He stared, discommoded and uncomfortable, however, into the primitive American kitchen, where Mrs. Newall had arrived before them to fuss with her cousin and serving girls at the hearth.

"Why, Meg. And Earl Carstip. Your Lordship." Her eyes grew with delight. "Do you care to see the details of our special feast-day cuisine? I am honored." She reached to the shelf for a small bound volume. "Here it is. The secrets come from these very pages. The real thing, I promise you."

"Fascinating," Carstip replied coldly, turning the book over and reading aloud from its title page: " 'American Cookery, or the art of dressing Viands, Fish, Poultry, and Vegetables, and the best modes of making Pastes, Puffs, Pies, Tarts, Puddings, Custards, and Preserves, and all kinds of Cakes, from the imperial Plum to plain Cake. Adapted to this country and all grades of life. By Amelia Simmons. An American Orphan.' " He stared at Mrs. Newall with flat blank eyes. "Yes, fascinating. But I believe you are wanted by one of your guests. The Secretary of State has arrived."

"Mr. Avery?" Mrs. Newall bloomed with pleasure, patting her curls with quick inspection. "Well. I will be but a moment, Earl. My cousins will be delighted to give you anything you care to have."

Carstip managed to wait until she had disappeared up the stairs. "Now, ladies, you are not to stay in the kitchen on such a glorious occasion as this."

He commanded the twittering, awed group of three with his customarily brittle voice so unexpectedly devastating that the women stopped their chatter and blinked at him, not knowing whether they were being proffered a favor or requested to descend to hell. They nevertheless made up their minds to act quickly when he added no further comment, and scurried up the stairs after Tabitha, leaving Meg alone in company with the victor.

"Now here we are," said Ralph in a monotone. "You and I, alone, Meg. As it is meant to be always. The thief and the injured party. Of course, you do not see it that way, do you? I suppose there can be another point of view. But shall we say, my love, that since you have freely taken what is mine, I, in fair retaliation, can recover what is mine." He strolled to the fire, where three huge wild turkeys were slowly turning on a jack. At its end, away from the heat, hung a small metal cage. Inside it, powering the jack, ran a tiny black and white spotted dog, ten inches high, running eternally so that the slats of the cage revolved from the spent strength of his tiny legs. "Yes, Meg." Ralph touched the snout of the dog through the wires. "I have been to a great deal of time and trouble finding you."

"You could not have looked very hard for something so trifling as a mere woman gone off with a few garnets." Meg smiled in dismissal of so preposterous a notion.

"Do not mistake me, Meg, as you so often pretend to do. Of course it was not the garnets, but the principle. You understand about principle? You have heard something of it, sweet little street rat in your fine dresses? Has not the chevalier explained it to you? Or Elise?"

"So that is how you found me." She recalled the look of unfinished business on Philippe's face.

"Isn't it amusing that we have friends in common at last." Ralph approached and crowded close in front of her so that she could not get around him. He slapped the book into her palm. "Here. Perhaps you can find in this the receipt for justice. Or shall I save you the trouble? Let me tell you, for my right to you is really a simple matter."

"*Right* to me?" Meg trilled and flicked her finger as though waving away some minor insect in the ai between them.

"Yes, my right," he repeated, gathering force. "Yo thought it right to take what belonged to me. Fo what payment, Meg? Is there no payment due me Meg, for my jewelry? For those beautiful jewels tha carried you across the ocean and dressed you and too you into so many fine homes?" He pressed he arms to her sides and lifted her to her toes. "Yo have always been mine," he whispered. "Now yo have made it legal. Yes. A fine point of law, but true one. It is called barter. You have made yourse exclusively mine. *Mine*. As you were born to be."

Small yellowish bubbles of spittle formed at tl sides of his mouth and signaled his frenzy. Yet sl was more able to stare at them than into his empt burning eyes.

“I am not yours. Or anyone’s,” she replied calmly, recklessly. “Put me down. Put me down!”

“Yes, I will put you down, why not?” He spoke slowly with his truculent, twisting smile. “I shall put you down and I shall take you home with me, and we shall be together at last.”

“And shall you marry me, Ralph?” she taunted, feeling strangely unreal with him in his madness. “Shall you marry me and escort me to President Jefferson’s New Year’s Day levee? Shall we walk together, arm in arm, on his front lawns?”

“But that is the very idea,” replied Ralph with alacrity as though she had read his mind. The recognition that he meant to do it jolted Meg a few steps backward toward the heat of the fire, which she did not feel. He grabbed her shoulders and shook her. “Of course we shall marry! And go everywhere and do *everything* together.” He squealed with the joy of the novelty. “And your Dick Fox. That cringing, miserable scum will be left to paint his bohemian heart out, alone, in his mental wilderness.”

At the mention of Dick’s name Meg felt a disheartening drain of confidence and a fresh stab of fear. “My poor artist cousin,” she said, in the hope of overing her tracks.

“Cousin, is it? A strange relationship for cousins.” e scowled with gleaming, lascivious disgust. “But ow simple it was to untangle your protests of innoence. Your lies. Everyplace I went and heard the ame Meg Watkins, there it was, linked with Fox. *inked.* I did not believe you in England. I do not lieve you here. This revolting Fox character, this aveling painter slop-pot, is beneath my contempt. shall squash him down, I tell you. Squash him down!” e lifted a wooden spoon and banged it viciously ainst the bellies of a number of empty pots from hich dregs of boiled canvasback ducks and oysters nt out a hollow, resounding rumble. He dropped e spoon and cracked its neck with his boot heel. “ou know I am a man of honor, Meg. I can be counted upon, completely counted upon, to mean what I say. To keep my word. There is such a thing, Meg, as broken hands. Both broken. Wrists. Knuckles. Fingers. And in such a fashion that a man may never recover to do his work properly ever again."

Meg clasped her fingers and squeezed them steadily together in the spaces between the knuckles, fighting to maintain herself upright and aggressive, to mask the sudden, violent quaking underneath. Any other threat from this maniac would not have fazed her. Anything. But to stand here and watch his imagination coiling around the target of Dick Fox was beyond her. Break his hands!

"I am sure I do not know what you are talking of," Meg responded, stiffly aloof. "This Dick Fox means nothing to me and never did. Not in the way you think." She swung her back upon him then and felt herself stagger from his sight, forcing her stomach down against the wrenching sensation of terror.

All of Boston seemed suddenly made of windows. At every moment she expected Carstip's ghostly face to rise from behind the market stall or float at her through the snowflakes. In her room she undressed nervously, looking for him inside the clothing curtains and sometimes, when she was overtired, beneath the bed. She feared him piercingly when she lay with Dick or walked the streets with Dick or even thought about Dick, as though Carstip had the devil's intuition and could penetrate her dreams.

"Why don't you tell Fox and get it over with?" pleaded Allan in his gentle way, walking with her round and round the inn's frosty garden where next spring's herbs lay beneath a carpet of twinkling white.

"I dare not." Meg shuddered. "He would go fo[illegible] him directly. It would be blood all around."

"I think your Carstip is a coward when it comes [illegible] fighting."

"Perhaps, but not Dick. Dick would take him [illegible] pieces with his fists. Then Carstip would find so[illegible] way to have him killed." Meg spoke decisively, glancing up at the window behind which Dick was sleeping late in the day. With no good weather for painting, there were only the dissection hours, and these had become infrequent from lack of suitable subjects. She felt the flush of a warm, miserable glow. "I must keep it secret from him. I truly must. One never knows how these matters can end. He could kill Carstip as soon as talk to him. And I remember the sight of that gallows too well!"

"Yes. But Dick would make a fine body for dissection." Allan laughed, patting Meg's arm to ask her forgiveness for the gruesome joke he was unable to resist.

"What shall I do?" Meg queried the sight of her snowy shoe tips. "Can I dare to brush Carstip aside, do you suppose? Would it be wisest for me to forget his threats? Perhaps if I let sleeping dogs lie, he will give up and go about his business. How marvelous that would be! If only . . . if only." She was musing more to herself than confiding in her friend. The echo of her words resounded with wishful thinking but had no foundation of possibility. Her chin dropped to her chest and she muttered, "I must not think about this oday. It is a big day for Dick when he wakens. Your nother is truly kind to help me so, when I have rought her merely a few of Dick's smallest sketches."

"Kind? Where do you think she gets it from?" Allan vinked, lifting Meg's collar to her chin.

"Yes, I know," Meg replied, smiling wanly. "She nherits everything good and beautiful from her oldest on."

Gazing up again and again, she finally saw Dick's noving shadow reflected in the panes. "There he is. must go to him."

"You needn't worry," Allan called after her as she roke away. "He will not refuse you this engagement."

Meg raced up the stairs, laughing like a child bringng Dick the gift of her news. She flung his door pen without knocking and sailed over to tie his cravat, umming a Yankee melody made up of street cries from the tea-rusk man and the fish seller, toppling Dick backward as she came at him with all her might.

"What's this, my lion?" he said, laughing. "I am attacked."

"Yes, you are! You are! Guess by whom! Guess what is happening for us this day! This very day!"

"You're not often in this mood. What's happened? Are you elected to the White House as the president's Ministress of Foreign Affairs?"

"Better, my darling. Much more important. You will love me when I tell you. Oh, I am so thrilled."

"When you are thrilled," Dick intoned, lifting his chin to evade fingers while she finished the tying, "I had better watch my steps."

"Oh! You! Don't make such a to-do. As though I hadn't an education of your likes and dislikes, enough for a college degree. Do you realize how long we have been together this December? A lifetime."

"What have you to tell me?" he asked, ignoring the flutter. "Where are we going?"

"Oh. You can see we are going somewhere."

"Am I mistaken?"

"You are absolutely correct." She kissed his nose.

"And keeping it to yourself."

"Yes. Yes." She kissed him again on the nose and lips. "I want to tickle you. I want you to be eager."

"In that case," drawled Dick, shaking his hair forward over his eyes, "I suppose I shall take another nap first, then have dinner. A brace of partridge would be tasty. Where's Allan?"

"Dick. You mean thing. You monster. Behave an I will tell you at once."

"A bargain," he said, backing with her to a chair sitting down, and pulling her onto his lap.

She loved it when he did this, when he had th time to hold her and give all his attention to what sh would say, to listen with both ears—to be hers. Stil she wanted to keep her secret for one moment longe as though it were the only tempting bait that held hi But then, as she studied his face with its work lin drawn around the mouth and indented around the deep, slanted eyes, when she absorbed again the meaning of his many hours of labor so hard won against cruel weather, stark conditions, and a society that made artists its servants, she settled down to a serious, respectful presentation.

"A note has come for me this afternoon, from Mr. Gilbert Stuart."

"Stuart the portrait painter?" Dick focused closely upon her with a new facet of interest.

"Yes, the very one, my sweet."

"How does he know you? Or should I ask?"

"You can ask whatever you wish. Allan's mother ıas done us the service, you see. Courtesy of her nterest in *my* fine manners." She felt herself becomıg lighter again. "We have an invitation for a visit vith Mr. Stuart. I believe he has a very strong interst in young American artists."

"But he is always in England. And we are British."

"Yes. And so he has, perhaps, an even stronger ıterest in young English artists."

"Of the Benjamin West school."

"Do you begrudge him his years of study with Benımin West?"

"I begrudge no man anything, love. But I cannot e that Mr. Stuart would much care for an Englishan in America when he is an American in love with ngland."

"Let us say it is the war's fault," she concluded tiently. "And that everyone neutral has sought refe here in America, including us, which is the truth, part."

"You know, my girl," said Dick with a gleam, uncing her on his knee, "I would be perfectly pleased meet with Mr. Gilbert Stuart."

"Not for his connections, I dare say," she prodded ıderly.

"For what I can learn of his technique, first-hand. u may find me rather ruthless, darling. That I don't e a damn who or what he paints or where or how it sells. He has a worldwide fame, however, which is to be respected because it is based on *worth*. Artistic worth. And that means everything to me."

Meg listened to him quietly. As though he had to explain to her his reasons! As though she had to reply! "I must go and touch up my looks and we will be off. Yes?"

"Yes."

"And may we take some of your pictures to show him? Yes?"

"Yes."

She carried the warm glow of Dick beaming at her all the way back to her room, and on her return to him, and in the carriage that went a slippery trip over icy cobbles down the many twisted courts, lanes, and alleys, to finally arrive at the carved front door of Mr. Gilbert Stuart's residence.

They were met, not by the doddering, venerable gentleman she had expected, but by a sprightly, venerable gentleman with a great, kind strength in his eyes that made it seem he would live forever. The famous presence had a practical cast that assessed Dick in a single eyeblink. As Meg watched the two together, she saw the instantaneous recognition of one hawk face by another. She thought how simple it could be for the legacy of art to pass from the old genera tion to its heir, via Dick.

The towering prime of manhood and its springy sen ior proceeded with their dishes of coffee to Mr. Stuart painting room. There on the wall, commanding eve other art work, hung the head likeness of Geor Washington, the figure and drapery left unfinishe yet utterly complete and serene in its mastery of natu Meg, for once, fell silent, content to listen and c serve.

"I see you are looking at my General Washingto said Stuart with a sharp twinkle. "I must tell you the embarrassment I had, at first, to get on with You might guess, from the great man's countenar the hard work it was to get him to speak on li subjects. However, I resolved to try, at all hazards, to make him laugh. Fine job! At last I hit upon it and told him the old Joe Miller story of King James the Second's journey to gain popularity, during which course His Majesty arrived somewhere that the mayor of the place was Baker and no speechmaker and had o be prompted. When a friend, to help him, nudged iis elbow and said, 'Hold up your head and look ike a man,' the blundering mayor repeated the adnonition to the king. Well, this stupid story had the equired effect, and from that time on with General Vashington, I had him on a pivot and could manage im nicely."

Meg could feel Dick relaxing as his gaze roved the oom, comfortably settling on the head sketches and nplements of painting that he loved, along with the ervasive odor of turpentine and the sweet linseed-oil iixtures. She thought that Dick, so interestingly atntive, was a quiet prompter to stories, and a fine, ppreciative audience for the artist who had roved the orld and met and painted so many eminent men.

"Miss Watkins, you would be interested in the picre I have of Voltaire from when I was a child. I member him sitting on the stoop of Mr. David ume's house at the end of the North Bridge in dinburgh. I was but a little boy following my educaon, and Mr. Hume would call me in to converse th him on all manner of philosophical subjects as came home from school. I dare say Mr. Fox here ll be much more inclined to bend an ear to the ct that I was the first person to set Sir Thomas wrence on the path when he arrived in London om Bath, quite a young man, now upwards of enty-odd years ago. Until the time we met, Sir omas had busied himself merely with drawings in ayon, pretty little things, of course, but of no real nsequence. Except that I saw at once he was a n of genius. One day, overlooking my own rudess, I said, 'Who makes you waste your time doing h *damned* things as these?' The poor young fellow's abashed look reminded me what a breech of politeness I had been guilty of, but soon we mended it and Sir Thomas was all a-going."

"Sir," said Dick, "you cannot tell me that the British school of painting is altogether so open-minded as yourself. Even Benjamin West, with his earth colors that he has learned to make from the Indians here, has not the full-bodied genius you speak of. He is the king's man and therefore president of the Royal Academy. That is the reason for his fame, not art."

"Benjamin West has many brilliant associates who have learned much under his tutelage, and I am one." Stuart smiled pointedly. "But show me your pictures and we shall see what there is to talk of."

Only a man such as Dick, replete with his own confidence and secure in the world of his own independence, could respond instantly and eagerly, unfurling a series of penciled works made, Meg saw with astonishment and horror, at the medical institution.

"What are these?" said Stuart, bending his sharp-nosed face to the sketches.

"These are the articulations of the cervical vertebrae, the neck bones and the collarbones, sir, tha curve down gradually, as you see it goes, into th lumbar region."

Stuart swung his head around and eyed Dick fro beneath beetling brows. "Are you a doctor, sir, or a artist?"

"How does a man learn to work if not from tl deepest, most hidden mysteries of his subject?"

"You are an Englishman. You could be an Italia Or an ancient Greek. You certainly and verifiab would never make a successful American with su an outlook." Stuart laughed. "These are remarkab What have you done to acquire such knowledg Stolen in, I see, to forbidden territory. I would n bandy these about quite fast, young man. I mys have painted generals in my time, from ma countries, and statesmen of every disposition in li

Yet I have learned nearly everything of anatomy from antique busts and casts and from such as Lord Elgin's Greek reliefs that are now gaining fame in London. I say yes, anatomize. But you must do the thing itself, too. Why have you not brought me some portraits? What are you doing, as I said to Sir Thomas, with these *damned* things?"

Meg stole a look at Dick to see how he was reacting to this chastisement. It was the first time, to her knowledge, that someone Dick respected in the art world had said anything close to what she herself had told him. Why, it was the very thing exactly!

But Dick sat relaxed, staring back at his challenger, absorbing the advice behind his steely, noncommittal gaze. The fine, chiseled features seemed to cut a crystal profile through the cool air, while he listened and thought and weighed everything, impassively on the surface.

"The faces I see of generals and such are not paintable," Dick replied with studied thought. "They are lazy, insipid, or hollow and cruel. Everything poor and hard and unworthy of the great legacy we carry with us from the ancients."

"Bosh," replied Stuart with the utmost matter-of-act dismissal. "Everything, everyone, is paintable. ou must make up your mind to it. And I mean what say. There is no face that hasn't *lived* in its own eculiar fashion. No brain that has not thought some *ea,* no matter how selfish, how shallow. There is no ull, no pair of cheekbones, no nose, no chin, that oes not harbor its *soul,* my fellow. And there you ave it. The soul through its character is what you ek. I say, get out into the world of action, however may seem to you, Mr. Fox, and paint it as it lies. ake everything. Yes, take it all at first. And adually you may come to select those persons in nom you may suspect greatness. But for that there a responsibility. You must bring to the subject your vn greatness in equal measure."

Dick had slumped against the chair back, his dish

of coffee neglected on a spindly-legged table beside his knee. The rugged, sensitive features had sunk deep into the black tides of his comprehension while he searched out, in the businesslike face before him, all the marrow of meaning it possibly held. The small muscles at his temple flicked with the intensity of concentration. In the hearth light Meg could see a bluish cast where the blood flowed close to surfacing. The dark hair, combed straight back, glossy and smooth as raven feathers, shaped the outline of his long ears sitting sleekly close to his skull. The carved face seemed like a figurehead pressing forth across dark waters, endlessly searching out some truth needed for the continuation of life greater than that lived on the mere animal plane. The ideal man lurking inside him was stripped bare of his protections and reached out cutting through the mist to find the illusive prize perhaps contained in the responsive brain of Gilber Stuart.

"You ask me to do portraits," Dick repeated. "Bu not for the fame. For the experience and growth c understanding." He spoke slowly, his mouth holdin each word, finding in every one a meaning. Unlik Stuart, Dick was not a man of easy speech. His min flowed through his brush.

"Stay with your dissections, yes. But return to th source of life *in* life."

Stuart rose, recollecting the cold in the room, an moved the burning logs about with a long poker.

"I will do it," concluded Dick, also rising, taking th sight of Stuart's back as his signal not to overstay ar tax the man with the heated intensity of their talk. ' will work from human faces. I will do portraits."

Meg listened in astounded silence. Could this be h Dick speaking so calmly, so conclusively, about pair ing people? She wanted to fling her arms around M Stuart's fine neck and cover him with thankful kiss —for he had put the world at her feet. How simp it would be now. Everything in its mercifully pro position. She managed to stand but felt a smile wid ing her mouth that would not be controlled as blinked from one man to the other, seeing not faces but the shape of Dick's future materializing before her eyes.

"I may meet you both again in the home of Mr. Newall one day soon," said Stuart, walking with them to the door. "When the weather eases and I have a day between my commissions. No, Mr. Fox, the profession of portrait painting is not a free-and-easy way of life. Responsibilities pile up misgivings, I can assure you," he concluded with gentle contentment.

"I hope *I* know my job one day," said Dick as the door opened for them, "as you know yours."

"My boy, my boy," said Stuart, patting Dick on the shoulder and laughing. "Your modesty is attractive but not required for me."

Then they were out in the street. Meg looked back at the house with its cheerful lighted windows, trying to realize the dream she had lived through. It had happened and was now past. She poised on the round cobbles underfoot, swallowing and crying with a poignant delight that welled in huge, engulfing waves carrying her between fits of sadness that she could not explain and ecstatic joy. *But I need not say a word to Dick about my feelings. He has found his own for himself.*

In a dizzy, heavenly glow she walked by his side, absorbed in trying to encompass the meaning of all that had transpired in a few short hours. Already she could see the important faces of Tabitha and Peleg Newall captured by Dick on canvas and elaborately framed. The thrill of accomplishment sent speechless raptures rippling through her flesh. She could not contain herself sufficiently to sit in a cab but insisted on walking a few blocks in the severe weather, feeling warm and protected in the wind, feeling immortal.

"You have finally accomplished your heart's desire." Dick smiled, pressing her hand between his coat sleeve and his side.

"You have accomplished yours, too," she answered with a passionate ring of sincerity.

"Somehow our goals have met at last," Dick answered. "That much is truth. I will paint because I must. But now I shall paint what you have wished for all this while."

"Isn't it divine?" she whispered. "Isn't it perfect? Aren't we the most fortunate, most enviable, happiest . . ."

Thunderous clattering of hooves dragged a giant, lumbering black carriage around the corner. Four slipping animals careened into each other and stumbled, struggling for balance on icy cobbles, but could not catch themselves and change direction. The driver, standing high in his box, hallooed in a voice that urged them on, snapping his whip with hellish stings that danced upon the wild-eyed creatures and drove them beyond control.

Meg sensed Dick react instinctively as he lifted and swung her against a fence. She grabbed the rails and glimpsed him running and leaping aside just in time to avoid the treacherous slash of iron horseshoes tha barely missed cutting him down. The carriage rumbled past and she exhaled with relief. But at the foot of th street it swung around and came at Dick again, with obvious, terrible intent. Before he could catch hi breath, on roared the horses, a wild fury of swingin heads, manes, and tails. Snorting nostrils flared, breat roared, as the driver skillfully aimed them directl where Dick stood, ten feet away from her along th low picket fence. Her gaze froze with horror. He ha but a hair's breath of time to leap over the bushes an roll away onto the snow as the two rightmost horse grazed the hedge with their shoulders, trampling an tearing up the roots.

Once again the carriage flew past, but as it wheel in its circle it came about more slowly, more delib erately. Meg, stricken with understanding, had prove what she was witnessing. When the carriage ra tled past her, she strained to peer inside its dark wi dow and managed to glimpse a single, jewel-ring fist resting on the head of a cane. The narrow cut the jacket sleeve was of a gold-embroidered cloth s had often seen before. As though she were sending message to its owner, the face leaned forward into the darkened frame. A mufflered, narrow, pale-complected profile shone for an instant in the glimmering, shifting light of the street lamp. The carriage was then gone around the corner, its creaking wheels growing faint.

Meg pressed her hands to her ribs, trying to open the cage there for breath to get in. The stabbing, choking pain gripped her. She could not dare think, yet her mind whirled with a buzzing commotion that made terrifying sense.

"What the *hell* was that?" Dick said, brushing snow from his sides and stumbling toward her. "You all right?"

"Fine," she gasped, barely audible.

"Are you sure?"

"Yes." The sound dropped from her like blocks of ice afloat in a dead, black sea.

"Drunken lunatic," Dick muttered, brushing Meg here and there. "You could think he was trying to kill us."

"Yes," said Meg. *Yes, one could.*

She stared away into the dark, listening rigidly for the sound of wheels to come around once more. She did not move, nor let Dick move until she was certain it had gone.

"I want to go home," she said, voice shaky, body trembling.

"Don't blame you, darling. Nasty, messy business. Sorry you were frightened."

She kept staring at him all the way back to the boarding house, staring, frightened, into his face, devouring him alive, pulling long gulps and drafts of the sight of him into herself, making his flesh her own, weaving the sound of his voice, the rough and smooth textures of his flesh, into her skin. She stared at him stupidly, violently, without letup and insisted on going into his room, where she undressed and climbed into his bed.

He came to her. She held him, at first quietly, lifting his head and staring through the darkness at the sight that was his face. Then said violently, "Make love to me," her demand cracking with sorrow that she could not withhold.

"But it's gone. Gone," he said soothingly.

She answered nothing, only groaned now and again, biting him, rocking beneath him, tying him to her by linking her legs around his waist, her arms around his neck. She sucked his flesh and took nips of it as though to keep the taste forever beneath her tongue.

"Dick. Dick. My Dick. Love me. Promise. You must always love me," she pleaded, the words like driftwood flung ashore in strange, barren ports.

"I do love you. What's got into you? This isn't my Meg. He didn't hurt us."

"I know. I know," she cried, sobbing helplessly. "Love me. Kiss me. More . . . Oh, more."

Hanging on to him through the night while he slept, she tossed wretchedly exhausted, sweating in the cold air, yet alert with staring eyeballs straining from her skull. Hanging on to his scalp, she gently pulled his hair to sense the feel of it one last time, and when he wakened, pressed her tongue into his mouth, upward, tasting the ridge of his palate.

"More. Again. Oh, love me. My darling. You are the perfect man. The only man. You're to be happy. You're to paint as you never have before."

She saw him peer groggily down into her face as a worried laugh lifted from his throat. "What is this nonsense? Go to sleep."

"I need you."

His body strained above hers. She took him and gave of herself in the most intimate positions, cuddled like a child to his long chest. Later, she rode him like a warrior woman, seeding and reaping her harvest both in the same moment. Lying passively quiescent beneath him, she stared up at the hulking strength above her that loomed almighty. Sometimes she glanced out the window, dreading the dawn she must inevitably meet there.

When she could bear to let him sleep, she hovered over him, leaning her chin on her wrist, then brushing her cheek along the curves of his back, finding secre places she had never kissed before. Finding him new, always new, afresh. *I will always love you. Oh, Dick. Oh, darling. Please never forget me.*

Day came, as it was bound to do, in long roseate fingers that gripped the black sky and squeezed from its darkness a slow, tawny drip of golden light.

And Dick still slept, peacefully down, down under. She stole from the mattress. Walking backwards, she moved toward the door, heedless of the tears falling swiftly down her pale cheeks, unable to tear her gaze from him, that single deep gaze she had held upon him all the night long. *I don't want to leave you,* she cried in her heart. *I want to stay and have you fight for me.* But that way lay madness, and his destruction.

With a single gulping breath, she moved swiftly, putting a door between them and letting go of Dick forever.

She knew what she had to do.

Chapter Thirty-one

HER COURAGE FAILED as she hurried into the bleak dawn, told a sleepy cabman, "King's Tavern," and climbed into the carriage. Any moment she might fling herself back into the street, fly home to Dick again, and waken later to discover another, less drastic solution. Then the stab of Carstip's threat broke through. She heard his voice clearly, and the vision of twisted, bleeding hands appeared before her. *As long as there is life in me, he will never touch Dick Fox!* she vowed with strength that dropped to her from the skies.

Numbly, she settled back in the seat, unable to deal with the prospect of giving herself over to Carstip and their future life together. Life! Her mind then plied her with pictures of Dick at his work, taking commissions, building the reputation he deserved. She kept herself busy with imagined sights of Dick flourishing and at ease, painting in well-lighted rooms, content with his achievements and befriended by Allan Newall. Should she write to him, eventually, and tell him where she had gone off to? Allan, in any case, would guess what she had done and why. Perhaps in a few months, when she had Carstip safely far from Dick on the other side of the Atlantic, she could write and say why she had run off without a word. Dick's habit of leaving *her* unexpectedly returned to haunt her now with a bitter irony. For the first time she understood how distractions could keep people from confiding in each other when it seemed most needed. Her mind balked blankly then, facing the dark chasm of her days ahead.

She arrived at the coaching inn where other carriages were starting out for different cities, everything in a hustle that reminded her that she, too, was soon to be gone. With the grit of a stiffened will, she found Carstip's rented apartment and swept past the servants into the front parlor.

Everything reflected Carstip in his usual state, the furniture stained by emptied wine decanters and strewn about with cards. She half expected to find him hanging drunk over one of the chair arms, his cronies sprawled asleep beneath the table. A girl no more than sixteen crept in to peep at her meekly from the doorway.

"The master is asleep inside," she offered when Meg stopped swinging around the room and looked at her.

"Asleep, eh? That's a relief."

They stared at each other and shared a moment o understanding, unspoken but ringing clear. Meg pu a coin in her palm and went the dozen steps throug the room swiftly, but with a dragging pull at her ankle still fighting to hold her back.

A connecting door stood ajar. Citron scent wafte from inside, along with a restless snore, more like th cry of a sick animal than like sleep. *I could stab him,* she thought abruptly, coldly, comfortably, and felt in her bag for something sharp. But she recoiled from the mistaken choice, as though the voice of a secret destiny were whispering some other directive in her ear. Then, again, her mind became numb. Her body moved without awareness, pushing her to his bedstead where she paused at the foot, glaring at the tumble of bedclothes wrapped and tangled around Ralph's embattled sleep.

She barely glanced at him for confirmation that the white face was indeed his. Then, whisking her gaze around the room, settled on a long, fine tailor's pin, which wouldn't really do. *Where is his sword? Where is his pistol?* She would risk the sound of gunshot. She would risk herself, her own life, for—peace.

The usual massing of squat jars, lotion bottles, boot hooks, combs, discarded shirts, and neck cloths filled every flat space and counter. Her hands began to tingle, as though testing their strength to throttle him. She turned her back to the bed, and reached for the needle. She could thrust it into an ear, an eye, a nostril.

As her fingers closed around its ruby knob, something caught her thigh and yanked her to the bed.

"What a pleasant surprise," laughed Carstip, bouncing her onto the mattress beside him. "Breakfast in bed."

"Ralph!"

"I dreamed you were coming, isn't that strange?" He raised himself above her, pinning her down with the point of his elbow pressed into the crook of hers till she grimaced and squirmed. "My butterfly. My beautiful butterfly," he whispered. "My butterfly on a pin."

"Let me up. You're hurting me."

"Did you intend to hurt *me,* my sweet? Of course not."

His face lowered toward hers. Darkness swept over her world. The tip of his tongue felt along the edges of her nostrils. She gasped from the horribly ugly torture he could contrive without half trying.

"Ralph! Ralph," she choked. "You can do what you will. But if you revolt me, how will it serve you?"

Her frankness was despair. Lying in his bed, in his arms, she had given all and had nothing more to fear.

"Revolt you?" He peered at her, the rusty eyes disconnected. "You toy with me."

"Here's something interesting you'll like," she said, quickly squirming out from under his face. "Look."

She undressed and pulled his head down between her breasts, pressing them to his ears, coddling him there between the warm twin cushions of flesh. She began to rock him as she might a child, remembering his weakness, hoping to play upon it and escape for as long as she could the venom of his triumph. Her hand crept to his mouth and pressed a finger between his lips. She felt him hesitate, then begin to suck on the tip over the nail, grumbling self-satisfied noises. But soon his shoulders stiffened. He raised himself, blinking closely into her eyes as though in a moment he would pluck out her eyeballs and study her brain.

"I have come to marry you, Ralph," she said softly before he could think of anything worse.

"Oh, don't I know it." He chuckled acidly. "Don't know that you miss me."

She refused to reply to his bait and lay back cautiously alert to deal with any mood that migh take him.

"I must have you. I will have you," he said. "B you won't go altogether unsatisfied." He stroked he nipples. "The life in Grosvenor Square is pleasing. Th idleness and gossip of London society will amuse yo We will do the house over and open our doors people who haven't visited me in years. I will dre you like a princess. We will be seen at Holland Hou for tea and hear the best conversation in all of E rope. Have you ever been to the theater, Meg? Wou you not like to sit in a box at Sadler's Wells and lo down upon the mob to see which honored ladies ha switched their lovers? I promise you, there will not be a minute wasted with *ennui*. When the season is on, we shall ride down to Brighton and stroll the promenade with the prince. Do you know he likes to drive a coach and six himself? And is not half bad at it, Ned says, for a prince."

Meg felt something rise in her throat as he rambled on, a suffocating swell of tears that never reached the surface but turned inward upon itself and dove darkly down into her heart.

"We shall be married in America," he said with beaming inspiration. "That will be quicker and amuse me much."

In all her life she had never experienced companionship before Dick. Now, on the threshold of her wedding, the absence of friends or relatives to confide in and make pretenses with was not missed. Could she say that the ceremony would have meaning for her? The American mode and figure were surely as strange as her own unfeeling heart.

Who were these people lined around the wall of the parson's room? Did she know them? The men and women were seated separately, not a smile to be found, reflecting the dingy gloom inside her. And here she was herself, seated at the bottom of the room, Ralph beside her, staring dazedly at the squat clergyman in top boots rattling on merrily from the center of the room, a chair before him that he held or leaned upon by turns. What was he blubbering of? Something about the Institution of Marriage.

"Now if you will please join hands."

Ralph's damp fingers crept to her palm. She minded nothing. A lovely wall had grown up around her that kept all feeling at bay. Was it the madeira? She had drunk enough to float and the fumes had risen, mortifying her brain.

"Do you promise to love, honor, cherish, and *obey?*"

"I do."

"I do."

She no longer sensed Ralph the man, but a stooped bundle in dark clothes next to the foolish, fluttering whiteness of her own gauzes. There came a general scraping of chairs. People stood while the cheery voice droned on in yet another prayer. She remembered that Silas Peddle had prayers, too. Beyond the parson's shoulder a drifting snow was fast closing off the window view.

Behind her someone said, "Our Presbyterian ceremonies are the loveliest of all, don't you think so?"

Now she was standing, with her hands at her sides. No one, however, came up to wish her well. Wasn't that what happened at weddings? Then a little boy came splitting in through the funereal silence, carrying a tray with two huge plum cakes. The guests began to scramble toward it, each shifting out a huge piece and bolting it down in lumps. Why were the Newalls not arrived? And all of Peleg's jolly fat friends?

"Are we in Boston, Ralph?"

"You silly thing, you're drunk. And here comes more wine. Why should we stay in Boston longer than we must, that disgusting place with its pretenses?"

"Are we in Massachusetts Bay?"

"Meg, we are halfway back to New York City and the ship to take us home."

"Then these are not our friends."

"We have no friends in America. I paid the best man three dollars to stand up for me. There he goes, away. Not so much as a thank-you. What could be better?"

"Nothing. Nothing. When do we go aboard the ship?"

"My darling wife." He spoke the word uneasily "You *are* drunk. Never seen you quite in such a state as this. How amazing, the changes that come over you in a flash. You are a never-ending source of interest to me. But I will not touch you until you are sober.

She was aware of her cloak being dropped upon her shoulders, and then the biting touch of snow sifting along her neck inside the collar. Going home t

England in a storm. Perhaps the ship would pitch completely over.

Were hours passing? Days? They seemed locked in the carriage, which stopped again and again as the horses drudged on endlessly through piling drifts. Were those clusters the rooftops of New York, blurred beneath their blankets of snow?

"You must decide upon an American vessel rather than a British one, your Lordship, if I may say so. Particularly in winter. As you can see by our advertisement on the wall, our *Betsy* is a first-rate hotel upon the water."

"How can American ships be superior to anything naval that is British?"

"Well, m'lord, you must compare them for yourself. In the British vessel the ladies are cocked up at the nether end of the ship, while in the American boats they are placed at the center of the motion, which is a merciful and considerate arrangement when things begin to pitch and toss."

"Mm, yes," Ralph drawled at the clerk without in-erest.

"But, m'lord, if you wish for a British vessel ex-clusively, may I recommend that you wait for an April crossing?"

"You may not recommend."

"Yes, m'lord. Thank you. Your tickets will be sent long to the hotel."

The snow had sunk over the horizon, sending back vapor of frothy breath that bellied out the sails verhead. Cranky, creaking sounds dropped from the anvas and spread across the huge flat decks. There ame a clinking of spoons and jingling of glasses ev-y hour or two, signaling that meals were to be the reat entertainment aboard. A wind curled around the assengers in sulky drafts, tugging the ship farther and rther from the quay while Meg stood at the rail, raining to see back to the gray outlines of land and ouses for as long as she could find them.

"Well, Meg, aren't you starved?"

"Not hungry at all, thank you."

"Listless girl," Ralph replied, displeased.

"I will take a glass of wine, thank you, if you can find one."

"Wine in these swells? Then we shall call for the basin."

"Wine, Ralph. Port. Canary. Madeira. Whatever they keep aboard. If there is no wine, then bitter ale. Or porter."

"How long do you intend to stay drunk?" he added irritably.

"I am not drunk."

"You are utterly demolished by liquor, my dear."

"Then perhaps I shall be dead in an hour."

"You feel too sorry for yourself," he replied with disgust.

"Then you must go to the other passengers for company."

He backed away from her with a look made uncertain by the whip in her voice. Aware that she had unsteadied him, Meg disappeared below decks to observe the panorama of green-faced passengers who could not raise their heads from their pillows. Two stoic gentlemen leaned over a board of chessmen. From somewhere forward came the piping of a flute.

"We'll be floating six weeks if it's a day," someone commented darkly.

One afternoon the sun shone overhead, full and clear. A great number of pistol and rifle shots resounded in a *feu de joie,* a celebration. Meg rode out the storms in a cloak of shepherd's plaid, never taking it off except at night when Ralph made suspiciously weak and futile attempts, driven off, it seemed, by horrible retchings of seasickness. While everyone cursed the weather, she found it excessively useful and hoped for pitches and tosses till they would drift into port.

How did the weeks pass? Springing and spinning through one high, whining gale to the next. Dinn hours rang with a fainter bell. People who had formerly rushed off to meals now stood with their heads bowed, mouths clinging like leeches to the sides of mugs.

"We're closing in upon shore, your Lordship."

"How can you tell it?"

"The fog, m'lord. Has a different kind of smell to it. And listen, you can hear birds."

True! True! Through the dismal soup came the ill-humored screech of sea-bird voices, riding with the naked masts back toward land.

"You see, Meg? You never thought we would make it safely. You expected, or did you hope, that we would be drowned at sea, but Piccadilly is straight ahead. Why, one can recognize the cut of the oval even from this bit of window space. Nothing has changed, Meg. Look, we are almost home."

Home! Grosvenor Square home for her? She had not ouched a drop of wine since reaching land and now lescended from the carriage to gaze upon the great nansion called home. Spring was trying for an early tart. The box hedges had turned a deep green. Glossy lackbirds popped along the tops of the leaves. She ooked up to the third story, recalling that night, a year go, of running up the steps so carelessly—so hope-illy!—to ensnare Carstip for the purpose of taking er to Dick in France. How wise she had thought her-elf! How wicked! How competent!

A straggle of footmen, postilion boys, and parlor-aids hung back, wanting to greet the returned aster and his wife, yet hesitating watchfully. Bags nd portmanteaus and leather trunks, their nailheads ittering, were wordlessly marched indoors. The rved portal with its shining brightwork opened to r like the mouth of a cave. Home! She lifted her ad high and her chin higher and stepped boldly nead into Renning Hall. The lady of the house fol-wed bundles upstairs as the servants thus showed r unwittingly into the dingy spread that was her own rivate room.

"You must behave in here," Ralph said behind her in a curious voice. "This was my mother's."

She waited tensely for what was to follow and heard him move off down the hall to leave her entirely alone.

"Now, Meg. Now, Meg. You mustn't trouble yourself with anything except writing cards and letters of invitation. Here is the list."

"Ralph, you are amazing. We are home for exactly one week and you expect me to make a fête?"

She was walking around the old-fashioned boudoir cluttered with porcelain statues of monkeys, fans, and parrots. Heavy chairs and a dark dressing table twenty years behind style supported half a dozen cases that stood open with gnawed, powdered wigs dropped in along with their protective mousetraps, as though worn only yesterday. Dirty windows overlooked the back garden, where an uncertain day flung drizzle and sun with mad, erratic interludes upon an old, leathern-covered carriage studded with nails.

"Besides which, you don't know how, eh?" Ralph smiled, seeming to catch the drift of her irritation. "My sweet wife has not been to the manor born. Well, there is nothing difficult, really. Pity my mother isn't alive to teach you," he said, fondling some white curls of a headdress. "She had a perfect command of the social graces. How will you ever take her place? Well, then. Can you write? Can you hold a pen steady, at least? Here. I have already sent Tom and Ned notice of my *betrothal,* and they have spread the word accordingly. You shall wet your feet one toe at a time, so to speak. To begin with"—he picked up a copy of the *Journal of Beauty*—"you must make friends among the Whig ladies. Choose whosoever looks most wholesome and appealing to your sympathies. I assure you she will be an old friend of my family and delighted to take into her fold the care and keeping of the Earl of Eggleston's *wife.*" He dropped prone onto the cushions of a cherry silk sofa, flu arms and legs wide, and began to laugh in a slow, grinding rip.

"Ralph, it only makes a fool of you to compare me with your mother," Meg said softly.

He stopped abruptly and hauled himself into a more sober mood. "You have brains, you see. That is the problem. You know what troubles me and that I cannot retrieve the past. God Himself could not." He struggled with the thought, growing awed and moody before it, then switched to a subject he could control. "You have never yet quaked before the *ton* of this city, and I don't expect it of you now. We will turn our home into a gilded tavern, refurbish the rooms, and put in some changes of furniture. You will tyrannize over the most notorious salon in London. But you must stop turning your head west to America. I see it in your eyes."

He slid to his feet and began pacing the carpet, sniffing from a vial of laudanum and dueling with mighty forces painfully colliding inside his head.

"I have done nothing," Meg protested. "What are you dreaming of?"

"What are *you* dreaming of!" he barked accusingly. "Will you *never* forget him?"

She fell silent before the truth. And she stood nobly, simply, before the vivid image of another man while Ralph came to her, and grabbing her arms, began slowly to shake her, as though with the shaking he would rattle her brains to destroy the only memory that kept her alive.

As long as Dick walks this earth, I can go on.

Yes, it was easier to manage a ball in her own *home* than to try to comport herself properly before the prince at Carlton House on her very first try. To manage the dishes and deportment in Renning Hall, to preside over a brood of sulky servants, came to her naturally and with the appearance of novel high style, simply because rumor would fly that she had learned it all in *America*. In a week of dusting into rotted corners, polishing silver pots and urns, and throwing light upon the Canalettos, she was teaching the servants that life had found a purpose, that this was now a woman's home, with a woman's bright taste. Brooding daytimes and drunken brawls were tempered by afternoons of whist among sheltered groups of urbane feminine society. The French doors were opened to the garden and the scent of wild roses blew in, while the stench of muddy boots was relegated to the kitchen.

"No, Ralph, we shall not have a *rout* for three hundred that would stifle this house to death, and myself along with it. Rather a dancing ball. We shall contrive a tea garden with Bengal lights over the walks. I hear Ranelegh has closed forever this past year while we were gone. How I loved the fairs. I can do something of that sort very nicely here."

She saw that Ralph was shaken by her ability to charm her way through doors that should have remained closed to her, marriage or no marriage, but he could not guess that she had another, more impo tant purpose behind her fêtes than mere entertainin This imprudent marriage was imprudent on Ralph part, hardly her own. The wives of earls, baronet lords, and dukes who arrived to whisper behind h back were connections, nevertheless. They boug paintings from Royal Academicians. They commi sioned portraits. They became patrons.

Patrons! There it was, that tyrannical yet magnet ing word. Were not men of wealth and taste interest in pictures from America?

"Now, if you will give me your list, my de *husband.*"

"List? I can rattle off my cousins and aunts a uncles to you faster than I can break this glass." tossed one long-stemmed beauty at the fireplace no purpose other than to hear the crash of his r lessness. "Did you say you could write or no?"

"I can write."

Sweetly smiling, and patiently, she sat at ease in light muslins, copying the names he spelled out for in a penmanship surprisingly swift and clear. The long trough of despondence in which she had lingered seemed, with the onset of spring weather, to be drying out, freeing in her heart the one ambition that lingered there always. The Royal Academy! How close she was to making acquaintanceships with its members on terms that even old Feargus could never have arranged for her.

"John 'Puddles' Stowe, that's the Duke of Livesly on my mother's side. . . . Albert Ryng. Elbows, they call him, which you will understand when you see the way he walks. The Earl of Freycaster. . . . Their wives are Maria and Caroline. . . . Then there's my uncle Eddie Lithgo. No title there. He was a youngest son. But owns thousands of wheat-growing acres in the north and never makes a dent into his fortune. . . . And Ned and Tom you know. And the Marquess of ell, if he's still alive. . . . And my uncle, the Duc Beauclew, whom you met in Paris. There's a start for you instantly."

Meg felt her hand tremble at the name. "Oh? Is the duc in London?" she murmured casually.

"Yes, indeed. I passed along White's the other day and out ran Bulldog Ruddy from the club to tell me expressly."

"By all means, he shall be our honored guest," Meg said, hanging on for dear life to the recollection of that familiar face. She happily continued to write, unconcerned with other names as her mind played swiftly ahead in happy expectation of the reunion, if, indeed, would approve and help with the plan actively taking shape in her mind.

Here it was, almost April. Songbirds hovered at the windowsills, drawn by the brilliant light to her party. ...e-colored barouches, coaches with golden crests, ...ll traps, and fashionable curricles bearing couples ...he finest couture clattered into the courtyard and ...led out into the street behind while drivers tried ...ly to quiet prancing horses.

The women glittered and their jewels outdid th chandeliers for lighting. Meg had never seen suc heavy clusters of rubies and diamonds shimmering i frizzed-out hair. Gay red cloaks or satin white one were flung aside, revealing the utmost in a spectacl of graceful, flowing, feminine costumes, modishl French despite the continuing war, in styles reminis cent of Napoleon's empress. The Empire waists fla tered most of the buxom figures and made etherea those who were actually slender. Arm spangles sli down from elbows to wrists as women came up t embrace Meg and work at their duty of welcomin her and making her one of their circle. She could hea the difference between their simpering speech and h own broader accent. The last, final touches of cla sical polish resisted her no matter how hard she pra ticed her mimicry.

"But when shall you come to a game of faro, m dear? Mrs. Hervey is the banker, and we do ha such a roaring time. . . . Will you visit us for whi little Meg? Can Ralph part with you for an afternoo or does he fear we will steal you away? Please try. . . . Have I not left you a card to my Wednesd afternoons? We have a remarkable Tokay mellow to perfection. . . . Will we see you at Carlton Ho for supper on Monday?"

On and on twittered the invitations while e gleamed, alive with the joy of new gossip and tense, important employments of whiling away after day. Meg hugged one and replied yes to next and said to the third that she would ask Ral How she had envied these women, and now she one of them, while glancing over their shoulders ery moment in search of the Duc de Beauclew.

Among the frieze jackets and the embroidered pels, she saw him enter at last. He looked more Fre than ever in his British evening dress and with fine white hair, more slender than she remembe frailer through the chest but sprightly, delightful, sparkling with joy to see her again.

"How beautiful you are, my darling child." He kissed her forehead, then held her away to study her with deep, satisfied smiles. "I am sorry la comtesse is not here to see you doing so well."

"Oh, I am, too. Let us take a glass of port together, my dearest uncle." Meg sighed for other times, drinking him in with the memories that the sight of his loyal face and courtly manners brought to mind.

"You must honor me with a quadrille. I am still a good dancing partner even in my ancient years."

The French flutes and the clarionets and the violins drew them close to the sportive couples engaged in clumsy or graceful encounters with the music.

"No, no." Meg restrained him with a hand at the last moment, unable to take her place on the floor. "I cannot bring myself to dance."

"You? Not dance? But why not? What has happened to the blithesome bird in one year that can keep you from dancing?"

Meg did not answer. He took her by the arm, gently leading her away from the crush and out into the garden, where the buzz and hum of insects were the loudest noises.

"Now you must tell me everything," he said, seating her on a bench beneath an ancient oak. "Do not keep back a single word from me, because I can tell if you do." He touched one gnarled but kindly fingertip to her cheek. His face changed from fatherly smiles to concern when he saw a droplet form and glisten at the side of her eye.

She looked at him mutely, beseechingly, then impulsively pressed her cheek against his lapel, fighting back the tears as she bit into her lip.

"You are not happy," he said with amazement. "You have married this crazee young man and he does not make you happy. You must tell your old uncle everything."

She could feel the warmth in him and his compassion, as he refrained from asking about Dick Fox. Her rust rose in deep, abiding comfort for the only friend he had in her new world. No longer could she squelch the need to ease her loneliness. An urge to talk, to hear her own voice speak out what was in her heart, took her and opened her.

"Yes, you are my uncle," she cried. "I can tell you everything. I can tell you, and no one else will hear a word."

"That is so. I promise it."

"Oh, you need not promise, Uncle. And yes, yes, I am unhappy. Desperately so."

"It must be Ralph. I will deal with him for you. Tell me of what."

"No. That's not it. It was my decision to marry Ralph. We were in America when it happened."

"That much I know. Rumors came to us. They flew in! And la comtesse looked at me and said: 'My English daughter has made a terrible mistake.' "

"Oh. Did she say that? Did she? But I am so sad. Yet it was not a mistake, Uncle. It was my only choice. I married Ralph because he was insanely jealous of another man . . . the man I love."

"Do I know whom you mean?"

"Of course. The only one, ever. Dick Fox. My painter. The one I have so long called *cousin*. And now, openly, proudly, I call him lover. At least to you."

"But, child, why did you not marry him?"

"If only I could," she wailed softly. "If only I could Perhaps you don't know it. Ralph came to America He looked for me. And he found me. He said he wanted me for stealing his jewels. He wanted me in exchange."

"But that is a terrible misfortune, and only half th tale. You see, *I* gave the money to Murier for thos jewels. Yes. I bought them for you, indirectly. It wa my money you had, though I did not want you t find it out at the time, for fear you might not accep And when Murier gave me the jewels, I then returne them to Ralph. So you see? He had his jewels."

"*And* me."

"But his lying is not the point, I suspect."

"No. Not at all. Any excuse would do. He lives

torment me. And succeeds. I will not pain you with the details, for I can deal with him. After all," she said, trying to smile, "my life has not been such a bed of roses that I must be weak in the face of some suffering. Oh, I can take it. Whatever he has to give, I can stand up to."

"Then what is it, at last? Why do you look so like death?"

"It is the fear in me, Uncle. The fear of the unknown, which I never could bear."

"What don't you know, then?"

"About Dick Fox. I left him in America months ago. And have heard nothing of him since. I don't know what happened to him. If he is doing well. If he is in trouble. Whether he is dead or alive. Must I tell you what Ralph tried? Oh, I blush to reveal it, he is your flesh and blood."

"You need not tell me about my nephew," the duc replied with grave understanding. "He is a wicked, wicked boy and has been so all his life. But have you not written to America?"

"Where would I receive an answer safely if I wrote?" she cried, at her wits' end. "Ralph has an uncanny way of intercepting everything I try."

"I see. I see." He patted her cheek and handed her a folded, lace-edged handkerchief. "If that is the case, perhaps I can help you. I shall write to America myself. We have friends in New York. Some Democrats manage to sympathize even with members of the *ancien régime*. And surely I can write to Elise. She will answer. She is a good spy, you know." He smiled gently. "Where is your Dick Fox?"

"I left him in Boston."

"The chevalier has interests in Boston, too."

"But no. Not le chevalier. He is a friend of Ralph's, and that is how Ralph got to me, I fear."

"Then I will write to Elise in private and caution her accordingly. She will contact my business agents and will discreetly inform them, with nothing set on paper. They, in turn, will call upon . . . ?"

"Let them try a Dr. Allan Newall on Tremont

Street. If anyone knows where Dick Fox is, Allan will."

"Fine. Then it is settled. No more tears?"

At four in the morning, when Meg finally got to bed, she lay awake bubbling with new hope and possibilities. What a fool she had been. How sluggard. Why had she never once thought to visit Maundy Bannish, who, if anyone, would have heard by now from Dick Fox?

But Ralph lay upon her like a pall and tracked after her throughout the house all the next day, as though sniffing something suspicious on the wind. His lips seemed to harbor the taste of blood as he lounged over the sideboard and sucked at a morning pot of beer while Meg, assuming a pose of nonchalance, sipped her chocolate and complained weakly of aches from their gala affair.

"They were all admiring my crepe dress," she twittered on. "I must go immediately and have six others made just like it, and that will put me in style for the rest of the month."

"Yes. You were divine." Ralph spoke through the foaming bubbles. "I will go with you to the dressmaker's and supervise the work. My taste is superior to your dressmaker's."

"That it is. But I would like you to see about some trousers for yourself. Mr. Beau Brummell is setting London on its ear, yet he is no handsomer than you." She turned her glance to the thin slices of bread and butter redolent on a silver tray, and played with one inspecting the whiteness of its flour.

"I will go with you to your dressmaker's," Ralph repeated firmly.

For two days there was no peeling him off as h turned away his barber, his tailor, his fencing maste and a furtive little man who looked like a pimp. The his cronies came and finally dragged him away to sho snipe in the Pimlico marshes.

Breathlessly, Meg waited half an hour till he w well gone on his way. Then she slipped out of h fine dress and into a dark bombazine, a more serviceable affair made up for her at a bargain. She could not risk taking one of her own carriages. The driver himself could cause trouble without realizing what he did. She tied on a tremendous poke bonnet to hide her face from the running footmen who might recognize her on the street, and then went out down a side road to find a cab that would take her without remark to St. Catherine's docks.

How long it had been. The crowded, ramshackle houses and the rank smell of river tides were so odd and familiar at the same time. She listened to the street cries and in a moment was transported to happier, freer days, lifetimes ago! when she ran in torn clothes, sometimes barefoot, to mingle, fight, and take her chances beside Dick. She was taking the same desperate chances today. Did her fine but hated state make a difference? *Oh, pray, Mrs. Bannish, be at home.*

She kept saying it over and over as she ran up the rickety steps, catching the hem of her dress on a sprung-up plank near the wall, while aggressive cats brayed at perfumes they had never smelled before.

She turned from habit to Dick's old room and was about to plunge headlong into it, for no good reason she could think of, when the caterwauling of some hungry infant came from inside, chasing her off.

"Mrs. Bannish? Mrs. Bannish!" she cried, rapping loudly at the proper door. "Please open. This is Meg."

"Who's there?"

"Meg. Meg Watkins."

"Why, saints preserve us!" breathed Maundy Bannish, pushing her hair back and tilting her head to squint up and down at the sight before her. "Meg Watkins it is! We thought you'd fell from the face of the earth. Feargus said so to me. Now what are you standin' out there for? Come inside. From the looks of you you're not starvin', but I'll give you as fine a dish of tea as you'll get in your other end of town. Why, I can see where you've been, child, and what you're up to." She was all pleasured grins, pushing aside bits of frames and pulling out one of the rockers from a host of wood shavings. "Here. Have a seat. Have a seat. Honest dirt won't kill you, as you know. What brings y'back, eh? 'Tisn't love for old Maundy Bannish. What's on your mind? Where is *he?*"

Meg felt her heart sink with a melancholy fall as she looked into the woman's welcoming but expectant expression. She had wanted a good homecoming and assurance waiting in the form of a letter from Dick. Mutely she stared into the shrewd but benevolent eyes and instantly knew the answer to the question she could not bear to ask.

"It's true I haven't a word from him and neither has Feargus 'less he's hidin' somethin' I don't ought to know. But I doubt it. Feargus isn't one to keep things to himself about that rogue Fox, since he's *my* boy, after all. Now here's your tea, there's a good girl. So you've been to America, is that so? You say he's still there? My, my. I wouldn't wonder that he's gone off to a wilderness with all the bloody doin's in this end of the world. I'd go myself, if I was a young man."

Meg sat glumly drinking her tea and answering questions when she herself had come expressly to ask them.

"But, dearie, he'll write us one day soon. What's there to keep him from it when 'twas us that put the bread and butter in his mouth? He may not be the sweetest sort, but not the desertin' kind, neither." Mrs. Bannish rattled on, drinking tea very soberly from a huge mug and easily believing every word of her expectations. "And you're in the fine upper crust now, eh, Meg? *You* can get us real pictures. Just to be copied, o' course. Never to be missed for a moment. And easily returned. A harmless trip. Quick and profitable." She cocked a covertly pitying eye upon Meg hunching tiredly, disappointed, over her mug. "You never do know. No, you never *do* know when Dick Fox'll see fit to drop us a line. He can't write to you even as he wants. Yet he may write to me or Feargus. Yes, he *may* do. You could be at this very doorst again next week, with me holdin' out a bit of paper to ye, callin', 'Look, Meg! Here's the very thing!' "

"This is almost the start of April," Meg replied sadly. "And not a word to you, either."

"Dick won't forget his friends. Oh, no, he won't," she blundered on enthusiastically. "Not old friends, anyway, like Maundy and Feargus."

"I left him in December."

"Hardly any time at all. Now see here. You must cheer up and do what I tell you. Dick Fox is comin' home to England very soon. *That's* why he hasn't writ. He's on the boat already and pukin' his guts up over the rail."

Meg stared into the never-ending fire that blustered and crackled in this dank hole of a room where spring was as damp and cold as winter. Had she lived like this? Had she lived as cheerfully as Mrs. Bannish and never known the difference until now?

"Supposing Dick is dead," she said sullenly at the fire. "Supposing Ralph Carstip *did* take his revenge to have the last laugh on *me*. Supposing I sit here in this room with you and the cat and that little dish of oysters she's eating, while Dick lies . . ."

"Hush, Meg. Hush. Why scramble your brains? Don't you think if Dick Fox were molderin' in the ground I'd feel it right here?" She slapped her hip. "In the very marrow of me old bones?"

"It's a question of faith, I suppose," Meg replied. "Why should I not believe you better than myself when I've been wrong so many times, too many times, about Dick Fox?"

"Then you'll do it. You'll bring us pictures, there's a deal." Mrs. Bannish clapped one spongy paw on Meg's shoulder. "And mark my word, little Miss Watkins, we'll be hearin' from your man one way or another." She fingered the bit of red material on Meg's dress fashioned from the old sash. "Luck always returns, didn't he tell y'so? You must believe it, since you're wearin' this."

"Yes, I believe," Meg replied stubbornly. "I believe."

Chapter Thirty-two

THE DUC DE BEAUCLEW'S TOWNHOUSE in Mayfair reflected the man, a safe harbor of genteel sanity, but with grand proportions and airy, rosy color that soothed disquiets rampant in a mere mortal's breast.

"Leading a double life can hold certain advantages for one's peace of mind," mused the duc with a philosophical smile as he directed a servant to remove a small Dutch painting from above the mantel on the library wall.

Meg came away from an urn of rain-soaked jasmine and St. Michaelmas daisies to study the dark earth tones of burnt umber, sepia, ocher, and sleepy, sinuous reds of the picture, unexpectedly revealed in the gentle splash of morning light. "I make no excuses for helping Mrs. Bannish," she said fondly. "I think the best part of my life must be over, and she recalls to me what once was mine."

"You remind me exactly of my own position during the Reign of Terror." The duc smiled. He motioned Meg to eat a bite of the toast she had been pushing around on her plate, neglected beside the settee. "One foot each in both worlds. Yes, it can be managed," he added with a decisive nod. "Let her have this Rembrandt copied. Let them make engravings of it. Then you will return it to me, and who will know ou[r] secret, eh?"

"You are so kind," she answered, hardly audible[.]

He waved a hand, dismissing it. "There but for th[e] grace of God go I. And yourself, perhaps. But yo[u] have not come today merely to beg a picture fro[m] my walls in the name of stealing. You want to hea[r] if I have heard something from America. I do have news." He went with small steps into a pale green alcove and riffled among some papers on a gilt-legged desk. "Here it is, Meg. From my agent in Boston. Come read it for yourself."

He held the page out. She rushed to him, snatching the paper and skimming it with a trembling intensity of concentration. "I can't believe it. Is this true? Left for England in February?" She read the words over and over, blurting, "This is almost April. He may be here this very minute. Dick Fox could be in London even now. What do you know of it? Has the *Mohawk* docked?" She was standing, then sitting, tossing the ringlets from her forehead, pressing a palm to her heart, catching breath, struggling against fits of dizziness that heaved the fluted folds of her white muslin dress.

"I could not have called you sooner." The duc smiled, removing the fluttering paper and squeezing Meg's fingers. "This has come to me late last night. I have sent to the city for further news this very morning. We shall hear it together. Now come, child. Take a glass of porter. You will meet with your painter again very soon. Should you not then be at the glorious height of your beauty?"

No amount of good sense would settle her. She could do nothing from that moment on, other than listen to the grinding progress of the clocks or run to the windows and peer out in mistaken hope after hope of having heard the arrival of a carriage.

Noontime came and went. She sent a message round to Carstip that she was delayed at the duc's residence, her scribbled writing dashed about distractedly with many blots on the paper. Not until two in the afternoon, when she thought she must be dead from the strain, did the longed-for message arrive.

"The *Mohawk* has reached these shores one week to Friday," announced the duc, who was nearly toppled over as Meg ran to him and flung her arms round his neck.

"He is here! Here!" she sang, and swung herself

in circular whirls, skimming about beneath the grave marble busts in their niches. "He is in London three days already." Abruptly she stopped and faced the duc with troubled eyes. "And does he not know where to find me?"

"Oh, he knows," the duc replied softly, sipping at some pale claret and tapping the round side of the crystal. "And hesitates."

"Yes, I understand you. He will not put me in danger with Carstip. I must go to him. I must!"

"So you shall. All things are possible in love and war. We will uncover his whereabouts directly." He penned a brief notice and sent it off with a liveried messenger. "That went to a friend of mine who must remain nameless, but who has a finger in every pie in London."

"Like Murier in Paris."

"Yes," the duc twinkled. "Like Murier."

Surrounded by ears and eyes, the duc nevertheless took longer than she thought she could live through, another three days, before turning up Dick's address in Portman Square, where he had settled, so the information went, with a number of heavy parcels, renting a huge bare barn of a place. No report could yet be made of his comings and goings, however, since he was a free citizen of the realm, much decorated during previous wartime engagements, and under no suspicion of spying for the French.

"Portman Square! That is a very good address," Meg noted with satisfaction. "He has learned a thing or two."

"Yes. You must congratulate him for me," the duc called after her as she flew out to his carriage. "And remember, I want to see his paintings."

His paintings. She could think of nothing but the man, the precious flesh and blood, destructible yet enduring, now only minutes away after ten thousand lifetimes of separation. All the anticipation that had built up sat in her throat, ready to burst into love song as it lay in mute ecstasy while she thought of him. S had lived without him and discovered the difference between mere dull survival and the shine of life. There was nothing to compare with love. No position, no wealth, could equal its sensation. Everything she owned, every friend she had made, every earned wisdom and hard-won prudence she would gladly throw away into the Thames for a single night in the arms of her lover, lying with her eyes closed and gaudy rockets bursting inside her. Yet . . . she was different. She knew she was different from the girl she had been last winter. From the child she had been all her life. The mad, scattering fragments of her eagerness to be with Dick could not rub out the torturous price she had paid to help preserve his survival, separate from her own. She could feel the tingle of strength in her that signaled the existence of her own unique *being* and her will to go on. She was rushing to Dick now, not for protection but as an equal with needs n many ways similar to his. Her willing degradation before Carstip had left her independent and strangely unafraid of him any longer.

Portman Square enfolded her with its crowd f closely built red brick houses. Dick had rented front ooms and a rear studio with northwest light that rifted down today in shrouds of smoke-filled sun. he paused, imagining how he must have regarded ith wry acceptance the familiar, grimy atmosphere home. Then she was lifting and dropping the nocker in a slow motion of suspense, clenching and nclenching her fingers with nervous apprehension that might not be here.

A moment later, she heard the impatient, springy otfalls crossing boards, and the air seeped out of r lungs in sudden release. Flashes of Mrs. Bannish pping her hip passed through her mind, and all nner of trivial, inconsequential images, as though were reviewing her old life before passing into aven.

"Meg. My God."

She leaped into his embrace as he stepped back and shed the door shut.

Now it was happening, as she had dreamed of it every night and lived with it daily—the sensation of his arms, the pressure and jump of his muscles, the leathery scent of his clothes, the creak of the belt round his waist as he lifted her, the dear, devouring mouth that knew everything, all her secrets; the living, breathing man of him absorbed her. A million words of endearment passed through her mind, but none formed on her lips busy with tasting his. Her body trembled, becoming weaker and stronger in waves, then sinking again with overwhelming gusts of rapture. Her palms pressed his stubbled cheeks, stroked his silky hair grown longer behind the ears. Her fingers spread and clutched his skull, holding his face still while she kissed his eyelids, his cheeks, his forehead, his ear lobes, devouring him and being devoured in turn. They stumbled and staggered back, bumping into a chair, knocking a table aside. Blind to everything else, they sank together to the floor and rolled on the carpet. She wanted to cry and laugh, and nothing came from her beyond gasps. His swift-moving hands were even larger, stronger than she had dreamed. Their movements slowed feelingly along her rib cage, expandin over the curve of her breasts. The meaning of passio burst upon her afresh, with a piercing possession tha she could not remember as being like this. *This!*— spreading in warm currents, flowing upward from he knees into her thighs, downward from her heart int her bowels, deeper, arrowing deeper, into the privat winding, writhing channels of desire that must be fille

She lay panting into his mouth, atop him, besi him, then beneath. Their clothes came away mirac lously, moved by swift, demanding fingers. Nake they touched in every part of the flesh, embracing wi love's expert assurance, with love's total intimac neglecting nothing, taking all. How she had hungere And while she lay rocking, sharing that which s could give to no other, the hunger grew. It grew ev in its highest point of fulfillment. Grew as she stretch beyond the measure of her possibility and cried w ecstatic pain into his ear. Her mind, her body, refu to release him. She must keep him, have him, again and again, while he, with his fine, rough hands and his deeply penetrating need, remained where she wished him to be for hours. There seemed no end to what she had to give. But then she became aware of the floor and its bruising hardness that knocked the bony parts of her arms. He lifted her to the bed. Begrudgingly, she released him to leave her and poke up the fire, for daylight had traveled over the rooftops and was gone.

"Did you do it?" he said with his back to her. "Are you married to Carstip?" He spoke calmly, but each word was a boulder of ice.

"Yes. But how do you know of it?" She lay on her side, watching the ruddy glow on his flesh, hardly daring to breathe as she waited for what was to come next.

"When you left me, there could be only one reason. Allan told me of Carstip's connection to his father and we went to Peleg directly, who obliged by finding what needed to know. Besides, it was easy enough to uess. And Carstip left me another calling card soon fter."

"Did he hurt you?"

"After he had taken you away, how could he hurt ne more?" Dick laughed with solemn bitterness. "No. he horses didn't run me down on the first attempt. nd his thugs couldn't burn my eyes out on the second. I am certainly fine. What about you?"

As he wheeled to study her, Meg dropped herself rone and hid her weary, frustrated cries in the crook f her arm. Dick had come home to England for her, r *her!* And it had nothing to do with his work!

"Darling, darling." He sat next to her on the bed, roking her back slowly with one finger, up and down e length of her spine. "Nothing keeps us apart, you e. Somehow or other, we do find each other eventually."

She heard the ring in his voice and, encouraged, ted her head. "Yes, yes. And your paintings? What d you bring? Why do you keep them facing the wall? Show them to me. Let me see what you accomplished in America."

"Everything!" He spoke triumphantly and went to turn them around, one after the other. "Look. I have landscapes for you. Finished ones. See? See how the water falls and the foliage flourishes." He laughed with a child's delighted pleasure, and with a more sonorous note of some deeper, serious bargain completed.

"They are magnificent," she breathed. "And large enough for the walls of great country homes. Why, these are the most astounding creations," she said, exclaiming at the half-dozen vistas of American wilderness that she had seen with her own eyes but which had never before been captured on canvas by an Englishman.

"And *these* will surely please you, my darling."

"Portraits? Portraits?" she squealed, pressing his hands with a thrill of fulfillment. "Indian faces. And Mrs. Clinton! Why, that one's Tabitha Newall in her old-fashioned mobcap, so very British."

"Yes. The original studies. The finished likenesse are hanging in their proper homes."

"Oh, Dick." Meg smiled, overwhelmed. "What ar you going to do with such treasures?"

"You know very well," he said quietly. "What yo have always pleaded for. I shall send two of these i to the exhibition at the end of this month—if I am no late in applying."

"The Academy exhibition?" she repeated, hardl daring to believe her ears.

"Is there another?"

His mock innocence appeased her. "Of course the will take them. The duc will see to it. But why onl two?" she persisted greedily.

"Because that is the limit they accept."

"Foolish committees," she said with derision. "Th know not what they miss. How happy I am. How lo it has been in coming. Dick, I always knew!" She ke gazing from the glossy canvases to his beaming ey "Which have you chosen?"

"This and this," he said, lifting out two panoramas of the Boston hills.

"And the others?" she said voraciously, eyes narrowing with ideas. "What shall you do with them?"

"Sell them, I suppose."

"Sell them? Really? Do you promise it?"

"I intend to, yes," he replied, smiling calmly.

"Then I have the very man to buy."

"Have you?" he inquired softly.

"Do you hesitate?"

"More than that, Meg, my darling." He came and kissed her in the crook of her neck. "I firmly, flatly, refuse to deal with anyone you know."

"But why?" Her voice rang hollow from the depths of disappointment.

"You can see it for yourself, I think. This Carstip. This madman. What would happen if he knew you had a part in my success? After all he's done to keep us apart. No, dear, it cannot be. I fear more for you than for myself. He thought he could take you from me back to England. But where can he run with you from here? No. The rat cornered will rise up on his hind legs and fight in whatever way he can find. I would not sleep one night through if I allowed you to put yourself in such danger."

"How can you say so? How can you think so?" she demanded, at her wits' end. "I will leave him today. You know I must."

"Hm. And the effect? More madness. His violent way is something to be considered carefully, Meg. Or we could live all our lives looking around corners for the revenge of Ralph Carstip. No. It's completely out of the question."

"What do you expect me to do? Stay with him? Now? Now that we are finally together at home and your future is assured? There is nothing more I want for than my freedom to be with you in a settled condition. And I *shall* have it."

"Yes. It will come to pass, eventually. But not through some impulsive burst of self-indulgence that could reap dire consequences."

"What do you propose instead?"

"As yet, I don't know," he said, moving to the table and carving cold mutton from a bone. "Besides, my future is not so assured as you may think. The picture-hanging committee has yet to approve my work. The world has yet to view it and pass its own judgment. My darling, I have miles to go."

"No. It is quite settled," she insisted with the blind enthusiasm of her devotion. "And for me to bring you a patron is not so exceptional as to raise Carstip's suspicions." She took a slice of the meat and bit into it with angry, unconscious hunger. "The Duc de Beauclew is *my* uncle, too, you see. He has adopted me, at least in spirit. It would hurt his feelings if I did not bring him here to view your paintings. Besides, he asked to see them before some other privileged member of the peerage captures you."

She was not to be talked out of it, nor threatened, nor frightened, nor delayed. Too much had happened, too much time had passed, for the prospect of Carstip's violent revenge to stop her from pressing on with the ambition so dear to her heart. Besides, Dick stood right there, on the brink of his success, with her or without. The pictures were painted. They were amazing in their spectacle. And he was willing at last to part with them to make his fortune.

Revealing all of this to the Duc de Beauclew within the walls of his own drawing room confirmed the grip Meg felt she finally had on a destiny that had too long eluded her.

"If he is willing to show his pictures, then I must have an appointment to go and see them. But, Meg, my sweet, you must run off now and amuse your neglected husband."

Meg glanced across at the faro players seated around small tables where dappled sunlight spread upon ladies' exposed white shoulders and gentlemen's colored jackets. A fat, bright blue fly buzzed along a mirror and bounced lazily against its reflection, finally landing on the mantel to rub its hind legs. She could hardly care that she presided over this gilded drawing room with its Chinese carpets, silver dishes of bonbons, and graceful statuary all sufficient to the taste of titled ladies accustomed to every surfeit and comfort of wealth. Beyond them at the open, double French doors, Carstip stood with his hands clasped behind his slightly stooping back. The tailor had outdone himself in creating a cut of jacket to fit like a second skin. Yet nothing could bolster Carstip or cheer him. He stood wracked by dreams of heaven only knew what, his sinking profile turned away south to the Channel, the whole of him somehow shriveled in recollections. *He looks stricken by a blight,* Meg thought uncomfortably. In a flash of speculation, she wondered again why he could never sleep with her since their marriage. Something held him frozen from it, some memory, some equation or unspoken terror. Until today she had been glad to dismiss the reasons and simply feel thankful that he had lost the potency, if not the interest, to fulfill his dreadful and twisted promises. Now, reminded of her legal duties and Carstip's lawful right, she wondered with foreboding how it must finally be resolved.

"You must not underestimate him," the duc added, areful of her feelings. "In your eager and laudable assion to help your lover, there is a husband who ust be considered."

"Dear Uncle, I do consider him. But he is forever aring at me and swallowing handfuls of pills that do t keep him from shaking with one ague or another. e has begun taking lessons from a ventriloquist and nds voices of Ned and Tom into corners of my bedom expressly to worry me. I cannot tell you what e. I must either ignore his queer behavior and go my way or else be driven mad by it." Meg glided er the words as they came up unbidden.

"This is not speech from the circumspect woman ave known." The duc pursed his lips with concern.

'Yes, I am different. I am changed. There is no ying the truth."

'You are his wife. That, too, is the truth. He still

possesses you. And you must take care both for your honor and for your safe well-being."

"I know it only too well, my dear, dear uncle." She smiled with fleeting dimples of love that suddenly dismissed her troubles. "Does that mean you will not come to see Dick's paintings?"

"Heavens, of course I shall. With all the bare house walls I have still to decorate? With my growing grandchildren who must have their faces done, and Gainsborough and Reynolds dead these many years? No, indeed. I look forward to viewing the work of your Dick Fox, and I expect he is as good as you say."

For half an hour the duc sat at the edge of his chair, examining in silence the landscapes and the portraits set out for his inspection at Portman Square.

"Why, sir, you have the very thing and are to be congratulated," he said at last, over his spectacles and stood with a spring to shake Dick's hand enthusiastically. "I will give you five hundred a year and you will paint all my family."

Meg, standing off beside an empty easel, watched with glowing joy and pride as the men she loved best in the world sealed the arrangement with glasses of port. She had all to do to restrain herself and not leap between them to clasp them both to her breast.

"You must do something for me, sir," continued the duc. "I must beg you to paint for me beginning immediately. There is a devilish big house up in Wiltshire that till now I have seldom visited, which wants historical subjects for the walls. I am a man of both French and British sympathies, as you know. What can you do for me?"

"Off-hand I might suggest something neutral start," Dick replied with an easy good will.

"Something American?" Meg put in, unable to control herself any longer.

"No, not American." Dick waved it off. "These are all I will ever do of those wild shores unless I revisit them one day. That page is closed."

"Then a classical theme, perhaps?" Meg persisted.

"No, no, my dear," the duc said. "Mr. Copley has ended the classical craze when he painted the 'Death of Chatham.' The days of dressing our native heroes in Roman togas are gone. But I might like a seascape, Fox, eh?" he said, blinking up at him. "This is a naval country and I have watery interests. A frigate in a storm would do me well."

"One is put in mind of Mr. Turner," replied Dick with faint reluctance to challenge the master.

"Yes. So one is," the duc agreed.

"And could do worse for a model, at that," Dick concluded.

"Much worse. And would you enjoy the privilege of meeting the gentleman? Since you wish to show at the Royal Academy this season, it is not too soon for you to meet with some of the influential members of that circle. Mr. Copley will have them to his house or us. It will prove a pleasurable and instructive hour or you, my boy."

Meg watched Dick agree, herself amazed at his ever-ending flow of good will these days, so different rom the dark, brooding character of time gone by. et even as plans were concluded for them to drink a ish of tea with the honored circle, Meg could tell hat something restless still stirred in the breast of her eloved. But what it was she could not quite be sure.

"You must take me along." She put herself for-ard now. "To see Mr. Fuseli, especially. We know ch other from the old days. And Mr. West, the merican, is much too interesting for me to miss. Why, have had such fine instruction from Mr. Gilbert uart in America, remember it, Dick? I would be uch put out if you did not include me on your vis-."

Had either of the men revealed the slightest hesi-ion, Meg would have withdrawn her plea with iet good sense. When they agreed, she let her eager-ss bubble visibly and could only grumble in private w she wished she could, as Mrs. Fox, invite them her own home.

This discontent was, however, of the mildest sort and soon blew away in busy expectation of an hour with the John Copley of Boston fame, now dwelling at St. George Street, Hanover Square, in the pulsing heart of her own London.

John Singleton Copley, in old traveling clothes, welcomed his guests to join the others. A white French bonnet, turned on one side and pulled over the ears, topped a yellow and red silk neckerchief with a large Catherine wheel flambeaued upon it, reminiscent of that worn by the street sellers peddling Malton oysters. Below this hung a faded cinnamon jacket that swung its old swallowtails as he pushed and banged himself about by means of a hickory stick with an ivory head. Always thin, pale, and a bit pockmarked, the face had now sunken away, revealing prominent eyebrows and small sharp eyes with a cast of humor undying upon them.

"This gentleman wishes to show at the exhibition?" He squinted at Dick. "I should suggest to you also not to neglect to have your work engraved. Engraved, man. For when you see two thousand prints very quickly sold, why, then fifteen hundred guineas fo the original work will be but a flyspeck of the ac quisition."

"But there is not the color in engravings to equa those of your own experiments," protested Dick i a mild way, his voice floating amiably around the clut tered workroom.

"That is so. I have experimented with the schoo of Florence and Venice for a long while, perhaps to long. And finally, I could write out the receipts f those lustrous hues in which Titian and Correggio e celled. But look at my works, sir. Look at my 'B and Squirrel.' I did that before the name of Titi ever was pronounced in my ear. Let me tell you a ta of portrait painting that will give you a lesson. O day a man, his wife, and seven children came rou to me, to be all included in a family piece. Well, s I did the portrait and the man said to me: 'It wa but one thing. And that is the portrait of my first wife, for this one is my second!' Said I: 'But she is dead, you know, sir. What can I do? She is only to be admitted as an angel.' 'Oh, no, not at all,' he answered. 'She must come in as a woman. No angels for me.' I added the portrait and some time elapsed before he came back with a strange lady on his arm. 'I must have another cast of your hand, Copley,' said he. 'An accident befell my second wife. This lady is my third, and she is come to have her likeness included in the family picture.' Well, sir, I complied. The likeness was introduced, and the husband gazed with a glance of satisfaction upon his three spouses. Not so the lady. She gave off angry cries and disagreement. Never was such a thing heard of, cried she. Out her predecessors must go. Well, sir, I painted them out accordingly, but hen what do you suppose? I was forced to bring acion at law to obtain payment for the portraits which vere no more."

"Mr. Fox will never paint out a face he has put ipon canvas." Meg smiled. "For they *are* all angels."

Mr. Benjamin West leaned into the conversation, aying, in his stately way: "Angels are those folks ith the most agreeable of human natures. I would ay that some angels I knew came to me in the shape f Indians when I was a very little boy, and they arved one summer for their annual visit to Springfield. hey were so amused by my sketches of birds and owers that they taught me to prepare the red and llow colors with which they painted their ornaments. nd then my mother added blue by giving me a piece indigo, so that I was in possession of the three imary colors. And the next angel I met was in the ape of a cat. For my drawings attracted the atten-on of the neighbors, one of whom said to me that much regretted having no pencils. When I inired what kinds of things pencils were, I was told ey were small brushes made of camel's hair fastened a quill. As there were no camels in America that could find, I could not think of any substitute, till

I happened to cast my eyes on my father's favorite
black cat and saw in the tapering fur of her tail
exactly what I wanted. Immediately, I stole off to
my mother's scissors, and laying hold of Grimalkin
very carefully and with proper attention to her feelings,
cut off the fur at the end of her tail and so made my
very first pencil. But that was merely the beginning.
For I soon stood in need of further supply, at which
time I then had further recourse to Grimalkin's back,
my forays upon which were so frequently repeated
that Father observed the altered appearance of his
favorite and lamented it as the effect of disease. When
in due course, I told him, with suitable contrition, the
true affair, he was much relieved and amused by my
ingenuity, so that if I was scolded, it was certainly
not in anger."

"You are fortunate to have had parents who en
couraged you," said Meg.

"Yes, indeed, Madame. But surely my greatest for
tune was in finding art. Why, I was so thrilled wit
the conception as a child that I would refuse to rid
behind a schoolboy on his horse. For I, the *artis*
would never ride behind *anybody*. The boy, in rep
to me, said his father intended to apprentice him to
tailor. 'But a painter,' shouted the boy. 'What sort
trade is that? I never heard of such a thing.' '
painter,' I replied, 'is a companion for kings and e
perors.' 'Surely you are mad,' replied the boy, 'f
there are no such people in America.' 'Yet there a
in other parts of the world. And do you really inte
to be a tailor?' I asked again. 'Most certainly.' 'Th
you may ride by yourself, for I will no longer ke
you company,' and with that, I alighted and imme
ately returned home by myself."

A mellow glow had settled upon the room of
mous faces gathered here, at the duc's behest, to p
informal judgment upon the work of a young ar
aspiring to election in the Royal Academy. So
portant was this preliminary impression that no m
tion was made of it, and the evening drifted by i

succession of tales and conversations upon every topic related to art, but none whatsoever concerning Dick Fox. It was sometime after ten o'clock that Fuseli, who had been studying Meg for a good part of the evening, shuffled toward her and peered into her face with a thrusting forward of his lion's head. "So it *is* you, by Gode!" he exclaimed. Meg glanced up at him with a flirting smile, although she had not reminded him of their first meeting for fear of embarrassing Dick. "Yes, it is indeed you. I remember how you left me with his sketches tucked beneath your arm. A good friend you are to the gentleman. And does he appreciate you, this poor artist? How different it is in these days from the ones of my own youth, when a painter lad with no prospects must be sent far away from the door of his beloved. How I sat in exile from my fairest heart, alone in a town full of soldiers, parsons, coal crushers, landladies, and shopgirls, with my head propped on both fists and my eyes filled with tears. . . . But these are different times, by Gode. Different times."

"Different times indeed, Mr. Fuseli," Meg replied with a cheerful lilt, though a stab of anger for her married state passed through her. She never fully accepted or believed in her betrothal, even when she was reminded thus, directly. For what marriage could she admit of, other than the true one of her heart? She gazed upon Dick, here and there in conversation, his face shining like a bit of silver flashing in a pond. She caught snatches of his conversation, heartfelt in tone, about the Royal Academy and its obligation to the standards of art. Some reminiscence reached her about old King George and his secret explorations years before, with Reynolds and West at Buckingham House, upon the best means of promoting the study of fine arts in the kingdom. It was there, at eleven o'clock at night, that the king expressed his readiness to patronize any association which might be formed to improve the arts. And it was here, this night, thought Meg, that these dignified members of the profession would open their gates to its latest and most serious aspirant.

Had a week flown by so quickly? Was the committee's verdict yes so soon? Then she found herself dropped from the clouds into a skulking, hellish state of misery as Carstip, so quiet and passive lately, began to stir around her and stalk her again.

"How long have I been gone from you?" she remonstrated, the edge of her mouth tightening with anger she could not suppress. "What is a week but a week?"

Carstip stood buffing his nails in her bedroom, breathing on his knuckles from time to time, lounging carelessly, as he often did when irritated, at the fireplace. "A week without the pleasure of your company is equal to a lifetime."

"Bosh." Meg slipped out of her bed before he would come upon the idea of entering it to poke her with odd, sharp objects. "Between your bulldogs and your fighting, prize monkey, you have not thought of me for a month. Two. Three! You have been off with Ned and Tom, leaning over the green tables, tearing away at your fortune as fast as you can go. Why, you have been home drunk every night for a fortnight. I have seen you in nothing but shirts stained with port and your jackets filthy as the ground. Now here you come, moaning to me about lost love."

"Well, it may be I am stirred by the boudoir gossip I hear about my fair wife when she quits he toilet table, tea, and cards." His gaze traveled everywhere except to her face.

Immediately she felt in his hints the cold wind o destruction brushing over her cheeks. She decided t forestall his accusation by shifting the subject to him

"Are you deceiving me with another woman?" sh said. "Is that why I never find you in my bed? O with it and clear your conscience."

A maid came in with horn combs and brush Meg flounced over to a stool and sat upon it, allowi the girl to begin work on her hair, in hopes that Ralph would find the situation too common and walk himself out.

But he had no such idea, ignoring the girl as he concentrated upon his own terrible hurts. "Deceive you?" he whined guiltily. "That has never come to pass. Not even on that miserable trip across the ocean."

"Then do I disappoint you?" She could barely hide the pleasure in her voice as she charged him with his impotence.

"So there it comes out." His mouth twisted with a snicker of misery. "You long for another man, don't you? Yes, long and ache and yearn. Tell me about it, dear wife. How you roll and pant in his arms every night behind my back. How you kiss and suck him, all over. But it was not always thus. Only of late. The last few weeks, I should judge, have turned you from me. For some *one* in particular."

"Spring," she said flatly. "Spring is in your blood. You need to ride out of town for the season before the influenza comes and takes you in your weakened state."

"Not spring at all." He began darting about the room, opening and slamming the drawers of her various cabinets as though expecting to find some important evidence.

"You must leave me in peace while I dress," she said finally, at the end of her patience.

"No, I shall not leave you in peace! And why should you dress? Where are you going this day?"

"The Duc de Beauclew expects me."

"Does he expect you every day? If he were not so very ancient, I should suspect him of . . ."

"You are disgusting."

". . . of conspiracy against me, mine, and my rights."

"Don't be ridiculous, Ralph! What can you be thinking of?"

He came toward her quickly, scowling into her face a distance of half a dozen inches. She leaned back to get away from him, to put space between their abrasive contact. He grabbed her abruptly, brutally, by both shoulders and spun her around in a single yank that sent her off balance and pulled her halfway from the stool. Behind her the servant girl gasped. Meg, feeling sorry for the wretch who had to witness these things, motioned her to leave. Instantly the child ran out, slamming the door behind her.

"Now that we are alone," Meg said quietly, "get it out of your system, Ralph. You haven't had a good blow at me for quite some while. I suppose it's due."

"Nothing is due that you don't deserve." His voice rising to strident notes, reminded her, as he often did of a wounded bird hanging precariously at the poin of death. "You always deserve what you get, my dear."

His curved hand shot out to catch her around th neck. It was a familiar act, but today she had no in tention of allowing that cold, flat thumb to press int her throat, pressing and pressing slowly, while he en joyed the sight of her struggle for breath. She caugh his wrist in her own angry grip and brought it dow to his side, holding it there steadily as he stared a her, eyes bulging with astonishment at her strengt and his weakened condition.

She sensed the danger of her game and let go him. Turning her back, she strode away to the windo where she could look out at the black and speckl birds flying free.

"It is the beginning of April," she said, changi the subject, "and most of your friends are packi for a jaunt to Scotland. Will you go with them th year?"

"Will you?"

She felt the entrapment. Leave London! She alized she dared not answer, not with the force th flew into her throat.

"I shall think about it," she hedged. "The lad tell me it is a dull, wet place with nothing to am but dull, wet hunting."

"Then why send me?" She had no answer and

added, "But don't I already know?" His voice cut and snicked the air. He came up behind her and repeated, "Don't I already know?"

She did not challenge him. There was that certain strength in her that stretched out beyond the reach of his suspicions. She waited.

"He has come back. Against every warning and l my heroic efforts, he is back, isn't he?"

Meg held her silence. It would be simple, too simple o pretend, which would only infuriate him further.

"I hear his name wherever I go. The Earl of Worth ells me of this new, young painter, all the rage. Lady tefton tells me of this dashing new painter recently rrived from America. Mr. Dance of the Academy nd Mr. Farrington are agog over this remarkable lent that spews such color, such verve, over a canas."

She felt him behind her, panting a hot vitriolic eath down her neck. Unreasoning fear for Dick aimed her, a fear she had not felt in many, many onths, as though she had waked, caged and helpless ainst the boiling, fuming spirit of a mad beast gone t of control.

"Even the Duc de Beauclew, the closest friend of family, my very uncle, has offered a yearly stipend this wretch. Everyone. Everyone! He ravages like lisease. He surrounds me. He eats alive everything t is fine and beautiful. He spreads his poison slowly, troying the finest brains of the realm. And you? And , Meg? Why so silent?"

He grabbed her and spun her to face him.

he stared at his eyes suddenly bloodshot, his whit-d face growing blue at the tops of the lips. A tic begun to tremble in one corner of a lower eye-vhile his hands closed slowly, more tightly, around arms, cutting off the blood supply so that her fin-tingled.

Vhat you say may all be true," she began coldly, ig inside, yet aware that she must find a way to shield Dick from this bedlam. "But one cannot kill a man for following the ways of his profession."

"What care I for his profession?" he screeched. "It is my *wife* he is after! And my wife that he has! Whore! Don't you lay with him every night of the week? Don't you spread your legs for him?"

As the words rang in her ears, and the profanity smeared a blurring pain over the true nature of her love, something snapped in her. Some chain that had linked her all this while to Carstip broke clean. A peace of huge proportions began to swell and lift in side her. She did not know how it happened or wher it came from, but now the decision was there, com plete and solid. With a great, wrenching pull sh yanked herself free and stepped back out of arm reach.

"Yes, Ralph. *Yes*, Ralph! Y-E-S!!" She whipped o the words, but they came softly with the fury an continuity of storm over seas. "I love him. I hav never stopped loving him. I will always love Dic Fox. AND THERE IS NOTHING YOU CAN D TO STOP ME. . . . Even," she said, hoarsely now, " you find a way to send my soul to burn in hell fc ever."

As though the man before her were no bigger a no more capable of following her than a cricket, s turned away from him and went off into her dressi room to take a shawl and leave the house.

Chapter Thirty-three

SHE WOULD never know how Ralph stood trembling and glowering at the door that slammed shut between them.

A startled humiliation passed across his eyes and melted their aggression, dissolving his fury to a whim-pering rage. Helpless bleatings squeezed up from his :hroat. His chest began to heave. He coughed in spasms, giving in to the well of filmy tears that rose ınd slid to the ends of his lashes. Swallowing motions ɔecame convulsive. He thrust his hands into his hair ınd began to pull at the roots, first above his fore-ıead, then at the neck, and finally, grasping firmly at he temples, shook his head wildly, eyes hard closed, ears spraying out into the air.

Then, quite suddenly, he stood dry-eyed and fro-en, the gaze blank and distracted by a deep, hidden ırmoil. His breath paused at the end of every exha-ıtion and he seemed to die there or hang suspended a dream, until he would think to draw air again. n itch started at the bottom of his chin. He began claw downward from jawbone to throat in long d marks, flinging his head back and moaning as lotches of a nervous rash began to spread.

"She won't," he whispered. "She won't do this to e. Not to me. Filthy bitch. Not to me! I'll ruin her st. Ruin her. Ru-in her!" He cast a searching stare ound her bedroom and dashed to the wardrobe ors hanging open. Plunging both hands in, he caught eat armfuls of her dresses, tore them from where ey hung, and swung them out into the room, fling- them over the carpet with all his strength. His vision caught a blur of silver, cerulean, cloud white, leaf green, wafting a scent of roses that made him cry out with the anguish of her presence so close to him, yet so completely gone. Panting, he jumped upon the tulles and satins, stamping both heels into them, screeching, "Whore! Whore!" with bursting attack, as though the woman herself were in the dresses. His boot tip caught in a twist of ribboned puffed sleeve. He stumbled to a low boudoir table, its oval mirror reflecting the rows of fragrant jars and bottles, the tiny pots of colored face paints. "Mother," he called hauntingly, and smashed his forehead into the mirror till his face crumpled with pain. Squinting in the trickle of blood, he brushed an arm and sent the little jars flying. They sailed away, banging into the walls, rolling beneath chairs and her bedstead. Fastening upon the bed itself, he yanked away the coverlets, wrapping them around in each other and heaving them out over the dresses. Staggering back to the wall, he stood gasping and surveying the scene, smiling slightly at the destruction he saw before him, licking absently at the tears and blood slipping to the ridges of his lip. "Why don't I feel better?" he panted.

The words renewed his force. He raced to find he underchemise and discovered another small garmen alive with her shape traced in the curves of the stays He held it, staring at the imagined sight of he body. A rough, wincing gasp escaped him. He clutche the corset to his face and buried his nose in the silke material, winding the laces around his head. "I love you. Oh, how I loved you. And I was faithful, thoug you never believed me." Loud, righteous sobs heave into the corset. With it clasped to his bosom, he shu fled to the bed and fell down, the garment benea him, wrapping his arms around it and trying to bri his legs up to encompass it, like a body. "I gave y everything. Everything," he sobbed. "Why don't y love me? But you will. You will! I'm stronger th you are. You'll see!" Anger built in his voice as talked to her image. Soon, while he stroked the m terial, he began to move it lower, rubbing it along his chest, his stomach, till he caught and grasped it between his thighs.

Lying prone, he rocked back on his knees and then straightened forward in a thrust, crushing the form beneath him and pounding into it. Over and over he worked his hips, beating her down with his loins, conquering her at last with his maleness. "Oooooooh, love me . . . love me . . . love me . . . you must."

He shuddered in one huge encompassing contraction that held him steadily pressed upon her, his cheek buried in the pillow, eyes wrinkled shut, mouth stretched in a taut leer of heavenly gratification.

Almost instantly afterward he lay asleep, profoundly silent and still. Drained and pale, his breath became a shallow, rapid struggle to catch up with his previous exertions. Gradually his grip loosened on the cloth and his mouth went slack, tongue lolling up to the edges of his teeth.

In sleep he began to dream.

The suffering brain, to ease its torment, conjured up pictures. Soon the nostrils began to quiver and widen, flaring like an animal sniffing conquest. His lips quivered. Snickers exuded from a widening smile. The elaxation of sleep became a tossing involvement in ome horrible, satisfying event. He sighed and sighed gain and tittered. A thin voice rose from him, crying, "Help! Help me! Oh, my head," high-pitched, weak, and hopeless. Then he laughed.

His laughter jarred him. He lay staring at the ceilng, awake but still dreaming, confounded by what ad come to him; by what he now knew must be one.

He shot up from the bed, raced to the window, and eered at the sky. The long, curving sunlight hung its four o'clock angle. A certain self-possession took ver now. He raked his hair back from his forehead, ade quick, jerky movements to smooth away the eases from his shirt front. He plunged over to her irror and stared at his clothes. *No. I can't go out like this. But first I will have dinner. God, I am famished.* He lunged from her room, darting glances up and down the hall.

"Pim? Jonathan? Emma?"

Not a servant in sight. He laughed with sneering knowledge of how they scattered, running from him like mice before a lion.

"Emma!"

His voice resounded along the paintings and flowered wallpaper. Proudly he thought, *How beautifully I have redone this coffin of a house.* Then remorse arose that became despair. *Why don't they let me live?*

"Emma! Where in blazing hell *are* you?"

He started down the broad staircase, sliding his palm over the dark, polished wood, feeling its warmth pleasant to his flesh.

"Emma!"

He wondered at her not responding, that she would risk his wrath when she well knew the rewards of laziness. *I shall not be annoyed with her today,* he thought. *I shall be kind. I shall surprise her and be kind.*

Creeping up the stairs from the servants' kitchen came the skinny, rigid figure of the child whom he had given a home. Her blonde, frizzy hair hung from its cap. Dark blue eyes peeped at him, then fixed upon the floor.

One day I shall make her pretty . . . if I maintain the inclination.

She came toward him stooping and frail, her narrow body holding back like a frightened cur forcing itself forward within arm's reach.

"Closer, Emma. Come closer. Don't be afraid.

He saw her swallow and creep ahead another inch How it angered him to see the fear.

"Emma, all I want from you this night is dinner. D you understand that?"

"Dinner, your Lor'ship?"

"I want you to go downstairs and tell Jonathan th

the master wishes *you* to bring him his dinner. In the morning room, Emma."

Her eyes widened with reluctance and confusion that told him how unheard of it was for such as the likes of her to carry the master's dinner.

"Yes, you, Emma. The very one."

He turned on his heel and went off to the morning room, for its windows faced in a westerly direction and at every minute he could watch the progress of :he sun. On most other days in spring, it was hot and stifling and dark. But today the grime had parted, evealing an odd, whitish sky without clouds. Thus ie waited, drenched in thought while wave after wave of discomfort passed bafflingly across his face.

Behind him he heard the rattling tray of his dinner rrive, conducted slowly through the doorway. "Serve ie, Emma," he said as she stood looking from his yes to the covered tureens on the table and pressig her palms to her skirt folds over the thighs. "What ave we here tonight?"

"I don't know, your Lor'ship."

"Don't know, eh? Let's have a look." He strode to e cover and lifted it. "Ah, yes. Pigeon in sauce *es-ñol.* Very fine. Do you like pigeon in sauce *español,* mma?"

"I don't know, your Lor'ship."

"Then let us find out." He waved to the birds ly-g beneath their glossy brown blanket. "Go ahead, ll off a leg. I said, pull off a leg," he called into her cking hesitations.

Judging the sound and sight of his insistence, Emma ged ahead with desperation and struggled to tear e a leg from the carcass.

"It's but a bag o' bones, your Lor'ship," she cried.

"No, no, Emma. It's a bird. A delicate creature. ry like yourself."

Finally she had the leg in her fingers and stood iging out bites that snapped and cracked between teeth. He sat in a large upholstered chair, swing-one crossed boot, watching her and turning every so often to view the sky with an impatience that could not be distracted even by the amusing play of Emma trying to be comfortable before him.

"Well, Emma? How do you like it? Is it good?"

"Oh, my, yes, your Lor'ship."

He sighed. "Your vocabulary quite bores me Emma."

"Yes, your Lor'ship."

The sight of the torn bird attracted him more than the girl munching it. He went and stood beside her tore off the other leg, and ground his teeth into it a she did, cracking the bones, too, and wiping his mout upon the side of his wrinkled sleeve. Soon he ha the claret bottle in one greasy hand, pouring straigh from the decanter into his throat to ease the woun of the long afternoon with increasingly longer draf of the wine. The band of pain around his head re laxed and gradually opened its grip.

When next he looked, the sky had grown dark.

"Aha. Now it comes," he muttered.

He wove up the stairs to his bedroom, thunderin "Pim! You bastard! Come help me to dress!"

Pim, a short muscular creature, leaped up from b low stairs, taking the steps three at a time, reachi his master easily and steadying him at the elbow.

"Damme, I don't need your help to walk," Ral shouted, yanking the arm free. "Get to my roo Take down the jackboots I brought from Americ

Spurred by a great swinging kick that missed hi Pim sprang ahead.

"Want the fawn breeches," Ralph said, the d closed behind him. "And a blue swallow-tailed coat."

"Breeches, y'Lordship?" Pim squinted at h "Y'ain't worn britches in an age."

"Want 'em tonight!"

In half an hour he stood sobered and observing effect before a full-length mirror. Clad in the unif of an American gentleman, he might be crossing Boston common on a Sunday afternoon. *I mis powdered wig,* he thought. *But a wig might be much and call attention to me when I least want it. This is very nice as it stands. I look like a foreigner, but not outlandish.*

"What do you think of the cut, eh, Pim?"

"Very uncommon, y'Lordship. Wouldn't recognize you if I didn't dress you myself."

"Excellent, Pim. That's the compliment." He glanced about the jumble of clothing, the shirts and ɪats he had tried and rejected. "Gloves. Gloves. Vhere are my leather deerskins?"

"Here. Right where we dropped 'em when we un-acked."

The deerskin fingers were smothering in the heat. wave of dizziness caught and spun him. He dug ıto a cluttered drawer and brought forth a bottle. This wretched worm that eats my brain," he whim-ered, and swallowed a handful of pills that rallied m. "Splendid. The look has worked out to perfection. nd what do you say, Pim? You have seen nothing this, eh? Your master has gone to bed with an tack of gout and has stayed in his room all evening, ı't that so, Pim?"

"The very thing, y'Lordship," Pim replied with ightly agreement. "An attack of gout in the knee ıes, Lordship. And in the big right toe."

With Pim cackling in his wake, he strode through door and down below stairs into the kitchen. Mov-with swift, confident eagerness to the hearth, he ked the coal box, calling, "Where is the tinder? Is re no tinder here, dammit?"

'But no, your Lordship," came the bewildered re-from a soot-blackened face astonished to see the ter below stairs.

No tinder?"

There's no need, your Lordship."

'e drove the box aside and rushed out into the garden, combing through the hedges and gather-ırmfuls of dry twigs, which he rushed to the heavy ıern carriage and piled inside until one seat was pletely covered.

"That'll do it," he muttered, glaring at the humi sky with satisfaction. "That'll set us up just fine."

The horses, always hitched and ready for his whim whinnied softly as he climbed up over the wheel t the driver's seat, lifted and jerked the reins. Respond ing before the whip touched them, they backed an wheeled and cantered away around the oval that le toward the more congested part of the city.

"She'll never know. Never know," he babbled "Then again, she will, when she thinks about it. She' feel my curse all her life long, and yes, she will know. He lifted his nose to the air and sniffed its soot darkness where public lamps failed to light the wa sufficiently. His skin felt hot and wet and prickle with anticipation. He half stood in the box, urgin the horses faster with the flicking whip. "I loved he But she never loved me. This will fix her. Th will . . ." His mind rattled with the fever he could n longer abide.

At Portman Square he reined the horses and s for an hour, gazing at the house across the way an lost in his reflections. How often he had done thi How often he had writhed in agony at the realizatic of her unfaithfulness inside this house. How he h spent days controlling the immediate impulse for sa isfaction, planning the ultimate conquest. And tod had come the miracle of method. A voice had spok in his sleep, predicting what was about to materializ He stared up at the new stars and felt through l flesh the infusion of a god's power. The world w created for his purpose, spinning at his command, wa ing eagerly to fill his need.

He dropped the reins and jumped lightly dov springing catlike with a speed and grace beyond t ordinary. The sensation of his movements thrilled hi He felt ten times larger, stronger, lighter. Ten tin wiser, clearer. All of his faculties were suddenly bu from their filmy matrix, dazzling with the perfect and clarity of a precious gemstone.

He banged open the carriage door, removed

armload of the twigs, and dashed across to the dark house. *If someone is inside,* he thought, *so much the worse for him.*

There was no one. The pair of villains were out cavorting in their social sphere, as he knew they must be. He could see them over their dishes of tea, prancing about with *his* fine painter friends. He could hear he innocent laughter from their unknowing faces as ie clambered around the staircase into the large studio n the rear, drawn to it unerringly by the smell of its urpentine fumes.

The room lay entirely dark, except for a splash of ıoonlight slanting through long windows and falling ver an easel. He scattered the tinder and stomped to ıe hearth. Bending to search out a lighted coal, he ɔund not so much as a single ember, the fire carelly doused. Annoyed, yet enjoying this futile precauɔn, he stuffed in twigs and brought from an adjoining om glowing coals on a shovel.

The lifting, crackling flame caught his fancy. In its ıncing light, he pranced about the room, kicking his ot through canvases carefully stretched on their ımes. "There you go, painter. And there. And there. *ıere's* your career. *There's* your exhibition." He fted one pushed-through picture and carried it to fire. Tossing it in, he watched the flare and spit of arks.

A thrill of intoxication overcame him at the sight of ıan's lifework being so easily destroyed by himself. strength and energy in his bones grew apace, eading out like the flame, all-consuming. The ıt blazed, reflected in his eyes. He sniffed the acrid ell of burning canvas.

"There is your career," he boomed, spreading his ıs to the magnetic light beginning to roar and rum- restlessly confined. "There is your lover, Meg. rthless in flames. *My* flames!"

.s he grinned with the glorious ruling force of his his manhood began to quiver, swelling and filling life. "My flames," he called again to the snappy, angry explosions. "Dance, dance, my flames. Beautiful flames. You know I loved her. I always loved her . . . and she is mine."

There came a tearing, roaring flash that exploded outward, bellying from the hearth in successive rolls that sucked the room's air into its voracious center. His mouth opened. His chest inhaled a scorching noxious heat. Gaping, he stood thus as though forever astonished, frozen in the melting heat, face and body reflecting the reddened light.

Outside on the streets of Portman Square, five dog trotting in a pack through the darkness stopped an began to skitter in circles. Running excitedly, tails lift ing stiffly, they raised their drooling jaws and we noses to howl at the delicious, torturous smell of mea roasting on the wind.

Chapter Thirty-four

"MY DARLING DICK," Meg crooned in the carria flushed with wine and joy. "How proud you ma me. Those Royal Academicians, they are nothing co pared with you. And how you have charmed . . . y with your brooding ways. Why, they understand y and love you." She subsided against his sleeve, gaz out the window at the velvet night carrying them ho with an easy pace. "Especially Mr. Turner."

"His genius has earned him the right to his scow

"But you are more elegant," she said, fiddling w his cravat. "And who is to say that your genius not surpass his when you have reached his yea She sighed contentedly against him. "What a pe time this has been. I can think of only one that will be more so."

"The day of the exhibition itself."

An excited gabble drifted in to them from the street ahead. Soon voices became strident and louder. Dick put his face to the window.

"This fine night of ours is filling with the stench of smoke."

"Then we shall go to Italy, if you like. Or Greece. want to see America one day again, Dick, as we vere meant to see it, you and I, together."

"My God, Meg," he called with his head out the vindow. "There's fire on the street!" He thrust the oor open and swung himself out to get a better view. Whip up those horses, driver. Move them!"

In a minute they had turned a corner and were aring at a wall of flame, once a small building, now crumbling shell, roaring and bursting explosively, cked up by the night wind.

"Dick, it's your house!" she screamed. "Your ouse!"

He was already down and running toward the line people working with the firemen, passing buckets water and rolling casks of water to be emptied onto e blaze. Three fire carts were being pumped at full eed, but the pitiful stream their horses flung onto flaming mountain seemed only to feed it, as though e water itself were fuel.

Meg leaped from the carriage and dashed after Dick, onized by what he would do. "Don't go in there. n't! You'll be killed!" she cried.

She saw him get as close as he could, stopped only a fireman who grabbed his shirt and pulled him ay.

"Don't try, sir. You can't go in there. It'll eat you ve."

Dick, pulling away roughly, again struggled forward, arm over his eyes, coughing, trying to butt through billowing smoke.

Meg, fighting toward the firemen, jumped onto

Dick's back. "You can't. There's no way in. Let's take buckets. Help pass the water on. There's nothing else to do now." Crying, coughing from the smoke, she realized he did not hear her and slid off him to put herself on the line that swung meager, slopping pails between vats of water and the crumbling house. She saw Dick with the firemen, a shovel swinging from his hand, his face already smeared black and glistening, eyes wild and single-minded. He crawled in close as he dared, working with the more experienced men, to draw the fire away by feeding it a path of wood leading out toward the street. The danger of surrounding houses catching fire depended on the whim of the wind. One moment the flames blew close to a larger brick build ing, then they leaned away, to sink with lusting voracious hunger back upon their own swelling orang belly. An eerie light, bright as day, was flung half way across the square and reflected from buildings o the far side. Everyone coughed. The acrid smell o charring wood blew about, mingled with the ironi smell of the dank but useless Thames.

Her arms ached. She felt the stinging swell of blis ters in the creases of her fingers and on her paln while she kept on swinging the pails. But the wate meant nothing as it disappeared into the pyre, co sumed like the house itself. Gradually as the nig passed, people exhausted themselves with the futi work. They began to dwindle from the line to sta back listlessly, helpless, awed, their faces streak and wet, while the flame became sated and cond scended to suck downward, curling less in fire a more in black smoke.

She watched Dick often testing the edges of the mains, trying to move forward, trying to find a w inside the shell, yet pulled back continually by sy pathetic firemen. Finally, as the sky lightened w dawn, he shoved two men viciously away and beg to clamber inside the smoking rubble.

"The roof will cave in on you, sir. Don't go there."

Deaf to all pleas for his person, he somehow found a way to manage and worked past the hole that had once been a door.

At the sight of him proceeding, Meg dropped the ax that had got into her hand and lunged after him.

"No, ma'am. It's forbidden."

"If he can, I can, too. Let me go." With hysterical strength she yanked her arm free and dashed inside after Dick, who had disappeared through the gaping doorway. She had the will of ten men. The smoking heat beneath her sandals meant nothing as she climbed over and moved around the fallen beams that hung precariously above her. The smoking frame of the building, what was left of it, creaked and teetered, occasionally dropping a post with the horrendous screech of a human being losing a limb. She was too tired, too obsessed to cry, yet the tears were rolling down her face as she picked her way along the tunnel of what had been a hallway, back to the empty, smoking bowl once his studio.

She didn't dare murmur a sound at the sight of him rummaging with insane persistence among the flaked remains. Gray, feathery curls wafted from his boot heels as he walked about, hoarsely saying, "Nothing . . . nothing . . . nothing. Not a frame. Not a scrap of canvas. Nothing left." He spoke in a rigid voice and sometimes bent over a dense heap of cinders or kicked into it, raising a gray mass of dust.

"Oh, God . . . oh, God. Help us," kept ringing in her ears from her mind's forlorn cry. And she, too, fell upon heaps of rubble in crazed hopes of finding the edge of a picture, some fragment of color, that could attest to what once had been. But everything was gone forever.

Yet neither of them stopped searching. Unwilling, still disbelieving, not able to give up, they sifted continuously around and around the dimensions of the studio as though a miracle were hidden somewhere under the blue-black wisps, if only they could see where to find it. Once, as she kicked, her toes banged against something harder. Dropping hopefully upon it, she pushed away the debris of ash and smoldering floor planks to look at what seemed, to her crazed mind, like the charred remains of a human skeleton. There was something skull-like in the shape of one frail part, and lower, a resemblance to curving hip-bones that she recognized from Dick's anatomical drawings. She turned over a succession of linking structures that could have been a spine. It made no sense to her, for Dick kept no servants. As she tried to lift it out, it crumpled to dust, disappearing back down into the indistinguishable mass as a dream dissolves when challenged by the hard facts of day.

Finally Dick stopped walking, stopped searching, and Meg stopped following after him. She came up beside him and he hung a heavy arm around her shoulder. Thus they stood together, silently looking about them, then looking at each other without a word, looking up at the sky opening overhead as the first beams of a bright red morning drove away the stars and the smoke.

He would sleep at the Duc de Beauclew's house, she said, if he could sleep. She would stay with him until their minds cleared and they could think what to do.

The duc was not at home when they arrived, filthy and strained beyond the limits of their strength. Each was shown by a servant to a room, and Meg lowered her aching body into a tub where she sat for dull, listless hours. She thought she must never sleep again Sleep would bring back the glaring, roasting heat and drive her mad. She called for coffee and drank alone, in silence, wanting to go to Dick yet aware that he needed privacy to pull together the fragmente inner soul that must face the destruction of his life entire work. His despair was hers. It ate throug her flesh to her heart and burned away the flesh her heart's tissue. What was he to do? All the precio paintings gone, and Exhibition Day a mere thr weeks hence.

How strange were the ways of Fate, to heave such a devastating obstacle into her path. She sipped her coffee, thinking bitterly that Fate was not the name of her adversary. His name was Ralph Carstip.

In the heightened, excited state of her exhaustion, there passed across her brain the recollection of how she had left him. Never before then had she flaunted her nonchalance, her separation, quite so openly. She had dared to walk out on him. Disgrace him, he would think. Yes. She knew his mind utterly. He would feel the destroying desolation of being abandoned and seek revenge as only he could find to do.

One of the duc's old retainers brought her a lime silk dressing gown embroidered with scarlet pheasants in the Chinese manner, as though the sheer opulence of the attire could distract her from the grief. She managed to smile and thank the woman, then went out to find Dick in his room.

He was standing at the window, hands clasped behind his back, feet wide apart, gazing up at the sky where long fragments of tattered cloud ran before the sun. It was his familiar place, and oddly, she managed to take comfort from it. The existence of his habit could assure her that life was not altogether tamped out but that some flowing current went trongly forth, underground and unseen, yet persistent nd influential and dependable, to be leaned on in imes when the mind lay cowed.

She approached him and he gazed down upon her. n his hollow eyes she saw the haunted, worldly con-ition. She put her cheek to his shoulder and rubbed . There was nothing to say. No comfort to give. No omfort existed in the world. And so they stood to-ther, side by side, sharing in silence the expanse of mute despond that each tasted to its bitter dregs hile the sun rose stronger overhead.

"I've had some coffee," she said at last. "It would good to have some more." Using this as an ex-se, she had some breakfast things brought in for ick to pick at whenever he could.

They sat and looked at each other for a while in more silence. Sometimes she stood behind him, lightly stroking the sides of his neck, bending over from time to time and kissing the top of his damp head. He caught hold of one of her hands. They drifted together to the bed and lay there cradled in each other's arms, each holding the other close with an impulsive need more intimate, more revealed, more vulnerable than any act of love they had ever shared.

She walked around the rooms in a brooding concentration of torment, waiting day after day for Carstip to confront her. *I will never go back to him again. I will never step foot into that house,* she thought with growing conviction.

"Where is he?" she said to the duc one afternoon. "Why doesn't he come to me and settle this once and for all?"

"Settle this?" the duc repeated, sipping his port as they strolled among the tiny flowers in the rock garden. "Seems to me everything is settled quite enough for one occasion." His voice was sad.

"He knows I am staying with you. He knows ever move I make, and always has, unfortunately. Perhap if I had covered my tracks, if I had been less sure o myself, this could have been prevented."

"The wisdom of hindsight breaks our spirit mor than the despair of a failed act. No, my dear. Yo did as you had to do. And who is to say you are t blame? At any rate, I did not try to stop you, eithe Yet well I might have. I could have discouraged yo in little ways and you would have heeded me, out respect for my years."

"Whatever is to be said," Meg whispered so th her voice would not carry upstairs to where Di napped, "I am miserable. And utterly without an id of how to proceed."

"But why are you waiting for Ralph before you p your wits together?"

"It's not that I am waiting for him, exactly, Uncl

She poured tea and sipped it tastelessly. "The thought of him follows me like a shadow wherever I go, whatever I do."

"You have always turned him out of your mind before this."

"And yet, isn't it very different now? I know my mind is made up to leave him. But when he discovers it . . ."

"That might not be for weeks."

"Why do you say so? He is unpredictable. I suppose he must have gone off in his rage with Ned or Tom, to find distraction with some sordid amusement. It is stifling here in London. Perhaps you are right. Anyone with sense would be gone. Why not Ralph?"

"So you must think what to do, child. For yourself. For Dick Fox. But Dick can take care of himself, I expect." The duc looked up to the window. "He is not idling, as you may suppose. That strange, unconquerable necessity of his will must find an answer to his wretched predicament."

"Oh, it is worse than wretched," she blurted. "It s hopeless."

"Hopeless?" The duc smiled. "I never thought to ear such words from you. After all you have done? After all you've been through? And only eighteen ears old. Why, you are just at the beginning of a ong, wonderful life."

"I wish I could see it that way," she said, watching great orange butterfly lollop over a carpet of mossy ock. "Tell me how you can imagine a good life for e when my beloved lies with his career in shambles ound him. Those pictures are irreplaceable. He has ld me himself that he cannot paint America with the me feeling if he is not there. The time is past. The irit flown. Vanished up in smoke," she mused in a wered, icy voice. "If I were to face Carstip now," e continued woodenly, "I know I could kill him."

The duc took the trembling cup from her fingers d set it down beside a dish of neglected tea cakes, ak and melting in the shifted sunlight. "Who's to blame you?" he said. "But that would not restore the paintings to their creator."

"Even so." She paced the grass path in a thoughtful circle and returned to face him. "You are quite correct, Uncle. There is no revenge that would help me. No mortal position I could take to recall what is gone. Do you know, when I was searching the ashes that horrible night, I kept thinking that if I could trade my life as a bargain to regain Dick's paintings, I would do so. And just as I was thinking it, I seemed to become deranged. My mind overwhelmed me and my foot kicked up some charred wooden planks that looked to me like the strange remains of a human being."

"Really," the duc said with interest. "What happened then?"

"It was beyond my comprehension, along with everything else. I was too startled by the hallucinatio to speak out and call Dick to help me regain my wits I simply gave in to the madness. As it gained strength I stared, as I thought, upon a crusty human skull. Oh yes, I know full well what a skull is like, for Dick ha shown me so many of his drawings, you know, i Boston, when he worked with his doctor friend upo corpses."

"This so-called skull was quite similar, you say?"

"Similar? More than that. My memory created a exact replica. Oh, I made a complete likeness. An not of the skull alone, mind you. Insanity drove f beyond the mere head and proceeded to knit up fuller figure. The remains of the post below it so changed into a link of spine bones, one after the othe all very intricate, exactly like the real thing, I suppos with a widening aspect at the bottom, you see, in t extended shape of hipbones. Yes, yes, Uncle. M mind did its work well. I could remember and rep every detail I have ever seen Dick draw."

"I see."

The duc stared at the grasses and into the da leafy shade beneath a spreading elm. He stood t for some while, intensely sunk in thought, which she was reluctant to disturb. She waited, content to watch the flying about of young birds trying their wings from a hidden nest up in some branch. The tiny things descended uncertainly, floundering in the air until they bumped the ground with wobbly relief. Instantly the mother descended in circles of sharp, chattering concern, nudging them to try again, to spread their wings and lift! lift away to their safe home. This they did after much struggling. Then, rising with a gather of maturing strength, they disappeared, accomplished, back into the nest.

"My dear girl," the duc said after some time. "I want you to look at what you have just confided. Look closely and see if your thought does not follow the same track as my own." He came toward her, linked her arm, and walked her off to the shade of the tree. "Now here it is. I shall put it to you bluntly, for that is the way I have come to know, of late. You are waiting for Ralph almost a week now and there is no sign of communication from him. You say this is very much out of his character. He usually follows after you at the very shadow of your heels. Especially since Dick Fox has returned and become popular. The success of Mr. Fox must be anathema to my nephew. It is everything he loathes and wishes to prevent, *n'est-ce pas?* And you yourself, obviously enthralled by your lover, have neglected Ralph shamefully, everyone can see it. The jealousy must fume inside Ralph, never quite so collected before. When you stampede out of his house, Ralph sees himself finally defeated, shamed beyond survival. Oh, it is all so tragically clear, Meg. You can see where I'm going. It was Ralph who intended to ruin Fox by destroying his work. That was the single way to get at you both at the same time. I am sure if Ralph could have killed Fox, he would have. Perhaps it was his cowardice, I don't know. Or his imagined, twisted love for you. In any event, he determined to destroy what you cherished most in life: the success and future fame of your fast-rising painter.

When you slammed out the door, these secret, seething feelings must have come unbidden to the surface of his nature and taken control of him. I can easily imagine him in his rash of temper, charging out of your bedroom and to the studio—which, by your own admission to him earlier, he knew would be deserted!"

"Uncle. Uncle, stop!"

She turned from him, unable to bear it any more. Blinking at the sky, she felt a shuddering recognition of the inevitable rising inside her.

"Yes, *ma chère*. It was no imagination, no dream, no insanity," he said with a whisper of kindness. "What you saw was the case."

Meg clasped her hands and pressed her teeth into the knuckles as different currents of her mind converged, drowning all sensible thought.

"You must not worry about it any more," he soothed. "I will see to what has happened and take care of everything. Ralph's affairs have always been in my hands. Please. You must simply accept."

Chapter Thirty-five

ACCEPT! Could she dare to believe that the worst was true for Ralph Carstip?

She ran across the lawn into the house and up to Dick's room. Shifting, shimmering smiles played across her eyes and mouth as new hope, new life, were resurrected in her heart.

". . . but if Uncle believes it," she concluded, fling ing her arms around Dick, "then it *must* be true. H is such a conservative man. Would he decide some thing so loathsome if he were not sure?" As sh spoke, she became more confident, pressing her opin ion upon her beloved and trying to awaken something inside him. "But I must prove it to you. I must." She touched the reserved and quiet face with her hands. "I will return to Renning Hall. Yes, I will! And find more evidence there, enough for our satisfaction."

Dick blanched, coming alive with antagonism. "It is your nature, I think, to dig for trouble. No. You will not go back. You will do nothing of the sort."

"Oh, yes, I will," she sang, smiling widely. "Because I know in my heart it is safe."

He watched her skeptically, then said, "I can see you mean to do it. Since you must indulge your impulse, I will go with you." He drank down a glass of port and filled another. "But it is courtesy to tell the duc what we are up to."

When they faced the duc with their intention, he said, "But of course. It is the curiosity that immobiles. I will go with you. We shall do it today."

The three rode off in a stiff and nervous silence, each not daring to speak out the contrary hopes, the dreads, the sadness, the cruelties, that rose in recollection, drifting across one face or another as they crossed toward Piccadilly Circus. A spring drizzle splattered the windows. The wet clatter of hooves grew loud on cobbles that glistened through patches of mud. It was a gloomy, dismal business that they were up to, said the duc's countenance, while Meg, prancing inside herself with intentions, seemed to look upon the ordeal as already concluded in her favor. Once or twice she thought, *What if we are mistaken?* But it could not be so. The universe, she felt, had emptied its full cup of oppression, and thus having tested her, would no longer try.

Pim opened the door to them, his expectant look instantly sullen when he saw her.

"Where is his Lordship?" Meg said immediately, her gaze sweeping the room for some sign.

"Why, bless me, I don't know, m'lady," he replied with the exaggerated ignorance that always kept him distant from her.

Meg gave him a quick, crucial inspection. He was Ralph's man and would reveal nothing to her. "Call me Emma," she ordered curtly.

While Meg and Dick went restlessly about in the drawing room and the duc poured claret, Emma crawled up from below stairs.

"Have you seen the master?" Meg asked softly. "Don't be afraid, Emma. Tell me when you have last seen his Lordship."

"I am sure I don't know, y'r Ladyship," she replied faintly. Then, beneath continued scrutiny, " 'Twere with the pigeons, y'r Ladyship."

"Pigeons?"

"The pigeons I brought for his dinner, right here i this very room." As she pointed at a round, richl carved mahogany table, her gaze became sharp an seemed to see again, like a nightmare, the image c another afternoon. "He commanded me to bring hir his dinner, he did. And I obeyed him, y'r Ladyshi Then . . . why, then he said I must taste a bite of th pigeon, m'self."

"And after the eating, Emma?" Meg coaxed gentl as the others listened but carefully avoided the pressu upon Emma of watching her directly.

"Why, and after all the eating, y'r Ladyship, he we upstairs."

"To his room?"

"No. Maybe."

"Why did you say no, Emma?"

"Why, y'r Ladyship? The upstairs maid and m'se we heard such a devilish ruckus."

"Where, Emma?"

"In your room, m'lady. But that's all I know," concluded, and shut her face into a wall that no qu tion or promise could budge.

At last Meg announced to the others, "I am gc upstairs to look about. Perhaps I can discover so thing."

"Not without me," Dick said behind her.

The duc's hand glided firmly over the baniste he followed Dick in resigned silence.

With a grinding urgency to face what she must, Meg flung open her bedroom door and stood there repelled, leaning backward from the shock of what confronted her.

"A madman's work," breathed Dick beside her.

"You do not know the half of what he is capable," Meg said. Trying not to step on the pile of her dresses, she lifted first one torn gown and then the next, searching in vain for some garment that had been left intact. "I can bear no more of this," she said in a sunken voice, and turning abruptly, dashed from the room, working hard to blot from her brain the images that followed after her. In brief flashes she relived the year of unreasoning violence, then peeled it from her, as hough at last she could shed that skin altogether.

The duc came after her with a rigid firmness on his ind face that she had never before witnessed. "I had o idea," he said, shaken. "Why did you not tell me?"

"And what could you have done if I had?"

Dick touched her shoulder with a gentle stroke of ympathy, but his eyes were hard with anger. "Have ou had enough yet, Meg?"

"Have you?" she retorted. Still needing to prove her oint, she proceeded to Ralph's bedroom with a certain ing bravado that made her capable, she thought, of itnessing any further spectacle that might be put bere her.

"This is quite enough," Dick said as they stood starg at Meg's undergarment on the bed. "If he has not rned himself alive in that fire, then he has flung himlf off a bridge somewhere."

"But this is my own flesh and blood," the duc whisred, spying the bottle of pills lying half hidden in the vers and reaching for them. "I do not understand. Velno's Vegetable Pills," he read. "For those afted with the scurvy, scorbutic eruptions, leprosy, and ier disorders arising from impure blood. To those, ewise, whose constitutions have been impaired by injudicious administration of Mercury. To those ose puerile indiscretions have already given birth to disease or sown the seeds of debility . . . And particularly to those, being married or on the eve of marriage, who are liable to entail corruption on their posterity, i must be a matter of no small consolation to reflect tha when all other medicines have failed, DeVelno's may be relied upon as a most powerful Alternative Purifier and Sweetener of the blood."

"Liable to entail corruption on their posterity." Meg repeated the words with a new and awful understanding.

"So that was it," the duc said. "He was a very il man, made desperate and crazed by his illness at th end."

"We've had enough, now, to convince us of every thing." Dick touched Meg at the waist and moved he gently from the room.

As they left the house, Meg knew it was foreve Her mind began to spin with a dizzying, giddy excite ment of freedom. The rain-blurred world outdoors be came suddenly clearer, as though everything wer freshly cut of crystal. She inhaled the growing promis of buds and shoots making their way up from the nou ishing earth. Yes, it was possible to live, live agai She turned her smile upon Dick and saw there the r flection of his joy for her. Yet deep beneath it swa the slow, settling pain of his own predicament that ne ther death nor freedom could abolish.

Obsession possessed her.

Plunged into the deepest challenge of her life, a with no hint of how to vanquish it, she looked do from her window at Dick in the garden, sketching i yet intently the huge lifting arms of the ancient el his tousled hair gleaming in the early light. The her bird of his genius still flapped its wings and rose to mightily without concern for the mere mortal man c quered by a strange tangle of human events.

As she stared at him her love rose in an overwhel ing wave. She saw them together as they had been St. Catherine's docks, in the fields of Hampstead, when she had run after him the very first time, to find him among the strung-up horseflesh . . .

"I have it." She rapped the wall with the knuckles of her fist, spun, and flew from the room, dress trailing lightly on currents of air as she flew down and out to him, going headlong, her eyes alive with fireworks of celebration.

"Dick, listen to me. Listen!" she cried, recklessly pulling the chalk and paper from his hand. "How many weeks do we have to the exhibition?"

"Why ask that, silly bird?"

"Tell me. Tell."

"Barely three."

"Three whole weeks. Oh, I knew it. You can do it. I know you can."

"Do what? What are you talking about?"

"You say you could never repeat your American paintings. My beloved, there is something you know better, much better than those wild scenes. Something you understand naturally, with your flesh and blood."

"Meg, you are blithering. Please sit down."

"You must paint *me!*" she cried, ignoring him. "Me! Yes. Of all things, you know my face best. You know every thought that flits behind it. Your hands have a million times felt and touched the bone structure. Of all creatures in this world, it is *I* who am a part of you. And, Dick, listen." She rushed on headlong so that he could not stop her. "You will paint me and it will work, don't you see? I am the wife, the wealthy widow of the Earl of Eggleston. I have given the finest, most elegant winter balls. I am known everywhere. Talked of everywhere. I am the center of this season's juiciest, most cherished gossip. Paint me, Dick, and you will take my face beyond April to make it live forever. Oh, paint me. Paint me! The gossip will rise to the heavens. Paint me, and my reputation will clear a path for your genius. Please. Can't you see it? Can't you?"

Her fingers clutched his shirt, shaking him, forcing, willing her energies into his brain. As she spoke, he turned his head slightly to one side and then to the other, watching the shadows shift across her mouth, the structure of her nose, her swaying hair that lifted slightly in a breeze. She saw and understood that he was exploring her face with the eyes of more than her beloved; with the eyes of an artist jolted into seeing, for the first time, the possibility of a subject in something he has lived with all his life.

"Meg, my beautiful animal," he said finally. "You know, it *is* true. You are more than beautiful. You are *interesting*. Your face *will* compel others, as it does me. Yes, I will paint you. I will. And I shall do as you say," he added calmly. "I will make your face immortal."

"Oh, I knew it. I knew!!" She jumped up and flung her arms around his neck, covering his face with kisses, smothering his mouth, his eyelids. But the rapture lasted only briefly. She stood back from him, and suddenly her tone was all business. "I must immediatel[y] get us a place to work. You must have a painting room The duc will give us something. He will give us the fin- est, lightest room in the house. Oh, where is he? I mus[t] go to him this instant."

By sunup the next day it was all settled. Servant[s] came and pulled away the furniture in the mornin[g] room. The new Sheraton cabinets, a sideboard, and gil[t] embroidered chairs were removed, everything gone, t[o] be carefully protected from the tails of paint that woul[d] surely fly in days to come.

Dick stood with hands in his pockets looking arour[nd] him, satisfied at the empty space covered by an u[n]furling, clear light of the new day. Then, wordless[ly] turning on his heel, he was off to the color man.

Supplies arrived.

"Put everything there, in that strip of sun," we[re] the only words Meg heard after the delivery.

For some hours she strolled about, watching w[ith] fascination while he cut and stretched canvas, nai[ling] it over the frame, then began applying the white ge[sso] ground, working methodically, with tempered fire. S[he] dared not speak to him, aware of the shifting interp[lay] of creativity gestating behind the broad, seemir[ngly] placid forehead. But the abstracted look of him told all. She could read every feeling. Her experience with Dick was so sensitive, so complex, that they could go for the rest of their lives without speaking, and still she would know his every thought and feel close to him. Occasionally he would glance up from his preparations and peer at her for endless moments, seeing her deeply, gazing far, far beneath the surface of her face, down into the shining places of her very soul. And she would gaze back at him, not smiling, not changing her expression, but perfectly relaxed, drinking in the reserves of his energy that meandered at random around her, their mutual fascinations meeting and blending into a single, unified existence.

One afternoon he began sketching. She sat or stood n different, lengthening shadows of the room, taking no ose, casually inhaling the fragrance of a harebell be- ween her fingers or reading from a volume lying open n her palm. Sometimes she reclined, merely gazing out t the vast stretches of green that rolled away into the ountryside hills, letting her thoughts wander over all e people she had become . . . for she felt now, with ick concentrated upon her, that she held the entire niverse in her own existence, to be revealed forever n canvas.

His sketches grew larger and became more detailed. he chalks and the burned sticks created profiles, semi- ofiles, and frontal faces of her. Sometimes the draw- gs were disembodied, sometimes full length as she lay a sofa. But always he returned with contemplation the simple, yet arrestingly languorous outlines of her ad, as though confident he could catch the total, im- ortal being of her between hair and bosom.

The process continued, growing as a child in its other's womb. Sketches became watercolors, splashed loose washes. The filled brushes lifted speedily from ter to color to paper and swung back, taking bits of t again on the hair tips, to blend miraculously with t, shining hues on the page. From the fleetest of out- es grew her likeness in its profoundest elemental sses.

He seemed glad for everything that occurred, speaking warmly to her or directing her to shift position with the most cursory gesture of a finger. Sometimes he would whistle when an odd change happened unexpectedly before him on the paper. She guessed it was good, perhaps miraculous, for then he seemed to forget her presence, even as he concentrated on its physical parts.

The watercolors soon were set in a row and contemplated for days without a word from Dick as he chos and discarded ideas. The happiness of work change and expanded, to include meditation and consciou judgment. She sensed the living, breathing process o creation happening as he nurtured the portrait in hi mind, where it grew and became complete, while pre cious time passed and he seemed to be doing nothing a all.

Then, one day, he was ready. He lifted a full-siz canvas onto the easel, stared at its blank whiteness i silence, stared and stared, motionless before it, as h projected the picture as it would be. All that neede doing was the actual effort, for in his burning face sh could tell that the picture already lived.

"Please sit on that stool, Meg, and talk to me."

She answered the request with silent compliance an in a thrill of expectation for the final work about to g under way. The place he had chosen was a simp straight-backed chair that supported her without bei seen. He directed her to turn her chin slightly, and s found herself gazing outdoors through the sunlight at small marmalade cat trying its claws upon the bark the old elm. Through the window she could also see t duc soaking his bones in the brilliant warmth. S watched him stand and stroll around the rocks with h hands behind his back, then settle down in the sha with some newspapers. He seemed thoughtful, yet e tirely satisfied, in the philosophical way he had of a cepting the world's unpredictable fortunes.

"Tell me what you are thinking now, Meg," D

said absently as the bristles began their first forays upon canvas.

She sniffed the familiar smell of paints and the various, mysterious components that held paint together, making it possible for colors to be spread upon cloth. The broad palette he held was, at this stage, quite neatly organized, generous dollops clearly separated into reds, yellows, and blues, the three primary tones that he would combine to capture her soul.

"I was looking at the duc." she replied. "He is an old man, very old. And he has learned a great lesson in his years, I believe. Allan Newall once put it into words for me. He was quoting Mister Benjamin Franklin, who said: 'A change in fortune hurts a wise man no more than a change of the moon.' "

"Benjamin Franklin, eh," Dick grunted in reply. He was not truly listening but wanted something in the play of her expression to remain and grow, to become nore defined, more revealing. "Those strange Ameri-:ans are ahead of us in many ways. Turn your head slightly this way. That's it. Yes. Right there . . . Now, f the light will stay but a moment . . . ah. We have it. Ve have it. . . . What was he saying? George Washing-on's fortunes?"

Meg laughed. "Benjamin Franklin."

"Lovely. That's the way to laugh, Meg. Beautiful. Vhen you laugh your lips wrap around your teeth in pectacular style!"

"Lips wrap around my teeth?" She laughed again, ware now that George Washington was a ploy to ckle her which had worked.

Despite the laughter, despite the talking, the days ew by too quickly, but in long, seemingly endless ses-ons of posing that began to wear on her. She could ardly believe that his energy did not flag but contin-ed to rise from some endless, sparkling fountain as he orked against the hours. Yet, when she felt tired, she oked at him and saw again into the future, saw her an on his chosen peak. Then her own energies re-rned with a rush, and she felt, in her way, like one of the gods who could call forth some marvelous instant in the endless ebb and flow of the world. She was becoming, as she sat for her portrait, a living part of history . . . and her name would be forever linked with that of Dick Fox.

"Here it comes now. Here it comes," he said on the final day. "I need three more hours."

"But the picture is required to be present this morning," she said, aghast.

"Is it? Yes. You are right!" He sent for the duc's footman. "Here, my man. Take this frame to the Royal Academy. Tell them the painting will soon come to fill it."

Three hours later, he said, "Now, Meg, you must look at this and tell me what you see."

She hesitated, as though glued to the stool.

"Yes, you are permitted to see it complete. Well? Well?" he barked, abrupt in his eagerness.

With a flush of comprehension she approached he likeness and stood, herself looking back at herself. Th painted image sat vibrant before a window fram through which, in the distance, a small fox could b seen approaching at a trot, its deep russet hair carryin the glossy color of the subject's tresses. But the languorous, arresting creature on the canvas was mor than the image of Meg Watkins; it was the fusion o Meg with the living being of Dick Fox, as througho their trials she had dreamed and known it must be.

"What do you say to it, Meg? Shall we call it 'Fo and his Vixen'?"

She shook her head yes! speechless, as tears spra to her lids. And he, beside her, was laughing at he patting her on the neck, pulling her into the crook his embrace while he handed her the edge of a smel paint-smeared cloth with which she tenderly, loving wiped her eyes.

Chapter Thirty-six

"YES, YOUR GRACE," said Dick at breakfast. "It is varnishing day at the Academy and I must be off to it."

"That is the thing, boy. You have fought your battle against time and won. Now you will place your picture among your peers, and they will respond according to your merits."

Dick accepted the challenge with an ease she had seldom seen recently. The high tension was gone from him, drained by the completion of work. His hawk face seemed a trifle gaunt, for he had neglected food or burned up its nourishment too quickly. She thought she glimpsed a gray hair at his temple, then laughed at herself for harboring the pompous notion that this young man before her was already venerable. Still, she couldn't deny that she longed for the security that came with fame and years. She had had enough of flying about the world and wanted them settled in their own great house, Dick working peacefully away while she entertained the subjects of his pictures, at tea.

"I wish I could go with you," she murmured over er cup of chocolate. "I would so love to see the first esponses. The amazement. The flatteries. Oh, Dick. You will be insufferable when you arrive home later. know it."

"Deservedly so," Dick replied without pause.

She sent him off with smiles and kisses, waving her ce-trimmed handkerchief out the door and peering fter the curricle as far as she could while Dick was orne away from her to Somerset House. For a moment she thought wickedly of following after, the old habit dying hard. But time had taught her how to be separate from him, and she forced herself to behave in a spirit becoming to the subject of the season's most notorious portrait.

The hours dragged. She could bring herself to do no reading, no shopping, no whist playing, as though her spirit were deposited within the body of her beloved and her attention engaged elsewhere.

When he finally returned, she opened the door to him herself, nudging the servant aside and taking Dick's hat and gloves, crying, "Tell me everything. Everything. Was Mr. Turner there?"

"Oh, yes, he certainly was." Dick smiled. "With some of his lovely landscapes. You know how it is with him. He has to stroll around the room watching the walls fill. What a racket of hammering. And he walks up close to examine every picture from beneath his brim, grunting at this one, silent before that one. And would you believe it? He takes up a bit of color and adds a great red blob to one seascape that is not his own!"

"What did the painter say?"

"Oh, he was flattered, I tell you. To have a stroke of Turner's brush on your canvas? That alone would make it imperishable. But there we all are, wondering what is to become of that lump of scarlet stuck in the middle of the waves, and no one daring to speak a word. Then, toward the end of the day, he returns to the picture and quickly fashions that lifeless thing into a little waterway marker. And damned if it didn't bal-ance out the composition amazingly!"

"Yes. What of yours, Dick?" she asked, trying t sound casual while they drank glass after glass of fin sherry uncorked for the occasion, and poured one fc the duc, whose footstep could be heard on the carpe

"Mine?" Dick replied with a grin. "Why, mine h simply stood in front of for a length of time, rubbing h neck beneath the dirty, spotted neckcloth he likes wear. And says nothing for a while and goes along, sa ing nothing but merely peering at the picture here a there from every angle he could think of, while I stand by saying nothing in reply, and him ignoring me like a boy who has sneaked in to the show uncalled for."

"Then finally?" urged the duc with a gratified little smile as he entered, took up his glass, and settled in the high-backed chair near the low hearth flame.

"Finally," Dick continued, "he turns, looks me up and down as if I were the painting, and says: 'You have conquered.' "

In her bedroom, she read the letter from Julien in Paris:

If I am to be of real use to you on the day of your glory, I must give you the advance news about fashion. Muslin and crepe in colors of white amaranth or lilac will be worn with little intermissions, like chemises, fastened round the waist with cords of silk, or as frocks, lacing or buttoning behind down to the bottom of the skirt. Instead of lace trim, they are trimmed with broad white net on the sleeves, neck, and bottom. No trains are worn. The gorgeousness of the stately name of haut ton *is now exchanged for a light and aerial costume of the* petit figurant. *The petticoats are always of silk, and short. The bosom is much exposed, except in the morning, which I do not think will apply to your case.*

"But it is not yet summertime for such a light cosne," moaned Meg to Emma, now raised to the posin of personal maid, and cowering from one corner the sunny room to the other in the discomforting uggle of becoming familiar with her advanced station life.

'You must trust your English dressmaker, m'lady," avered Emma, watching Meg walk the room in a nd dress of saffron-worked muslin, its train swishing eep luxurious trim of white lace over the carpet.

'How does it seem to you, Emma?" She lifted the ck lace veil and fastened it up on one side with a nelian pin. "Do you suppose this will do?"

"Oh, you are a picture, m'lady," Emma breathed.

"No, not a picture, Emma," Meg laughed at the girl and at her own nervousness. "I am the flesh and blood."

"Meg? What are you doing so long?" Dick's voice resounded from downstairs.

She dashed to the door and called, "Only one moment more. I am putting on my hat."

He had bought her a Grecian turban for the day, ornamented with gold and silver and turned up in front, that she fitted over the profusion of her hair. "I think this is too fussy," she gasped, and pulled it off, to take up another in white satin, with white ostrich feathers lifting and swaying above. "But I must wear the one he bought for me." She gasped again and tore off the second to return to the first. "He will have a showy nature this day. And so must I!" Then, turning to Emma, "What do you say to that large silk shawl? It is only to be worn for evening, I know. But is this not a formal occasion to me, much more important than an evening event? I must wear it. I must. But no. I don't want to look foolish beside him. I must seem elegant and at the same time casual . . . Oh, I am blundering about jus like you, Emma. What has become of me?"

Observing herself with one final, harried stare in th mirror, she found the long, graceful image reflecte there of a woman, not a girl, with a proud carriage an firm chin lifted dominantly above the dilemma of co tume. *They will notice,* she thought. *But they will notic the Vixen, and I could appear in red fur pelts and tail, for all anyone would dare to criticize!*

"Good-bye, Emma. I will return to you later, much finer lady than you see before you now."

"Oh, good fortune to you, m'lady. And to the gentl man, too."

"Why, thank you," Meg replied softly, touched.

She hurried from the room, dress train skimming t broad stairs as she glided down to Dick waiting at bottom, one gloved hand gripping the banister, h combed smoothly back from the dark but unlined bro

He stood tall, in a fitted dove-gray coat that revealed the astonishingly broad expanse of shirt front with its sparkling white cravat. The elegant trousers shaped his narrow waist and complimented the straightforward maleness in a way that no dandy could ever achieve. The shining boot tips showing beneath were tapping impatiently upon the lowest step.

"Here I am," Meg chirruped. "Let us be gone before the fête is started."

The duc had driven on ahead so that the two of them would arrive alone together. What would they find there? she wondered, riding in the carriage and looking at every turn for some glimpse of the king, surely also on his way to Somerset House. *There is no equality anywhere in the world as great as ours,* she thought, *where even a street wench can rise from the gutters to sit beside her true love, recognized and spoken to in the highest circles of the first city of Europe.*

"What goes on behind that beaming face?" Dick aid after a while.

"April twenty-ninth, eighteen hundred and four," she eplied, smiling at his peaceful countenance.

"The day of our christening?" Dick laughed.

"Something like that."

For all they tried to make light of it, they fell silent hen they reached the red brick house on the Strand here vast, stately porticos, carvings, and pillars wel- med a thousand people from the domain of the com- onwealth. The nobility and gentry, arriving in their aret and black carriages with gold-painted coronets on the sides, doffed their high hats and swung fash- nable canes, strolling with their ladies bedecked in aceful, waving plumes of lilac, buff, blue, pea-green, d white. Straw hats in gypsy shapes, pink silk hats, arkling diamond ornaments, gold combs, all flowed vard the exhibition, everyone intent upon the pre- w of paintings that would be shown tomorrow to the neral public. They formed a crescent at a distance w, to watch the spectacle of the privileged expanding ore them.

Upon Dick's arm, Meg approached the formidable staircase that once she had envied as the very gates to heaven. Passing between the huge statues of Apollo and Hercules, Meg touched the tiny strip of red she had sewn inside her dress and felt herself blessed from above by the figures floating in ovals of sky-blue. Then with a breathless thrill, up the long, steep steps she rose to the entrance hall of the exhibition rooms themselves, where huge full-length paintings had been hauled by ropes. At each landing a gold chair waited for Queen Charlotte to rest upon when she visited. Would she be here today?

They entered the humming turmoil of the Great Room, its walls hung with pictures that reached upward from the floor along the curving wall to the top that seemed miles away, where light shone in from a circular expanse of windows.

"Shall I tell you what is going on here?" Dick said a[s] Meg stared around her, overwhelmed by the confusion[,] the puzzle and abundance of pictures, frame touchin[g] frame, that unrolled before them.

"Where are *we?*" she asked. "Where are *we?*" Sh[e] looked up into his knowing grin and controlled her self[-]centered absorption. "Yes. I know. I must become fa[-]miliar with the work of our friends, too."

"Exactly," Dick said with approval. "Let us sta[rt] right in. Over there, you will see your old acquaintanc[e] Copley has two large pictures, whole-length portraits [of] Mrs. Montague and her brother. Sir Lawrence has [a] whole length of Mrs. Siddons, done with an admirab[le] simplicity, and one of Mr. Kemble and Mr. Curt[is]. There are three from Shee, that one of Lord Moira."

"Infinitely superior to the other two," Meg add[ed] with instant expertise. "Which look to me exceedin[gly] commonplace and affected, without novelty or forc[e]."

And so it went on between them, while exchangi[ng] "Good day to you, Lord Willingsly. Fine afterno[on,] your Grace. And here comes Westall, Smirke [and] Hoppner."

"Why, Mr. Hoppner. How delighted I am to

you. I understand that you have had a course of ill health."

"My dear lady, how kind of you to think of me when the prince is on his way up the stairs this very instant and all eyes are upon him."

Meg felt her heart leap into her throat. The prince, come to the exhibition this day!

"He always enjoys the preview, m'lady," added Sir George Beaumont. "I shall be delighted to present you o him when he has caught his breath."

Meg felt her fingers grow cold and tingle. Words aded in her ears as the handsome, rotund presence rrived, his high-combed, reddish-brown curls brillian-ned and gleaming in the light from the great handelier. His clear, gray-blue eyes took in everything ood-naturedly, with a sweeping pleasure that ex-ected to find only the most cultivated excellence in hat he observed. There flowed and shimmered about m an aura of sparkling elegance that came up from s very soul to shine through the gold buttons, the gold naments, the gold embroideries, that enlivened his ue coat lapels, his wide waist sash, the embroidered ousers. He seemed a living yet sculptured creation, vertheless very human in the softening chin line and eet, childlike rosy lips, a man in his middle forties o wanted so much to smile and teetered on the brim laughter if only someone would provide him with the use.

"We understand there is artistic scandal in our midst s day." His cheerful voice rang clearly through the sh around him. "We have with us a new artist, is that ' A bright star on the horizon threatening to out-nk all the other stars in our artistic constellation? o is this young man?"

Meg felt the floor sink away from beneath her as stioning faces turned from one to another in the wd. Finally Benjamin West came forward, saying, our Majesty, he is right here, standing almost before . Mr. Richard Fox? Are you not there, sir?"

Through tear-dimmed eyes she watched Dick step

out from the group, striding without a moment's hesitation up to the very pinnacle of his life as he approached and met face to face with the future king of England, the two gazing upon each other with mutual satisfaction and confidence. It burst upon Meg's consciousness that the honest, uncompromising integrity and truth to himself that had kept Dick steadfast through so many painful years was now upholding him on its most solid foundations in front of the world that receded a pace to make room for him.

"Your Majesty." Dick's voice came loud and proud and clear as he bowed before the magnificent presence.

"Ah, sir. So you are the Fox we have heard of. And where is your esteemed picture? Let us see it."

Calmly, but with a beam in his eye, Dick led the prince directly to where the portrait had been hung miraculously at eye height upon the line, then stood silently aside to allow an uninterrupted view of the very soul of his being.

Meg, rooted to her spot, watched Majesty pose with his unequaled, cultivated eye before the image of herself. But what she focused on was Dick together with the prince, the lean Adonis and the aging Adonis in company, as she had always dreamed it, Dick comfortable beside splendor as though he himself had been born to the court.

"I see before me Fox, but where is his Vixen?" Amused at his own play with words, the Prince of Wales repeated, "Can Fox show me his Vixen?"

In the material light that was the real world, she saw Dick turn and gaze directly upon her. Flashing with a special, secret glory, he extended his arms and walked to her, saying, "Your Majesty. Here is Mrs. Watkins, the only one. This is Vixen herself, in life. Have I caught her, can you tell me?"

"You have caught her in the picture," replied the prince, delighted. "That much I can readily say. Very readily. It is an extraordinary work."

Meg stood as proudly as her consort, tall and steady and stilled in the glow of Majesty upon her and in the higher light of her love upon her.

"Have you caught your Vixen in the fields? That is the question, Fox. Perhaps the answer is too discreet a one for you to make me clearly."

The prince, surveying her, seemed to relish with his unabashed gaze every inch of her being, from the trimmed lace upon her sleeves to the cut of her figure beneath the garments. She knew she was being measured by the uncompromising eye of the first connoisseur in all of Europe.

"What do you say to it, young woman? Are you Vixen? And is Vixen quite captured as yet?"

"Your Majesty, the hope of a vixen is always in her ree condition, do you not agree?"

She felt him studying her reply and the sight of her ace as she spoke. Then, standing back and with the nuff box in his hand quite forgotten, he answered, "I e you are the Vixen indeed." His painted cheeks inkled-with many delighted smiles that spread outard from his person in ripples of agreeable laughter rough the entourage around him. "Yes. The Vixen eaks with a vixen's quick wit. Will you come to pper tonight at Carlton House at one o'clock, Lady? nd bring Mr. Fox with you?"

"Your Majesty," Meg replied, subsiding speechlessly to a slow, respectful curtsy he quite enjoyed, while e continued gleaming as though they were old friends d would parade the Steyne together in Brighton, now at the season was here.

"And you, Mr. Fox. This ravishing portrait impresses elf unalterably upon the mind. It makes me happy t I have given a chandelier to the Royal Academy its proper illumination. Are you a busy man? You ist be, sir. Do you suppose you could manage a likes of your sovereign one day quite soon? I shall tell ı what I have in mind." He waved three white fins to motion Dick toward him. "It is a great, whole gth, life-size. Perhaps twice or thrice life-size. Do ı see what I am thinking? Long have I been considıg how much I should enjoy a portrait of myself in army uniform. The one I wore in Egypt against

Napoleon in battle, that venomous but glorious day when we vanquished him and believed that peace was to be ours forever. I am put in mind of those days sometimes, and regret there is no memento to animate my imagination upon the subject."

"A great full-length thrice the size of life would suit your Majesty," Dick replied, the light in him changing to his characteristic, examining expression of study. His sociable pride had done its proper work. Now it was gone, dissolved by an intensity of new considerations as the next portrait began to take shape, while the indulgent man and the disciplined man strolled through the great rooms together, not chatting in a courtly way, but talking with the serious enjoyment of art shared between them.

"You must see me in my costume. The Tenth Dragoons, you know," the prince expounded with longing, full strength upon him.

"Yes. I understand what you miss," Dick was saying. "I was in the Twenty-third. You have that commandin stature which makes a uniform the more convincin But it is the bone structure of the face. The way you eyes are set into their sockets . . ."

They were going on and on, Meg saw, while a crow of gentlewomen with their escorts closed around he Here were the Marquess of Kell, and Albert, ar others, all recognizing her and preparing themselves f renewed yet different acquaintance, saying: "This is fine a day for conversation. Will we see you at Ho land House, Lady Margaret? I trust you have plans f taking a place where the air is healthful in summer

It was all a buzz in her ear. She saw the tops of t two heads, swaying distantly beyond the crowd, deep the discussion she had always known would come pass. It seemed to her then that she, too, must hold her end of things at this moment, when the social mate of life was at its peak. . . . But in the living of in the experience, taste, and savor of it, she felt fleeting, fickle joys that were the thrills of life pass l cool water through her heated grasp. Never would carefree days be as simple as they were. Only in the work would she live, and survive herself in this best of all possible times. But not only in the work would she forever stay beside Fox, his Vixen.

Dear Reader,
If you enjoyed this book, and would like a complete list of Ballantine's exciting romantic fiction, we would be happy to put you on our mailing list. Simply print *your name and address and send to Ballantine Mail Sales, Department LE/RF, 201 East 50th Street, New York, New York 10022.*

A Gift of Romance

Six novels of passion . . . fire . . . and triumph!

Available at your bookstore or use this coupon.

CAROLINE, Cynthia Wright 27323-0 1.9
A stormy tale of wild innocence and raging passions set in th post-revolutionary America of the 1780's!

THE DARK PRIESTESS, Juanita Coulson 24958-5 1.9
A fiery saga of desire and treachery set in fabulously wicke Babylon at the threshold of history!

FLORA SWEET, Jeannie Sakol 25055-9 1.9
Turning from New York's decadent music halls, a young woma braves a thousand dangers as she searches for one passiona love across America's wild frontiers.

THE PRICELESS PASSION, Angela Lang 25397-3 1.
Set in 16th century France, a beautiful young woman is to between two fierce passions — her cause and the man s loves!

ODILE, Robert F. Joseph 25953-X 1.
The blazing story of a proud Creole beauty and two power men set against the sweeping panorama of the Old South war!

THE FOX AND HIS VIXEN, Viveca Ives 27325-7 1.
A saga of fiery wills and enduring love set against the turbuler of the Napoleonic era!

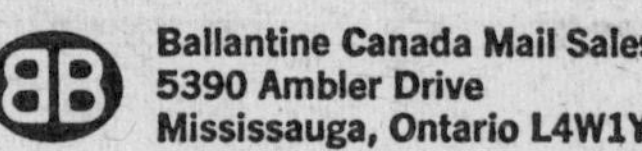

Ballantine Canada Mail Sales
5390 Ambler Drive
Mississauga, Ontario L4W1Y7

Please send me the books I have checked above. I am enclosi $.. .... (please add 50¢ to cover postage and handling Send check or money order—no cash or C.O.D.'s please.

Name____________________

Address____________________

City__________ State__________ Zip__________

Please allow 4 weeks for delivery.